Author's Note

Everyone knows that at the famous Little Bighorn battle in 1876, Colonel George Armstrong Custer and all his men were wiped out by the Cheyenne and Lakota warriors . . . or were they? There has always been a persistent legend that one soldier escaped. Indeed, the body of one cavalry officer was never found. That much is history.

What you are about to read is fiction—this author's version of that timeless legend and the Indian girl that cavalry officer loved. It is also the romantic saga of that officer's half-breed son, Colt Shaw, who is forced to go to Boston to take his rightful place in his wealthy father's world. Waiting there is the prim Samantha MacGregor, the fiery-haired beauty who thinks she's been hired as governess to a child, not a grown savage male. There'll be plenty of fireworks and conflict as Samantha attempts to civilize Colt. The virile and dangerous half-breed has a few things to teach Samantha, too!

Also by Georgina Gentry

Published by Zebra Books

TO TAME A
SAVAGE

Georgina Gentry

ZEBRA BOOKS
Kensington Publishing Corp.

ZEBRA BOOKS are published by

Kensington Publishing Corp.
850 Third Avenue
New York, NY 10022

Copyright © 2002 by Lynne Murphy

ISBN: 0-7394-2717-2

Printed in the United States of America

This novel is dedicated with great respect to the brave men, both white and red, who fought valiantly through the Indian Wars of this country and whose bones lie often unmarked and forgotten throughout the West.

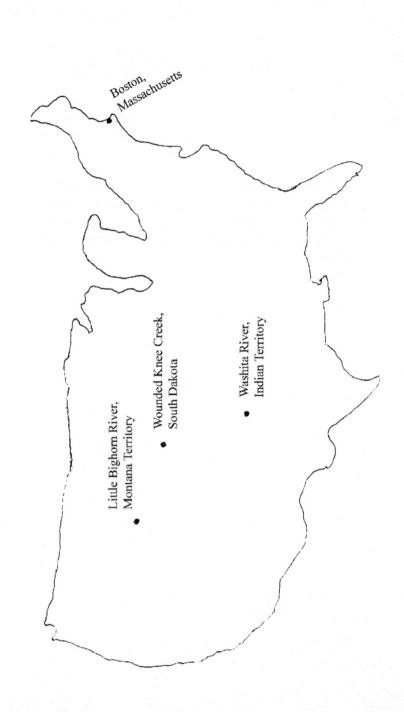

Boston, Massachusetts

Wounded Knee Creek, South Dakota

Washita River, Indian Territory

Little Bighorn River, Montana Territory

PART ONE

AUSTIN'S STORY

One

Colonel Custer had just given orders that the cavalry would attack the Indian camp at first light.

If they all didn't freeze to death first, Captain Austin Shaw thought, as he shifted his weight in the saddle and hunched his body against the icy wind. Behind him, he heard the other Seventh Cavalry horses crunching through the hard crust of snow as the men moved into position. The officer next to him cleared his throat and Austin whispered, "Sir, don't you think—?"

"We've already discussed this, Captain." Lieutenant Colonel George Armstrong Custer's blond curls were hardly visible under the fur cap. "There's been enough parlaying with the Cheyenne and their allies already. We've got our orders from General Sheridan."

"But shouldn't we wait for the Kansas troops?" Austin insisted.

Custer's pale blue eyes glared back at him. "With this blizzard sweeping across the plains, no doubt the Nineteenth Volunteers are lost in the snow north of here. We wouldn't have found this camp ourselves if it hadn't been for our Osage scouts tracking that war party through the snow."

Austin had to agree with that. They had left Camp Supply to the north days ago and had been fighting their way through the drifts. They'd lost many horses to the weather already and some of the men were suffering from frostbite.

Captain Benteen rode up just then, a frown on his moon-shaped face, his white hair hidden by a buffalo skin hat. "The troops are ready, sir."

Austin noted that Benteen's tone was barely civil. Everyone knew that Benteen disliked the senior officer and hated serving under him. George Armstrong Custer had changed in the last three years, there was no doubt about that. Austin had known Custer for many years. They had both attended West Point and served together during the Civil War.

"Good," Custer nodded. "Is the band ready?"

Benteen started to say something, then seemed to think better of it. "Yes, sir."

Austin chewed his lip, keeping silent. Only Custer would charge into battle with a brass band playing; it was one of the quirky things about his personality. He'd been in disgrace since his court-martial last year, and Custer was determined to clear his record. His old friend, General Sheridan, was giving him that chance now against the warring Plains tribes.

Austin's fingers felt numb inside his gloves and ice clung to the whiskers of his roan horse. God, he wished he could take shelter away from the relentless prairie wind with a hot cup of coffee to warm his stiff hands and a pipe full of fragrant tobacco. However, no one was allowed to smoke right now; the scent might carry to whatever sentries were in place . . . if there were any in place. So far, there was no indication that anyone in the sleeping Indian village had noted the approach of the cavalry. The wind howled relentlessly, biting into Austin's face and blowing drifting snow past the waiting troops and on toward the sleeping camp spread out along the Washita River.

Somewhere a dog began to bark and the waiting soldiers behind him cursed softly. There was no way to know whether the barking came from an Indian mongrel or one of Custer's beloved greyhounds that had come along on the march in case he got the chance to hunt.

Custer muttered under his breath to his men, "You've got your orders. We can't lose the element of surprise."

Austin wheeled his horse to return to his troops. He signaled them silently as the dog continued to bark. They were taking a chance, he knew, by splitting their forces in the attack because no one knew just how many warriors were camped along this river. It was difficult to know that, with the visibility so poor. What in the hell was he doing out here when he had a fortune and a luxurious estate waiting for him back in Boston?

He knew the answer: because his mother was in Boston and he loved the freedom of the army life and the vast expanse of prairie. Summer Van Schuyler was out here, too, but not in this camp, he hoped. He had loved her all his life, but when she had made her choice, she had run away with her half-breed warrior, Iron Knife. Austin could only pray that the pair and their children were riding with another Cheyenne band, far, far from here. If they weren't, he couldn't do anything about it now.

In a tipi by the river, Wiwila lay sleepless as she had been for hours. Nearby, her stepbrother, Runs Away, snored heavily, still under the effects of the liquor he'd drunk last night to seal the marriage bargain for her.

Wiwila sighed and moved restlessly. Though she and her brother had ridden in from the Lakota a few days ago and she was part Cheyenne herself, this had not been her choice. Today she was to wed Go Dog, a Cheyenne brave who had offered ten ponies to Runs Away so the brave could make her his second wife. With Wiwila's parents both dead, her drunken brother had realized her beauty was a commodity with which he could bargain. The Lakota and the Cheyenne-Arapaho were long-time allies, united against their common enemies. With her Cheyenne-white-Lakota blood, Wiwila had paler skin than usual and gray eyes, gray as a wolf's pelt. Go Dog hungered for her and her stepbrother had driven a hard bargain.

Wiwila looked toward her sleeping brother again, gritting her teeth. Tonight, she would be sharing a lodge with the cruel Go Dog and his other wife. She pictured herself under the grunting, ugly brave and shuddered, then half rose up on one elbow. *Could she possibly catch a horse and escape?*

To where? she asked herself. It was a long way back up to the Dakotas through this terrible winter weather and she would never make it. That didn't leave her much alternative except to surrender her virginity tonight to the dirty, homely Cheyenne brave.

Outside, a dog barked and the sound echoed above the wind. Wiwila sat up and looked around the lodge in the cold coming dawn. Why was that dog barking so insistently? Most animals were curled up out of the wind asleep, just like the tribe. She slipped on her moccasins, dreading going outside to relieve herself. Grabbing a fur robe, she wrapped it around her, and went out, the howling wind taking her breath away. The snow still fell in a shadowy swirl so that even the trees swaying in the gale seemed like bare, stark bones. She crunched through the hard, frozen crust as she made her way to a haven of bushes that broke the icy blast.

The dog still barked. Probably it had jumped a rabbit. The camp was asleep, nothing stirring except herself, Wiwila thought. There was no need to get up with a blizzard blowing across the barren plains. Only a day or two ago, after she and her brother had arrived in camp, a Cheyenne war party had ridden in with scalps and booty from a raid against white settlers in that place called Kansas. When she felt herself pitying the dead women and children, she hardened her heart. Though Wiwila had picked up a little of the white language from missionaries and trading posts, she knew the white eyes were not to be trusted. Hadn't they proved that at Sand Creek four winters ago? Old Chief Black Kettle had ridden over to Fort Cobb a few days ago to ask for refuge for the peaceful element, but had been turned away.

She started back toward her lodge. The dog barked even more insistently and Wiwila stopped suddenly, all her senses alert. She stood there shivering for a long moment, then laughed out loud at her fears and continued trudging through the snow. Of course there were no enemies out there in this terrible storm. Everyone knew that white men, like the Indians, settled in by their fires until the cold weather was over. War was for warm days when the warriors could make their medicine and strip down to a breechcloth and paint for the fighting.

In the distant, blinding snow, shadows seemed to move. She strained her eyes, but now saw only swirling flakes. Somewhere, a horse whinnied and the dog barked again. The hair on the back of her neck rose. Something was not quite right. She must wake her brother and warn the camp. Wiwila hurried into the lodge, fell on her knees, breathless, and shook Runs Away roughly. "Brother, something's wrong."

He opened one bloodshot eye. "What you say, woman?"

Now she felt ridiculous. "I—I don't know why, but there's a dog barking and—"

He struck her then, cursing as he knocked her across the lodge. "You disturb my sleep for a silly woman's fears? You want something to fear, think about Go Dog taking you tonight." He laughed coarsely, rolled over, and went back to sleep.

She struggled to control her indignation, knowing she was powerless. Wiping blood from her mouth, Wiwila stood up, uncertain what to do now. Her stepbrother was right; all she had to fear was her wedding night. She decided she would rather die than marry the ugly Cheyenne her brother had chosen. Despite the weather, she would steal a horse and flee the camp.

Very quietly, Wiwila grabbed up her fur robe, a packet of dried pemmican and a knife. She was tempted to stab the sleeping man, but knew it would only bring her more trouble. Runs Away owned an ancient gun but it lay under his arm and she feared to wake him if she tried to take it. She stepped outside, straining to see in the swirling whiteness.

Were her eyes playing tricks? Off in the distance, vague forms moved and a sound drifted to her ears on the wind. She must be losing her sanity; the noise was discordant and shrill, not like Indian flutes and rhythmic drums. Abruptly, she recognized the sound from the times she had been in trading posts and forts.

"Soldiers!" she screamed even as she recognized the distant shapes coming into focus, blue uniforms and charging horses throwing up sprays of snow as they galloped, breaking through the brittle crust of drifts while a brass band played loudly. "Everyone wake up! The solders come!"

Even as she screamed, she knew it was too late. The Long Knives were thundering down on the village, their guns echoing as they fired.

Was that a woman's scream or was it only the wind? Austin galloped through the snow toward the river. What did it matter? he thought as sleepy Indians began to tumble out of tipis and grab for weapons. Austin aimed and fired at a warrior who was pulling a soldier from his horse. He saw the girl now, a tall figure wrapped in a buffalo robe standing out in the snow, screaming and gesturing. He felt a flash of admiration at her bravery in trying to warn her people, but it was already too late. The Seventh Cavalry swept down across the encampment like a deadly scythe. Half-dressed warriors ran from lodges, shouting to each other as the soldiers' guns roared. Women stumbled outside, screaming and adding to the noise and confusion. Austin felt sick to his stomach, but then he remembered the dead settlers up in Kansas, and gritting his teeth, he fired at the warriors. If he didn't kill them, they would try to kill him. Women ran now to gather up children, struggling through the deep drifts, hoping to reach safety. Some of the soldiers fired wildly, making no distinction between women and men.

"Don't kill the women and children!" He shouted the order, but the cold wind blew his words back into his mouth. A brave raised his rifle, aiming at Austin. He felt the bullet whiz past his head and he shot the man dead. *What the hell was he doing here, anyway?* Austin swore and wheeled his horse past another brave who came at him with a lance. The lance barely missed Austin and took out a soldier riding behind him. The soldier shrieked in agony and fell. Austin shot the warrior, spurred his roan forward, and cursed himself for staying with the cavalry after the war instead of returning to Boston.

Boston. It seemed a million miles away from this desolate prairie battleground. Were his friends in this camp? Oh, God, he hoped not. No, he must not think of that now, he must keep on fighting, because even in the dim light and confusion, it was evident that there were far more Indians in this camp than the Seventh Cavalry had bargained for. Damn Autie Custer for his recklessness!

Near him, he heard Major Elliott shout, "Here's for a coffin or a brevet!" as he and his platoon split away from the charging troops and rode off into the blur of snow.

"Stop!" Austin yelled at him, but the wind blew his words away and the reckless young officer and his troops disappeared into the blizzard. Austin hesitated, wondering

if he should go after them. It was foolhardy to split off that
way, just in hopes of winning a medal or a promotion.
Around him, soldiers fired, horses reared and whinnied,
churning up the white powder, and over the screams and
shouts, the brass band blared out "Garry Owen," Custer's
favorite tune.

We are killing people to music, Austin thought. It seemed
so ridiculous that he paused, reining in his roan. Indians
were running, some making it to the horse herd, hoping to
escape. Ahead of him, an American flag flew over a buffalo
skin lodge. *Had they accidentally attacked the wrong
camp?* His ears rang with the noise of rifle fire and the
scent of burnt powder choked him. Then there was no more
time to think, he was fighting for his life as the surprised
warriors organized and began to defend their camp. Women
screamed and gathered up children, trying to flee. Babies
cried out in terror, dogs barked frantically, horses reared
and plunged, whinnying as they struggled through the deep
drifts or were wounded and fell.

Through the confusion and the slaughter rode George
Armstrong Custer, his yellow hair gleaming under his fur
hat as the dawn lightened the sky while the brass band
played its peppy tune.

This might be my only chance to escape. Wildly, Wiwila
looked around, trying to decide what to do next. Runs Away
stumbled out of his lodge, looking confused and uncertain.

"Brother, what should we do?"

He cursed and pushed her away. "You're worthless if Go
Dog doesn't survive. Look out for yourself!" With that, he
shoved her aside and ran toward the stampeding horse herd.

She was on her own. Could she catch a horse and escape?
Even as she thought that, her brother swung up on a running
bay and rode out, not even looking back as he abandoned
her to her fate. She must get out of here before she was

killed. Wiwila began to run, stumbled, fell. She lay there a moment, gasping for air, feeling the chill setting into her bones. She must get up and run, risk being shot, or she would freeze to death lying here. Either way, she would die.

Wiwila stumbled to her feet, still clutching her precious bundle of supplies. Ahead of her, a woman with a baby strapped to her back was attempting to mount a plunging, terrified gray horse. It would be so easy to grab the reins, take the horse. Encumbered as the woman was with the child, she couldn't defend herself if Wiwila stole her horse. Wiwila rushed forward, grabbed the gray's bridle, then hesitated, listening to the screams of the baby.

"Here," Wiwila shouted, "I'll hold him, you mount up!" The Cheyenne woman looked surprised, then nodded. Wiwila helped her up on the horse, handed her the baby, and watched the woman gallop away, knowing she had just lost her own best chance for escape.

Galloping toward her now was a handsome officer on a roan horse. She paused, frozen in fear and defiance, knowing he was too close for her to escape him. If he were going to kill her, she'd just as soon be shot in the chest as the back. She stood her ground and glared at him, then began to sing a Lakota warrior's death chant.

His hazel eyes blinked, startled, and he rode on past her, firing at retreating warriors. She whirled in disbelief, looking after him. The horse herd had scattered now, making it impossible for her to catch one. As she watched, old Chief Black Kettle, with his wife mounted behind him, galloped across the shallow, frozen river and headed to safety on the far side. They didn't make it. Soldiers' rifles rang out and the horse stumbled as the pair slid off to fall partly in the muddy water that was turning as pink as the coming dawn, as pink as the blood-stained snow Wiwila stumbled through.

There was a captive white woman and her child in the camp. Wiwila knew the Cheyenne had taken her on a northern raid. Now in the distance, she saw the white woman and her frail little boy running toward the soldiers. Shots rang out and she and the child stumbled and fell, smearing the white, white snow with crimson. With all the confusion and the gunfire, there was no way to know which side had killed them. Around Wiwila, people were falling and dying. She grabbed up a lance from a fallen warrior, forgetting about escaping her fate as an unwilling bride now, concerned only with surviving. A soldier rode toward her on a chestnut horse, swinging his saber. She remembered only that he had light-colored eyes and his pale face grinned as he reached to cut her to pieces. Abruptly, Wiwila brought her lance up. The soldier's face registered horror and he tried to rein in, but it was too late. She threw the lance hard and impaled him. He was dead even before he tumbled from his horse.

If she could just catch that horse, she'd be safely away from here. She ran after it, but the beast, panicked no doubt from the warm scent of blood running down its saddle, reared as she grabbed for the reins.

From a distance, Austin watched her as he reloaded his rifle. The slender Indian girl had just killed a soldier and no one could blame Austin if he shot her. Yet even as he brought the weapon to his shoulder while managing his plunging horse, he hesitated. He remembered the beautiful girl now, the one who had been so defiant only moments ago, the girl who had tried to warn the camp. Any moment now, she would swing up on that horse and escape. He paused, torn by inner conflict, admiring her bravery, yet knowing his orders were that women and children were to be captured.

He galloped toward her, spooking the chestnut horse as she tried to mount up. It plunged away, leaving her standing in the snow, facing him. He could see her face now, her skin lighter than the other Indians, her eyes gray as a summer storm. Her defiant yet frightened expression betrayed the fact that she expected him to kill her. He reined in, looking down at her, trying to decide what to do. She had earned the right to escape. Deep in his soul, he was tempted to capture one of the cavalry horses wandering about and give it to her. *Austin, are you crazy?* he thought.

Somewhere, a bugle sounded recall and the din of battle faded. He looked down at the girl. "You speak English?"

She glared back at him without answering.

"Of course you don't. What a stupid question," he muttered, wishing he could take that look of fear and horror off her face. "You are safe now," he said slowly. "You will not be killed."

She stared back at him, then lunged at him. He got a quick glimpse of metal as she brought a knife from under her buffalo robe and tried to plunge it into his leg.

"Dammit!" Austin wheeled his horse as the girl attacked, the blade flashing in the morning light. The horse reared in surprise as Austin spurred it and he fell from the saddle, grabbing the girl in self-defense as he went down.

Austin caught her hand as they struggled for possession of the knife. "You crazy girl! I'm trying to help you!" Still she fought and bit and they rolled in the snow, but Austin was stronger and ended up on top. He lay on her, his hand holding her wrist as she struggled to stab him. She had a woman's softness and the warmth of her was a comfort to his chilled body. When she seemed to realize she couldn't win and lay still, breathing hard, he looked into those gray eyes and realized she had some white blood.

He twisted the knife from her hand even as she turned her head and sank her teeth into his wrist. "Damn you!" he swore, jerking away from her. For a moment, he was tempted to slap her senseless. She certainly expected he would beat her now—her wide eyes told him that. He was torn between admiration and anger, yet he was a Boston gentleman born and bred and could never hit a woman.

"Hell!" he said and stood up, reached down, and jerked her to her feet. "The battle is over," he said. "Do you understand? No, of course you don't." He brushed the snow from his blue uniform and mounted his horse, trying to decide what to do about her.

The bugle sounded again. Austin drew a sigh of relief. He had thought Custer's orders ill-advised. Sometimes Custer had more bravery than brains. But then, that fiery officer hadn't made his mark in the Civil War and risen all the way to a general's stars by being cautious. However, Custer could be foolish, too. He had been downgraded from general to colonel after the war, and had just survived a court-martial.

Leaving the girl staring him and with the bite on his hand still throbbing, Austin found his horse, rode back to the officer in charge, and reined in, saluting sharply.

Custer leaned on his saddlehorn, smiling in satisfaction at the dead Indians scattered across the frozen landscape. "Looks like we took them by surprise."

"Good thing," Austin snapped, "since there seems to be hundreds of them camped up and down the river."

The colonel shrugged. "They're in no mood to fight—they're on the run."

Lieutenant Tom Custer rode up just then, his fair skin red in the cold wind. As he saluted, he said, "We lost a few men, but they've lost more."

Austin looked around, a sick feeling in the pit of his stomach. "Anybody seen Elliott since he took his men off down the river?"

A long pause. Benteen galloped up, saluted. "What's this about Elliott?"

"He's missing," Austin said. To George Custer, he said, "Colonel, I request permission to go look for Major Elliott and his men—"

"You'll do no such thing," Custer snapped with a shake of his blond curls.

"But, sir," Benteen protested, "they—"

"We've done what we came to do," Custer said. "I can't risk more men looking for a squad that may already be dead."

Austin gritted his teeth and watched Benteen exchange glances with an Osage scout. Custer wasn't as popular with his men in the Seventh Cavalry as he had been with the Wolverines of the Michigan brigade. Autie's attitude had changed, too, since he'd been demoted from general down to colonel as the army cut its budget. Austin sighed with resignation. "Sir, we await your orders."

For a long moment, there was only the sound of the wind and a few faint cries of dying Indians. Most of the warriors had fled, no doubt even now regrouping to attack the smaller white force.

Custer stroked his blond mustache in thought. "We've got to get out of here before they regroup and realize they outnumber us. Captain Shaw, take some men and gather up whatever women and children are still in the camp."

"Sir?"

"You heard me. If we've got hostages, the warriors aren't apt to attack us as we head back toward Camp Supply."

"Sir, what about the Indian horses?" Benteen asked. "We can't drive that big herd clear back to Camp Supply and—"

"Shoot them," Custer said.

Benteen's eyebrows went up. "Shoot them?"

Austin winced. He liked horses.

"Are you deaf, Captain Benteen?" Custer shouted and his fair complexion turned an angry red. "If the braves recapture that herd, they've got the advantage. You've fought against mounted Indians enough to know that. Let our Osage scouts pick out a few for their personal use, keep a few to mount the captive women, and shoot the rest."

"Autie," Austin blurted, "I don't think—"

"Captain Shaw," Custer's eyes were as icy cold as his

tone, "I would hate to think you were guilty of insubordination."

Austin swallowed hard to choke back his anger. "Yes, sir."

Custer nodded in curt dismissal and whirled his horse, riding away. Austin looked into the sullen faces of the other officers. He was gut-sick of the carnage of war. "When it comes time to reenlist, I just may retire."

Tom Custer laughed, his red face even redder in the cold wind. He had a reputation as a carouser. "Shaw, if I had your inheritance, damned if I wouldn't be in Boston right now at some fancy tea party. You're loco to stay."

Austin felt his face burn and one of his fists doubled up inside his glove. Some of the other officers, jealous of Austin's wealth and aristocratic background, would never let him forget it. "You heard the colonel's orders," he snapped. "Let's carry them out."

The others frowned and saluted, then rode off to deal with the horse herd. Austin wheeled his horse, looking out over the bloody battlefield. In the distance, he saw a slight figure struggling through the snow away from the camp. He recognized the girl who had tried to stab him. His wrist still throbbed, but he felt a grudging admiration for her pluckiness. She was determined not to be defeated, no matter how bad the odds.

A sergeant rode up just then and saluted. "Orders, sir?"

Austin saluted automatically, his gaze still on the girl. "Take some troops and start gathering up the women and children for hostages. Colonel Custer wants us out of here before the Cheyenne realize they outnumber us and regroup."

"Yes, sir." The grizzled sergeant spurred his horse and rode off.

Austin watched the girl in the distance, still struggling through the snow. She might get away, but she'd freeze to death out there on the prairie with no food or shelter. He nudged his horse and started after her.

She looked back over her shoulder in alarm, and attempted to quicken her step. Austin put spurs to his roan and loped through the snow toward her. "You, stop!"

She glanced back, spat in the snow, and kept moving.

Damn her, just who did she think she was? Austin was abruptly more than cold and tired, he was angry. How dare this slip of a girl defy the power of the U.S. Army? Off to one side, he saw the soldiers gathering up the forlorn group of survivors. He would insist this girl obey him.

"You there! Stop!" he yelled again as he rode closer.

Wiwila glanced over her shoulder at the blue-coated officer coming after her. She tried to quicken her step and fell in the snow. For a long moment, she didn't move. She couldn't outrun him on foot, so she might as well lie here and let him shoot her. No, she mustn't give up so easily. If she could just outwit him, perhaps she could figure a way to return the hundreds of miles to her Lakota people.

The officer was right behind her. She could hear the roan breaking through the hard crust of snow. "You there, I said stop!"

She would pretend she didn't understand English and keep moving. Maybe if she kept walking and he followed her, she could lead him out to where a warrior might be hiding, waiting to pick off a stray soldier.

"You there," he yelled again, "I said stop!"

She glanced back at him. He was tall, with wavy brown hair and hazel eyes. The brass on his blue uniform told her the man was a captain. He leaned from his saddle and reached for her. No doubt all the women were to be raped by the blue coats. She would not lose her virginity so easily. Wiwila attempted to dodge away, but he was strong. She fought him as he lifted her to his saddle before him.

"Damn you, I'm trying to help you!"

She answered by attacking him with teeth and nails,

causing his horse to neigh and rear. He was an expert rider, she thought, almost as good as a Lakota warrior. He managed to keep his seat while twisting her arms behind her, rendering her helpless. "I ought to leave you out here to freeze to death," he muttered as he wheeled his horse and started back toward the center of the camp where other soldiers were burning lodges and supplies, shooting horses. A bewildered little group of women and children stood surrounded by a guard as the others burned the camp and gathered up the others.

Wiwila took a deep breath and yelled at the women in Lakota, "If we can delay them, our warriors will regroup and come back to save us!" They looked at her, puzzled and defeated. She tried to think of the Cheyenne words and could not remember them.

The soldier laughed. "You must not be one of them, my little minx. It's plain they don't understand you."

"Lakota, me," she snarled at him before she thought, looking over her shoulder at him.

His handsome face furrowed. "You speak English?"

She must not give herself away. Wiwila stared up at him as if uncomprehending. Her ability to understand the soldier talk might be the only thing that could save her later.

Her officer rode over to two other soldiers where they were joined by an officer chief with yellow hair.

The moon-faced one looked her over. "Where'd you get that toy?"

"I was saving her life, that's all." Her captor sounded embarrassed.

The red-faced one snickered. "Let's both save her life a little tonight when we're back in camp."

If Wiwila had had any doubts, she had none now. Tonight, the bluecoats would use her for their pleasure!

Two

Austin felt the girl in his arms stiffen. Did she speak English or was it only Tom Custer's tone she understood?

George Custer frowned. "Let's stick to business right now, shall we?"

Tom looked away from the girl reluctantly. "That white captive woman and child are dead."

Austin felt sadness and shock. "God, we didn't know there were white captives—"

"Stop feeling so guilty, Captain," Custer said. "It isn't our fault—things like this happen in war."

"Sir," Benteen's pale eyes blinked, but the distaste for his senior officer was there, "we're ready to ride out."

Behind them, red flames contrasted with the white snow as the Indian lodges and supplies burned. A soldier galloped up to a fire, threw in a beautiful beaded doeskin dress.

"Such a waste," Austin blurted without thinking as he watched the white leather dress burn. "These people will starve the rest of this winter."

The others scowled at him.

"Captain," Custer said with a slight smile, "that's the idea, to bring them to heel as General Sheridan ordered. Now take your hostage and add her to the group."

"Yes, sir." He saluted as best he could while holding onto her, then reined his horse around and rode over to the frightened, silent women and children. "All right, I leave you here." He let her slide down the side of his horse; she crossed and joined the others, glaring back at him.

As he started to ride out, he noticed four small children—children of mixed blood. Plainly they were frightened, but trying hard not to cry. He blinked, unbelieving. No, it couldn't be. Then they looked up at him and his heart fell. Oh, God, no.

Austin dismounted, ran through the snow to the shivering children. "Lance? Garnet?"

The small, half-breed boy looked up at him, his eyes as pale blue as his mother's had been. Clinging to him was a smaller girl and a pair of identical twin girls.

Austin squatted down. "Don't you know me? I'm your mother's friend, Austin Shaw. Where's your mother?"

The children hesitated; the boy seemed to recognize him.

It had been two years since Austin had seen these children back in Boston the night he had helped the beautiful socialite, Summer van Schuyler, escape on the train with her Cheyenne lover, Iron Knife. Now here were four of their five children all alone, cold and frightened.

"Where—where are your mother and father?" he asked again, but he was certain he already knew. Iron Knife would have protected his little family to the death and Summer would never have allowed herself to be separated from her children, unless . . . "Lance, answer me! Where's Summer Sky?"

Little Lance hesitated. When he finally spoke, he seemed uncertain of his words as if he had not used the English in a long time. "Father had grabbed up Storm and gotten away, but Mother was wounded and called out to him. He handed my brother over to our uncle Lance Bearer and went back for her."

Tears came to the big, blue eyes although the child, who was hardly more than eight years old, struggled manfully. Garnet, the little beauty, was no more than seven. She stood with her arms around the twin toddlers. In a haze, Austin tried to remember the twins' names. "Lacy." He struggled with his emotions. "Lacy and Lark. Oh, God, don't tell me your parents are dead?"

They didn't answer, they only stared back at him in numb shock. His vision blurred and his throat seemed to swell shut. It wouldn't do to have the Cheyenne women see an officer break down. He wanted to scream and curse and hit someone. That wouldn't help. He looked out toward the battlefield. "I—I've got to find them."

The sergeant standing nearby cleared his throat. "Beggin' your pardon, sir, our instructions are to get these hostages mounted and ride out."

Austin had never known such inner pain as he felt now staring down at the four children. He had loved Summer Van Schuyler all his life, but her heart had belonged to the big Cheyenne half-breed, Iron Knife. She had known the dangers of living in an Indian camp; known them all too well, but she had loved her warrior more than life itself. "I must bury them," he whispered.

Lance looked up at him. "Our people will bury them in the Cheyenne way."

"Yes, of course." Austin blinked hard, but still the tears filled his eyes, blurring his vision. "Children, I—I'll take you to your grandfather. You remember your grandfather?"

Three of them looked at him blankly, but Lance smiled in recognition. "The one with the big house far away?"

"Yes. He'll be glad to see you. You're safe now." He turned away so that no one could see him cry. Summer, he thought, beautiful Summer Sky. Once she had been engaged to Austin, but she had returned the expensive sapphire-and-diamond ring the day she rode away with Iron Knife.

Well, if he could do nothing for Summer, Austin would make it his duty to take care of her children. If things had been different, these children might have been his. He looked out toward the battlefield, all bloody and gray with smoke against the snow along the river. It made Austin feel better to know that wherever Summer lay, she was in the arms of her Indian lover; safe in death, forever safe in Iron Knife's embrace. Austin did not want to see her body, all broken like a frail bird. Little Lance was right—the Cheyenne would honor them in their own way.

He cleared his throat. "Sergeant, get some horses and blankets for all these hostages and look out well for these children. As soon as we return to camp, I'll escort them to their grandfather in Boston."

"Yes, sir." The burly sergeant saluted.

Austin dropped to one knee and hugged Summer's children to him. "It's going to be all right," he said softly, although he didn't know how. He hated the Cheyenne then, hated them for causing her death, and yet, this life had been her choice. As she had said to Austin as she left with her Cheyenne lover: *My mother told me once that if I ever found a once-in-a-lifetime love, I should run after it, damn the consequences and not look back.*

Austin swallowed hard, remembering. "Good-bye, children," he said. "I've got to return to my troops, but the sergeant will look after you on the ride. Everything will be all right now." He was lying, he knew; nothing would ever be the same again—not for him, not for these children.

He mounted up and rode back to his outfit, fighting to keep his broad shoulders from shaking. He must not break down right now, not with so much to do, so many responsibilities, and Cheyenne and Arapaho warriors waiting to attack the troops all the way back to Camp Supply. Abruptly, he hated all Indians, hated them with a sorrow-driven rage that was past reason. His beloved Summer would be alive now if she hadn't chosen to live among the Indians.

He reined in and rejoined the officers. Benteen stared at him. "What's the matter? You look like you just lost your best friend."

"She was more than that," Austin murmured.

"What?"

"Never mind." His memories of the fragile blond girl who had returned his ring and run away with the Cheyenne dog soldier were too precious for Austin to share with anyone. "Let's get the column moving, shall we?"

They rode out then through the snow, heading back north, their little group of hostages riding silently in the column. He looked back over his shoulder at the dead Indians and ponies strewn across the churned-up drifts now pink and splotchy with blood. Fire still licked its greedy way through the lodges, furs, and supplies the soldiers had burned and smoke rose in black clouds through the bare skeletons of trees. Austin had never felt such inner pain, knowing that somewhere behind him along the Washita River lay the only girl he had ever loved. "Oh God, Summer," he whispered, "I only hope you know I'll take care of your children."

Her children. There were five, he remembered. Who was missing? The dark little boy known as Storm Gathering. Storm had looked more like his Cheyenne father. Storm was still with the Cheyenne and there was nothing Austin could do about that.

He rode up beside Custer.

After a moment, the colonel asked, "What's the matter? You getting soft? You've seen dead people before."

Austin swallowed hard, not wanting to imagine his old love lying dead back there along the Washita. "You remember that time you came to a party at my family's estate before the war?"

"Yes, lovely party." Custer smiled.

"There was a girl, my fiancée."

Custer brightened. "Beautiful blonde? Yes, I remember her. The one who broke your engagement to run away with some Indian and—"

Austin nodded. "I didn't know they were in this camp. They're both dead."

The other shrugged. "It happens in war, and make no

mistake about it, this is war. We were just following General Sheridan's orders."

Damn the orders. Damn General Sheridan. But of course, Austin only nodded, his shoulders slumped. "Yes, it's war. There's no way the Plains tribes can ever live peacefully next to white farmers who are bent on plowing up the ground to plant wheat and corn."

"Not unless the Indians will submit to living on reservations."

Austin remembered the tall, handsome Iron Knife. "The Cheyenne are a proud, independent people. They'll never settle for living off the white man's charity."

"They'll have to learn," Custer yawned, "or die."

"Then most of them will die," Austin said, and he hated the Indians all over again for their gritty determination. Because of them, his Summer was dead. He stared at the snow as they nudged their horses into a trot. "I have four of Summer's five children among the hostages. I want to accompany them to Boston to turn them over to their grandfather."

"Sorry, Captain," the senior officer shook his head as they rode, "I can't spare you right now. With the Cheyenne on the warpath and me being shorthanded from all the desertions, I can't let you take a furlough."

"Autie, we've been friends a long time."

"Then you should know better than to presume on our friendship," Custer snapped, his pale eyes hard as blue glass. "I understand your feelings, but I still can't spare you. You can put the children on a stage and tip the driver to look after them. Wire ahead so their grandfather will be expecting them."

That was the logical thing to do, Austin knew, yet he wanted to do so much more than that. "Yes, sir."

Custer cleared his throat. "I'm sorry, Captain. I know you must have loved her very much."

Austin winced and closed his eyes. He did not want to

share his pain with anyone. As soon as he got those children on a stage, he was going to drown his sorrow into oblivion; get so drunk that he couldn't remember his name or anything from the past . . . at least, not until he woke up the next day.

The wind howled as if it, too, were mourning and it seemed a long, long trip riding back through the snow before they reached Camp Supply. Austin checked on the children often. That responsibility was the only thing that kept his grief under control. He could barely stand to look at the captive Indian women, hating them now. It wasn't fair that they were alive and his love was dead. He knew it wasn't logical, but hating them gave him something to focus on and took some of his grief away.

When they reached the camp, Austin asked again for a furlough so he could accompany the children back to Boston and was denied. He explained to little Lance why he could not go, cautioned him to look out for his sisters, then at dusk, put them in a comfortable wagon with a mounted escort that would accompany them farther north to connect with the train. Ironic, Austin thought as he waved to the wagonload of children as it pulled out through the snow, the building of the train tracks across the plains was one of the things causing the Cheyenne to go on the warpath. The tribes were smart enough to know that the coming of the train meant more white people arriving to fence off the land for towns and farms.

Austin stood and watched the wagon pull out. He stared after it until it disappeared into the darkness, then went to the crude tent where the telegraph was located.

"I've got to send a wire to Boston," he said. It wouldn't do to have the children arrive at Silas Van Schuyler's big mansion without the stern old robber baron knowing they were coming. Austin chewed the pencil for a long moment, trying to decide what to say. A telegram seemed such an emotionless way to tell of the tragedy, although old Silas and his oldest daughter were estranged. The rich Bostonian had hoped Summer would marry Austin, who was equally rich and prominent.

He chewed the pencil for a long moment, finally writing a terse message that Summer was dead, the children were on their way to Boston, and that little Lance would tell Silas what had happened when the children arrived.

With a heavy heart, Austin handed the message over and went outside into the darkness. It was still cold and snowing, but the troops were safe from attack now because of distance and the Indian women hostages they were holding. He did not want to think what might have happened to the ambitious Major Elliott and his troops who were still unaccounted for.

Austin returned to his tent where he got a big bottle of fine brandy out of his locker and proceeded to get very, very drunk. Outside, as darkness deepened, he could hear the soldiers laughing and singing. And why not? They had had a great victory over the Cheyenne and their allies at the Washita River and their losses had been light, considering. They would have to return with reinforcements to look for the missing Elliott and his men, who were most certainly dead.

Austin laughed bitterly. The reckless young Elliott had been willing to risk his life for a promotion. What a fool!

He staggered out into the darkness toward Custer's tent. "Permission to speak, sir." He attempted to salute, but had to grab the table to keep from falling.

His old friend looked up from the paperwork in front of him. "Austin, you're drunk."

"Not as drunk as I'm gonna be."

Custer sighed and put down his pen. "Since we're West Point schoolmates, I'll overlook your impudence."

"I want to resign from the army," Austin said, swaying on his feet. "The army kills people."

"That's its job, remember? Go sleep it off, Captain."

Austin shook his head and his vision blurred. "Can't sleep. Feel rotten."

"You'll feel better tomorrow," Custer said softly.

"How the hell would you know?" Austin's voice rose in sad anger, but he didn't care. "You don't even drink."

Custer leaned back in his chair and fingered his blond mustache. "Yes, and it keeps me from behaving like a drunken fool as you're doing now."

"Maybe you didn't understand, Colonel," Austin's voice rose, but he was past caring. "The woman I loved was killed out there today."

"Get hold of yourself, Captain," Custer's tone was cold as steel, "before I forget we're friends. We're both soldiers and soldiers follow orders. Our orders were to hit the Cheyenne and hit them hard, and we did that."

His head ached. "I hate Indians and I hate fighting Indians."

"I hate it, too," the other officer shrugged. "It's not nearly as noble a fight as what we just went through in the South, but the army chooses to send us out here. If I had your money, Austin, I wouldn't have reenlisted. I've always wondered why you did."

Austin was having a difficult time thinking clearly and he was not sure of the answer to that himself, except that he loved the wild, free landscape of the West. "If I were still at home, I'd have to take over some of Father's factories and deal with my mother and I'm not her favorite son."

"You get those children headed for the train?"

Austin nodded and murmured, "Those should have been my children, but she chose him instead."

"You'll feel better tomorrow," Custer said. "Go to bed."

"Can't sleep," Austin said stubbornly.

Custer stood up. "Well, most of the camp's not asleep, either—they're all celebrating. It's cold outside, but there's a lot of warm women among the captives and some of the officers are enjoying them tonight."

Austin paused, blinking as the words sank in. That was all those enemy women deserved, to be enjoyed as the spoils of war. "Serves them right."

Custer took his arm and led him out of the tent. "You'll feel better tomorrow. War kills people and this is war. We're both soldiers, helpless in the hands of Congress and the voters who want the Indians corralled so white men can have the land. Good night." He returned to his tent.

Austin swayed on his feet and looked out toward where the captives huddled around fires, guarded by soldiers. He looked at the bite mark on his arm and remembered the Lakota girl. She had white blood, but her eyes were gray, not blue. He hated her then, hated her for being alive while his beloved Summer was dead. Damn the Cheyenne, damn the Lakota, damn them all. If it weren't for the Indians, Summer would be alive.

He felt dead inside himself and it scared him. He wanted to feel alive, feel anything but this pain and black despair that enveloped him. He looked toward the captives again. It had been a long time since Austin had a woman, and even then, it had been a meaningless thing with a paid whore and he'd been ashamed afterwards. Suddenly, he wanted a woman, wanted her softness and warmth against him through this cold, lonely night. A man never felt as alive as he did when he was mating. It was an instinct as old as time itself.

Austin stood there alone in the darkness a long moment as the cold wind whined around him like a sobbing woman. He thought of death and yearned for the warmth of life. He took his pipe from his pocket, filled it with fumbling hands, tried to light it, but the icy wind blew the match out. With a muttered curse, he gave up and put the pipe back in his pocket. He didn't mean to, but his steps led him crookedly toward the captive camp, crunching through the snow. The sergeant came to attention, snapped him a salute.

"At ease, Sergeant, I've just come to inspect the captives."

"So have some of the other officers, sir," the sergeant laughed. "Some of them Injun females is right pretty."

Austin looked out at the captives huddled around their fires. For a moment, he didn't see the girl and the horrid thought crossed his mind that maybe one of the other officers had already taken her. He didn't like the idea, didn't like it at all. If she was left out here, one of the officers might still choose her.

Then he spotted her huddled down behind some of the others and pointed her out. "No one's taken her?"

The sergeant shook his head. "Several tried to, but she fought like a bobcat and they backed off, afraid she was more than they could handle."

"That's the God's truth. She bit the hell out of me when I caught her this morning."

The girl was looking at him now, her gray eyes reflecting the firelight like some wild thing, her long black hair shiny as silk. Her beautiful face betrayed no emotion.

"Bring her out."

The sergeant hesitated, doubt on his face. "Are you sure, sir? She's a hellion and you've had a little too—"

"I said bring her out!" Austin snapped and glared at the man.

The sergeant shrugged and nodded to two soldiers standing guard. "Bring that hellion out for the captain's pleasure."

They both looked at Austin questioningly but he nodded. "Yes, I'll take that one."

The Cheyenne women parted as the soldiers walked toward the fire. A pretty one jumped up. "I go with him," she said. "The officer will buy me presents if I sleep with him."

The soldier turned and looked toward Austin, but he

shook his head. "No, I want that mixed-blood Lakota girl with the gray eyes."

The sergeant said, "What do you suppose she was doing among the Cheyenne?"

Austin shrugged. "Who the hell cares? She was at the wrong place at the wrong time." *Just like Summer,* he thought, and chased the thought from his mind.

The soldiers each grabbed one of the Lakota girl's arms and jerked her to her feet, but she fought them.

"Don't hurt her," Austin yelled. *Hell, what did he care if they roughed her up a bit? Didn't he intend to do the same?* Then he realized that her courage and defiance had attracted him more than her beauty.

She fought the pair as they dragged her over to face him.

"Anyone speak her language?" Austin asked.

The other white men shook their heads.

"Never mind, sir," said the sergeant. "You won't need to communicate much for what you've got in mind."

The soldiers laughed and Austin felt himself flush. The girl glared up at him. It was evident she knew what was coming and that he would bed her only after a fight. No wonder the other officers had passed her up.

Austin hesitated. In spite of his drunken anger, he was born and bred a gentleman. Abruptly, he felt ashamed and started to tell them to send her back to her fire, but at that moment, she spat at him and came at him with her nails.

Austin caught her wrists and they struggled a long moment before he subdued her.

"Sir," the sergeant said, "maybe you ought to choose one that's more willing."

Austin held onto the girl, looking out at the Cheyenne women. Several smiled at him, eager to be an officer's toy for the evening.

He was drunk and he knew it. Austin Shaw, the gentleman rapist. Gone was all thought of protecting her from the other officers. In its place was the warmth and the fire of this gray-eyed hellion stirring a desire in him such as he hadn't felt in a long time. "No, I want this one. I'm going to treat her like the little savage she is. I think I can tame her."

He started away from the fire, staggering a little as he walked, dragging the girl along as she fought and clawed him.

The cold wind whipped his breath away as he pulled her toward his tent. *Summer. Summer. Summer.* He felt dead inside and in terrible need of vengeance against these savages.

The mixed-blood girl sat down in the snow, making it impossible to drag her. Damn her anyway—he would have his pleasure to take away his pain. Austin picked up the girl and started off toward his tent again. She was tall but slender; all warm, soft curves, nails and flashing teeth. It would be like bedding a bobcat. What in the hell had he let himself in for? He must be drunker than he realized. Well, it was too late to back down now. If he took the girl back to the prisoner compound, the soldiers would snicker.

He entered his tent, tossed the girl on his cot, and turned to close the flap. She tried to run past him and he grabbed her, her doeskin dress ripping down the front as they struggled. She fought him and managed to claw his face. He pushed her down on his cot where she lay, glaring up at him.

"What's your name?"

"Wiwila." She spat it at him.

"What does it mean?" He felt awkward and clumsy.

"Spring."

Spring. Yes, it was a good name for the beauty. "You know why I've brought you here." He reached for the bottle of brandy. "You want some?"

She shook her head and glared back in silence.

"So you do understand English," he muttered. "Well, I want some, I want a lot." He took a long drink, then wiped his mouth and studied her. She was smaller than he had realized, but more beautiful, too. Her hair had come loose and fallen around her shoulders in a black cloud and her defiant gray eyes glared back at him like a wolf bitch.

Drunk as he was, he realized suddenly that he had picked the most beautiful among the captive women . . . and certainly the most dangerous. What the hell had he been thinking? If he passed out while he was enjoying her, she'd try to kill him. He had always been cautious and careful. Tonight, he didn't care about danger; he welcomed anything that would take his mind off his grief.

Wiwila glared up at him, her arms crossed over her breasts, protecting them from his gaze. He was very, very drunk, and she sensed the anger and the sorrow in the man. She had understood when she saw him with those half-breed children that he had lost someone he loved with all his heart. Later, she had overheard the Cheyenne women talking about the yellow-haired girl who had belonged to a dog soldier named Iron Knife. Wiwila could have felt sorry for this man if she didn't hate him so much for being a soldier.

Like any white man, he saw her only as an object for his night's pleasure. Tomorrow, he would toss her back into the pack and choose another to warm his blankets.

This white man seemed to be stunned by her nakedness. He reached out and caught her hand, pulled it away, stared at her bare breasts, then jerked her to her feet. She struggled, but he pulled her into his embrace and his mouth covered hers, forcing her lips apart. As he put his tongue inside, she could taste the brandy and feel the heat of him as he molded himself against her. His hand went under the torn buckskin, caressing along her back as he buried his face in her hair. "Beautiful," he murmured, "and so warm and alive."

She felt the maleness of him probing against her and she

knew that he intended to take her virginity. Then again, if the soldiers had not attacked the camp, she would be giving her virginity to Go Dog tonight, courtesy of her stepbrother. Now she was not even sure either of the cruel warriors were alive and she didn't care.

She let the soldier kiss her, wondering if he was drunk enough that she could find a weapon in this tent, kill him and then sneak away from the camp. It would be a while before the camp settled down for the night. She had to buy herself some time. If she resisted the officer, he might send her back to the captives where she'd be under the watchful eyes of guards. She must do whatever it took to stay with him a couple of hours more. She knew what it would take, even though she hated this man. Very slowly, she molded herself against him and didn't fight him as his shaking hands caressed her breasts.

"God, you are desirable," he whispered and she raised her face to his and let him kiss her, putting her hot tongue between his lips. He gasped and shuddered, ran his hands up and down her body feverishly. "You're not Summer," he said. "She's dead because of Indians, but you're my prize tonight and by God, I intend to use you." His voice trembled with his grief and need.

Wiwila let him pull her to his cot.

"You know what I want, don't you?"

"I know." She looked up at him, her voice calm though his was shaking like his hands. *I will do whatever it takes,* she thought, *and then I will kill him and escape.*

"You speak English?" He swayed on his feet.

"A little."

He flushed then. "You know why I brought you here?"

Damn him, he was just like all men, thinking only of his lust. She only shrugged, pulled off her torn buckskin, and lay down on the cot. "I am here for your pleasure."

He stood looking down at her, his brown hair tumbled in his hazel eyes, red with grief.

He took another drink, as if for courage. For a long moment, he only stared at her in the dimness of the starlight filtering through the tent. Then he unbuttoned his pants and lay down on her, not even taking off his boots. His blue wool uniform scratched her tender skin as did the brass buttons. She resisted the urge to push him off onto the floor as he molded his hard body into her soft curves.

His hands were everywhere, running up and down her body, tangling in her hair as he kissed her. Wiwila resisted the urge to bite him when his tongue invaded her mouth. The hard maleness of him pressed against her thigh insistently. "You're shivering," he whispered against her lips and she could taste the brandy on his lips. "Are you cold?"

"What do you care, white man? Get on with your pleasure." She closed her eyes and waited for him to rape her. Was he wearing a knife in his belt? Could she stab him even as he enjoyed her? This might be her only chance to escape, so she must trade her virginity to this hated soldier for the chance she needed.

He was struggling to mount her, trying to put his maleness into her, but he was failing. He was too drunk, she thought suddenly. Although she had not had a man, she had heard the married women giggling behind their hands and whispering, so Wiwila knew that too much liquor could sometimes make a man unable to perform.

"Pretty," he murmured again, still trying to enter her small body, but his voice was fainter, as if he were fighting to stay conscious. His mouth went to her breasts, caressing them with his tongue as he struggled to make his body obey his mind. Then very slowly, his head sank against her breast and he lay still, breathing heavily.

Wiwila held her breath, waiting. He was a big man and his unconscious weight was heavy even as his day's growth of beard scratched her skin. She waited a long moment to make sure he was unconscious, and reached up to run her hand through his brown curls. The officer did not move.

With difficulty, she wiggled out from under him and stood up, naked and shivering. "Dirty bluecoat!"

She was cold without his warmth against her. She stepped away from the unconscious young officer in distaste, then grabbed up her doeskin dress from the floor. The soldier lay still, snoring now in his drunken stupor.

Wiwila ran her hands over his body until she found the knife in his belt. She would cut his throat and leave him to drown in his own blood. Outside, one sentry called to another and they both laughed, talking about how the officers were enjoying the Indian women right now. One of them said he hoped tomorrow night the soldiers could have the women if the officers were tired of them. She tucked the knife inside her torn dress and peeked out through the tent flap. The camp had too many sentries and she was a long way from the horse herd. Over in the distance, she could see where the Cheyenne women were bedded down in the open. They had a fire, but their camp didn't look too comfortable. If Captain Shaw hadn't chosen her, she would be out there in that miserable camp right now.

She looked back over her shoulder at the unconscious officer, considering. Asleep, he looked like a small, tired boy and very defenseless. She paused. He wasn't going to wake up anytime soon. She could easily plunge the knife into his unconscious body. With the knife in her hand, she hesitated, decided not to kill him, then was angry with herself for her weakness. She ought to cut his throat and take his scalp. What was holding her back?

He made a noise in his sleep as if he were sobbing and she thought of the girl he had loved, dead now back at the Washita. What was that to her? And yet . . .

No, she would let him live, just slip away, catch herself a horse and go. Wiwila started out of the tent. In the shadows, a sentry shouted, "Hey, someone stop that girl!" She made a run for it, her moccasined feet crunching across the snow as fleet as a doe, but soldiers were coming from every-

where. Two of them grabbed her. She fought and bit, trying
to stab them with the knife, but they overpowered her and
there was no escaping.

A bluecoat twisted the knife from her hand none too
gently. "Someone better see if the captain's all right."

A soldier went running to the officer's tent.

Good thing she hadn't harmed him, she thought, or they'd
be killing her right now.

The other yelled back, "He's okay, but he's out cold."

"Don't wake him—let him sleep it off." Several soldiers
had gathered around now.

An ugly one with buck teeth stared down at her, lust
bright in his eyes. "You must have been some fun, honey."
To the others, he said, "You suppose the captain would mind
if we sampled her, now that he's through with her?"

One of them spat in the snow. "Captain might not like
it—he might want her again. Put her back with the others."

Wiwila swore a Lakota curse. She should have stayed
with the captain; at least it was warm in the tent. Now the
soldiers dragged her back to the Cheyenne and tossed her
inside the circle. The women looked at her with distaste.

One of them said, "Lakota slut, you please the soldier."

"It was not my choice," Wiwila snarled. Why hadn't she
killed him when she had the chance? She went over to the
fire and huddled down, shivering in the cold wind. She
should have stayed with the officer; he would have kept her
warm through the night. In the morning, he would be in a
bad temper when they told him she had tried to escape. She
flexed her fingers, all bruised from the struggle for the
knife. Wiwila smiled to herself. She had discovered white
men's weakness; they all wanted to sleep with her and she
would gladly sacrifice her virginity for a chance to escape.
Sooner or later, she would get another chance to steal a
weapon and next time, she wouldn't hesitate to cut a throat.
She might kill that hated captain yet!

Three

The bugle blowing reveille just before dawn brought Austin awake with a start. He tried to sit up, but his head thudded like a war drum and his mouth tasted like an old wool blanket. "Brandy," he groaned aloud, remembering with a sigh. Austin never drank much or joined the other men when they set out to get uproariously drunk. Why had he done that? Then he remembered everything that had happened yesterday and his heart lurched. Iron Knife and Summer Sky were dead, killed in the battle at the Washita River.

He tried to push that sorrow from his heart as he put his aching head in his hands. What else? There had been an Indian girl. Even as he flushed at the memory, he looked around, uncertain as to what had happened. He was a Boston gentleman; he couldn't have raped a woman. No, not even an uncivilized savage. All he could recall of last night was that Summer was dead and how warm and alive the Lakota girl had been in his arms.

Outside, he heard footsteps crunching through the snow and a shadow fell across his tent entrance. A soldier cleared his throat. "Captain Shaw?"

"Come in." Austin tried to stand as he attempted a half-hearted return of the soldier's salute.

"Colonel Custer requests your presence, sir."

Oh, God, what did Autie want? Austin managed to suppress a groan. "Tell the colonel I'll report immediately." Austin saluted and the soldier spun on his heel and left.

Austin stumbled outside, got himself a pitcher of icy-cold water, and splashed his face. In the camp, everything seemed to be all hustle and bustle, soldiers hurrying about, horses on the picket line stamping and whinnying in the cold air. He wished he had time for some coffee, but Custer would be annoyed if his order weren't followed promptly. His head was still pounding as Austin made himself presentable and strode to Colonel Custer's tent. "Captain Shaw reporting as ordered, sir."

Custer looked up from his crude desk and frowned. "Sit down. You look like death warmed over."

"Thank you, sir." Austin sank into the folding chair across from the colonel and sighed. He had never felt so miserable in his whole life.

"Don't thank me, Captain," Custer snapped. "I was merely trying to get a chair under you before you fall down." The pale eyes glared into Austin's hazel ones.

He didn't know if a reply was appropriate or not, so he sank back in the chair and watched Custer pick up his steaming tin cup and sip the coffee. Austin could smell it from here. He wished the senior officer would offer him a cup, but Custer did not.

Moments passed. Austin wanted to take out his pipe and light up, but the other's annoyed expression told him he'd better not presume on their long friendship. Outside, the sound of the camp drifted to him—horses being saddled and wagons hitched up.

Colonel Custer stared at Austin a long moment before he spoke. "Austin, if you weren't a personal friend, I'd have your head for what happened last night."

Austin wrinkled his brow, trying to recall last night. It was mostly a blur of brandy. "I—I'm sorry, sir, I really don't remember—"

"I guess not!" Custer's voice was as cold as his face. "I quit drinking long ago, I suggest you do the same."

So he did know about the girl. "I'm sorry, sir, I'm not sure—"

"You took a Lakota girl into your tent last night."

Austin felt his face flush. "So did some of the others, I think."

Custer stood up, paced the tent. "But you were different, Captain. You were so drunk, you passed out."

He couldn't deny that, so he only sat staring at Custer's steaming coffee, wishing he had a cup.

"When the sentries caught her slipping out of your tent, she was armed with your own weapon. It's only luck that she didn't kill you or one of the others in her escape attempt."

Now Austin did groan aloud. "I—I had no idea."

"No excuse." Custer paused in his pacing and glared at him. "In the meantime, the whole camp is talking about it. If you hadn't served so well in the Rebel rebellion, I'd have you up for a court-martial."

"Yes, sir." He tried to remember last night, but only small details came back to him, the naked beauty of the Lakota girl, how her breasts had tasted, how her bare skin was like brown satin . . .

"Captain, are you listening to me?"

"What?" Austin jerked up. "Yes, sir."

Custer pulled at his blond mustache. "Since you endangered the whole camp and everyone knows about it, I have to punish you, despite our friendship."

"Yes, sir." It was all Austin expected. In his mind, he pictured himself involved in a court-martial, being forced to return to crowded, civilized Boston.

The girl. What had happened to the Lakota girl for trying to escape? Even as he thought it, Austin was annoyed with himself that he cared. She was an enemy and he was lucky she hadn't killed him.

"The Seventh is pulling out this morning, accompanied by additional troops," Custer said. "We've got to continue our campaign and find out what happened to Elliott and his men."

Austin's heart leaped. He yearned to go with the Seventh. His love of the West had kept him in the cavalry. "I'm looking forward to serving, sir."

Custer glared at him. "You aren't going."

"What?"

The other shook his head and resumed his pacing. "The Kansas volunteers finally made it in, but I don't think much of them. I'm going to use them to guard the Indian prisoners and escort them to Fort Dodge—"

"Begging your pardon, sir," Austin said before he thought, "but what has that to do with me?"

Custer glowered at him. "It has everything to do with you, mister. You are going to ride along with those volunteers, making sure Cheyenne warriors don't intercept them and free the prisoners."

"Go with the volunteers? But, sir—" Austin protested.

"Did I give you permission to speak?" Custer shouted. "I could be putting you up for court-martial this morning. You're getting off light. If we weren't old friends . . ." He let his voice trail off.

Austin felt suddenly nauseated. He was being drummed out of the Seventh while they continued their journey to the battle site where Austin hoped to bury the remains of Summer Sky and her love. "I beg the colonel to reconsider. I want more than anything to continue on this campaign—"

"Dammit, Captain, don't argue with me!"

Austin winced. He had pushed the other man too far. "Yes, sir."

"Your orders are that you will help the Kansas volunteers escort some fifty prisoners up to Fort Dodge. Now get out of here."

The interview was finished. Custer's hard, expressionless

blue eyes told Austin that. Austin stood up, snapped a salute. "Yes, sir."

He left the tent, swaying a little as he walked through the snow.

Outside, men were running about, readying wagons and saddling horses while the bugle blew. The sun peeked out behind gray clouds, but the wind was still chill across the dirty snow. He welcomed the cold wind across his face as he faced the harsh reality of his situation. He was in disgrace and lucky the Lakota girl hadn't murdered him as she attempted her escape. He wondered for a moment why she hadn't killed him.

Austin's head still throbbed as he got himself a cup of coffee at the cook's fire and returned to his tent. He sat down on his cot and wrapped his cold fingers around the steaming tin cup, then sipped the strong brew gratefully. Back in Boston, the maid or a butler would be serving coffee with sugar cubes and rich cream right now, along with omelettes and the finest sweet rolls from a silver platter in the large dining room. For a moment, the thought tempted him; then he remembered that his mother would also be seated at that table, and he flinched, thinking the army coffee in a crude tin cup tasted better at the thought.

He got out his pipe and lit it with trembling hands as he sipped the coffee, realizing just how disgraced he was. Austin Shaw, who had always been so cautious and conscientious, had acted like a damned fool and now would pay the penalty. His mood was as deep as his sorrow over Summer's death. He was disgraced. It was all that Lakota girl's fault, he decided. If she hadn't been so tempting and so pretty, he would have drunk himself senseless, passed out in his own tent without creating trouble, and this morning, he'd be riding out with the Seventh. Damn her anyway.

* * *

He didn't feel any better an hour later when he and the Kansas men assembled on the snowy parade ground to watch the Seventh Cavalry ride out to the jaunty tune, "Garry Owen."

One of the officers of the Nineteenth Kansas Volunteers strode over, saluted him. "Captain David Payne at your service, sir."

Austin gave him a halfhearted salute. The volunteer was younger than Austin, with dark hair and eyes.

"Colonel Custer tells me I am to take my orders from you." Plainly, Captain Payne didn't like that.

Austin sighed. "We leave for Fort Dodge immediately."

"Nursemaiding a bunch of squaws along the route is going to make it tough."

Austin winced at the epithet, but he didn't correct him. Austin wasn't feeling very charitable to Indians. "And we might be ambushed along the way by Cheyenne warriors attempting to get their women back."

"Yes, sir."

"Tell the men we leave as soon as you can get the captives mounted. Dismissed."

"Yes, sir." The other saluted and left.

It was all Austin could do to keep from groaning aloud as he returned to his tent to pack his things. With his head hurting and his heart sick, he was going to have to sit a saddle all day, heading away from where he wanted to be, and in disgrace besides. Damn that Lakota girl for causing him so much trouble!

Finally, the troop was assembled. Austin sat his horse, looking over the Kansas volunteers. They were a poor lot as far as he was concerned, even if they were organized by the Kansas governor. They'd been no help at all to Custer in the attack at the Washita, having gotten lost and delayed in the snowstorm. The Indian women and children were mounted on old, thin nags as they were herded into the line of march. He saw the Lakota girl in the group and was slightly annoyed with himself that he couldn't remember her name and wasn't sure if he'd even known it. He was both shocked that he couldn't remember using her for his pleasure and whether the experience had been worth what it was costing him.

He studied the silent women. Mostly Cheyenne, a few Arapaho and Kiowa, they sat their horses and glared back at him with closed, stoic faces. The children were also quiet and frightened. "Anybody here speak English?"

The women looked back at him, not answering.

They were defying him and the thought annoyed him. He ran his hand across his aching forehead and motioned to the Lakota girl. "You. I know you speak English."

She only looked at him, not denying or agreeing. Someone in the little group tittered and Austin felt himself flush all the way to his ears. She was defying him, humiliating him in front of the soldiers and the captives. "I know you speak English," he snapped at her. "Tell them they will not be hurt, that we are only going to take them up to the fort and detain them for a while. You tell them that."

An amused smile played across her lips. "If I told them, they might not believe me because I am an outsider."

"Tell them anyway!" Austin almost shouted at her.

The girl shrugged and spoke to the assembled women. They looked distrustful, but a little more relaxed.

Austin rode to the head of his troops, but he was certain he could feel the girl's gray eyes boring into his back. Custer had been right; Austin was lucky the girl hadn't killed him before fleeing his tent. Probably if she'd had time, she would have.

Wiwila watched the tall officer pass as he rode to the head of the column. He was furious with her for humiliating him before all the people, but she didn't regret it. It was all the hated bluecoat deserved. The captain was handsome for a white man, she decided, and there was an air of class about him, so unlike the brutish soldiers in the camp. He was attracted to her, she could tell, and angry with himself because of it. *Could she use that to her advantage?*

She still planned to escape, but she wasn't sure when or where she would make that attempt. If her would-be Cheyenne bridegroom were still alive, he might make an attempt to recapture her. The thought made her shudder. Better to be a white officer's slut than the chattel of the ugly Cheyenne warrior. If she could escape, she could make her way north to her aunt and uncle, who probably had no idea that the stepbrother had forced her to go south with him.

A Cheyenne woman said in a loud whisper, "I heard the captain bluecoat is in trouble over that Lakota wench."

"Ah? How so?" came an eager chorus of voices.

Wiwila's ears pricked up, but she looked straight ahead and made no notice that she had heard.

"I heard two soldiers talking. She almost got away and she had stolen his weapons."

The old woman next to her reached over and poked her. "Is that true?"

Wiwila shrugged and nudged her old horse along.

"She had a chance and didn't kill him?" asked an old hag. "Just goes to show she's more white than Lakota."

There was a murmur of agreement.

Wiwila ignored them all with dignified silence. There was no point in reminding these jealous women that the Lakota and the Cheyenne were old friends and allies. The women thought of her as more white than Indian.

She watched the officer's back as the column rode along through the snow. So he was in trouble because of her. Well, it was all he deserved.

Austin had never been as miserable in his whole life as he was on this ride. The wind was chill and his head pounded with every step his horse took. Worse than that, he had seen the curious way the silent women had regarded him and figured he was the butt of gossip. He had seemed to feel those cold, gray Lakota eyes drilling into his back throughout the day. Damn her anyway. She was as beautiful today as he remembered her and if he closed his eyes, in his mind he could see her as she had looked lying naked on his cot. He ran his tongue over his lips and remembered the taste of her nipples and the heat of her mouth. As bad as he felt with his hangover, desire still surged in him when he recalled the brown satin of her skin.

Then Austin felt a rush of guilt for wanting the girl even though the woman he loved so long ago lay dead back at the Washita River. He tried to push the thought of Summer and the pain of her loss out of his mind. He concentrated on the hate in the eyes of the Lakota girl and his anger at her to block out everything else.

It was a tedious ride that day but finally they camped on the prairie, still a long way from the fort.

Austin rode about the temporary camp, inspecting and giving orders. "Captain Payne, keep a sharp guard out tonight in case they try to escape."

"I reckon you'd know more about that than I would."

"What was that?" Austin snapped.

"Nothing, sir." The other snapped to attention.

A titter ran through the captives and the soldiers were fighting grins. The Lakota girl looked amused. Austin's face burned. He'd been a respected officer until he'd been tempted. He owed her vengeance. "As you were, Payne."

"Yes, sir. I'll get things taken care of." The volunteer officer saluted.

Austin leaned on his saddle horn. "Make sure the women have enough blankets and food."

"Whatever you say, sir, but some of the men think they'd be less trouble if we kept them a little hungry and cold."

"I don't care what the volunteers think," he lied. Hadn't he been acutely conscious all day of the way the men kept whispering together and watching him? Hell, and all over one gray-eyed half-breed girl.

They set guards and built fires as darkness settled in. Austin got his tin plate of stew and hardtack and sat before his fire alone, nursing a cup of steaming coffee. His headache had faded, but his mood was as grim as the weather.

When he looked up, he could see the captive women lying down around their fires, except for the Lakota girl. She was watching him with those cold, gray eyes. What the hell was she thinking? Was she only sorry she hadn't killed him when she'd had the chance or had she heard of his disgrace and was enjoying her triumph? What difference did it make?

The wind picked up and Austin shivered, then got up to do a final inspection of the camp. When he walked past the captive women, she looked at him. He wasn't sure what she was thinking and was doubly annoyed that he cared.

He retired to his tent, but he couldn't sleep. The cold wind seemed to be crying as it blew about the corners of the canvas. He lay on his cot, smoking his pipe and watching the tobacco glow as the fragrant scent drifted around him. He wondered if the girl was awake, too, and if she was cold. He forced himself to remember that she had almost cost him his army career last night, if not his life. Finally he knocked the ashes from his pipe and dropped off to sleep.

He was awakened in the middle of the night by a sentry's shout, then the sound of running feet outside. Austin sat bolt upright as footsteps ran to his tent.

"Enter!"

Captain Payne was breathless as he saluted. "Sir, we've lost a prisoner."

Austin blinked the sleep from his eyes. "What?"

"We did a count just now—one is missing."

"Just one?" Somehow he knew.

The man nodded. "The Lakota girl."

"She get a horse?"

"No, sir, she must be afoot. There's small tracks leading away from the camp."

Austin ground his teeth. "As cold as it is out there, she won't survive long. I won't have the whole camp aroused to chase after one lone woman."

The other shrugged. "That's what the men say. What's one squaw more or less?"

Austin winced at the word. "Tell the guard to keep a closer watch on the others, but I don't think the rest will be stupid enough to try it."

Stupid or brave enough, his inner voice said. She was the most stubborn, untamed creature he had ever run across.

"Yes, sir." The captain saluted and went out.

Austin lay back down, listening to the wind howl around his tent. Only that gray-eyed girl was crazy enough to try to get away in this cold, and without a horse. No doubt they'd find her frozen body at daylight within a mile or two of the camp. In his mind, he saw her body crumpled in the snow, the long black, hair blowing in the wind. The gusts howled again and shook the tent. Austin lay in the warmth of his wool blankets and pictured the girl struggling through the drifts without a buffalo robe or food. She'd die out there tonight.

Damn her. After a long moment, he swung his feet over the side of his cot and reached for his boots. Then he stuck his head out of his tent and yelled at a passing orderly. "Private, saddle up my horse."

"Sir?"

"You heard me! I'm going after that half-breed girl!"

"But Captain Payne said you said—"

"Never mind what I said," Austin snarled. "She may be a chief's daughter and as such, she's a valuable hostage."

"Yes, sir. I'll saddle your horse."

Austin sighed as he listened to the man's footsteps

crunching away in the snow; then he reached for his heavy buffalo fur overcoat and his rifle. He didn't believe for a moment that she had any status among the others—they certainly didn't treat her as such. He ought to let her die. Even as he thought that, he strode out into the snowy night. Only a few campfires flickered red against the white snow and the darkness. Here and there sentries walked their posts. Over at the captives' circle, the women and children huddled under army blankets, asleep.

The private brought Austin the roan stallion and he mounted up. "Where's her tracks?"

The soldier pointed. "Heading off to the west, sir. You want a squad to accompany you?"

It would be wise, Austin thought, but he shook his head. "No use getting all the men up. She's probably dead by now, but I'd better make sure." The thought upset him and that surprised him. She'd been nothing but trouble from the first time he laid eyes on her.

Austin rode over to the west of the camp, staring down at the small footprints in the snow. The wind cut into his face like a knife blade and he shivered. Damn her for getting him out of his warm blankets. Did she think she was going to walk all the way back to Sioux country? Was she desperate or just plain stubborn? In the meantime, headquarters wouldn't care if he delivered one Indian woman more or less. He ought to go back to his warm bed and let her reap what she so richly deserved. Even as he thought it, Austin knew he couldn't do it. Nudging his horse into a walk, he began to follow her tracks, so apparent in the moonlight reflecting off the white, white snow.

There was no sound save the howling wind, the noise of his stallion's hooves crunching through the hard crust of snow, and somewhere, a lonely coyote wail. The sound twisted his insides. If the girl fell and lay very long unconscious, lean predators would move in for the kill. Austin checked his rifle again to make sure it was loaded. The chill wind cut through his warm fur coat and stole the breath from his lips. He paused to look down at where her steps had hesitated and she had fallen in the snow, gotten up and moved on. Angry as he was, he also had a growing admiration for the spunky renegade. She didn't have a chance of getting out alive and she must know it, but it hadn't stopped her from trying.

He kept his horse moving, his gaze searching the drifts ahead for the small footprints. How far had he come? Austin reined in and twisted in his saddle to look behind him. He had lost track of the camp and its life-giving fires that were somewhere in the swirling blizzard behind him. The thought crossed his mind that he could get lost out here and become a victim himself. The West was an unrelenting mistress and anyone who took her for granted sometimes paid with his life. The snow had drifted, blown by the chill wind. In places, her tracks had been wiped out and he had to ride on, guessing his path until he again picked up the barest outline of her small moccasins in the white snow. If he didn't find her soon, he might not find her at all with the swirling drifts erasing her tracks. He came to another place where she had fallen, gotten up, and staggered on. With his heart beating hard, he urged the big stallion forward.

Up ahead, he saw a shape move like a shadow through the blizzard, then another. "Wiwila?"

The wind blew the sound back into his throat, leaving him breathless. The shapes turned and looked at him, their yellow eyes gleaming in the moonlight. *Wolves.*

Swearing, Austin grabbed his rifle and sent the predators scurrying as he fired. What had they been trailing? He urged his horse forward through the drifts; then he saw the small, dark form lying motionless against the whiteness.

Oh, God. Austin dismounted, ran to her. She lay crumpled in the snow, her black hair blowing in the wind. He was certain even as he reached for her that he was too late; the Lakota girl was dead.

Four

"Damn you for your stubbornness!" Austin knelt in the snow next to the motionless body, then gathered her into his arms. Her face was as white and cold as the ice. "Did you hate me that much that you'd die to get away?"

No answer. Austin shut his eyes as he cradled her against him and in his mind, he saw his beloved Summer lying back there somewhere on the Washita with the wolves prowling about the dead bodies. At this moment, this slim, helpless girl represented all the dead Indians, all the wrongs that his society had done against them. He held her against him and wept. "Damn you! Damn you anyway!"

At that moment, she stirred ever so slightly and he paused in disbelief. He put his head against her breast and heard the slight heartbeat. She was alive, but just barely.

Quickly, he opened his fur coat, pulled her inside it, then stood up, carrying her. She was chilled and stiff against the warmth of his body. Awkwardly, he tried to stride through the drifts back to his horse, but it was slow going. She weighed hardly anything. He swung up in the saddle, looking down into her pale, motionless face. "Don't you die on me," he muttered, "don't you dare die on me!"

She made no answer and did not move. He covered her with his coat, holding her tightly against his muscular chest. He could feel her thready pulse as he turned his horse and paused. All around him was nothing but swirling whiteness and a howling wind. Which way? He was no longer certain where he was or how far he had come. The blizzard had obscured his horse's tracks, so there was nothing to guide him. Even the distant campfires were no longer visible.

More wolves had joined the ones he'd scared away. Lurking near, they set up a howling as if they sensed that soon they would get the girl, her rescuer, and his horse. The roan nickered and laid back its ears. "Steady, boy," Austin murmured with an ease he did not feel. He'd been a fool to ride out here alone and he'd lost direction. Perhaps he could follow his own tracks. He only rode a few paces before he realized it was hopeless; the blowing snow had wiped out his stallion's hoofprints. Even if a patrol came looking for him, they would have no tracks to follow. The hair stood up on the back of his neck as he realized that all three of them might soon be a meal for the lean predators.

The girl in his arms stirred, burrowing unconsciously into the warmth of his embrace. Austin held her against him tightly as he tried to decide what to do next. "You'll be all right," he lied. "You're safe now."

None of them were safe; he knew that and it was a long time until dawn. Never before had he felt so helpless and so conscious of the fact that he was a foreigner in this harsh prairie country. He'd come out here to save this girl and now he might die, too. A sudden peace settled over him and he looked up at the sky. For a long moment, the wind quieted to a whisper and he seemed to feel his beloved Summer's presence. "If you're here with me now," he whispered, "help me make amends for the Washita by saving this girl."

For a long moment, there was nothing and he despaired. Austin was not a religious man and now he felt like a fool. Then someone seemed to whisper in his ear: *Trust. You are not going to die.*

At that moment, his panic subsided. Calm and inner peace spread through his being, allowing him to think. The answer came to him, clear as water in a brook. *Trust. Think. Turn your horse loose and let him find the way.* Holding the unconscious girl close with one hand, Austin loosed his hold on the reins. "Okay, boy, take us back to camp. You know the trail better than I do."

For a long moment, the horse did not move, its muzzle high as it sniffed the wind. Austin wavered toward despair. Maybe he hadn't had a sign from God, maybe . . .

Abruptly the horse began to walk. Austin was almost certain it wasn't the right direction. Suppose the horse was taking the wrong path? He almost grabbed the reins, but then he seemed to hear Summer's high, sweet voice: *It will be all right, Austin. God and I will take care of you, always.*

He nodded and held the girl close. If the message was wrong, if the horse missed the camp, the three would all freeze to death before dawn. He closed his eyes and listened to the wolves howling behind him, eager for the horse to stumble and fall. He lost track of time as the roan moved and the cold wind stole the very breath from his lips, but he felt such an inner peace that nothing else mattered anymore. The girl in his arms stirred ever so slightly, warmed by his big body, but Austin only held her close and kept riding. Finally his horse paused and Austin was almost afraid to open his eyes.

For a long moment, he saw nothing and his heart sank. Then, in the distance, he thought he saw a pinpoint of light. Had he been mistaken? Was his pathetic hope seeing light where there was none? "Keep going, boy," he whispered.

The roan obliged, moving slowly through the snow. Austin hardly dared to breathe. For a long moment, the light disappeared and he feared he had imagined it, but no, ahead, the light appeared again, brighter now and flickering. His horse whinnied and somewhere in the distance, other horses answered. The camp! They were approaching the camp! As they rode closer, Austin realized that the flickering lights were campfires. "Thank you," he whispered.

In minutes, he was within shouting distance. "Hallo the camp!"

Men scurried about. "Captain, is that you?"

"Yes, and I found the girl!"

They hurried to meet him as he rode into the camp circle, and one caught his stallion's bridle.

"Thank God," Captain Payne shouted. "We were about to send out a search party."

"Wouldn't have done any good," Austin said with certainty as he dismounted. "The tracks were wiped out in the snow." He stood there holding the still-unconscious girl.

"Oh Lord, sir, is she dead?"

"Not quite. Get me some warm broth and some brandy." He strode toward his tent, ducked, and laid her on his cot, knelt by her side. What was her name? A Lakota word for Spring. He searched his memory. "Wiwila, can you hear me?"

No answer. Austin lit a stub of candle and stuck it on his small travel trunk. Then he began to rub her hands and arms. What was he supposed to do? He wasn't certain. The buckskin dress was wet from snow. Austin pulled off her wet moccasins and began to rub her feet. They were such small feet and like two blocks of ice. A burly sergeant entered just then. "Here's your hot broth and brandy, sir."

"Good. Get me some warm stones from around the fire."

The man nodded and ran out.

Austin bent over her. "Don't you die, you hear me? Summer sent me after you, I know that now. I don't want my efforts to be in vain."

He put his arm under her head and lifted her. Her gray eyes flickered open, then closed again. She moaned aloud, the sound as sorrowful as an abandoned kitten, as if she had just realized that her escape had not worked.

The sergeant entered just then. "Here's your hot rocks, sir. I've wrapped them in blankets."

"Good." Austin laid the girl down and took the stones.

"She gonna die?" The fat sergeant peered down at her curiously.

"She'd better not! Now get out of here!" Austin turned to tuck the warmed rocks in all around her, then decided the wet dress had to come off. He took his knife, and cut it off while trying not to look at her bare body. Then he tucked the warmed stones and wool blankets around her. She moved ever so slightly and the color began to come back to her pale face. "Can you hear me?"

No answer, but she took a deep breath.

"You little idiot, you almost got us both killed." He put his arm under her head and shifted her. Her long eyelashes fluttered ever so slightly, hinting that she had regained consciousness. "Here's some brandy."

The girl resisted without opening her eyes, but Austin was persistent. He dripped the brandy between her lips very slowly and patiently.

She coughed and gasped, her gray eyes opening wide. "Hate you," she murmured.

"I'm not too crazy about you either," he muttered, wondering if Summer had really wanted him to save this untamed savage. "But it'd look bad on my record if a prisoner dies. Here, I've got some broth."

She was shivering and turned her head away as he held her up and spooned the savory beef broth between her lips. The blanket slipped down and he could see the soft curve of her breasts as he held her. Her eyes, as they glared back at him, were hard as gray granite, but the soft lips trembled and he saw vulnerability there. "Go away."

"I've got no place to go, lady. We're in my tent and if you think I'm going out in that blizzard, you're crazy."

She pulled away from him and snuggled back down in the wool blankets. "I hate you, damned soldier."

Austin sighed audibly. There was no reasoning with this woman. "You could at least be grateful I saved your life."

"Rather be dead than prisoner," she whispered so softly,

he had to strain to hear. Then she closed her eyes and began a rhythmic heavy breathing.

What had he expected? This girl wasn't the type to be grateful for being recaptured. She was like some wild thing that had to live free or die. Maybe he hadn't done her such a favor after all. On the other hand, he could not have lived with himself if he had not tried. Somehow, it seemed a small payback for the slaughter of Indian women and children at the Washita.

Now that she was safely asleep, Austin realized how wet and cold he was himself. He changed into dry clothes, got himself a bottle of brandy and his pipe. He was tired, but he couldn't sleep. He tamped his pipe full and lit it, leaning back against her cot as he sat on the floor. Outside, the wind still howled and rattled the tent, but inside, he was at peace. He sat savoring the fragrant tobacco as he smoked and sipped the brandy. He listened to the girl breathe. She hadn't been grateful, but he would do it all again if he had to. Fate had thrown the two of them together and he sensed somehow that she was his responsibility, for a while anyway. The thought almost made him groan aloud. He didn't need a burden like this. Well, she was only his problem until he got her up to Fort Dodge and after that . . . what about after that? He'd turn her over to the commander at the fort and she'd be their problem, God help them!

He smoked his pipe and watched her lovely face in the slight glow of the candle. He knew what her fate might be at the fort. The pretty Indian woman would end up warming some officer's blankets.

Austin frowned. She would resist, some drunken officer would try to tame her, and failing, would beat her into submission and enjoy her anyway. The thought made him wince and he reached out and brushed her tumble of black hair from her eyes. Now that he had rescued her, he felt a protective guardianship.

He listened to her even breathing and touched her hand.

She was warm now. Sitting on the floor, Austin shivered and thought about how warm and naked she was beneath those blankets. The images tortured him, but he let his mind linger over the thought.

His pipe had gone out. He emptied it and put it in his pocket. Then he blew out the candle, laid his head against her arm, and dropped off to sleep.

The next day, the sky cleared and the weather warmed a bit. Wiwila was returned to the prisoner compound without so much as a thank-you from the cold, gray eyes. Gray as a wolf's coat and as wild as that animal, Austin thought. He ignored the curious looks the other men gave him. If they thought he had enjoyed her during the night, none dared say so. As they saddled up and started north again through the melting snow, the prisoners were sullen and silent.

The rest of the trip was uneventful and miserable. It was bad enough to be in disgrace with all the men knowing Custer had sent him on "squaw duty" as punishment, but the way the girl glared at him both annoyed and depressed him. All during the trip, he could feel her angry gaze on his back.

At Fort Dodge, the prisoners were put in a fenced compound with some crude sod cabins for their use. Austin reported to the commander. "Captain Shaw reporting in with the Cheyenne women and children, sir."

The gray-haired major snapped him an annoyed salute. "At ease, Captain. Now just what the hell am I supposed to do with them?"

Austin shrugged. "Just hold them awhile, I suppose, until Custer's sure the warriors are going to go peacefully to the reservations."

The other snorted. "That could mean forever."

Austin didn't answer.

The other chewed his lip, thinking aloud. "Well, maybe it won't be so bad. After a few days, perhaps we can turn them loose around the fort. It'd be nice to have some women to clean our quarters and entertain the men." He winked.

"I wouldn't trust them, sir," Austin frowned. "They'd just as soon put a knife between your ribs as look at you."

The other grinned. "From what I hear, you have personal experience along those lines."

Austin felt his face burn red-hot. "I wouldn't listen to gossip, sir, if I were you."

"Quite so." The major stood up, suddenly serious. "I know your history, Shaw, and a man of your breeding and background wouldn't take up with some filthy squaw, no matter how pretty she is."

Austin started to come to Wiwila's defense, then realized how that would look to the major, and decided not to add to the gossip. "If the major pleases, I have reports to write."

The other nodded. "Dismissed, Captain. Perhaps in a week or two Colonel Custer will be back and you can rejoin your outfit."

Austin saluted. "I hope so, sir." He turned sharply and went out. He tried not to look at the prisoner compound as he returned to his quarters and began to write a report of his trip, but his mind kept going to the girl. There was a wire waiting on his desk that told him the children had arrived in Boston. Austin drew a sigh of relief over that. Old Silas Van Schuyler was rich and powerful; Summer's children would lack for nothing. He put his face in his hands and tried not to think about their mother.

The weather warmed slightly and the snow melted. The major gave orders that the Indian women were free to come and go about the post, but to keep a watchful eye on them. Austin ignored them completely. Soon it was evident that some of the women were occasionally sharing soldiers' blankets for money or trinkets. The soldiers had not seen women in a long time at this bleak outpost.

Was Wiwila giving away her favors for coins or pretties? Austin didn't even want to think about it, but late at night in his lonely bunk, he could think of nothing else. One night, driven by a hunger he could not suppress, he went to the prisoners' quarters. Wiwila sat on the floor against a wall. The other women looked up, smiled, and nodded knowingly to each other.

Austin felt his face flush. To the girl, he said, "Can we go outside and talk?"

She glared up at him, shrugged. "We have nothing to talk about, soldier."

The other women giggled behind their hands and Austin took out his pipe, holding it awkwardly. "Are you—are you pleased with your quarters? Can I get you anything?"

She looked up at him. "I want to return to my Lakota people. Can you get that for me?"

Damn her for being so obstinate. "Not yet, but maybe eventually if they decide the warriors won't attack us."

She shrugged, her voice sarcastic. "Thanks for nothing, you white scum."

The women smiled at his humiliation and he felt like grabbing up the girl and shaking her. At that moment, he wanted her in his bed more than he had ever wanted a woman in his whole life, but he wasn't sure how much to offer her. It would be embarrassing to be turned down in front of all these women. Austin turned and strode out into the night, tamping his pipe with angry frustration. He should pick one of the other captives for his pleasure. Certainly there were plenty of them who were willing. Some of them had winked at him just now. More than once at night, he had lain in the darkness and heard a woman's soft laughter through the thin walls of the officer's quarters. The problem was, none of the other women appealed to him.

Austin returned to his room and flopped down on his

bunk, smoking his pipe, his body tense with need. He heard footsteps outside his window and went to look out at the darkness. A sergeant walked past, his arm around one of the Cheyenne girls. Evidently, they were headed for the cavalry barn. Austin returned to his bed and lay staring into the darkness, thinking of the pair making love in the soft hay.

He should have been more insistent with the Lakota girl. Maybe she had only been toying with him, hoping to raise her price. At this moment, he would have paid a king's ransom for the warmth of her soft body in his arms, but he didn't have the nerve to face the amused scorn of all those women again. He closed his eyes and willed himself to sleep.

He came awake suddenly, puzzled and wondering what had awakened him. A small noise outside his door, then another. Presently the sound and footsteps moved on down the hall. Puzzled, Austin got up, tiptoed to the door, and peeked out. In the dim light, he recognized the Lakota girl in the embrace of a tall captain. Austin gritted his teeth. The thought that she would spend the night in the other officer's bed made his hands tighten into fists.

Then the pair turned slightly in the darkness and Austin realized the officer had his hand over her mouth. "Quiet, honey," the tall officer whispered, "until we get to my room. We'll have some fun then." He sounded drunk.

The girl struggled, making a soft noise of protest, trying to break free.

Austin stepped into the hall. "What's going on here?"

"Nothing," the other man said, but he didn't take his hand off the girl's mouth. "You know we've all been enjoying these Injun women."

In the dim light, the big gray eyes begged him for help.

Austin took a step forward. "I don't think the girl's willing. Why don't you choose another?"

The ugly captain laughed. "Because this one's the prettiest—you know that, Shaw. Everyone says she's been your bed-warmer for the trip up. Now don't be selfish."

Austin took a deep breath for control. "Let her go."

The other man backed away, still holding on to the girl. "What's with you? I'm not going to hurt her—I'm just going to enjoy her a little."

"No, you're not." Austin shook his head and moved two steps closer.

The other man frowned and swayed on his feet. "Now, Shaw, you aren't going to start a ruckus over this little honey, are you? We can share her tonight, if that's what's bothering you."

"I said let her go."

"Not 'til I get what I want from the little bitch."

Austin moved then, quick as a lightning bolt. He grabbed the girl and flung her to one side, even as his fist connected with her captor's jaw. The girl did not cry out, but the officer swore and charged at Austin. "You bastard! What's wrong with you? She's just a squaw!"

This might cost him his army career, but Austin looked into her terrified face and his rage made him reckless. He sidestepped the ugly drunk and hit him again. They rolled and fought in the hallway. Men came to their doors, stuck their heads out, yawning sleepily. "What's going on?"

The drunken officer staggered to his feet, wiping the blood from his mouth. "I wanted to share Shaw's Injun slut and he ain't willing."

"That's right!" Austin snapped. "Now get out of here and I'll take the girl back to the compound."

The captain swore under his breath, then limped away.

Austin looked at the gaping faces up and down the hallway. "Break it up. There's nothing more to see here."

Doors closed reluctantly. He stood alone with the girl

still cowering against the wall in the semi-darkness. Austin took her arm and looked longingly toward the door of his own room. He had won the right to bed her fair and square and to the victor belonged the spoils!

Five

Austin tightened his hold on the girl's arm, looked down into her eyes, then back toward his door.

She shook her head. "You pig! You save me so you can use me yourself."

"Shh! You'll wake all the men!"

"None of them are asleep and you know it."

Austin frowned. "You could be a little grateful."

Her lip curled disdainfully. "One soldier between my thighs is much like another. I am not grateful for that."

"Okay, I'll take you back to the compound." He led her out the door and across the gravel. Her flesh was warm against his hand and he wanted her more than he could have thought possible.

As they passed a storage building, the girl paused and turned toward him. "On the other hand, if you'd help me escape, I would do what you wanted."

He looked down at her, took a deep breath. "How do you know what I want?"

She laughed in a way that made him hate her. "I know what you want, soldier boy—what that other one wanted also. If I would let you do that, would you help me escape?"

He hesitated, assessing her. She must have read the urgent need in his eyes because abruptly, she slipped her arms around his neck, stood on her tiptoes, and kissed him. For a moment, Austin was so startled that he could not move, but she leaned into him, molding her soft curves against his body, her hands caressing the back of his neck, her mouth opening against his, her tongue teasing along the curve of his lips.

For just a second, he resisted; then he moaned deep in his throat and jerked her hard against him, kissing her with all the wild hunger that had been building in him since the moment he had first seen her. His hands went inside her dress, fumbling, then caressing her breasts.

Against his lips, she whispered, "We could go to your room or to the barn where the soldiers take the other women."

His heart pounded so hard, he was certain she could hear it. His hands shook as they fumbled with her clothes.

Her warm breath stroked his cheek. "Help me," she begged, "and I'll please you in ways you can only imagine."

Oh, he could imagine all right. Too many times late at night, he had pictured her under him, all warm and eager. "How—how much do you want?"

She laughed against his lips and rubbed her breasts against him. "Not money. I told you—help me escape."

His manhood was turgid and throbbing with need. He would tell her anything, *anything* to get her under him. He need only lie to her. And yet, he drew back, took a deep breath, shook his head. "I—I can't do that."

She pressed the curves of her body into his. "Why not?" she purred. "They'll think I did it on my own."

He sighed at the feel of her nipples against his chest and almost promised her. If he were to die five minutes after he had taken her, he might count it worth it. "I can't. Ask for money, trinkets, anything but that."

She pulled away from him, angry now. "I don't want anything else."

"You ask too much." He stepped back, abrupt and furious with her in his frustration.

She seemed to be appraising him with those wolf-gray eyes. "Other soldiers would have lied and promised."

He shook his head, damning himself for his old-fashioned ethics. "I am a man of honor—I couldn't do that."

"Not even to bed me?"

He clenched his teeth a long moment. "Not even to bed you," he said.

She laughed, then regarded him seriously. "You do not speak with a forked tongue. That is rare in a bluecoat."

"I know. I'm a damned fool. Now let's go back." He was cursing himself for not lying to her, taking advantage of her desperate situation for his own pleasure. He was a damned fool all right.

He walked her back to the compound. "After tonight, there'll be even more gossip."

She looked up at him, amused. "That I am your woman?" She was taunting him.

"Damn you, I don't find it funny." He started to leave.

"Captain," she called softly.

"What is it?" he turned and looked at her.

"Pilamaya. Wakan Tanka nici un."

Austin blinked. "What does that mean?"

"Never mind." She turned and fled into the compound.

Damn her for teasing him, playing with him. Austin strode back to his room. He lay on the bed, his body hard with desire. When he closed his eyes, he saw her naked, leaning over him, her hair a black tumble, her breasts brushing against his eager mouth. He rolled over on his belly and was even more miserable because he could almost feel her under him and he ached to mount her, then thrust and thrust until he exploded in a spasm of pleasure. It was a long time before he dropped off to sleep.

Wiwila couldn't sleep. *Pilamaya. Wakan Tanka nici un. Thank you. May the Great Spirit go with you.* She had blurted it out to the white soldier without thinking. Now she lay in her blankets listening to the other prisoners sigh and mumble in their blankets. Half of her hated the bluecoat because he would not help her escape. The other half gave him grudging admiration because he had been unwilling to lie even to bed her. It had been a long time since she had met a man of such honor. In the old days, the best of the warriors had been such men, but slowly, the white man was corrupting many of them. She thought now of the captain with his pale hair and hazel eyes. If he were a Lakota warrior, a good name for him would be White Wolf.

The night deepened, a cold, crisp night, and she dozed. Abruptly, a noise brought her awake. The shadow of a man loomed over her. White Wolf. He had come to her after all. For a split second, she almost reached for him, welcoming the passion she had seen banked behind those hazel eyes. Then the rank scent of the man came to her and she opened her mouth to scream as he clapped a dirty hand over her mouth.

"Be quiet, my future bride! I am here to rescue you."

Go Dog. The realization hit her like ice across her soul. She began to struggle, but he slapped her hard. "Be silent, little fool! Do you not realize I have come to save you?"

Dazed, she could only stare into the cruel face as he swung her up in his arms and turned to go. "I have a horse waiting just beyond the compound."

He was taking her away to slavery in his blankets. "No," she struggled as he strode toward the horse, "no, I don't want to go."

"You would choose being a prisoner of the bluecoats?" Go Dog snorted with disbelief, but kept walking. "You have gone loco, but I will take you anyway."

She tried to scream out as she struggled, but he hit her in the mouth, hard, and the taste of her own blood left her gasping with pain. "No, I—I—"

He clapped his hand over her mouth, threw her across his saddle. "Shut up or I will beat you!"

The bay horse loped away in the cold, starlit night, but still Wiwila struggled. She realized then she'd rather be a prisoner of the bluecoats forever than stuck in a Cheyenne camp with this ugly warrior.

Too late! She was helpless against his strength. As they galloped away, a bluecoat sentry yelled, "Halt! Who goes there?"

The bay horse did not slow down. The soldier fired after them, but it was too late and Wiwila knew it. The Cheyenne warrior had come after his bride and now she wished she had given the White Wolf soldier her virginity. Now it would be taken by this brute she hated.

The sentry shouting and the sound of gunfire awakened Austin from a troubled sleep in which he was making love to the sultry Lakota beauty and she was oh-so-willing and responsive. Barefooted, he ran to his door and yelled to a passing sentry, "What's the noise about?"

The sentry shrugged. "Seems one of the guards thought he saw a lone Indian on the outskirts of the camp. You know how the shadows play tricks on you, sir, when you're new on the post and it's late and you're alone."

Austin nodded. "That's a fact." In the cold starlight, he could see his own breath floating on the air. "Well, if there's anything to report, get back to me in a few minutes."

The other saluted and strode away, the snow crunching beneath his boots. Austin closed the door, went to the fire and poked it up, warming the room a little. Then yawning, he returned to his bunk.

It was only the next morning when they did a prisoner count that the sentries realized one was missing. A crusty

old sergeant came to inform Austin as he finished his breakfast and immediately he pushed his plate back, cursing.
"Damn her! I should have known she'd pull this!"

The grizzled soldier looked at him curiously. "You know
who it is, sir?"

"Oh, I'll bet I know who it is, all right!" He reached for
his topcoat and followed the sergeant out into the cold.
"Damn vixen has plotted to escape from the first."

The two of them walked across the parade ground toward
the compound. "Whose horse did she steal, anyway?"

The other shook his head. "Don't think there's a horse
missing, sir—at least, none reported."

Austin scratched his head, deep in thought. Maybe it
hadn't been Wiwila who escaped. After all, she wasn't
strong enough to cover the hundreds of miles to the Lakotas
without a horse, but she was just stubborn enough to try.

He faced the Cheyenne women and children, their stolid
brown faces betraying nothing. His gaze swept around the
compound, hoping against hope to see her, but it was as he
suspected. Again, he cursed himself for not investigating
further last night. "All right, when did the Lakota girl sneak
out?"

No answer. They stared back at him.

"I said, who helped her?"

Again, they only looked at him, hatred in their eyes and
maybe amusement that the bluecoats had been bested.

"We'll get her back, you know," Austin snapped at them.
"She can't get very far alone and on foot."

A ripple of contemptuous laughter skittered through the
women. "Not alone," muttered an old woman. "Her man
came for her."

"What?"

No one answered.

The words sank in. The Cheyenne warrior had stolen
her. Tonight, she would be his woman in every sense of the
word. The thought upset Austin more than he was willing

to admit. He turned to the sergeant at his elbow. "Sergeant, get a squad—we're going after her."

"Sir?" The older man looked incredulous. "Are you sure you want to do that? After all, it's only one little squaw, and they might be layin' a trap for us."

Austin felt his face burn. "Of course you're right, Sergeant. I can't expose my men to danger just to recover one Lakota girl."

The other nodded. "Just let her go, sir. I doubt Colonel Custer will notice one prisoner more or less."

They turned and left the compound together.

"Sergeant, you don't understand," Austin muttered. "I'm already in hot water with the colonel. This escape could get me broken in rank, so I've got to get the prisoner back."

The other hesitated. "I understand, sir."

Austin cursed himself for a fool. All that was important to him was retrieving the girl. "See that my horse is saddled—I'll go alone."

"Beggin' your pardon, sir, but is that wise?"

"Maybe not, but I can't put soldiers at risk because I let a couple of Indians outwit me. There's enough snow on the ground that I can follow the tracks easily."

The grizzled sergeant looked at him as they walked. "And suppose it turns out to be an ambush, sir?"

Austin chuckled. "Then someone can send my mother a medal and tell her what a hero I was. She'd like that—I've always been such a disappointment to her."

Within minutes, Austin was mounted up with a few supplies tied to his roan horse. As he rode away from the fort with a cold wind whipping him, he was having second thoughts about what he was doing.

"I should forget about the defiant little bitch," he muttered to his horse. "She plotted to get out of this camp, so she should be very happy."

Still, what he remembered was that Wiwila had wanted to return to the Lakota, not become a bride for a warrior she didn't like. He cursed himself for his desire; no, it was more like lust, he thought, being cruelly honest. Ever since the death of Summer, he had been in an agony of grief and it had become a terrible need for a woman—not just any woman, but the stormy, tempestuous Lakota girl. He must be losing his mind; a Boston gentleman with a lust for the fiery savage. He knew deep in his soul that he yearned to be the first man to take her, to tame her.

The weather warmed as he followed the trail and the day lengthened. After a while, the tracks slowed as if the warrior was convinced he was not being pursued, so he rode at a more leisurely pace. The tracks led off to the southwest as if the warrior were riding to join up with the Cheyenne band that had fled the Washita River that day. Austin reined in once and looked around at the cold, barren prairie. "You damned fool! You're liable to top a hill and find the whole Cheyenne nation waiting. Forget about her and go back to camp. There's pretty Cheyenne prisoners aplenty who'd happily warm your blankets for a few trinkets." That was true. How stupid and stubborn of him to want the one who had spurned him.

As the day lengthened, Austin was more and more aware of how far he was from the fort and any help. The snow lay in drifts and the wind picked up. Somewhere a coyote howled. Austin shivered and pulled his coat collar up around his ears. He had never felt as lonely as he did at this minute.

Along toward dusk, his horse paused and snorted. Immediately, Austin came alert. "What is it, boy?"

He stood up in his stirrups and surveyed the vast expanse of treeless emptiness. He'd have to find shelter from the night cold. In the distance, he could just make out a tipi set up in a small grove of trees with a wisp of smoke drifting from a camp fire. Austin dismounted, ground-tied his horse, and reached for his rifle. He would scout out the area, make sure it was not a trap. Cautiously, he crept forward. It was a single tipi, with only one paint horse tied out front and no one in sight. After a few minutes of watching, Austin crept forward to investigate. From inside, he heard sounds of argument. He recognized Wiwila's voice and a man's but he could not understand the words except her tone told him she was terrified yet defiant.

His heart was beating hard enough to hear, Austin thought. With his knife, he slit an opening in the tipi and looked in. The girl lay half naked on her back, fighting off an ugly brave who was struggling to force himself between her thighs. Even as Austin watched, she sank her teeth into the man's arm and the warrior screamed in angry surprise and struck her.

At that point, Austin forgot caution. He lunged for the man, jerking him backward, pulling him away from the girl. They fell through the ripped tipi out onto the snowy ground, but Austin never let go. He saw the flash of steel as the other pulled a knife, but it was too late. Strong in his fury, Austin stabbed the Indian and stabbed him again, leaving him dead and bleeding scarlet against the snow. For a split second, he yelled in triumph, fighting an obscene urge to scalp the man in victory, then recoiled in horror at the thought. He was becoming a savage himself.

"Wiwila," he said and crawled back into the tipi through the growing darkness. "Wiwila, are you all right?"

She was sobbing and in answer, she held out her arms to him. He gathered her into a protective embrace, holding her naked body close and shushing her tenderly. "It's all right," he whispered. "Everything is all right for both of us." He knew it was true as tears came to his eyes. He could let go of his grief now over Summer's untimely death; this girl needed him more.

She sobbed uncontrollably, burying her face against his chest. "He—he came for me. I didn't want to go, but he forced me. I knew you would come, White Wolf."

"White Wolf?"

"It is a name I have for you."

He liked it. He liked it much more than his civilized name. He held her close, rocking back and forth with her, whispering soft things into her ear. "You'll be all right now," he said. "I'll look after you."

She only trembled and for a long time, he held her close. They needed to return, he knew that; they were vulnerable out here on the windswept prairie alone, but the way she clung to him made him never want to lose her again.

Finally she quieted. "What—what do we do now?"

It was dark inside the tipi. "Nothing tonight—it's too late. I'll put the horses out of the wind; fix some food."

"There's a rabbit Go Dog shot this afternoon," Wiwila volunteered, "and maybe some pemmican."

"Good. I've got some coffee, so we'll have a feast. Let me go take care of the horses."

He left her and went outside. The dead brave still lay there. Austin touched him, counting coup like any Indian warrior. *White Wolf, she had called him.* He felt freer and more fulfilled than he had in a long time. The thought horrified him. Could he be the same Boston aristocrat who had graduated from West Point and was heir to a great fortune? He had just stabbed a man to death and had counted coup on him. This country was changing him and the thought unnerved him.

Austin dragged the body into a ravine and tossed branches and leaves over it, then staked both horses to graze in a sheltered place in the grove of trees. When he came back to the lodge, Wiwila had built up the fire and had a pot of coffee boiling. In the darkness, they settled into their cozy lodge and ate, then sat staring into the flames.

Then she leaned back against his chest with a tired sigh and without thinking, Austin brushed her hair from her face and kissed her hair. She looked up at him, her full lips half-open. "What happens in the morning?"

Austin sighed. "You know what I'm supposed to do—I return you to the prisoner compound."

"And if I don't want to go?"

For a long moment, he said nothing, only pulled out his pipe and filled it. "I could always give you the Cheyenne's horse, let you escape, tell the army I couldn't find you."

"You would lie for me?"

He smoked his pipe in silence for a long moment. "It is not an honorable thing to do."

"I know that." She laid her face against his chest.

"But for you, I would do it," he said finally, smoking and staring into the fire.

"White Wolf, would you go with me?"

"Me?" He looked surprised. "Where would we go?"

"To the Lakota," she said simply. "Other white men have turned their backs on their kind and joined the tribes."

"They'd kill me."

She shook her head. "No, they would think you brave to ride into their camp and join them."

Austin thought about it a long moment as he smoked and she seemed to sense the longing in him.

"White Wolf?"

He shook his head. "I couldn't do it," he said finally. "I have duties and obligations among my own people."

"Oh." She sounded disappointed. "I thought when you came after me, well . . ."

"Well, what?" He knocked his pipe out in the firepit, slipped it in his pocket.

"I thought you wanted me."

She looked up at him, her hair a black tumble above the tawny brown of her skin, her lips ripe and wet.

"You know I do," he whispered and bent to kiss her.

She had not expected his kiss to be so gentle, not with the lustful way he had looked at her over the past few days.

Wiwila put the tip of her tongue against his lips and he gasped. At that instant, she slipped her tongue inside.

He gasped and pulled her against him hard. She had not meant to develop feelings for this bluecoat, and yet, he had come to her rescue several times in the past few days. Perhaps, she thought as she kissed him, it was only gratitude.

He took a deep, ragged breath and pulled away. "What is it you want from me?"

"Want?" She looked up at him in surprise, seeing the uncertainty in his hazel eyes. "I am grateful, that's all."

She saw the stormy expression in his handsome face. Perhaps he was angry with her or, maybe, with himself. "You're not a whore. You don't have to pay me back."

The moment was lost. Wiwila pulled back and shrugged. "Can't you just accept my gift for what it is and not question every little thing?"

"I'm afraid I'll be sorry later." He leaned back against a pile of buffalo robes. "Let's sleep and at dawn, we'll head back to camp."

"All right." Was she annoyed or disappointed or only surprised? Wiwila wasn't sure herself except that she was shocked that she had almost given herself to this enemy.

They settled down in the snug warmth of the lodge with the wind howling and blowing snow outside. During the night, the weather grew colder and she found herself curling up against the white man for his warmth. She was only dimly aware that he wrapped his arms around her and pulled her into the circle of his embrace. She felt safe and protected and warm there as she drifted back off to sleep.

It was almost dawn when she awakened with his face against her hair and his hand on her breast. She opened her eyes and looked up at him. His eyes flickered open and she saw the need there.

"Wiwila?"

She knew the unspoken question in those words and in answer, she slipped her arms around his neck and pressed herself against him. She would lose her virginity in the next few minutes, she knew, but there was no man she would rather give it to.

Six

She did not need to urge him. The bluecoat made tender love to her, hot and urgent. Her need was as great as his. She had not known that a woman could want a union as urgently as any man, yet she found herself spreading herself, pulling him on top of her.

He hesitated only a moment above her. "Are you sure?" he whispered.

"Very sure," she gasped between clenched teeth. "I want it—I want you!"

He came into her then, very slowly, as if afraid he might hurt her. Wiwila came up off the fur robe, pulling him down into her. The sudden thrust tore through the silk of her virginity and she gasped.

He paused, his voice unsteady. "I—I didn't mean to hurt you."

"Take it," she said, "I give you my virginity!"

At that moment, he surrendered to his own need and came into her hard, again and again.

It was pain and pleasure and an overwhelming need such as she had never felt before spiraling her to a dizzying summit before he thrust into her one last time and gave up his seed in a surge of passion. Wiwila locked her legs around his hard-driving hips so that he could not escape from her body until he had climaxed in a hot rush; then she, too, surrendered to the moment, her body quivering as she met his, her passion every bit as stormy as his own.

After a long moment, he collapsed on her, breathing hard. They lay locked together, listening to the cold wind blow outside the cozy lodge.

He sighed and sat up. "My God, what have I done?"

"I wanted it, too," she reminded him.

He shook his head and sat up. "I feel like a barbarian. This was not honorable."

She straightened her clothes, wondering for the first time if she had been stupid in surrendering to the moment. She had just given her virginity to an enemy. "You've wanted me from the first time you saw me," she reminded him.

He looked down at her, his handsome face uncertain. "And I still do, God help me, I still do!"

He gathered her into his arms, kissing her face, her breasts and the passion built in her again so that she pulled him down to her, urging him on. He took her a second time, this time, longer and more passionate so that she was clawing his back, begging for release before he finally brought her to the summit of ecstasy.

He seemed ashamed to look at her now as they lay there listening to the wind outside. "We've got to get back," he said finally.

"All right." She began to gather up her things, thinking she had misjudged him. Now that he had enjoyed her, he would be like other white men and cast her aside because she was Lakota. Well, it was no more than she expected.

Outside, the snow had stopped although it was still cold. She dressed, then the soldier wrapped her in a warm buffalo robe and saddled both horses.

"Are you ready?" He avoided her gaze.

She only nodded.

He lifted her to the Cheyenne's horse and as he did so, he looked up at her a long moment. "I'm sorry," he said gently. "I had no right."

She only shrugged, wondering if he was sorry that he had taken her or only sorry that she might try to obligate him in some way. She was not sure herself how she felt about him. "Soldiers use Indian girls all the time—it's not important."

His face reddened as their eyes met, and the muscles in his jaw clenched as if he were angry or insulted. "Yes, I suppose it was no more than that."

He mounted his own horse and they did not speak again as they began the long miles back to the fort. She watched his broad back as he rode ahead of her and remembered the feel of his hard body against hers and the hot eagerness of his mouth on her breasts. She had wanted this enemy in the most primitive way a woman can want a man and it both surprised and shocked her.

Once back at the fort, the officer dismounted and led her horse over to the compound. The guard on duty saluted.

"At ease, Private. I'm returning an escaped prisoner, that's all."

"Yes, sir." The younger man's eyes were bright with curiosity. "Major Nelson's looking for you, sir."

She watched the captain flinch. "All right."

He came around and lifted her from her horse. For just a moment, he held her close as he lowered her to the ground, his eyes never leaving hers. In that moment, she remembered the heat of their mating and knew that there would never be another man, red or white, who could make her lose all sense of reason the way he had. "Good-bye, White Wolf."

He didn't answer, merely nodded to the guard. "Take care of her, soldier."

"Yes, sir."

She turned and looked back, but White Wolf was riding away, returning the horses to the barn.

When she was turned out in the fenced compound, the Cheyenne women sneered at her with stony faces. "You become the bluecoat's whore?"

She didn't answer. Yes, maybe that's all she was to him, but for her, it was growing into something more.

Austin cursed himself as he went to the barn to turn in the horses. The major wanted to see him which meant he was in serious trouble. What a fool he had been. He had jeopardized his whole career over a Lakota girl who had no doubt submitted to him in the hopes of bettering her situation at the camp. Worse than that, what he had done was low and without honor, and Austin Shaw had always prided himself on his honor. Now he was no better than the most base and evil of the soldiers, preying on the beauty and vulnerability of the captive women. Well, he wouldn't let that happen again.

With a sigh, Austin crossed the parade ground and reported to the major's office.

The old man's face was stern. "Shut the door, Captain."

"Yes, sir." Austin stood on one foot and then the other while the older man glared at him.

"You have been off the post without permission?"

"Yes, sir, but—"

"I don't want to hear excuses!" the other barked.

"No, sir."

The major stood, clasped his hands behind his back, and paced the floor, the light gleaming on his bald head. "I don't know what's happened to you, Shaw. I hear you used to be an exemplary officer, but now you do things that make me doubt your sanity. I know Custer sent you back here because you had created problems on the Washita campaign."

He wasn't sure if he was expected to answer, so Austin

said nothing. He had never realized silence could be so loud.

The other paused, fixing him with a steely gaze. "Gossip tells me a girl you were once engaged to was killed there, so I can sympathize with your feelings, but leaving the post yesterday without permission is too much, just too much." He shook his head. "Do you have an explanation?"

Austin took a deep breath. "One of the captive women was abducted, and I went after her."

"What's one squaw more or less? Frankly, I'll be damn glad when we can be rid of all those Injuns. I hear we may be shipping them on to Fort Hays. Well, good riddance! I don't mind you men pleasuring yourselves with them, but—"

"Begging your pardon, sir, it was more than that." Austin knew he should not have interrupted the senior officer, but he hated the thought that the major thought of his emotions toward Wiwila as some dirty, shameful thing. Was it more than that? He wasn't sure himself.

The major sighed, sat back down, and motioned Austin to a chair. "Cigar, Captain?"

Austin shook his head. "I have my pipe if you don't mind—"

The other waved him permission. "Captain Shaw, what you have done, on top of what happened at the Washita is very serious business. You could be court-martialed, or at the very least, broken in rank."

Austin paused in filling his pipe. "I know that."

The major lit a cigar and stared at Austin as if trying to see inside his brain. "I don't understand you," he said and shook his head. "Gambling your whole career the way you've done the last few days."

"I don't understand it either," Austin admitted, lighting his pipe. His thoughts went to the mixed-blood girl and he knew he would do it again if need be, rescuing her from any man who would take her from him. She was his—*his*.

"Perhaps your mind is stressed," the major said more kindly, watching him closely. "You've been out on the plains a long time and before that, you were in some of the biggest battles of the war, right along with Custer."

He didn't want to remember the hell of the Civil War or killing Indians. Austin said nothing, not wanting to contradict the superior officer. He didn't think he was crazy or stressed; it was his passion for the fiery, dark girl with the wide, gray eyes that had made him throw caution to the wind.

"Captain, I know your family." The major leaned back in his chair. "I wonder what they would say about your strange behavior all because of some Injun girl?"

"She's not just any girl," Austin blurted.

"Be that as it may," the major smoked his cigar, watching the smoke drift, "she's certainly not appropriate for someone of your station. A plaything, maybe, that you can tire of like a kid with a bowl of cheap candy. Do you understand me, Captain?"

Austin swallowed back his anger. "Yes, sir."

"Good, then this discussion is finished." The older officer stood up. "Enjoy your brown tart a little while longer, Captain, then forget her."

"But, sir—"

"You heard me, Captain Shaw." He bit off his words.

"Yes, sir." Austin saluted, spun on his heel, and left the office.

The major stared after him and sighed. Being out on the desolate plains too long made men lose their judgment . . . or even their minds. A shame, considering that Captain Shaw was from such a prominent family. Maybe if he gave Austin a long leave back East or asked Custer to reassign him to a more civilized post, the captain would come out of his malaise. The major smiled. As an old friend of Austin's father, that was the least he could do.

* * *

Austin left the office seething at the major, but he knew the man was only doing his duty. In a way, he was right; Austin had been acting like a damned fool ever since the Washita campaign. Was it grief for the lost Summer Van Schuyler or was it lust for the Lakota girl? He didn't want to delve any further into it, he decided, as he did his duties about the post. There was little happening in the cold with most of the troops away on manoeuvres.

That evening, he went to supper at the mess, saying little and ignoring the talk of the other officers.

"I had a pretty Cheyenne last night," Captain Tasley stroked his sleek mustache and leered at Austin. "What about that Lakota girl—Shaw, she worth my time?"

Austin bristled. "Don't you put your dirty hands on Wiwila or I'll kill you."

He heard the sudden silence and realized the other men were staring at him with curiosity.

Tasley laughed. "That good, hey? We've all just been sharing the women around—"

"I meant what I said," Austin said so softly that the others seemed to be straining to hear.

Captain Tasley sneered. "I guess that makes it pretty clear—that squaw belongs to Shaw and nobody can sample until he tires of her."

Austin came up off his chair suddenly, turning the chair over in his anger. The chubby officer next to him grabbed his arm. "Shaw, pay him no heed."

"I'll kill him if he touches her," Austin said again and left the table. Behind him, he heard Tasley, "Why, I believe he's serious about that Injun girl."

Another snorted with laughter. "Shaw? He's a Boston blueblood. It's unthinkable, but men get pretty lonely out here after a while, you know, and sometimes go loco."

Austin went out into the night and slammed the door. Everyone seemed to be certain he was losing his mind. Now that he thought of it, he had doubts himself. He had thought that once he had enjoyed the girl's lush body, the hold she had on him would be broken, but incredibly, it was even stronger now and he hated her for it. Who was taming whom? As dusk spread across the cold landscape, Austin returned to his quarters, built up his fire, and poured himself a glass of fine port wine. He settled in with a book and his pipe before the fire and tried to read, but he couldn't keep his mind on the story.

Out in the hall, he heard laughter and talk. Austin got up from his chair, opened the door slightly, and saw two fellow officers leading Cheyenne women into their quarters. Probably many of the officers would be choosing girls tonight just as they had other nights to provide amusement. So victors had always done with vanquished women.

The thought crossed his mind that some officer such as Tasley might ignore his warning and take Wiwila to his bed, returning her in the morning like some paid whore. The thought caused him to slam his book shut and reach for his glass of port. From down the hall, he heard faint laughter and music. Austin fiddled with his pipe, imagining what was going on in some of those rooms. In his mind, he saw Wiwila again as she had been last night: her naked, ripe body; her breasts offered to his eager mouth; the hot wetness of her as he had thrust deep into her velvet place. Abruptly, he needed a woman in the worst way. There were some blowsy white whores in a filthy place on the edge of the fort grounds, but the thought sickened him.

He heard someone walking down the hall and went to the door, opened it. A young corporal passed.

"Corporal?"

The man turned and saluted. "Yes, sir?"

"Your business here?"

The other reddened. "I was delivering a girl to Captain Tasley, sir."

Austin's breath seemed to stop. "Was she Cheyenne?"

"Yes, sir. It's Saturday night. Can I, er, bring you a little company?"

He wanted to say, *No, certainly not. It's despicable,* but he couldn't say it. Austin took a deep breath. "Well, I could use a girl to—to clean my quarters."

A knowing smile touched the corners of the other's mouth. Austin wanted to hit him for it. "Yes, sir. Any particular type, sir?"

"The Lakota girl, you know the one?"

"Yes, sir, the one with gray eyes? I'll fetch her." The young man saluted and left.

Austin leaned against the doorjamb and cursed himself for a weak, rutting fool. He was no better than any of them and these women were helpless captives. God help him, he didn't care; he wanted that girl in his bed. She had become an obsession. Maybe if he enjoyed her one more night, it would break his fascination. Austin stripped off his shirt, filled his washbasin, and began to wash. There was a knock at the door.

"Come in."

"Here she is, sir." The corporal had the girl handcuffed as he led her in. "I hope she can clean your quarters to suit you, sir." The young man grinned in a knowing way that made Austin want to strike him.

"You may go." He studied her. He had forgotten how slender she was; tall but defiant, even now as she stood before him in chains. Her face was a closed book. She did not smile or exhibit any recognition.

Austin felt his groin tighten. "I'm sure she'll do, Corporal. You may pick her up in the morning." He held out his hand for the keys.

The corporal saluted, handed him the keys to the handcuffs, went out, and closed the door. The silence was awkward. She stood there in the handcuffs, looking up at him. He wished he could know what she was thinking.

Now he was the one who was ill at ease. "You know why I had you brought here?"

"Of course. You want to sleep with me."

He felt his face flush hot. He was the one with power, but somehow, it didn't feel that way. "I—I wanted a chance to explain about last night."

Her face was cold with scorn. "No need for regrets."

"All right then—we understand each other."

She looked up at him, her gray eyes defiant in her beautiful face. "It's not as if I have much choice. I'm trying to survive."

He felt his face flush and wanted to shake her, demand if that was all it had meant when he had taken her in that tipi in the snow, but of course, he had too much pride. He unlocked the handcuffs and nodded toward the washbasin. "Clean yourself up."

She paused, rubbing her wrists. "And you will watch?"

He didn't answer. She understood his hunger too well.

"All right." She pulled off the ragged deerskin shift and tossed it across a chair, then walked over to the washbasin near the fireplace.

Austin took a deep, shuddering breath as he watched her in the dim glow of the fire. She was naked, her brown skin like silk as she soaped herself. He watched her wash herself, his need growing as he stared at her. Finally he crossed over, caught her to him, her skin wet and soapy. She put her hands on his bare chest.

"Damn you," he muttered, "for making me want you until I have no pride and no honor, nothing except my need for you."

She said nothing, only opened her lips against his nipple, biting there until he shivered with excitement as he ran his hands up and down her soapy body, then he swung her up in his arms, kissing her wet breasts over and over. Wiwila looked up at him, arching her back so that she offered him her nipples for a feast of passion. He sucked them hard until she groaned and caught his head in her hands, holding him against her breasts, not wanting him ever to stop. "White Wolf," she whispered, "make love to me."

"You little vixen, I wish I knew if you were sincere," he muttered as he knelt and laid her on the bearskin rug before the fire.

"Would it make any difference?" She writhed on the soft fur that felt so good beneath her naked body as she let her thighs fall wide apart.

He cursed softly. "You know it wouldn't. I'd have you whether you cared about me or not."

She didn't know herself how she felt about this conqueror who could use her body without her permission. Still, she held her hands up to him.

With a groan of surrender, he fell to his knees and kissed the insides of her thighs over and over again. She caught his head between her two hands, guiding him to her belly, where he put his warm, wet tongue in her navel and then began licking downward. She tried to close her thighs, but he put his forearms on them so they were wide apart and she couldn't close them. His hot breath moved down her thigh and then he put his mouth on her mound. She started in surprise, tried to draw away, but he would not be denied. His mouth and tongue invaded her, teased her until she surrendered to the feeling and held his face against her, urging him—no, demanding—that he kiss there, suck there, thrust deep into her with his hard, hot tongue.

She climaxed with a shuddering moan and with that, he quickly unbuttoned his pants, not even taking them off, his need was so great. She saw the passion deep in his eyes as he thrust into her, riding her relentlessly. She clawed at his bare back as he rode her hard, deeper and faster until he climaxed, meshing his wet body with hers as they writhed on the soft fur.

Then they lay together on the rug in the firelight, his arm under her head, his other hand caressing her breast. "I never knew a man could want a woman like I want you," he muttered and he sounded angry.

His anger puzzled her. "Have I not pleased you?"

"Yes, dammit, yes!"

"Then why are you so angry?"

"I don't know." He came up on one elbow, looking down at her. "Because you're so unsuitable—so completely and impossibly unsuitable. It can never be more than this, do you understand?"

She reached to touch his face. "Have I asked for more?"

He laughed without mirth. "You're not in a position to ask for anything. You're my prisoner, a pet to play with when I have need of you."

"And do you need me?" she whispered.

He cursed again, gathering her into his arms, kissing her face over and over. "I'll tire of you, I know I'll tire of you if I just use you enough."

"And then the other officers can have me?"

He paused, frowning, then shrugged. "Of course. What's one soldier more or less to an Injun girl?"

She struck him across the face then and he grabbed her wrist, pulled her to her feet. "Don't try my patience, you gray-eyed bitch! You're here for my amusement, remember?"

She didn't smile. "And when you drop off to sleep, I may cut your throat and escape."

He laughed without mirth. "I've already locked up all the weapons. Besides, I still have the handcuffs, remember?" He swept her into his arms, carried her to his bed. He walked over to pick up the handcuffs, came back to the bed, put one on her slim wrist, then locked the other to the iron bed post. Then he proceeded to strip his clothes off.

She lay watching him undress. He was all man, wide-shouldered, lean-hipped and with a big, turgid manhood.

"Take a good look," he said through clenched teeth. "I'm

going to have my fill of you tonight so I can forget about you tomorrow before you cost me my career."

She looked up at him calmly, seeing the uncertainty behind his hazel eyes. "You won't forget me, White Wolf, not after what we've shared—"

"Stop calling me that!" he snapped as he lay down on top of her. "I am Captain Austin Shaw of the very civilized Boston Shaws and I can never be anything else."

She had hoped for more than he was willing to give; she knew that now and tears welled up in her throat. He was after all, a white officer and she was a lowly, mixed-blood Lakota girl, good only for his amusement. He need never know it meant so much more than that to her.

He caught her free hand and kissed her fingertips, slowly sucking each of them in turn in an erotic manner that made her breathe faster. She could feel his hard manhood pulsating against her thigh as he tilted her head back and kissed her, forcing her mouth open so that he could explore her throat deep with his tongue and would not take no for an answer . . . as if she wanted to say no.

Instead, she sucked his tongue into her mouth, touching his tongue with hers.

Her touch seemed to ignite more fire in him. He caressed her breasts, playing with them, teasing them until they throbbed and then he mated with her again, riding her slowly and deliberately until she was gasping for relief before he finally spilled his seed deep within her. Then he lay on her, gasping.

"White Wolf," she whispered, "I am your woman and will always be."

"Don't say that," he snapped, pulling away from her. "I'm using you, don't you understand? That's all it is."

"Not to me."

He snorted with derision. "You would say anything to improve your lot."

"Then use me and forget about me . . . if you can."

"I can and I will," he answered and began to make love to her all over again, virile and rough in his need.

After a while, he fell asleep on top of her. She lay in the firelight, looking at the man's face as it smoothed out and became vulnerable again. Without meaning to, her free hand came up and stroked his cheek. He smiled and settled deeper against her. She reached to pull the blanket up over both of them and it crossed her mind that she would be happy to sleep with this man in her arms for the rest of her life. Then she muttered a Lakota curse, knowing that he was a bluecoat, a killer of her people, and she was only an Injun slut to him. Some elegant, back-east white girl would become his permanent woman. All she would have were these few nights while he appeased his hunger for Wiwila's body.

She didn't sleep. She lay with him in her arms, watching the frowns of his face smooth out until he seemed younger. No man had ever been so protective and gentle with her and White Wolf had aroused passion in her that she hadn't known she was capable of.

Sometime in the night, she awakened and realized he was unlocking the handcuffs. "You can stab me and escape if you want to."

She didn't answer, only opened her arms to him and they lay curled in a warm embrace and drifted back off to sleep.

The next morning, he was silent, watching her without speaking as she dressed and he returned her to the prisoner's compound. She clung to the fence and stared after him. "White Wolf?"

"Don't call me that." He paused and looked back at her. "We're from two different worlds and that can't change."

"I know." She stared after him long after he had left.

Austin ate his breakfast without talking to the other officers, lost in a jumble of emotion. A private came into the mess hall, clicked his heels, and saluted.

"At ease, soldier," Austin said.

"The major would like to see you at once, sir."

"Dammit, what is it this time?" Then, without waiting for an answer, he nodded. "I'll be right there."

He watched the soldier go, wondering what the senior officer wanted. Camp gossip had surely told the old man that Austin had taken full advantage of the use of the prisoner just as the major had recommended.

He went to the office, was ushered inside, and saluted. "Captain Shaw here as requested, sir."

The major leaned back in his chair, smiled. "I have a special favor for you, Captain Shaw."

"Sir?"

"You don't need to thank me, but I've arranged a furlough for you."

Austin tried not to react with shock. "A furlough, sir? I'm sorry, but I don't think I—"

"You've been out on the plains too long," the major said. "You need to return to civilization for a while, get your perspective back, maybe call on some elegant young ladies who will be having coming-out parties this spring."

Austin shook his head. "Sir, you don't understand—"

"No, Captain," the other's voice turned icy, "this is an order. There's a supply wagon headed to meet the eastbound train in thirty minutes. I want you on that wagon."

"But I protest—"

"You heard me!" the major bellowed, standing up. "You'll thank me later. Now get your gear. I don't want you to miss that train. Dismissed."

"Yes, sir." Austin snapped him a salute, turned, and left. He wouldn't have time to say anything to the Lakota girl, he thought as he strode toward his quarters. Even if he did, what would he say? He didn't know himself. Well, maybe it was better this way. It was evident the major was worried about him.

Austin went to his quarters and packed his things. He barely made the wagon as it was pulling out to meet the train that would take him back to Boston. He tried not to think of her, but he found himself looking back toward the fort as he pulled away. Wiwila had said she was a survivor; now she would have to look after herself. She would do that admirably, he thought. Any of the officers would be glad to give her protection and little gifts for the privilege of enjoying her body just as he had done. The thought made him so sick, he almost jumped off the wagon as it turned the bend and drove away from the fort. Then it was too late. In a few hours, he would be on a train headed back to Boston.

Seven

Robert Shaw closed the door against the cold Boston wind and stood staring at the telegram the messenger had just delivered. "Hmm."

"What is it, dear?" Tiny Elizabeth Shaw paused as she descended the stairway, wheezing from her tight corset. "Not bad news, I hope."

"Well, yes and no." He rubbed his ruddy forehead. "Let's adjourn to the library and we'll discuss this."

"Oh dear, there's something you're not telling me. Is it—"

"It's about our son, but it's a little strange." He escorted his wife into the estate's large library and gestured to the butler to bring tea.

Elizabeth sat down, wringing her small, nervous hands. "Now tell me. Is it from Todd? Is it?"

"It's about Austin."

It was evident she was now less interested. Todd had always been her favorite son. "Has Austin been killed? I always told him it was crazy to stay in the army when you could make such a good position for him with any one of your companies—"

"Please, dear." Robert shook his head and gestured for silence until the portly butler had brought in the tea tray and left, closing the doors behind him. "It's a telegram from the major at Fort Dodge. He's sending Austin home on furlough."

She brightened and began to pour tea. "Why, that's good news. After we heard that Summer Van Schuyler had been killed in the attack on those savages, I was afraid—"

"There's a reason the major is sending Austin home." Robert pursed his lips thoughtfully. "He says Austin has done some very strange things lately, almost to the point of being discharged. He thinks his mind must be under severe stress."

"Oh, my! It's because of Summer's death, isn't it?"

"He doesn't say that." Robert reread the telegram and rubbed his ruddy face. "The major thinks a furlough will do Austin good."

She sipped her tea thoughtfully. "Dear, why don't you use your influence to get Austin reassigned to some civilized place like Washington, D.C. until his enlistment is up?"

"He wouldn't like our meddling." Robert brushed his white hair back from his forehead. "After all, he's a grown man and—"

"Do this for me, dear." It wasn't a request, it was a command. She leaned back in her chair, pleased with herself. "Now maybe he'll forget this foolish army career and take over your business interests as I always thought Todd would."

Robert sighed. Elizabeth had always favored their younger son, which led to friction between the parents and both boys. "You know Todd isn't likely to leave Denver. He's happy working on that newspaper."

"I want both my boys right here where they can look after me in my old age."

Robert hesitated. How could he tell his wife that her smothering personality was what had driven both of their sons from the house? Robert had long since resigned himself to being under his wife's thumb, but he could not blame his sons for escaping their mother's grasp. "All right. I know a couple of senators I can contact. In the meantime, let's try to make Austin's visit as pleasant as possible. No prying questions or attempts to influence him."

"Why, I'd never do such a thing." She looked genuinely shocked and hurt. "When is he arriving?"

"Day after tomorrow." He stood up, walked to the fireplace, and tossed the paper into the flames. He felt guilty about interfering in Austin's life.

"Good," she said and finished her tea. "You contact all those important people at the capitol and get him away from those horrid savages and I'll begin planning a welcome-home party."

Robert whirled and looked at her askance. "Perhaps you didn't understand. The boy may have severe nervous and mental problems. I'd think Austin would need peace and solitude."

"Nonsense! He needs to get back into the kind of social life that is expected of people of our station. With Summer dead, maybe he can finally quit mooning over her and look about for a suitable match. Hmm." She set down her teacup. "There's that congressman's daughter, and the banker's niece." She clapped her hands together like a pleased child. "Yes, I must have a party for him."

Robert Shaw sighed and fell silent, knowing that when his wife set her mind to something, she could not be stopped. "Very well." He pulled his fine gold watch from his pocket. "Look at the time. I've got to get down to my office."

Wiwila stared out through the fence at the windswept prairie. The officer had not been to see her for several days. Perhaps now that he had bedded her, he was tired of her. She could expect no more from a bluecoat.

A private came to the gate. "The captain wants you."

She smiled. So White Wolf still needed her. She was unsure of her feelings for him, but certainly his quarters were more comfortable than this prisoner compound. She followed the private out.

But the room the private escorted her to was not familiar, nor was the officer standing looking out the window with his back to her.

"Here she is, Captain Tasley. I'll wait outside."

"No need." The officer turned around and smiled and Wiwila's heart sank. It was the captain with the mustache. "You're dismissed, Private. I may have to interrogate the prisoner for an hour or two."

"Yes, sir." The man left, closing the door behind him.

"I'm Captain Tasley." He came over, smiling. "Do you speak English?"

"A little." Wiwila shrank back against the door. She already knew from his cruel eyes what it was he wanted.

"Would you like some whiskey?"

"No. I would like to go back to the compound."

He paused in pouring himself a drink. "That would be a stupid thing to do." He sipped his whiskey. "That's a miserable place."

"Where is Captain Shaw?"

The man threw back his head and laughed. "Why, he's gone. Didn't you know that?"

"Gone?" Her heart sank as she shook her head.

"I can only imagine what he told you, but of course he didn't mean any of it." He sat down on the edge of his desk, watching her and smiling. "He asked for a transfer and has gone back East."

Did this bluecoat lie? She wasn't sure. "He—he is not coming back?"

Captain Tasley shrugged. "No. I think maybe he has gone back to marry some pretty, white girl."

Her world seemed to shake and she grabbed hold of the

back of a chair. "He said the white girl he loved was killed at the Washita."

The man put down his liquor and stood up. "I know he bedded you, but surely you didn't think a rich, white officer could be serious about you?"

She didn't answer, waves of shock still washing over her. *White Wolf. Oh, White Wolf.*

Captain Tasley grinned, came over, and stood looking down at her. "You're just a pretty little squaw, meant to be a plaything for an officer. I could make life here very comfortable for you."

She blinked. "You and me?"

"Sure." He reached out and tangled his fingers in her hair. "You warm my bed and please me, and I'll make sure you get trinkets and extra food. Do we understand each other?"

As he bent his head to kiss her, she shoved him away. "No, never, you white pig."

He grabbed her, jerked her to him. "You brown slut! You let him bed you and now you'll do the same for me."

When he tried to kiss her, she brought both hands up, clawing his face until he stumbled backward, cursing. "You bitch! I'll make you pay for that!"

"You touch me again, Captain, I'll scream so loud, all the soldiers will come running."

He backed away, breathing heavily and wiping at his bloody face. "All right, you wait for your soldier who's never coming back. There's plenty of other Injun women in the compound who'll be pleased to have my gifts and warm bed." He strode to the door, threw it open, yelled at his orderly, "Sergeant, come take this filthy squaw back to the prisoners."

The grizzled old sergeant came in, looked at the officer's bloody scratches, and took Wiwila's arm. As she was led out, the captain yelled after her, "He's not coming back, you hear me, slut? You'll regret passing up this chance!"

She didn't answer as the sergeant led her away. "Is it—is it true that Captain Shaw has gone to Boston?"

"It's true." The old sergeant sounded sorry for her.

Wiwila was proud. Defiantly, she lifted her chin and blinked back the tears as she was returned to the prisoner compound. It was a long time until spring and maybe she was going to be miserable and cold, but that wasn't what hurt most. She hadn't realized how much White Wolf had come to mean to her, and now he was gone, perhaps to marry a white girl. Wiwila would never see him again.

Austin sighed as the carriage drew to a halt in front of his parents' red-brick Georgian mansion. The footmen were taking down the Christmas decorations. Strange, he didn't remember the holidays passing this year. In early January, Boston seemed more cold and barren than the vast plains country he had grown to love.

The thin, old driver came around to open the door. "Here we are, sir, and if I may say so, the staff is right glad to see you home."

"Thank you, Hemmings." Austin stepped out and went up the walk, deliberately not looking toward the vast, ugly Victorian estate down the street. Summer's home.

The portly butler met him at the door and took his coat and hat. "Ah, belated happy holidays, sir, and I'm pleased you're safe and sound."

Austin patted his shoulder and smiled. "It's been a long time, hey, Williams?"

Then his parents were rushing to meet him. "Oh, Austin, we're so glad you're here."

He hugged them both. "I don't know what I've done to deserve a furlough, but of course, I won't be staying long."

His parents exchanged covert glances, which puzzled him.

Robert Shaw's ruddy face turned a deeper red. "Come

in and let us look at you. Williams, we'll have coffee in the library."

Austin let them lead him into that vast room and they all settled before the fire. Now the three of them looked at each other as if they were not quite sure what to say.

Austin cleared his throat. "You're both looking well."

His mother twisted her hands together and looked first at his father, then at him. "And you, Austin, are you well?"

What had caused a question like that?

"Of course. A little sad, perhaps, after what happened to Summer."

"Well," his mother sniffed, "I always said a girl who would throw over her fiancé for a half-breed, penniless Injun should have known that—"

"Mother," Austin said and tried to keep the cold anger from overpowering him, "please don't speak that way about her. Iron Knife was a fine fellow. I couldn't blame her at all for choosing him over me."

His father looked from one to the other, evidently nervous at the tension between the pair. "It was a sad thing, a very sad thing."

"Nevertheless," Elizabeth persisted, "I can't imagine anyone giving up a life of privilege in a civilized society for some Injun—"

"Enough!" Austin stood up suddenly, startling the butler as he entered with the silver tray so that coffee sloshed out of the pot. "I'm going to my room and we will not discuss this again."

He strode out of the room and behind him, he heard his father's annoyed voice. "Now, Elizabeth, see what you've done?"

"Me?" The fake innocence in her tone made Austin grit his teeth as he crossed the hall toward the stairs. "I was only trying to make conversation. Everyone else in our circle of friends is saying the same thing."

Austin went upstairs to his comfortable old room, threw

himself across the bed, and stared at the horses galloping across the walls. This vast estate, all the factories and wealth, someday this would all be his and Todd's. Like Todd, Austin didn't want that burden. Todd had escaped to Colorado. Would he himself ever be free?

Austin looked out the window at the falling snow. Snow. When he closed his eyes, he saw Wiwila riding through the white drifts, wild and beautiful and untamed. He hadn't realized how free he felt out on the prairie. No, he could not blame Summer for returning the priceless sapphire-and-diamond ring that had been in his family so long and running away with the Cheyenne dog soldier. What had happened to that ring? Oh, yes. It was in the vault at the Lester jewelry store downtown.

Summer. He must make arrangements to visit her children tomorrow and see how they are doing. He wondered how many days he would have to stay for this furlough and then felt guilty that he already wanted to leave.

The next morning at breakfast, he mentioned that he had sent a note over to the Van Schuylers and intended to call there this morning.

His mother acted as if she might say something, then her husband shook his head ever so slightly. "All right, Austin, whatever will set your mind at ease."

"Mind? It is simple courtesy, that's all." Irritably, Austin helped himself to honeyed ham off the silver tray the butler offered him. "Besides, I want to see how the children are doing. Have you seen them?"

The pair shook their heads. "Not since we called on them after we got the bad news. Silas seems pleased to have that oldest boy with him."

"Of course," said his mother, buttering a pastry, "the Van Schuylers won't be able to attend the party, since they're in mourning, but—"

"Party? What party?" Austin paused as he poured cream in his coffee.

"Well," his mother smiled, warming to her subject, "I thought since you hadn't been home in a while, I should give a party so you could see all your old friends—"

"I wish you had waited to see what I thought," Austin snapped. "I'm really not in a mood for parties, Mother."

"Oh, but it will cheer you up. And I've invited that congresssman's daughter, and the investment banker's niece, and—"

Austin sighed. "Mother, you never cease to amaze me."

"Me?" She touched her breast with one birdlike claw, so very innocently. "I was only trying—"

"I know what you were trying," Austin said and threw the fine linen napkin across the elegant china plate. "You must stop planning this immediately."

"Stop?" his mother wailed, "I can't stop. Why, the invitations are already out and the young ladies have begun to reply."

His father looked sheepish and shook his head. "I tried to talk her out of it."

Austin had always known who was really in charge of the household. Tiny, nervous Elizabeth Shaw always got her way.

"If you insist on giving this party, you can do it without me." Austin stood up.

Elizabeth began to gasp for air and fan herself with her handkerchief. "I'll be humiliated. Everyone in society will be talking about it. Quick, Robert, my dear, my smelling salts!"

Austin glared at her as his father scrambled to do her bidding. "I am not in the mood to dance with a bunch of giddy young ladies who are after the Shaw fortune."

His mother quite forgot she was on the verge of fainting. "I'll have you know," she declared staunchly, "I haven't invited any young ladies who don't already have money."

"I'm interested in neither merger nor marriage," Austin said, and left the dining room. Damn her anyway. He wondered again how long it would be before he could return to his post. Last night, he had dreamed of Wiwila, and on this cold, bleak morning, he missed her pretty face and smiled to himself to think of how his mother would react to his bedding the mixed-breed savage girl. Well, Mother would never know. In the meantime, no matter how much he protested, he knew if invitations to a homecoming party had been sent, there was no way to avoid attending. It would cause too much gossip.

Later that morning, he paid a call on the Van Schuyler household. Silas was looking quite old, but his youngest daughter, Angela, was turning into a beautiful young woman who looked unhappy to be wearing mourning.

The butler ushered Austin into the music room. He paused, looking around and remembering that this had been Summer and her dead mother's favorite room.

The three of them settled before the fire.

Austin sighed. "I'm so sorry about Summer."

A frown crossed the old man's face. As he aged, his lean face with its prominent hooked nose looked more and more like a hawk. "It was bound to happen—she was such a fool when she could have made so many good matches."

"Father, I always told you Summer was not a chip off the old block," pouty, blond Angela reminded him.

Austin looked around the room, remembering the harp and the times Summer had played the piano for him. "Following one's heart is what one must do to find happiness."

"Happiness?" Silas snorted. "She didn't find happiness, she found death."

Austin winced. "Perhaps whatever happiness she got from her marriage was worth the price she paid for it."

"Poppycock!" Silas frowned at him. "I'm surprised at you, Austin. You were the boy who had his feet on the ground, so practical. I expected you to leave the army once the war ended and come home to run your father's businesses, since Todd refused to."

He didn't want to discuss any of that right now. "How are the children?"

Angela frowned. Austin realized she was almost a young woman. "Lance is taking up entirely too much of Father's time and I'll never turn that Garnet into a lady."

"She's jealous," Silas said. "Angela liked having everything to herself."

"It was my heritage," she insisted. "And then here come these little Injun kids—"

"I'd like to see them." He must not lose his temper.

Silas nodded. "The butler is fetching them both."

"Both? But there were four of them—"

"Oh, we decided we couldn't handle the twins," Angela explained. "We've sent them to that ranch in Texas—you know, the relative you told us about?"

Austin was horrified. "You split the children up?"

Silas yawned. "I wanted Lance, of course, and maybe we can make a lady out of Garnet, but Angela convinced me we couldn't deal with two toddlers. Yes, we sent Lark and Lacy to Texas."

Iron Knife's sister. Cimmarron, Austin thought. The Durango ranching empire was one of the richest in the Texas hill country. He wished suddenly that he'd sent all four of the children there.

The two children entered, smiling shyly. For a moment, Austin almost didn't recognize them. Lance's black hair had been cut and Garnet's had been curled and tied with ribbons. Both were dressed in the finest velvet and little handmade shoes.

Lance walked right up to him and stuck out his hand while Garnet curtsied. "How do you do, sir? I remember you were a friend of my mother's."

Austin was taken aback. Lance was every inch the elegant little heir. He shook hands solemnly and looked toward

Silas, who beamed proudly. "Oh, he's a corker, all right. I'm already preparing him to take the helm someday."

Austin caught the look of jealous annoyance that crossed Angela's face. He leaned closer to little Lance. "And is that what you want, young man?"

"Certainly, sir." The child looked at him calmly, confidence bright in his pale blue eyes. "I have already promised Grandfather I will double the Van Schuyler fortune for us."

"See? What did I tell you?" Silas beamed. "Now Garnet here is pretty enough to make a fine marriage—"

"If you don't mind, Grandfather," Garnet said, "I'd like to choose my own path."

Silas frowned and, in an aside to Austin, grumbled, "Too much like her mother. Headstrong, a bad thing in a woman."

Austin shook his head and remembered Summer, then thought of Wiwila. "Some of us like a little spunkiness in a woman"

Angela appraised him frankly, fiddling with her lace-trimmed handkerchief. "I hate it that women who could run companies are not even considered by old-fashioned males."

Austin caught the tension between father and daughter and cleared his throat in the awkward silence. "Well, I must be going."

Immediately, both children's faces darkened with sadness. Austin knew then that they might not be as happy in this plush environment as he had hoped. However, there was nothing he could do about it; after all, Silas appeared to be a doting grandfather as well as a very rich one.

Garnet peered up at him. "Will you come again, Mr. Shaw?"

He patted her head. "Of course, my dear. Your mother would have wanted me to see you whenever I'm in town."

The three adults stood up.

Silas said, "Will you be in town long?"

Austin shook his head. "Colonel Custer will be needing me. I was lucky to get a furlough."

The hawk-like face frowned. "The sooner he can get those savages wiped out, the better. I hold my daughter's death against them and that brute she ran off with."

"It wasn't like that at all," Austin began, then decided not to debate the issue. After all, this family was in mourning.

The butler escorted him to the hall and Austin left, haunted by how civilized Summer's children had become in just so short a time. Of course, they were very young and perhaps didn't realize the finality of their loss.

The next day, Austin had a house call from old Dr. Diggs, which mystified him. From the questions the man asked, Austin suspected the old man was exploring his sanity, which baffled him even more. Dr. Diggs left finally, telling Austin to get plenty of rest and relaxation. "I'm perfectly all right, sir," he insisted, but the old man only looked grave and nodded.

"Your mother is worried about you," he said.

Of course. "My mother hardly knew I was alive the first twenty-some years of my life," Austin said wryly, "but now that my younger brother doesn't seem in any hurry to return from Colorado Territory, she's suddenly very concerned about my welfare."

The old man hooked his thumbs in his vest. "Your mother loves you."

"My mother is smothering me," Austin said firmly.

"Your enlistment will be up soon?"

Austin took out his pipe. "I plan to reenlist, no matter how much my mother tries to stop me"

"Hmm." The old man paused in gathering up the contents of his black bag. "Think hard about that, my dear boy. You have a fortune waiting for you here and an easy life.

Once you have recovered from the loss of Summer Van Schuyler, all the finest ladies in Boston will be attempting to catch your eye so you can make a suitable match."

"It is comforting to know that all of Boston has my life planned out for me," Austin said dryly.

"You didn't used to be sarcastic," the doctor said quietly. "What's eating you, Austin?"

"I wish people would stop being concerned," Austin said as he tamped tobacco into his pipe and clamped it between his teeth. In his mind, he saw Wiwila's dark face, her gray eyes. *A suitable match.* God, his mother would swoon if she even guessed that he had bedded a Lakota girl.

"If you say so." The doctor paused in the doorway. "I'll see you at the party Saturday night. It'll provide a bit of entertainment in this dull, cold weather."

Austin frowned. "Perhaps the weather will turn so bad that no one will attend."

The other man chuckled as he went out the door. "Not hardly, not with a rich, eligible young man hosting it."

Austin stared after him for a long moment, then lit his pipe thoughtfully. Maybe everyone was right. As soon as his latest enlistment was up, Austin could expect a luxurious life here in Boston and pretty young women vying for his attention. *Suitable young women.* His mind went to Wiwila again and knew that she could never fit in here, even if he dressed her elegantly and hired a tutor. The elite class he had been born into would make her miserable. There were some chasms that love could not leap.

Love? Whatever was he thinking? He frowned and went to the window to stare out at the snow. He had merely bedded the savage girl, just like soldiers often did with conquered women. He owed her nothing, nothing at all. Yes, he would attend his mother's party all right and look over the eligible young ladies. He'd be a fool to pass up the easy life and the aristocratic white wife that fate and his station in life had in store for him.

Eight

Despite Austin's objections, his mother went right ahead with her plans for a party. Like his father, Austin found himself bowing to her demands rather than fuss with her. And so it was that on the appointed Saturday night, he put on his best dress uniform and came down the stairs.

The company was already arriving, servants bustling about with glasses of champagne, while a fine string quartet played in the oversized ballroom. Austin hesitated at the bottom of the stairs, dreading the evening. He saw his tiny, iron-willed mother, resplendent in diamonds and creme satin, greeting visitors in the front hall.

But she spied him. "Ah, here's our handsome soldier home from the Indian wars. Austin, do come meet Congressman Beasley and his daughter."

The congressman looked overfed and stupid. His pretty daughter looked thin and stupid in a pale yellow dress that flattered her brown hair. Austin pasted a smile on his face, although he didn't feel like smiling, and did as his mother bid.

The young lady could hardly contain herself as she smiled and curtsied. "Oh, Mr. Shaw, we've all heard about the savages. You must tell us your exciting stories."

Austin bowed. "I'm sure it's not nearly as exciting as you think." He thought of dead Indian women sprawled in the snow, and screaming, hungry children.

"Oh, but he's being modest," his mother insisted. "I'm sure he will be pleased if you'll save a dance for him on your dance card."

Austin gritted his teeth. "Of course," he murmured. "Later, perhaps. I wouldn't want to keep you from a bevy of admirers, Miss Beasley."

The ravishing brunette fluttered her fan, looking disappointed. "Of course. Father, shall we mingle with the other guests?"

They drifted on and Elizabeth Shaw frowned and began to scold him in a whisper. "Austin, how could you? I've gone to a great deal of trouble to give this party for you."

"You gave it for yourself, Mother," Austin said coldly. "Let's be honest about that."

His father walked up just in time to hear the exchange, then pulled out his pocket watch absently and checked the time. "Now, please, let's not have a scene."

"Father," Austin snapped, "if you wouldn't continually let her have her way—"

"Not now," his mother said through clenched teeth, then walked over to greet new arrivals. "Why, it's the mayor and his two beautiful nieces. I can hardly wait to introduce them to my son."

The fat mayor beamed. "And they are both anxious to meet him."

There was no hope for it, Austin thought sullenly. He must play the part because he was in a trap his mother had set and unless he made a scandalous scene, there was nothing to do but be charming. With a sigh, he moved forward to be introduced to the two giggling young beauties.

After that, he retreated to the refreshment table for some very fine champagne and caviar. There were the best of cheeses and small cakes on the glowing, priceless silver trays. Out on the floor, couples danced to the music while some of the older men headed to the billiards room. Maybe after a decent interval, he could go join the men for a whiskey and a quiet pipe before the fire, but right now, he must be the hero, resplendent in his blue uniform with the gleaming captain's bars.

"Hello, cousin." Austin turned at the fawning tone and tried not to frown as he recognized Bosworth Shaw. He'd always thought there was something sleazy about young Bosworth.

"Hello, Bosworth, I didn't realize you'd be here."

"Just because my family's not as rich as yours?" Bosworth's handsome face showed an ill-concealed envy.

"No, of course not," Austin said, "it's just that we haven't seen each other in quite a while."

Bosworth frowned. "Because I couldn't afford to travel in your circles. But I'm ambitious—I'll get there yet."

"Good for you," Austin said and wanted to be rid of the ne'er-do-well, disagreeable relative. His mother had always had a soft spot for his cousin, which surprised Austin, but then, Bosworth always flattered women into believing anything. "I see several wealthy young ladies looking this way. I'll wager they hope you'll ask them to dance."

Immediately, his cousin brightened. In an aside to Austin, he whispered, "Which one has the richest father?"

"That one over there." Austin indicated a plump, homely girl standing forlornly on the sidelines. "Her father is Leland West—made a fortune in shipping."

Bosworth grumbled, "Why is it the ugly ones always have the money?" Without waiting for an answer, he crossed the room and bowed before the wallflower. Austin could just barely hear him asking the girl to waltz.

In the long run, Cousin Bosworth would be wasting his time, Austin thought with satisfaction. Leland West would certainly check out the man's reputation before he would allow him to court his daughter. Austin had heard that some of Bosworth's business dealings were a little shady. Austin returned his attention to the buffet.

"Austin?" He turned to face a handsome younger man who smiled as he offered his hand. "Remember me?"

Austin searched his memory for this aristocratic blond man as they shook. "Oh, yes, Peter Lester. Why, the last time I saw you, I think was in the park. You were pushing a hoop, as I recall."

The younger man laughed. "I've grown up a bit, as you see. I'm in medical school."

Austin blinked in surprise. "Medical school?" The Lesters, he recalled, had been in the jewelry business for generations. "Are your parents upset?"

Peter frowned as he took a glass of champagne. "I'm afraid they are, but they'll get over it. A man has to follow his own heart, after all."

"Sometimes that's not practical," Austin said ruefully, thinking of the pressure from his own mother to take over the Shaw enterprises.

"Perhaps," Peter shrugged, "but a man only has one life to live, and damned if I'm going to spend it behind the counter of a store selling diamonds to rich ladies who already have too many."

Austin sighed, watching his own mother's jewelry gleam across the ballroom, remembering the magnificent sapphire-and-diamond ring in the Lester company safe. "My mother would say one can't have too many diamonds. Besides, as you get older, you'll find sometimes fate steps in and changes your plans."

His companion's face mirrored chagrin. "How clumsy of me. I had quite forgotten about Summer Van Schuyler. I'm sorry to hear of her death, old man."

Austin flinched. "Thank you. I'm getting past it, but yes, it was sad."

Young Lester touched his shoulder kindly. "Sooner or later, you'll meet another girl and she'll be wearing that ring we're holding for you."

Austin didn't answer. He tried to picture Wiwila wearing

the ring and shook his head. His mother would faint at the thought of a savage wearing the Shaw family heirloom. Not that he ever expected to see Wiwila again. The thought made him as sad as losing Summer. He didn't want to think about either of them, so he turned and looked toward the dancers. "Well, Peter, I suppose we must both do our duty and dance with some of these young ladies."

"I think they are all here to meet you. After all, you are the most eligible of all the men in Boston right now."

"So my mother tells me," Austin said grimly and started toward the bevy of giggling beauties waiting across the room.

It was a Monday morning several weeks after the party. Austin heard the front doorbell ring as he came down the stairs. The old family butler was hurrying to answer it. He turned as Austin descended the stairs. "Mail for you, sir."

"Me?" Austin paused in surprise. "I'm not expecting to hear from anyone." He took the letter and opened it, groaning aloud as he saw the official heading. "Oh, hell, I'm being reassigned to Washington, D.C."

He crushed the letter in his hand and went into breakfast, tossing it on the table.

His mother looked up from her tea. "What's the matter, dear?"

"Custer must be angrier with me than I thought. Major Nelson has had me reassigned to our nation's capital."

He saw his parents exchange glances; then his father averted his eyes and returned to spreading apricot jam on his toast. "Well, son, maybe it's for the best."

"Yes," his mother nodded, "you'll like Washington in the spring—they say it's beautiful and for a young man in your position, there's scads of social opportunities."

Austin sighed and sat down, nodding to the butler to

pour him a cup of coffee. "I'm not interested in social op-portunities. I'd like to return to the West."

His father picked up the newspaper and began to read. His mother smiled. "Oh, Austin, you can hardly refuse this assignment, and maybe after a few months—"

"I think I'll write Custer and see what I can do to make amends. I liked serving with him."

Elizabeth looked at her husband anxiously. "Robert, do say something."

Robert looked at him over his paper and cleared his throat. "Is that a wise move, son? To question official or-ders? Wait a few months and see what happens."

Austin considered.

"And," his mother said brightly, "you might decide you like Washington and it's close enough that you could come home on leave now and then."

"What do you think, Father?" Austin looked toward him.

Robert Shaw cleared his throat and pulled out the gold monogrammed pocket watch he always carried. "Look at the time. I think I'd better get down to my office and see how Mr. Hall is doing."

Austin felt vague annoyance. "Hiram Hall has managed the business very well for years. We could talk if you don't hurry off."

Robert Shaw's florid face turned even redder. "I—I really must go." He got up and left the table.

"Now, Austin," his mother said, "this might be a good assignment for you. Bucking orders doesn't seem too wise."

"I suppose you're right," Austin concluded reluctantly. "Very well, toward the end of the week, I'm off to Wash-ington." He sipped his coffee and thought of Wiwila. He'd expected to have forgotten about her by now. Sometimes at night, he dreamed he was locked in a passionate mating with her and she was as wild and untamed as ever. No, of course there could be nothing permanent in that union. His mother had been worrying him to death asking him to call on one young lady or another, accept social engagements that he didn't want to attend. All the eager young society misses seemed stupid and silly to him with their endless gossip of parties and fashion. Yes, he needed to escape from this house. As his father had suggested, Austin would take his assignment in the capitol, and later he would ask for a transfer back to the West.

At the prisoners' compound at Fort Hays where the Indian women had been moved, conditions grew better as spring came on and the weather warmed. The guards were more tolerant now, Wiwila thought, and had relaxed the rules so that the prisoners could wander about more freely. She'd heard talk among the soldiers that Yellowhair Custer's campaign had been successful and that sometime soon, the prisoners would be released to rejoin their kin.

She shrugged the news off as she went about her duties. She really wanted to stay and see if White Wolf returned to the fort. She had a special reason for wanting to see him.

Captain Tasley had also been transferred to the fort. He tried to strike up a conversation, but she ignored him.

He paused and laughed, taunting her. "Still waiting for the elegant Captain Shaw to return, are you?"

"You have news of him?" She didn't mean to ask, but she couldn't help herself.

He stroked his mustache and grinned. "I told you he was never coming back. Word is, he's been sent to the city of the Big White Chief. No doubt he has a white love by now."

Wiwila shook her head. "He said he cared for me."

"You stupid squaw!" Tasley sneered. "He's rich and can have any white girl he wants. He's used you like any squaw and tossed you aside. Why, right now, he's probably about to marry some beautiful, high-class society girl."

It might be true. She blinked back tears and turned away so that the hateful officer would not see her pain. "Even if he never returns, you will never bed me," she said and walked away.

He yelled after her, "Stupid brown slut! You could live good if you'd just be nice to me."

She didn't feel very well, so she didn't pause to argue with the man. What he was hinting at was dirty and what she felt for White Wolf was wonderful and pure.

Life in Washington, D.C. seemed exciting yet dull to Austin as late spring turned the trees green. He was assigned to special duty on the new President Grant's staff, which he suspected had been arranged by his mother. On his weekends, he was invited to a social whirl of parties, but he often wandered alone along the Potomac or over to Arlington where hundreds of Union dead had been buried on the lawn of Confederate General Robert E. Lee's estate in a deliberate attempt to keep that rebel from ever living there again.

At a White House social event, he was hailed by a tubby man. "Captain Shaw, what a surprise to see you here."

"An, good to see you, too." They shook hands as Austin searched his memory. Then the man was joined by a pretty yet vapid-looking young brunette. "Why, hello, Mr. Shaw. We haven't seen you since your party several months ago."

He remembered the shallow prettiness of the girl and the stupidity of her congressman father. "Oh, yes, Miss Beasley, I could never forget you."

She fluttered her eyelashes at him. "Nor I you," she cooed. "I had so hoped you would call."

Austin could feel the sweat breaking out on his face. He had no interest in the vain and silly girl. "Well, you see, I was transferred to Washington suddenly, and that gave me no time to make any social calls."

She simpered at him. "Yes, your mother told me at the party that you'd be going."

Austin blinked. Of course the girl was confused. He hadn't gotten the telegram for several weeks after the party, but he decided not to point that out.

Congressman Beasley hooked his thumbs in his ample vest. "You're lucky to be here instead of out West dealing with savages," he grumbled. "The army's wanting more money to feed Injuns. I'm in favor of buying bullets instead."

"Maybe if we'd feed them, we wouldn't have to fight them," Austin said.

"Big waste of taxpayers' money," the congressman huffed. "Well, I see a businessman who owes me a favor. I'll leave you children to chat."

He was gone before Austin could extract himself. He stood first on one foot and then the other, struggling to be charming to the silly beauty.

She smiled up at him and took his arm. "Let's walk. It's so crowded in here."

He didn't know what else to do but walk with her out on the lawn of the White House. "It is nice to see you again," he said lamely, wondering how fast he could extract himself and leave.

She gave him her prettiest pout. "Now that you're in Washington, I'll expect to see more of you."

"Perhaps," he mumbled, "but I have a great many duties." He let his mind drift as they walked among the gardens, remembering another, more spirited girl. Strange, it was Wiwila who came to his mind these days, not Summer.

". . . and what is your opinion of her?" Miss Beasley paused under a giant oak tree.

"What?"

"Mrs. Grant. Isn't she ugly?"

Austin looked at her blankly. He had no idea what the hell she was talking about. "What?"

"You know, silly boy," she slapped his arm with her fan

and smiled coquettishly. "She's cross-eyed. I do hope she doesn't bring ridicule to our government."

Miss Beasley was not only shallow, she was cruel.

"I doubt that very many of us are concerned about the First Lady's looks."

"Well, I am. Appearances are important. She's not very stylish, either."

"As you are?" Austin asked and the girl evidently missed the irony in his tone.

"You flatter me, sir." She giggled with delight. "Oh, Mr. Shaw, you must come to the house some Sunday afternoon when we are having a lawn party."

"Maybe sometime," he said vaguely, hoping he would never have to see this vapid girl again. "I really should return you inside, Miss Beasley. I'll wager all the young men are furious with me for taking you away."

"You men in uniform are so dashing!" She giggled again and Austin escorted her back so quickly, she was breathing hard when they stepped inside. Austin flagged down a passing lieutenant. "Ah, Mr. Dawson, I'd like you to make the acquaintance of Miss Beasley."

Miss Beasley giggled again and curtsied. "Oh, Lieutenant, I was just telling the captain how dashing you men in uniform are. Tell me, what do you think of the new president's wife?"

"Ma'am?"

"Duty calls," Austin said, beating a hasty retreat. "I'll leave you in the capable hands of the lieutenant. He's from a fine old family, you know."

Miss Beasley fluttered her eyelashes at the younger officer. "Oh? Mr. Dawson, you must come to our house for our Sunday lawn parties . . ."

Austin drew a sigh of relief and disappeared into the crowd, mopping his brow. The shallow Miss Beasley was just the kind of girl his mother would choose. He went outside on the terrace and lit his pipe, thinking about the vast expanses of the West. He hadn't realized he longed for the open plains and the freedom so much. He hadn't realized how much he longed for Wiwila.

It was late May when he got a letter from Colonel George Armstrong Custer. Puzzled, Austin took it back to his quarters to read.

Dear Austin:
I miss having you in my unit as I ride this glorious West. I presume you were angry with me for disciplining you. Was that the reason you asked for a furlough and then a transfer? Speaking as an old West Point friend rather than as a superior officer, I would like to arrange to have you back on duty here as I try to keep the Indians corralled. However, if you are having too much fun at that fancy posting, I'll certainly understand . . .

Austin let the paper flutter from his nerveless fingers. . . . *you asked for a furlough and then a transfer.*
How could he have been so stupid? Of course his mother had arranged it all. Why hadn't he picked up on that from the silly Miss Beasley at the White House social? He didn't know whether to be angry with his mother or with himself for being so easily duped. Visions of the wild, free plains came to his mind and along with that, another of a dark and beautiful girl he had left behind at the fort. He wasn't sure what it was he felt for Wiwila, maybe only that she filled the lonely spot in his heart once reserved for a totally different girl.
Immediately, he went to send a telegram.

To Colonel George Armstrong Custer: There's been a misunderstanding. Do whatever necessary to get me reassigned to the Seventh Cavalry. I'll come as soon as you can make the arrangements.

Then he went back to his room and began to pack. His heart sang, yet his soul was angry with his mother for interfering in his life and his father for not objecting to it. Yet he couldn't fault Robert Shaw too much; Elizabeth could be a very domineering, determined woman. Well, all was well that ended well. It might take a few days for the transfer to go through, but sometime in June, he would once again be at the fort. The thought of seeing Wiwila again made him smile for the first time in a long, long time. He did not need to make any decisions yet; she would not expect him to do so. It would be enough that they were together.

Wiwila wished she felt better now that summer was coming on. The weather was turning warm and though the prisoners were less closely guarded, the quarters were crowded.

Then came the early June day when the rumors that had been circulating were pronounced official. Although Yellowhair was back from his campaign and papers were being stuck on bulletin boards, only a few of the Indian captives who spoke English understood that they were about to be released. They were given a little food, a few supplies, and some old, second-rate horses as the officers announced that they were now free to return to their warriors as long as there were no further raids.

The women and children reacted gladly as the knowledge was finally understood and everyone around Wiwila talked of plans to rejoin their tribe. She tried to be happy, but she had little reason except that Captain Tasley would no longer be taunting her. She certainly didn't want to join the Cheyenne.

Her thoughts turned to her distant Lakota people. Her cruel stepbrother was dead at the Washita but she might still have an aunt and uncle among the Sioux. It was a long way and she was not certain she felt well enough to travel, but there was no longer any point in staying at the fort. She was convinced now, after all these months, that what Captain Tasley had said was true: White Wolf would never be returning. Not that he had promised her anything; it was only that she had grown to care about him and wondered if there was any chance that he might feel the same. Probably he had found a beautiful white girl and had forgotten about the brown girl who had warmed his blankets.

Now she must do whatever it took to survive with someone else depending on her. As the Cheyenne women mounted up and rode out toward the south to join their warriors, Wiwila headed her old nag to the north, toward the land of the Lakota. For herself, she would not have been concerned, but she must find a friendly refuge. After all, her belly was swelling with White Wolf's child.

Nine

Austin returned to the West to ride beside his old West Point classmate, George Armstrong Custer, still unsure what to do about the untamed, black-haired girl, Wiwila. Not that it mattered. He arrived at Fort Dodge and went quickly to Fort Hays, only to find the army had freed the hostages and they had scattered to the four winds. There was no way to track her. It was just as well, he told himself; they were from two different worlds and she could never fit into his.

The months passed and more and more, Austin's sympathies lay with the Indians who were gradually being rounded up and placed on reservations as the government signed treaties and then routinely broke them, sending the Plains tribes on the warpath again.

As the months turned into years, he thought of Wiwila often, and looked for her at every Indian village without success. His common sense told him it was for the best, but still, he couldn't get her out of his mind. Sometimes if he were lonely and drunk enough, he would wake up in the morning in some whore's bed, but he did not marry. Somehow, he compared every white girl he met against Wiwila and each came up lacking. He wrote polite letters to his mother now and then to check on the progress of Summer's two children at the Van Schuyler mansion. The tone of his mother's letters was quite cold. She scolded him repeatedly for passing up the opportunities in Washington to go chase Indians with a bunch of "scruffy soldiers." And after all she'd done for him and his brother, who was also so ungrateful, Todd wouldn't even come home from Colorado to visit.

It all changed that November day in 1872 when Austin got the telegram about his father's death:

Huge fire in Boston. Stop. Your father dead of a stroke. Stop. Please come home. Stop. Love. Mother.

Father dead. Austin collapsed on a bench, staring at the words. He wished now he had been a little closer to his father, but he had not respected the man for being so weak and indecisive. Austin went immediately to apply for emergency leave home.

He arrived in Boston to find an area of forty acres of downtown burned to the ground, including the landmark old Trinity Church.

Clad in fine black silk of mourning, his mother met him in the entry hall as Williams answered the door. "It's about time you got here," she scolded. "Todd arrived yesterday."

Some things never changed. Only her favorite younger son ever did anything right, but even Todd had shown an independent streak in the last few years. "Mother, don't start on me before I even put down my suitcase."

"Start on you? Oh, you terrible boy!"

Austin decided not to point out that he was no longer a boy. He nodded to the butler and handed over his overcoat before following her into the library. Todd stood up from the sofa, greeting him warmly. "Long time no see, brother."

"You both should come home more often," their mother snapped as her sons embraced.

The two men exchanged glances. Austin bit his lip, deciding it wasn't wise to point out the fact that they both might come home more often if she'd quit scolding them like bad children.

Todd moved to the sideboard. "Would you like some brandy?"

Austin nodded and closed his ears to his mother's scolding. "May I see Father?"

"He's laid out in the parlor," Todd said gently. "Would you like me to go with you?"

"Please." Austin finished the bracing snifter of brandy and the three went into the parlor to see Robert Shaw, laid out so pale in a fine silver casket, flowers everywhere. The scent was sweet, too sweet. Austin had never felt as sad as he did now, thinking of lost opportunities.

Then they returned to the library.

Elizabeth said, "Everyone says it will be the biggest funeral Boston ever saw"

"I'm sure that pleases you," Austin said and poured himself another drink, ignoring Todd's warning look.

"Of course it does," she said with smug satisfaction and dabbed at her eyes. "We are, after all, very important people in this city. However, the bishop is out of town and we'll have to settle for a nobody to do the services."

"I'm sure Father neither knows nor cares if the preacher's not on the social register," Austin said acidly.

Todd took his arm. "Come, big brother, let's get a bite to eat. You look done in."

Frankly, Austin was already totally exhausted from dealing with his mother. "Yes, let's eat in the kitchen."

As they started out of the room, Elizabeth said, "I don't know why you boys always wanted to eat with the servants. It's degrading, that's what it is."

They ignored her and walked to the kitchen to share some

cold roast beef, warm cookies, and the few good memories they had of their father.

Later, the three gathered in the library. Elizabeth Shaw was grim-faced and stern. "I don't suppose either of you is returning home to take over Robert's business?"

Todd shook his head. "Mother, we've already been through this. I've got a good job on the *Rocky Mountain News* as a reporter and I'm doing a little prospecting. Sooner or later, I expect to make a big strike."

"Hmmph!" Elizabeth sniffed, then went to the big walnut desk and opened a drawer. "Austin, your father wanted you to have his gold watch. I don't know why he chose you—I would have given it to Todd."

"I think Austin should have it," Todd said loyally. "He is, after all, the oldest son."

Austin's eyes blurred with tears as she brought it over and put it in his hand. He ran his fingers across the monogram. *R.L.S. Robert Lewis Shaw.* "It's a fine watch. I'll cherish it always."

"Finest Lester Jewelry ever carried," his mother said with satisfaction. "Robert bought it when his first mill began to make a profit. He hoped it would be passed on."

Austin turned away and sat down on the leather sofa before the fire. He didn't think he would ever have a son, but he didn't want to dispute with his mother. "Tell me what happened."

"What do you care?" she snapped. "You should have been here to look after the Shaw business."

"Mother," Todd said, "that's not fair."

She gave her favorite a warm smile, then frowned at Austin. "They tell me an abandoned hoopskirt factory at the corner of Summer and Kingston Streets caught fire and it spread. Robert was so worried, he went down there."

"He got caught in the fire?" Austin asked.

"No, he had a stroke trying to help the firemen." His mother sounded annoyed. "I don't know why he bothered— Boston has plenty of firemen to spare, and after all, our buildings were not in danger."

The two men exchanged glances. Austin turned the gold watch over in his hand. It brought him comfort somehow. "I am sorry," Austin sighed, and felt guilty that he didn't want to come home and run the factories.

"Poor, poor me," she wept, "a vulnerable widow, helpless in this cruel world."

Elizabeth Shaw was hardly helpless; she could probably run the business as well as she ran his father, but Austin knew better than to say so. "Hiram Hall has always done an excellent job of managing the mills and I'm sure he'll continue to do so."

"Dear Cousin Bosworth has pointed out that the mills could be making more profit if old Mr. Hall weren't so lax with the way he runs things."

Austin started to speak, then decided against it. He had never understood why his mother liked his disreputable relative so much. Bosworth had never shown much talent for anything except flattering women and making questionable deals.

"I'm having a sick headache," Elizabeth wheezed, "with all these people calling and flowers being delivered."

"But you get to be the center of attention," Austin said. "You always liked that."

"Brother," Todd stepped in quickly, "wouldn't you like to take a carriage ride and see the destruction?"

Austin didn't really want to look at the burned-out ruins, but it would get them out of the house. "Of course."

Their mother went upstairs to lie down and Todd called for the carriage. As they drove along the cobblestone streets, he said, "You'll be shocked when you see the devastation."

Austin was shocked. They toured the area and were standing in the middle of the street, staring at the burnt ruins, when a man leaned from a passing carriage. "Austin? Todd?"

Austin turned. "Peter Lester? How in the world are you?" The carriage halted and Peter got out, shaking hands with both of them.

"I'm so sorry to hear about your father."

"Thanks for your concern." Austin noted his friend looked older but happy and well. "Did you finish medical school as you planned?"

"Yes, and I'm trying to decide where to set up practice. I might even decide I want to be an army doctor."

Austin nodded. "The army needs good doctors, but the money's in a fancy practice here with the best people—"

"Now you sound like my parents," Peter said ruefully, shaking his head. "Are either of you coming home to take over your father's business?"

"No," Todd said. "I'm happy in Colorado and I guess Austin's returning to the cavalry."

Peter eyed Austin keenly. "The cavalry sounds exciting. We might just meet again someday at an army post out West."

"You won't regret it," Austin said and remembered Wiwila. He still missed her.

"I'm sorry I won't be at the funeral," Peter said, "but I've got patients in the charity ward to look after. That reminds me—I've got a meeting. What time is it?"

Austin pulled out the fine gold watch. "Three o'clock."

Peter nodded with approval. "I see you have your father's watch. He was always so proud of that."

Austin choked up, suddenly unable to speak, regretting the fact that he and his father hadn't been closer.

Peter patted his shoulder. "Our jewelry store was hit," he said softly. "I've just come from rescuing things from the safe." He walked over to the carriage and returned with a sturdy box. "I'd better give you that sapphire ring for safekeeping."

"I don't want it." Austin shook his head, but Peter put the priceless ring in his hand anyway.

"At least hold onto it until Father gets the store rebuilt—then you can put it back in the safe if you want."

"All right." Austin tucked the ring in his waistcoat without looking at it. There were too many memories attached. "Is the store insured?"

"To the hilt." Peter smiled. "That's the one good thing for the Lesters. Well, I must be off."

The men shook hands again and the Shaw brothers watched Peter Lester get in his carriage and leave.

Todd took Austin's arm. "Come on, brother," Todd said gently, "let's go back to the house."

They returned to their carriage, neither saying much as they drove. The horses' hooves sounded loud in the silence. Austin stared off into the distance, sad about the loss of his father and what might have been.

The funeral was long, tedious, and expensive. Elizabeth Shaw loved to be the center of attention and she was, resplendent in fine black silk, a mourning veil, and jet jewelry which Queen Victoria had made so popular as proper mourning attire. Everyone in town who mattered was there, including the Van Schuyler family. Little Lance and Garnet were dressed in the most expensive of clothes and their grandfather seemed to dote on them. Austin was glad to see them. Silas Van Schuyler said that he had corresponded with the Durangos in Texas who reported that the twins, Lacy and Lark, were doing well. That left Austin wondering what had happened to Storm, the most Indian of all the children. He hadn't run across him yet riding with the Cheyenne, but he knew the little boy was out there on the plains somewhere.

They buried Robert Shaw in Mount Auburn Cemetery, the final resting place for all the wealthy people in Boston.

Afterward, back at the family estate, friends gathered to console each other. Elizabeth appeared to enjoy herself hugely. Cousin Bosworth was there, prowling about, making contacts and mingling with anyone who looked prosperous.

Bald, chubby Mr. Hall was bereft as he sought out Todd and Austin. "You can be sure I'll look after the business as I always have."

Austin nodded. "You know we have complete confidence in your abilities."

The man hesitated, fumbling with his hat. "I wish I could say that about your mother."

"Nonsense," Austin said a little too heartily, knowing his mother had never really liked Mr. Hall. He suspected she was jealous of Robert's close friendship with him. "You will keep running the mills as always."

Late that night, after all the guests were gone and their mother had retired to bed, Austin and Todd shared a drink before the library fire. "I wish I had known him better," Austin sighed. "So many lost opportunities—"

"Stop feeling guilty," Todd scolded. "Mother will lay that on us soon enough. I'm sorry that she never treated you well. I didn't want to be her favorite, you know."

Austin patted his shoulder. "It's not your fault, little brother. Will you be leaving tomorrow, too?"

"As soon as the will is read and I can sign papers."

"Papers?"

Todd looked at him earnestly. "Austin, I'm on the verge of a big silver strike and I expect to be a very rich man. I want to sign over every bit of this estate to you."

"I don't need it," Austin shook his head, "and it will upset Mother if you do."

"To hell with Mother," Todd said and sipped his drink

and frowned. "Someday you may have children and I want them to be comfortable."

"I doubt that I'll ever marry," Austin said and thought of dear Summer and his lost Wiwila.

"Nonsense. Now let's have another drink for old memories and old time's sake before we retire."

"Here! Here!" Austin said and held up his glass.

There were no surprises at the reading of the will, although Cousin Bosworth showed up and seemed disappointed that he was not left anything.

"I had hoped Uncle Robert would remember me," he said. "You know, just some small, sentimental something."

"Like a fabric mill or two?" Austin said sarcastically.

"Austin!" his mother scolded, "that's no way to talk to poor Bosworth."

"Thank you, Aunt Elizabeth," the cousin sobbed. "I am so broken up about Uncle Robert's death."

Austin rolled his eyes at Todd as Elizabeth glared at him. He knew he would catch it later and sure enough, after Todd had caught his train and Austin was preparing to leave, she confronted him in the library.

"How dare you accept all Todd's inheritance."

Austin sighed loudly. "Mother, I didn't accept it. In fact, I want none of it. Todd was very obstinate. As far as I'm concerned, we can put it all in your casket when you go."

"You ungrateful boy," she wept, "and after your father gave his life to building all this for his sons."

Austin was not moved. He had watched her dominate his father all these years with her crying and fainting spells. Instead of anger, he could almost feel sorry for her. "Mother, we are not ungrateful, we are simply leading our own lives. Neither of us wants these mills and factories."

"I can't run all this alone." She fanned herself with her black lace handkerchief.

"You have Mr. Hall," Austin reminded her.

"But I've no grandchildren to inherit it," Elizabeth wailed. "What good does it do to spend a life building wealth when there's no generation to inherit it? Look at Silas Van Schuyler—at least he has a grandson, even if he is Injun."

"Stop using that word, damn it!" Austin flinched as he filled his pipe. "Lance is a fine boy. He'll make the old man proud someday."

"One of you could at least marry and give me some grandchildren for my old age. I've done so much for you!"

Austin had had enough. "Mother, you and I are going to have a talk that we should have had years ago."

She blinked. "I haven't any idea what you mean."

Austin lit his pipe and fixed her with a steely gaze. "I'm talking about the time you and father used your influence to get me transferred to Washington, D.C."

She took a deep breath and didn't look at him. "I have no idea what you're talking about."

"I thought we were going to be honest," Austin said. "I'm well aware that in the winter of 1869, you very deliberately used influence and money to get me transferred to our nation's capital."

She bit her lip and gasped for air. "I— I think I'm going to faint. Someone find my smelling salts."

"Stop it!" Austin said sharply. "You've used that a million times to keep from being honest, but this time, it won't work. For God's sake, at least own up to what you did."

"Very well, then, since you insist on making such a mountain out of a molehill," she sniffed and sipped her tea. "Your father and I were beginning to doubt your sanity after Summer Van Schuyler's death. We got you a furlough."

"I doubt Father's role in this," Austin said. "I'm sure it was all your idea."

She put down her cup so hard, it rattled the delicate china.

"All right! I'm guilty! Guilty of wanting to do what was best for my son. It was for your own good."

Austin looked skyward a long moment and smoked his pipe. "Lord protect me," he whispered finally, "from people who are doing things for my own good."

His mother rushed to her own defense. "Well, Summer was dead and I thought now you'd be mentally free to think about marrying someone else. I thought you might meet someone at that party, and then there were all those eligible young women we knew of in Washington—"

"Yes, I know. I saw the dimwitted Beasley girl at a White House party."

"Well, what was the harm?" she asked. "You ended back out West anyway, just a few months later."

"A few weeks too late," he muttered, thinking about Wi-wila and how she'd been gone when he returned, and how he had looked for her these last three years in vain. The mixed-blood Lakota girl was not "suitable" so his mother would never understand. He was very weary suddenly, and knew that nothing he said would make any difference. "I'll be returning to my unit in the morning."

"And what about me?" she wailed. "Here I am, left all alone, a helpless woman—"

"Mother, you were never helpless," Austin said. "You have run everyone else's life, but you're going to have to stop. I suspect you could take over Father's many businesses and run them better than anyone."

Elizabeth thought a minute, wiping her eyes. "I'll show you both I don't need you, I don't need anyone. I suppose I never did, really."

"And that's the sadness of it," Austin said gently. "You never needed any of us . . . except to further your own ends."

"I don't have to listen to this, you ungrateful whelp. I'll do just fine without you." She sailed out of the room and up the stairs.

Austin sighed and smoked his pipe. She was, after all, his mother, but she had interfered in his life for the last time. They could never have a good relationship unless he was willing to let her run his life as she had his father's. He wanted more happiness than he had had.

His mother was cold and Austin was polite as he said goodbye the next morning and left for the train station.

Austin sat on the train, staring out the window, and reached in his jacket for his pipe, fumbling in surprise as he brought out the diamond-and-sapphire ring. Damn. He'd quite forgotten about it. Well, he'd hang onto it for safe-keeping and put it in a bank vault if he ever got to a big city again. The light caught the stone and reflected its blue color. He dropped it back in his pocket and took out his pipe. As he smoked, he stared out the window, watching the changing scenery with a growing unease.

Many generations ago, on his mother's side, there had been an ancestor hanged as a witch at Salem. Although he never discussed it with anyone, he sometimes wondered if he had inherited the woman's unholy abilities. On a rare occasion or two, he had had a vision about some event that came to pass later. Now he had that same disturbed feeling.

Greasy Grass. The words popped into his mind and he blinked. Grass was never greasy. What had caused those strange words to come to his mind? He leaned back against the scarlet horsehair seat and smoked. In his mind, a hand-some warrior on a paint horse dashed onto the scene. The warrior wore many coup marks and his war paint was light-ning strikes and hailstones splashed across his body. The paint horse frolicked and reared, tossing its head like an animal that had been grazing on loco weed.

Austin jerked awake. *Had he been dreaming with his eyes open?* There could be no meaning to that dream, he decided; it was only some warrior he had seen in his many years on the plains. It meant nothing at all. He knocked the ashes from his pipe and closed his eyes, sorrowing for the father he had never really known very well and now he never would. His mind went to Wiwila and his thoughts brightened. It wasn't impossible that someday he might still find her. And if so, what then? He pushed her from his mind and concentrated on rejoining the Seventh Cavalry in the West.

Wiwila watched her son playing with a toy bow. She had named him Cincala, which meant Colt in her Lakota language. He was three winter counts old now, a fine, strong boy, light-skinned with eyes as gray as her own. She lived still with her old aunt and uncle; although several warriors had wanted her for a wife, she knew that no man save White Wolf could ever fill that empty place in her heart.

White Wolf. She never expected to see him again, but when she looked into her son's handsome face, she saw the captain all over again and remembered the few nights they had made love before he went away on the Iron Horse forever. Things were not good for her people now and were gradually getting worse. The white men made treaties, then broke them over and over. She had no way to know what would finally happen, but all she could do was follow the buffalo with her people as the herds dwindled, and hope that the Great Spirit, Wakan Tanka, would take care of them.

The next several years passed slowly for Austin as he served on the plains. He yearned for peace, but there was none as more and more whites flooded onto Indian lands. In 1874, he accompanied Custer and the Seventh Cavalry up through the Dakotas to find out if reports of gold strikes were true. When word leaked out that some traces of the precious metal had been found, greedy prospectors trespassed on Indian lands and there were more war parties raiding settlements and taxpayers complaining to the government. Congressman Beasley seemed to be leading the charge to annihilate the red devils, at least he led it in the newspapers. Of course, he did not bother to come out West and investigate, but then there were no votes for him out West.

Austin watched the unrest with growing alarm, knowing that it was inevitable that an Indian war might break out. He had given up the idea of ever seeing Wiwila again although he looked for her in every passing Indian face and more than once, he had hurried after some slim, black-haired girl, only to be disappointed when he grabbed her arm and saw it was not the Lakota girl. Occasionally he would awaken in a cold sweat, reliving that dream that he had first had on the train returning from Boston, but none of it made any sense and he shrugged off his witch ancestor.

Then came the hot summer of 1876 when the Seventh Cavalry rode out of Fort Lincoln in the Dakotas, and right into disaster.

Ten

It was a hot day as the Seventh Cavalry rode away from Fort Abraham Lincoln in Dakota Territory with the band playing Custer's favorite: "The Girl I Left Behind Me."

Austin had been having nightmares for several weeks, and now he felt misgivings as he led his troops into the lineup. Certainly most of the others were in high spirits, looking for some action to break the monotony of camp life. Several of the women, including the lovely Libbie Custer, rode out with the men for the first day before returning to the fort.

Austin's feelings of foreboding persisted as the days passed and the troops rode farther west. Somewhere out on the plains were a few desperate Cheyenne and Lakota bands that the Seventh would hunt down and force onto the reservations. As time passed, Austin lay awake at night under the stars, dreading sleep, because with his sleep came those uneasy dreams. *Greasy grass.* The wild, loco pinto horse, the warrior all painted with lightning bolts and hail. Yes, and his mother standing silently, all dressed in black next to a closed coffin with a gleaming medal in her hand while church bells rang and echoed through his brain.

What added to his sense of foreboding was that in the last several weeks, his treasured gold pocket watch had been stolen. It had disappeared from his saddlebags one night and he was not sure which of the soldiers might have taken it. There was no way he could search a whole regiment, so he kept silent, hoping camp gossip would finally point out the culprit. Nothing happened. After that, Austin took the sapphire ring and wore it on a string around his neck under his uniform, afraid this last memento of his past life might disappear, too. His nightmares persisted.

Finally, he went to Custer one evening as they settled into camp and told him about his troubling dreams.

His old friend threw back his head and laughed. "Austin, you must be getting old. We're not going to have any problems dealing with these scruffy savages. We'll be joined by Crook's troops, and Terry's. We'll execute a classic pincer movement, catching the Indians between us."

"But Autie," Austin sat down in a folding chair and lit his pipe, "I had a distant relative who was burned as a witch, and I keep having this unsettling vision."

Custer laughed. "Well now, about this dream you had— you said there are church bells ringing?"

Austin nodded. "I don't know if that means it's Sunday or maybe there's a funeral."

"Or a wedding," Custer scoffed.

He should have known Custer wouldn't believe him.

"If it were a wedding, why is there a coffin—?"

"Oh, yes, with your mother standing beside it." Custer grinned. "Did you see yourself in it?"

Austin shook his head. "The coffin was closed."

"Maybe it was your father's funeral you were reliving."

"Maybe." It was a logical explanation, but it didn't explain his sense of impending doom. He wiped the sweat from his face.

"June is too hot for chasing Indians." Custer pushed his hat back. His hair was cut short this time, Austin noted, not the long yellow curls the general had once favored, but then at thirty-seven Custer's light hair was thinning. "I'm worried about you, my friend. Perhaps Summer Van Schuyler's death back in '68 unsettled you more than you realize. Maybe you shouldn't reenlist next time."

Austin snorted and smoked his pipe. "And what would I do? Return to Boston and play nursemaid to my family's fabric mills?"

"I wish I had such an option," Custer grunted. "The only income I have is the army, and I married a judge's daughter. Libbie is used to the best. You know how shaky my army career has been the last few years."

Austin didn't say anything. Custer had been court-martialed once, often reprimanded, and had his career saved by his old friend, Phil Sheridan. Only a few weeks ago, Custer had testified before an investigation in Washington, D.C. "The fact that you pointed out that President Grant's brother, Orville, was mixed up in corrupt government deals didn't endear you to this administration."

Custer shrugged. "Maybe in the next election, the other side will make a comfy place for me back East. Libbie would love that." One of his many greyhounds wandered up and Custer patted it absently. "Know any jokes we can play on my relatives? I love a good practical joke."

The general sometimes behaved like an overgrown boy, Austin thought, and there were a number of Custer relatives on this trip: Tom, the rowdy cavalry captain, his brother-in-law, Lieutenant James Calhoun, younger brother Boston, and George's nephew, Autie Reed, who was only sixteen years old.

Austin stood up. "I wish I could convince you there's trouble brewing."

Custer played with his dog. "Now you sound like our Ree and Crow scouts who tell me how many, many Sioux are ahead. If I was worried, would I have left our Gatling guns behind?"

"That concerns me, too," Austin said.

"Don't be such an old lady," Custer said and made a

gesture of dismissal. "Those guns are heavy and slow us down. We've been chasing Indians for almost ten years. Believe me, it will be like it's always been. They hit fast and run, we'll chase them, and maybe, with any luck, we'll kill a few."

"All right, but I'll feel better when this campaign is over." Austin saluted and left the tent.

That night, as he slept, something awakened him and he realized he had been dreaming of church bells ringing. He must start attending services regularly once he got back to civilization. He lay there, staring up at the clear night sky, thinking about lightning and hailstones and wondering why. The word "rosebud" came to his mind. Why was he thinking of roses? Summer's mother had had a lovely rose garden—maybe he was remembering walking through it. *Greasy grass,* he thought. Those words didn't make any sense at all.

Maybe Custer was right; he was either becoming too cautious or perhaps was losing his mind. He thought of his ancestor who had been hanged as a witch and shivered, though the late June night was warm. It was a long time before he dropped off to sleep.

Private Willie Ratley often watched the officer in ill-concealed envy. It wasn't fair, wasn't fair at all that Captain Shaw had been born into a life of wealth and privilege while Willie, who even looked somewhat like the aristocratic captain, tall and brown-haired, had so little. Willie had grown up in the slums of New York City and couldn't read or write, while Captain Shaw had gone to West Point. Well, at least he had the captain's watch. Willie grinned and felt in his pocket for it. Carrying it, he could pretend he was a wealthy blueblood from a rich, upper-class Boston family. And later, he might trade it for plenty of whiskey at some trading post. Anyone with half an eye could tell it was gold and the best quality. It pleased Willie that he knew the captain was mystified as to who had taken it and he would never know. It now belonged to Willie Ratley.

The next day, the troops mounted up and rode on through the sweltering June heat. Austin tried to remember what day it was and couldn't, except that it was late in the month. *What difference did the date make?* Custer had estimated they would be meeting up with Terry and General Crook in a few days, depending on how fast they traveled. The renegade Cheyenne and Sioux would be caught between the three army columns and soundly defeated.

Rosebud Creek, Montana Territory.
June 17, 1876

Less than forty miles to the south on Rosebud Creek, General Crook and his men had paused for mid-morning coffee as they rode to meet Terry and Custer's forces.

Abruptly, shots echoed and re-echoed. Caught unaware, General Crook realized now that he was trapped in a narrow valley with riders along the rim. Around him, all was chaos, horses thundering through the camp, painted warriors, lots of painted warriors. "We're being attacked! Men, form a defense!"

Even as he shouted, he could see his outnumbered soldiers wavering, the attacking Sioux warriors shooting and riding them down. There were more enemy than he had ever seen before on the surrounding hills, galloping toward his unprepared troops.

At that moment, Crook's Crow and Shoshoni scouts came riding to the rescue, shrieking war cries, shooting the attacking Sioux with deadly accuracy, driving them back. For a few minutes, the scene was total confusion and then the Sioux began to give ground, retreating, leaving a field littered with dead and dying soldiers and Indians. The Crow shouted victory chants as they pressed the attack, chasing the Sioux from the scene, riding after them to kill more warriors and steal their horses.

General Crook leaned against a rock and sighed with relief, taking a deep breath as he surveyed the scene. The air was filled with the scent of blood and gunpowder and wild roses that grew brightly pink along the creek.

A shaking lieutenant ran to him, saluting. "They're on the run, sir—the Crow scouts saved the day. Shall I organize a pursuit?"

Crook snorted and wiped his sweating brow. "Are you joking, Lieutenant? We've got a lot of dead and wounded and there must be thousands of those red rascals. We'll have to regroup. We're out of any future fights."

The lieutenant looked about uncertainly. "You're right about that, sir. Shall I try to get a message through to Colonel Custer to warn him?"

Crook shook his head. "With as many Sioux as there are out there, we'd never get a rider through to Custer. The Seventh is on their own, I'm afraid."

The other chewed his lip. "Then God help them."

Crook nodded, surveying the death and destruction around him as shots faded in the distance as thousands of Sioux warriors rode away. "Yes, may God help them."

Austin had been unable to shake his grim premonition as the week progressed and the Seventh Cavalry rode deeper into the vast prairie landscape. The June days were so hot, he was drenched with sweat under his uniform; when he looked out across the plains, the heat undulated until he seemed to see waves rising up from the ground and blending into the faded denim sky.

On the other hand, Custer appeared to be having a wonderful time. He was in high spirits, often telling great stories to Mark Kellogg, the newspaper reporter who had come along to cover Yellowhair's next victory, or playing practical jokes with his many relatives who rode with the column. Brother Tom was a hard drinker and a troublemaker, but the soldiers knew he had won two Medals of Honor during the Civil War and they respected him for that.

They kept the column moving. Late in the month, the Ree scouts were shaking their heads as they dismounted and studied tracks. Austin leaned on his saddle horn and watched them. "What's the matter?"

Bloody Knife, the young Ree who was Custer's favorite scout, shook his head. "Heap no good. Many enemies."

Custer rode up just then, his face red from sun. "What's the matter?" His voice was terse, impatient.

Bloody Knife repeated his comments.

"So what?" Custer shook his head. "We've all fought Cheyenne and Sioux before. They use guerrilla tactics, hit and run, and we'll have three regiments. Why, the Seventh Cav alone will make them scatter like scalded pups!"

The Ree scouts looked to Austin for support.

Austin cleared his throat. "Perhaps he's right, sir. Perhaps we should delay until we're sure just how many of them we're up against—"

"Delay? Nonsense!" Custer snapped. "We saw a Sioux scout yesterday and worse yet, he saw us. If we don't move fast, he'll warn them and they'll clear out."

Austin wiped sweat from his face and tried again. "Maybe like Bloody Knife says, there's a heck of a lot more hostiles than we realize."

Custer surveyed him with the same look he might give a village idiot. "Captain Shaw, how many years have we been fighting Indians together?"

"Since right after the Civil War, sir, but—"

"Exactly!" Custer crowed triumphantly. "And in that time, have we ever seen huge groups of hostiles stand and fight like a regular army?"

Austin shook his head. "No. What they lack in weapons and manpower, they try to make up in hit-and-run attacks."

Mark Kellogg rode up on his mule just then. "What's happening, General?"

Custer gave the newspaperman a triumphant smile. "We've picked up the scent. You shall have one great story soon. I'm going to give our nation an overwhelming victory to celebrate its centennial."

The newsman beamed. "I can just see the headlines now. I've already sent a dispatch back saying, 'I go with Custer and will be there at the death!' "

Custer nodded. "And so you shall. You'll probably get a better job than that little *Bismarc Tribune*."

The middle-aged civilian brightened. "This will do it."

Austin sighed and reached for his pipe. With the press along, Custer would be in his element. The newspapers loved George Armstrong Custer; he always gave them good stories for their front pages.

Custer took off his hat and wiped his hand through his blond hair. "Well, gentlemen, let's get going. We don't want those savages to escape!"

Custer was so afraid the lone Sioux scout would alert the hostiles and they would flee the three-pronged trap that he drove his men relentlessly. The cavalry had ridden all night and by morning, both men and horses were tired.

Austin listened to the grumbling around him, then gathered his courage and rode up beside Custer, who sat Vic, the fine-blooded sorrel with the four white feet and blaze face. "Sir," he saluted, "the men are hoping you'll give us and our mounts a chance to rest and make sure General Terry has time to catch up—"

"Not a chance!" Custer's fair skin grew red with annoyance. "I'm not going to let the Sioux escape. We'll keep riding until we make contact. There's a creek up ahead in the valley, the Little Bighorn. We can rest and water our horses there."

Greasy grass. The words came to Austin again and he blinked. He must be losing his mind. "But we've yet to connect with Crook's forces—"

"That's his problem," Custer snapped. "I'll share no newspaper headlines this time."

Yes, sir." Austin saluted and returned to his troops. The loco painted horse galloped across his mind.

Benteen and Major Reno were grumbling and second-guessing Custer as usual. Austin didn't care for either of them and he figured the feeling was mutual.

Reno glanced up. "What'd the old bastard say?"

"We'll keep riding," Austin said.

A groan went down the column of tired men.

Bloody Knife, the young Ree scout, rode in.

"Bloody Knife," Austin said, "Custer says we're going to the Little Bighorn River."

The Indian's face remained immobile. "Heap Sioux and Cheyenne," he grunted. "Crazy Horse's men."

Crazy Horse. It was the horse of his dreams. Only it wasn't a horse at all, it was a warrior. Austin had a sudden premonition. "What's the Indian name for that creek?"

Bloody Knife looked at him. "The Greasy Grass."

Benteen's moon face frowned. "Are you all right, Shaw? Your face is white as cotton."

He had just been told the spot where he would die. Should he tell the others? It would panic them and besides, there was always the off chance that his intuition might be wrong. There was still no explanation for the church bells. He managed to swallow. "It—it's just the heat."

"And it'll be worse by afternoon," Reno grumbled. "The men and the horses need rest."

Austin took a deep breath. He was calm now, knowing his fate. "They'll get rest at the Little Bighorn," he said quietly, "a long rest."

* * *

The sun moved relentlessly across the sky in the June heat. As he rode, Austin heard bells in his mind, church bells. He turned to the soldier next to him. "Anyone know what day it is?"

The soldier looked surprised. "The twenty-fifth, I think, sir."

"No, I mean the day of the week."

"Sunday, sir. If I was back home, I'd be in church."

Sunday. The final piece of the puzzle. Somehow, Austin was surprised at how calm he was. He had been given all the clues now and knew his fate. However, he must try to save his troops.

He galloped his horse up beside Custer at the head of the column and saluted.

Custer gave him a careless salute. "What is it, Shaw? I'm estimating we'll meet the hostiles sometime this afternoon."

Austin cleared his throat. "Sir, I've got to insist you listen to me about my dream—"

"Look, Shaw, I believe you're losing your mind." Custer frowned. "When we get back, I'm putting you on sick call."

"Colonel, please listen to me," Austin implored. "I have a premonition we're riding to our deaths."

Custer turned his head and gave him a sharp look. "Shaw, we're always riding to our deaths in the cavalry. You knew when you joined up there's always a chance of that."

Austin wiped the sweat from his face and shook his head. "You misunderstand, sir. What I'm saying is that I have a premonition that great disaster lies before us this afternoon at the Little Bighorn River."

Custer's face turned a furious red.

"Shaw, get one thing straight—I have all the trouble I can deal with without you going loco on me. Now keep your mouth shut about your crazy dreams and get back to your column. Let's concentrate on the enemy, shall we?"

Austin started to say more, then hesitated. No one would believe him. "Yes, sir." He saluted and rode back to join his troops. He was going to die today. He looked around as he rode, wondering why he had never given much thought to what was truly important, or ever really enjoyed every hour of every day of his life. Now that he was certain he had only a few hours left, he savored the scent of the wild roses along the trail, the sight of a butterfly against the faded sky. His thoughts went to Wiwila, Spring, the mixed-blood Sioux and Cheyenne girl. He remembered the taste of her lips and the warmth of her embrace and regretted that he had never found her again. If only . . . no, he must not think of that. Who was the poet who wrote: *of all the words of tongue or pen, the saddest are these, it might have been?*

He fell into line ahead of his troops, his musings keeping him occupied as the sun moved higher in the sky. From up ahead, there was excitement, a scout's galloping horse. He hailed the scout. "What's going on?"

The Indian shook his head and made sign language. "Heap enemy ahead," he said and galloped away.

Custer called his officers to join him. "All right, this is it, men. There's a Sioux village ahead of us—the scouts have seen the smoke from the campfires. We're going to surprise them."

Austin took out his pipe and lit it with shaking hands. "You aren't going to wait for General Terry's or Crook's column to join us?"

Custer scowled at him. "And let the hostiles escape once they spot us? Benteen, you will take charge of the extra troops and the pack train. Reno, you will take your column and ride at full gallop through the village. I'll go down the valley and come around the other side. It's about what we did all those years ago at the Washita."

The officers nodded and saluted. Austin reported back to his men then, led them over to join Custer's charge. Tom Custer was there as well as young Boston, Autie Reed, Custer's nephew, and James Calhoun, Custer's brother-in-law. Hurrying to join them on his mule was the newspaperman, Mark Kellogg. "What a story this is going to be. One for the history books!"

"You have no idea," Austin said, then fell silent and listened to the sudden trumpet blowing the charge. Ahead of them lay the valley of the Little Bighorn River, green and lovely. Austin wondered if the grass would feel soft when he fell and whether he might only be wounded and then be tortured to death by the hostiles.

Now there was no time to think as he spurred his roan and they charged toward the Indian camp. In the distance, Austin heard the faint sound of the trumpet of Reno's command as that column charged toward the village. As Austin led his men at a gallop, he got his first good look at the acres and acres of lodges. "Oh, my God! Look at them! There's thousands, not hundreds!"

Around him men hesitated, fired. In the Indian camp, Austin saw men running and shouting as warriors grabbed up weapons and prepared to face the soldiers. The smell of gunpowder choked him and the gunfire was as loud as thunder. He felt cold sweat running down his back as he led his men through the sweltering June heat.

In the confusion and swirling dust, their charge faltered.

"Sound recall!" someone shouted. "We've got to set up a skirmish line!"

Austin's horse reared and neighed. It was all he could do to stay on the nervous animal's back. Near him, he saw Custer, his face red in the afternoon heat as he turned Vic back up toward the high ground. Around him, men tumbled from their horses and in the distance, warriors rode at a gallop, their war cries terrifying. Here and there a warrior screamed in agony and fell from his horse as a soldier's aim hit true. It seemed only minutes before the men had retreated in utter confusion and panic to a barren rise with no trees or brush for cover.

"Dismount!" someone yelled. Austin dismounted, hanging onto his panicked roan's reins. Around him, horses were going down as they were hit by stray bullets or killed by terrified soldiers to provide some bit of shelter against the deadly rifle fire and rain of arrows.

Custer seemed cool under fire. To Austin, he shouted, "We've got to have reinforcements and more ammunition!"

Trumpeter Martin saluted. "I'll try for it, sir."

Austin and Custer crouched behind a rock, looking at each other a long moment. The chances were good Martin would be killed trying to reach Benteen with the extra men and packs of ammunition now held in reserve.

Custer fumbled through his pockets in frustration. "You got anything to write on?"

Austin barely heard him over the roar of gunfire and shouting, but felt in his pocket, found nothing.

Lieutenant Cooke shouted, "Here, sir, I've got a notepad. Tell me what to write!"

Austin looked over Cooke's shoulder as Custer dictated: *Benteen: Come on. Big village. Be quick. Bring packs. W.W. Cooke. Adjt. P.S. Bring packs.*

Custer jerked it from his fingers, handed it to Martin. "Good luck. Remember, we're depending on you, soldier."

Martin nodded, swung up on his horse, and was gone.

Crouching behind the rock, Austin watched him disappear over the horizon. They were surrounded and cut off now. There was no way to know whether Reno had been successful with his charge or not, but if Benteen didn't get here with reinforcements quick, Custer's men would be wiped out.

Austin reloaded his rifle. It jammed, and cursing, he pulled out his pocket knife and dug the cartridge out of the old, inferior weapon. When he looked around, he could see other frantic soldiers doing the same thing. When a pocket knife blade broke, the soldier was out of luck. From the gunfire, Austin could tell some of the Lakota and Cheyenne had new, repeating rifles.

He was going to die today; he had known that from his visions. Somehow, that knowledge did not disturb him much—he didn't even care if he died a hero. All around him, wounded men moaned and dead men lay sprawled at grotesque angles among dead horses. Nearby, he spotted the colonel's younger brother, Tom, aiming his carbine at the brightly painted warriors who seemed to be creeping closer and closer. God, he was thirsty and he wasn't sure what had happened to his canteen. Somewhere in the swirling dust, a wounded soldier moaned for water, then fell silent.

We shouldn't even be out here, Austin thought; this is Indian land—why couldn't we just leave them the hell alone? *This whole regiment is going to die because we keep stealing their land.*

Custer interrupted his thoughts with a shout. "We should be hearing Benteen's forces coming. What time is it?"

Austin reached automatically for his gold watch, remembered it had been stolen. "I don't know—I don't know how long Martin's been gone."

Custer wiped sweat from his pink face. "Martin probably didn't make it," he shouted over the noise of gunfire and screaming men and horses. "We're all going to die if Benteen doesn't get here with the extra ammunition."

"Let me try," Austin shouted back. If he were going to die anyway, he might as well die trying to get help for these trapped men.

Custer shook his head. "It's suicide. I can't ask you to do that, Austin."

Once, a long time ago at West Point, they had been friends with such bravado and high hopes. "Autie, old friend, someone's got to ride for help, so I guess I'm the one. I've got a pretty fast horse, even if it is spooky."

"Then go!" Custer shouted back. "We can't hold out here much longer without help!"

Austin needed no urging. His roan was neighing and rearing, but Austin managed to mount. The horse took off at a dead gallop, with Austin only half in the saddle. He started back toward that rise where Benteen and his forces waited. How far was it? Three miles? Four? Five? He hadn't a chance of making it, he knew that, but anything was better than waiting here to be picked off one at a time. Even as he rode, bullets whistled around him as warriors spotted him.

Damn Autie Custer for his foolhardiness; Austin gritted his teeth and hunched low in the saddle. He'd pulled this once before on the Washita almost eight years ago, but that time they'd been lucky. This time, Austin knew their luck had run out. His roan was lathered and blowing, the smell of horse sweat strong in Austin's nostrils. Dust blew up from the churning hooves, coating Austin's sweating face. He didn't know if his fate allowed him to save the regiment, but at least he'd get a medal for trying. Hadn't his vision included his mother standing next to that closed coffin, all dressed in black and holding a medal in her hand?

His terrified horse was difficult to control. Off to his left, he saw a line of Lakota riding toward him, determined to cut him off before he could get through to Benteen for help. They were closing the distance rapidly, their war-painted horses fresher than his after the column's all-night ride. Somewhere, he heard drums beating and chanting as warriors made medicine. *It is a good day to die.*

No, no day was a good day to die, Austin thought, spurring his horse on. He wanted to live; oh, dear God, how he wanted to live! He reached up and touched the ring hanging on a thong around his neck. *They say when you are about to die, your whole life flashes before your eyes,* Austin thought as he glanced again at the approaching warriors and knew he couldn't outrun them. In his mind, he remembered Wiwila, the beautiful, tawny girl he had loved and lost. As his last thought, he wondered what had happened to her. He had loved her so.

He wasn't going to be able to outrun these Lakota. He knew it now, but he had to try. He hoped it would be a quick and painless death. Everyone knew that wounded soldiers would be tortured. And then there was no more time to think because, glancing to one side, he saw a warrior raise his rifle, heard the shot, and felt the pain as it grazed his head. Numbly, as his horse hesitated and stumbled, Austin reached up to touch the wound, saw the blood on his fingers through his failing eyes, and then tumbled to the ground and knew no more.

Standing next to the now-fallen Custer, Willie Ratley hesitated and stared after Captain Shaw galloping away for help. It was going to be too late, Willie knew. Around him, men were screaming and falling, writhing in pain. They were surrounded on this little rise with no cover save dead horses and the Indians were creeping closer. Willie, in his terror, could see the garishly red-painted faces as the warriors crouched and crawled toward them.

In the distance, he saw three warriors chasing after Captain Shaw. They were gaining on the rider. He'd never make it to the soldiers on the hill. Willie watched the captain desperately urging his horse forward, while the warriors on fresher horses rode him down. A rifle shot echoed through the valley and the captain hesitated and fell from the saddle as his horse stumbled. Captain Shaw had been Custer's last chance.

Willie Ratley would do anything, *anything* to live. Maybe if he threw down his rifle . . . he tossed it away. Yet around him men fell as they were picked off, one at a time. If there were any wounded, the Sioux would torture them. Now Tom Custer stumbled and fell as he was shot, landing near his dead brother.

The watch. Willie still had the captain's fine watch. Maybe he could trade it to the Injuns for his life. His hand shook so badly, he could barely take it from his pocket. The hot sunlight gleamed on its gold.

"Look what I have!" he yelled, holding it aloft in desperation. "Look, I'll give it to someone! It's gold! You know about gold?" He was the last one standing among the soldiers. Willie Ratley pasted a smile on his sweating face and ran toward the crawling warriors. "Look, it's gold! You can have it! You can—"

He looked up at the sound of thundering hooves, then half-turned toward the sound. A garishly war-painted brave on a spotted pony galloped toward him, the breeze fluttering the feathers on his long lance.

"No!" Willie waved the watch clasped tightly in his fist. "No, you don't understand! I want to surrender! I'm a friend of Injuns! I—"

The rider bearing down on him did not hesitate; the sharp point of the war lance gleamed in the hot sun. Willie screamed in terror and turned to run. His last memory was of agony as the lance impaled him and he tumbled to the ground.

Eleven

In the Indian village, Wiwila and her son, Cincala, were caught in the noise and confusion. "The soldiers are coming! The soldiers are coming!"

Not quite sure what to do, she watched the warriors grabbing their weapons, riding to the attack. Women ran about, gathering up their crying children, attempting to catch horses galloping through the camp in confusion.

"Come, my son, we must gather our things and make ready to escape!" Cincala was almost seven winter counts old, tall and strong. He was as handsome as his father, but his eyes were like hers, gray as a wolf's coat, his hair black as a moonless night. As she took Cincala's hand, she saw the soldiers galloping toward the camp, but a small group of Cheyenne rode to block them and the soldiers hesitated halfway through the camp and began to retreat. In the distance, she saw the dust of other soldiers, who appeared to be encircling the camp. It's the Washita all over again, she thought in panic, remembering the confusion and death. At least this time, it was the middle of the afternoon and the people had a few minutes' warning.

As the charging soldiers hesitated, she heard a panicked soldier shout, "Major Reno, what should we do?"

"Retreat!" The officer looked terrified as he waved and shouted. "Get across the river and back up to the bluffs!"

There was no way to know how many soldiers there were.

"Come, my son, we've got to get out of here!" She ran with the other terrified women to lodges. She couldn't leave their food and robes behind; they would need them desperately, and yet she was sacrificing precious minutes that she might need to escape the slaughter. Around her swirled screaming women and crying children attempting to gather their things and flee the village while their warriors held off the soldiers at the cost of their lives.

"Mother," Cincala shouted, "what shall we do? I want to go fight the soldiers, too!"

"No, my son, you must live to fight another day! Let us forget the lodge and catch horses." She glanced at him proudly as they ran. This tall, sturdy love child was her only memory of a deathless love affair with the officer called Austin Shaw so very long ago. Cincala meant Colt in the Lakota language and she thought it a good name for her handsome, mixed-blood son. Her Colt would grow up to be a stallion of a man.

Around them, dust rose as women grabbed precious food and tried to saddle horses. Gunfire erupted and horses reared and neighed as the warriors reorganized. In the distance, warriors were already singing victory chants as they rode to the attack. She could see the dust swirling as the bluecoats retreated. Wiwila took heart. There hadn't seemed to be that many soldiers and the whole valley was covered with hundreds of Cheyenne and Sioux lodges. She caught a rearing bay horse that had belonged to her dead uncle who had walked the Spirit Path only a few suns ago. "Here, Cincala, here's a horse for you."

The handsome boy swung up on it, looking much at ease on the back of the big stallion. "When I am older, I will kill many bluecoats."

"Your father was a bluecoat," she reminded him as she caught a palomino mare and struggled to mount.

Cincala sneered. "White men! I wish I'd been sired by a great warrior like Sitting Bull or Crazy Horse."

Bluecoats. Wiwila felt a twinge of sorrow for the white women who might be widows soon. Plenty of her people had been widowed and orphaned by soldiers in the last several years. With her old aunt long dead and her uncle killed only nine suns ago at the place the whites called Rosebud Creek, Wiwila and her child had been struggling to survive. When this battle was over, she would choose a good warrior and wed him to provide food and shelter for her son.

She motioned for Cincala to follow her and they rode through the camp. Women were still gathering up things, but the panic had slowed.

"What has happened?" one called.

Wiwila shook her head. "I do not know!"

Just then, a warrior galloped into camp, singing a victory song and immediately, women began to smile and make the trilling sound that always greeted triumphant warriors.

Wiwila stopped him. "What of the soldiers?"

The warrior smiled and waved his lance. "We have chased the soldiers who rode into our camp back up to the bluff, where they are trapped. The ones attempting to surround the camp have retreated and are now being killed."

Wiwila blinked, trying to feel glad, but she did not join in the victory trilling. In her mind, she saw wailing widows, both red and white.

An old woman shrieked, "Let us go out to cheer our warriors on. We will rob the bluecoat bodies, take their horses and guns."

"This is foolishness!" Wiwila argued. "If there's soldiers and our men kill them, more soldiers will come. We need to retreat from this place and put much distance between us and the bluecoats."

A young warrior rode into camp, shouting, "The battle goes well! I go to count coup and take scalps. You women may help yourselves to their blankets and food."

The women shouted in triumph. "It is only just, after

they have killed so many of our people. Come, Wiwila, they will have good things to steal!"

Wiwila hesitated, glancing at her small son. They were the poorest in the village and if she did not find a husband soon, she and her son might starve unless she could find some booty on the battlefield that she could trade for supplies. "Come, my son, we will go see what we can find."

The pair joined the women and old people who were now riding out to the valley. Even as she approached, she saw the women were mutilating the bodies in revenge, stealing the soldiers' clothes and boots.

She choked back her revulsion and dismounted. In the distance, the echo of gunfire still echoed through the hills as the warriors attacked the other trapped soldiers. A young brave, painted all scarlet and yellow, galloped up, shouting in triumph and waving a scalp. "We have the others trapped, but they are holding out. We are losing many good men in attempting to take their position."

Wiwila shook her head. "We should be retreating," she shouted to all. "More soldiers will come."

The young brave shrieked a battle cry. "If they come, we will kill them, too."

Wiwila sighed. Most of these people had never been around whites. They had no idea how many there were and that in the end, they could not defeat them. "Come, my son, gather up any food or weapons that we can trade."

Nearby, two women were stripping a body. The soldier had fair hair and reddish skin. There was a bullet hole through his head and another in his chest. Wiwila took a good look at him and gasped as she recognized him. It was Yellowhair. She saw the small "7" on many of the guidons and saddle blankets the Lakota were gathering up. Austin Shaw's regiment. For a long moment, she had mixed emotions, remembering her soldier. Long ago, he must have returned to Boston and a white girl who would give him proper children.

"Mother, why are you crying?" little Cincala asked impatiently as he took hardtack biscuits from a soldier's saddlebags.

"I—I don't know," she lied and turned and walked away quickly, sickened at the sight and smell of dead horses and white soldiers. Behind her, a woman yelled in triumph and shouted that she had found a good pistol and a pair of boots. Two women argued over a fine horse that grazed nearby, its cavalry saddle covered with dried blood.

Wiwila walked even faster, leading her horse away from the carnage. Many of the soldiers had been scalped for victory trophies and the women were still mutilating the dead white bodies in revenge for the many friends and relatives they had lost.

Cincala trailed along behind her. "Mother, you acted as if you recognized a soldier. Did you know him?"

She nodded and swallowed hard. "It was Yellowhair, one of the worst enemies of our people. Your father sometimes rode with Yellowhair."

"And was he an enemy?"

Wiwila shook her head and kept walking across the prairie. "No, he was kind and good."

"But he left us," the child said bitterly.

"He went back East," Wiwila acknowledged. "He did not know about you or I think he might never have gone."

She wasn't certain of that, of course, but she thought it might make her small son feel better. She didn't want him to feel he'd been tossed aside for a white son.

The pair was almost alone now, walking through the buffalo grass on a vast expanse of prairie. Ahead of them lay a dead bluecoat, his roan horse munching grass nearby.

"Look, Mother, here is a Long Knife no one has found. We will be rich with his horse and supplies."

"Yes, that is good. We need everything we can get to survive." Wiwila hesitated, looking down at the broad back. The dead man lay on his face and even though she needed to take his weapons and boots, she could not bring herself to strip the body and leave him without dignity as the women behind her were doing.

At that moment, the soldier moved slightly and moaned.

Wiwila started, but her son said, "He is alive! I can kill him and count coup on him!"

"No!" She caught her son's arm, trying to decide what to do. She couldn't bear to take part in the killing of a wounded man, and yet, when the others found out he was alive, they might want to take him back to the village and torture him, extracting vengeance for all the wrongs they had suffered at the hands of the whites.

The man moved again.

"Quick," Wiwila said, "son, get his canteen."

Her handsome son paused and looked up at her incredulously. "You would try to help this killer of our people?"

"Just do as you're told!" Wiwila knelt beside the bluecoat. She wasn't quite certain what to do. She couldn't kill the man herself, nor could she walk away and leave him helpless and suffering, especially knowing that when the others found him, they would either kill him or torture him.

Cincala brought her the canteen. She reached out hesitantly, touched the prone body. Yes, he was alive, all right; his white skin was warm to the touch. "Son, help me turn him over."

Her small son frowned, then obeyed. With a mighty effort, they turned him over even as he cried out in pain.

His face was so bloody and dirty, she did not know whether he was handsome or ugly. Around his sinewy neck on a leather thong, he wore a magnificent blue stone ring. She knew it was fine quality, the kind of ring a rich white girl would wear. She could trade that for food or blankets at some questionable trading post. His eyes blinked open, then closed again. They were hazel.

Wiwila poured a little water on a scrap of his torn shirt and wiped his face clean. Then she stared down at him, unbelieving. No, it couldn't be. She looked closer. Yes, it was Austin Shaw. She wanted to hug him and beat him with her fists for all the anxiety and broken dreams he had cost her; instead, she could only stare at him. What to do now? A surge of jealousy went through her, thinking of him leaving so many years ago to marry a girl back East. Why did he wear her ring around his neck?

"Son, go get a travois—we are taking him to the village." She poured a little water from the canteen on a scrap of his shirt and wiped the blood from his face.

"Why are you keeping this bluecoat alive?" he asked.

Wiwila took a deep breath, wondering how to tell him. There was no other way except to blurt it out. "This soldier is your father."

"Then I should kill him for leaving us!" He grabbed up the soldier's pistol but Wiwila reached out and jerked it from his hand.

"No, perhaps he had no choice."

"The chiefs will want him dead," the child growled.

"Not since he is your father," she answered, but she was uncertain. "Others will remember that he was always kind to the captives. Not all white men are bad. Now do as I say!"

Cincala ran to get a travois while Wiwila wiped the blood from his face. "White Wolf. Oh, White Wolf, please don't die." The soldier was still unconscious, but seemed to be coming around. Once his hazel eyes flickered open and he looked up at her momentarily before they closed again. Strange, Wiwila thought. He had not looked terrified at seeing a brown face so close to his; he looked as if he were surprised he was still alive. She brushed his light hair from his forehead. He looked older and more careworn than when she had known and loved him so long ago, and though she wanted to deny it, she knew she loved him still, even if he now belonged to some white woman.

She took her wet rag and wiped the wound on his head

while breathing a sigh of relief. The bullet had only grazed there. Other than that, she could find no other wounds. The blue ring seemed to mock her with its hint of a beloved white girl. Wiwila cut the thong that held it around his neck and slipped it inside her doeskin shift. She wasn't sure what to do with it, but she didn't want some warrior to take it from him as a prize of war.

Cincala returned with a horse and travois and the two of them dragged him onto it and started back to the village. In the distance as the sun moved toward the far horizon, an occasional shot still echoed as the warriors kept the trapped soldiers pinned down.

As word spread through the camp, people began to gather. "Wiwila is a great warrior woman! She has brought back a captive for us to torture."

"No," she shook her head stubbornly, "this is White Wolf, my son's father. You who were at the Washita remember he was good and kind."

Several women nodded. "Au! Yes, we remember White Wolf—he was good to the captives."

A young warrior blocked her path. "I will kill this blue-coat!"

Wiwila pushed between him and his prey. "You may not do this without the chiefs' permission."

There was a long moment of silence and Wiwila held her breath. She was not sure what any of the chiefs would say and there was not much she could do if this young brave took it upon himself to run his war lance through the man. In the distance, she heard occasional rifle fire as the warriors kept the trapped soldiers busy.

"This is White Wolf," she said again. "You, Pony Running, should remember him. He was kind to you and your mother many moons ago at the Washita."

The warrior hesitated and she could see the memory coming back to him. "Yes, I remember. I was a small, weak boy and this soldier gave me food and blankets."

A murmur of approval ran through the crowd.

A warrior galloped up. "We are to begin moving the village," he ordered. "Scouts have brought us word that another soldier column is coming and will be here in maybe two or three suns more."

More murmuring from the gathering crowd. With their attention diverted, Wiwila led her horse away to her lodge. She had an hour or two, she thought, to help this man she had loved more than life itself. She did not know what the chiefs would say about allowing him to live, but if he became conscious, perhaps he could sneak away as soon as it became dark. The hot sun was already slanting low in the hot afternoon sky.

She took him to her lodge and with her son's help, washed the soldier's face, put an ointment on his head wound, and bound it with a torn piece from his blue shirt. If White Wolf were to escape, he would have to blend in with the others. A man riding across the prairie in a blue uniform would attract every warrior in the tribes. She still had some of her uncle's clothes, although custom demanded that she burn them. "Help me, Cincala. We are going to get rid of his soldier clothes."

The small boy looked as if he would ask a question, then sighed and began to help her. When they finished, White Wolf was dressed as a Lakota warrior in buckskin with his own dirty, bloody clothes piled up and burned. Outside, the confusion grew as people followed orders to move the camp.

"Cincala, take the soldier's horse and trade it to someone. Right now, it will bring a premium in food and supplies—then help me load him on that travois."

It took a little time, but with hard work, she and her son had their lodge packed up and were joining the stream of all the bands of the Lakota and Cheyenne as they began a steady but slow retreat from the camp to the safety of the distant north, far away from the approaching column of soldiers. White Wolf. She looked at him fondly as he slept. His face was tanned and there were care lines etched around his hazel eyes, but he had not changed much in all these years, except that he appeared sad. Perhaps his life with the white girl had not been happy. Well, even with that, she could not hope that he would care enough about her to stay. She could only hope to help him escape.

Soon the warriors joined the column as it went north, the Cheyenne dog soldiers bringing up the rear as always to protect the women and children should the column be attacked.

It was almost dusk when Pony Running rode up beside her. "How is White Wolf?"

"Alive," she said.

"Perhaps the chiefs will grant him mercy," he suggested. "I will speak for him."

"Pilamaya. Thank you," she said softly. Wiwila turned in her saddle and looked behind her. "That was Yellowhair's forces the warriors killed."

The man shrugged. "He was foolish to attack us without sending scouts to see how many warriors there were."

"Did you kill all the soldiers?"

He shook his head. "We surrounded another group up on a bluff and they took heavy losses, but we could not overrun them. When we heard another column of soldiers was coming, we dared not stay to fight."

Wiwila shook her head. "This is going to bring much trouble to our people."

"What else could we do?" the warrior shrugged. "We have been pushed and pushed, lied to, robbed, driven onto reservations. There are times when a man must stand and fight, even when it costs him his life."

She nodded.

It was the middle of the night before the chiefs signaled

along the line that the people were far enough away to be safe from pursuit by the soldiers. They set up camp, danced the scalp dance, and the hungry children feasted on the soldiers' rations while the old men held the soldiers' weapons and talked of golden old days and their many battles. Defeating the soldiers had given them hope that they might yet avoid the bleak, horrible reservations where the whites hoped to cage them up. Freedom—it was everything.

In her lodge, Wiwila and her son tended to the unconscious soldier. The night had turned chill and she had lit a small fire in their tipi to make a little broth. The soldier's hazel eyes blinked open and he stared up at her in puzzlement. "Who—who are you?"

She stroked his dear face. "I—I am Wiwila. Do you know me?"

His eyes were blank and after a moment or two, his brow furrowed and he shook his head ever so slightly, then moaned aloud and reached to touch the wound on his forehead.

"Don't," she caught his arm. "You have been wounded, but you will be all right."

"Wounded? How?" He looked puzzled.

Wiwila took a deep breath. "Don't you remember?"

He shook his head. "I—I only remember riding hard, afraid I was going to die." He paused and his brow furrowed. "My name? I do not know my name."

What was happening? Surely he knew his own identity. Could it possibly be that he did not remember anything because of the wound to his head?

She cleared her throat. "You are White Wolf and you are in the camp of the Lakota."

Instead of reacting with terror, he relaxed and murmured, "I am White Wolf, yes, I seem to remember that name." He looked up at her again and she saw he was straining for an elusive memory. "I—I think I know you . . . or maybe I don't."

A tiny hope came to her heart. "You know me," she whispered. "I am Wiwila, your woman."

"Wiwila," he repeated and then he smiled. "Spring, yes, I remember you. You had skin like satin and soft lips."

She took his hand. "I am your woman," she whispered.

His hazel eyes softened. "My woman. I think I have been looking for you a long, long time."

"And now you have found me," she murmured and she leaned over and kissed his lips. It was as wonderful as she remembered it all these long, lonely nights.

His big hand reached up and tangled in her hair and he kissed her deeper. "Wiwila . . . Wiwila."

She must not dare to hope. Any minute, he might regain his memory and know who he really was and long for a white girl far away, but tonight, he belonged to her and that was all that mattered right now. "I will get you some food, my husband."

She got him a bowl of broth and helped him sit up to eat it. He was weak but he seemed better. As he ate, he glanced up toward Cincala, who had just entered. "And who is this fine young warrior?"

"Your son, Cincala," she said and waited. Maybe now he would suddenly remember that he was a fine, rich soldier from back East and wouldn't want a half-breed son, but White Wolf smiled up at the boy.

"Cincala," he whispered. "What does it mean?"

His son knelt by his side. "I am Colt."

White Wolf reached up in puzzlement to touch the boy's shoulder. "I am proud to have this fine son," he said and seemed confused; then he looked toward the lodge door and listened a moment to the sounds of dancing and cele-bration outside. "What are we celebrating?"

"Do you not remember the battle? You were wounded," Wiwila said and held her breath.

He shook his head and reached up to touch the bandage. "I remember nothing except my head hurts."

"Then rest," she said and took the bowl from his hand. "Tomorrow you may remember more"

He nodded and lay back down.

Wiwila caught Cincala's arm and led him outside. "He remembers nothing from his past," she said.

Cincala frowned. "I am not sure I want a white father."

"If he never recalls his past, he could live among us as a Lakota," she said, hardly daring to dream and hope. "He does not know he was a soldier and we have destroyed all the evidence." She thought of the fine blue ring sparkling in her clothing. It was the only thing that connected White Wolf to his past and she was tempted to throw it away, yet she knew it was valuable and there might come a time she would have to trade the ring for food or blankets. "Swear to me, my son, that you will keep the secret in case his memory never returns."

The boy looked incredulous in the moonlight. "You intend he stay?"

"I love him too much to let him go," she confessed and was ashamed of her deceit, and yet, she would have done anything to keep him.

Her son looked at the people gathering around the fire, dancing the scalp dance and feasting. "But now you must face the chiefs. They will surely want to kill him."

Her chest grew tight. White Wolf was not strong enough to try to escape. Even if she went with him to try to help him, could he make it? And once they were safely back among the whites, would he toss her away and return to his white woman as he had done in the past? There was no way to know and while it tore at her soul to think of him in some white girl's arms, she could not bear to see him killed. "If they decide to kill him, we will help him escape later."

"That will cause us much trouble among our people," Cincala argued.

"I would risk my life to save him," she admitted, "and maybe he would want us after he is safe."

"He never wanted us before," the boy argued. "Does he not have a white family?"

"I—I don't know for certain." In her mind, she saw a naked girl in his arms, a girl with the palest white skin and yellow hair. White Wolf was kissing her breasts and making love to her. The thought caused her great pain and Wiwila shuddered. Yet she loved him enough to save him, even if she was sending him back to that white girl's arms.

The rhythmic drums brought her out of her thoughts. The tribal chiefs were gathering. She took a deep breath and straightened her shoulders. It was time to plead her case for her man's life before the tribal council. If they would let her, she loved White Wolf enough to trade her life for his. "Let us speak to the council," she said quietly. Then, taking her child's hand, she walked to the big fire where the whole tribe waited silently.

The drums began a steady beat as the chiefs sat down on their ceremonial blankets, all resplendent in war paint, feathers, and beads. "Come forward, woman," ordered one.

She took a deep breath for courage and motioned her son to sit down cross-legged before she strode through the silent, hostile people to face the leaders. Sitting Bull was there and as she stopped, the great chief Crazy Horse rode into the camp on a war-painted pinto pony. His face was adorned with jagged lightning marks and his powerful body decorated with yellow war paint and white hailstones. His medicine was the powerful prairie storms. He strode to the fire and sat down, staring at her with dark eyes.

Old Sitting Bull studied her a long moment. "You dare to save a white soldier's life?"

She must show no fear. "He is White Wolf, the father of my young son."

A murmur of disapproval went around the circle, but

Sitting Bull held up a hand for silence. "Why did you not kill him as we did the other soldiers?"

"I said he was the father of my son. White Wolf is good and brave—many of you know him from the Washita."

A few heads nodded and a murmur ran through the crowd.

A visiting Cheyenne ally stood up. "The woman speaks true. The white soldier kept others from killing some of the women and children at that battle with Yellowhair."

Another warrior jumped to his feet, bristling with anger. "Yet he still rides with the soldiers. I say we kill him slowly to see how brave he is."

A louder mutter of approval from some of the men. Wiwila turned her head and looked toward the tipi. If she could not save him, did she have the courage to plunge a dagger into her helpless love to save him from a slow and agonizing death?

"He does not know who he is," Wiwila said. "I think he would be content to live among us as a Lakota warrior."

A buzz of excited chatter, then Crazy Horse motioned for silence. "This is a loco man?"

All knew the loco ones were protected by the gods and no tribe would anger the gods by harming a crazy man.

Yet she could not lie. "I—I don't know if his mind is gone or if he is crazy. I only know he seemed tormented when I knew him long ago and now he seems at peace."

There was a long silence and the chiefs looked at each other. Finally old Sitting Bull said, "We will retire and smoke and talk about this. We have had good medicine today and we do not wish to break it."

Wiwila heaved a sigh of relief as the chiefs got up and retired to a nearby lodge. At least now White Wolf had a chance to live. She could only pray that the chiefs decided in his favor. She glanced toward her son, who gave her an encouraging nod. Already, he was accepting the fact that he had a father. Cincala had been a lonely child, one of the few in the camp without a father to guide him, although her elderly uncle had done his best.

In a few minutes, the chiefs returned and settled before the fire. "Woman, stand up."

Heart beating hard, Wiwila approached them.

Sitting Bull said, "We all know it is bad medicine to kill the ones who have lost their minds—it enrages the Great Spirit. Therefore, this soldier is protected by our own laws." He paused to let his words sink in. "However, from this day forward, the white soldier is dead. As of today, he rides with us as a Lakota warrior named White Wolf."

A shout of approval went up around her and she had to blink back tears of relief. It would not do to weep before the council. She waited for a lull in the shouting. "It is agreed," she said, "that the soldier no longer exists and none of the tribe must ever acknowledge that he ever lived. As of today, he is my man, White Wolf, a Lakota warrior, for as long as he will ride among us."

More cheers as her son ran into her arms. She had saved Austin Shaw's life, she thought; now, would he be grateful enough to stay, or would he regain his memory and return to his white world? She couldn't know and at this moment, she didn't care. Soon it would be dawn and the Lakota would stay on the move, escaping from the hordes of vengeful soldiers who would surely be on their trail. She went to her lodge to care for White Wolf and gather their things for the march tomorrow. All that mattered to her was that for a few days at least, he was hers to love.

Twelve

Montana Territory
Tuesday, June 27, 1876.

General Terry's column halted and he squinted up at the blistering sun and wiped his face as he addressed the officer next to him. "Dr. Lester, shouldn't we be seeing some sign of Custer's forces by now?"

Peter paused, looking toward big birds circling in the distance. "I would think so, sir. What are those?"

The others looked toward the slowly circling birds as the June heat wafted up. Peter could feel the sweat running down his back and licked his dry lips. He sometimes wondered now if he should have stayed in his family's jewelry business back in Boston or at least begun his medical practice among the rich and elite. Yet he'd been inspired by Austin Shaw's descriptions of the West and Peter loved the freedom of these endless plains. He hadn't seen Austin in several years and he was looking forward to visiting with him when they joined up with Custer's column.

A grizzled scout rode up beside them and strained his eyes, shading them with his hand to stare off in the distance. "Good God, buzzards."

There was a silence. Peter felt a chill go up his back from the man's tone. Circling buzzards couldn't be good.

The general cleared his throat. "Maybe they've found a dead buffalo to feast on."

Peter Lester knew there hadn't been many buffalo around lately—the Plains tribes were starving.

The scout combed his fingers through his dirty beard. "What do you want us to do, sir?"

General Terry considered. "Let's ride ahead and investigate. Pass the word down the line for every man to be quiet and on the alert."

In spite of the heat, Peter had a terrible, cold premonition as the column rode forward silently. A mile up ahead, they found a wounded bay horse wearing a cavalry saddle with a Seventh Cavalry blanket. An arrow was imbedded in the saddle.

Peter said it without thinking. "Oh, my God, isn't that Captain Keogh's horse?"

The scout rode over and grabbed the bay gelding's reins. "Yep, it's Comanche, all right. The captain thinks the world of this horse."

"Bring him along then," the general snapped. "And pass the word to have weapons at the ready."

The valley was silent except for the squawking of the circling buzzards. In the hot sun, the gaunt birds threw giant shadows across the vast prairie. In another hundred yards, they came across a dead Indian and two dead horses.

The general sighed loudly. "Oh, dear God, something terrible has happened. Let's send out some advance patrols—there's no telling what lies ahead of us."

Peter Lester saluted. "Sir, if you don't mind, I'd like to go along. There may be some wounded men ahead."

"Of course." The general nodded, but the look on his stern face indicated that he didn't think they would find wounded men. Peter rode out with the patrol while the column waited. They kept a sharp lookout as they rode. Then they found a dead soldier lying sprawled on his belly, his back a pincushion of arrows.

The captain in charge of the patrol nodded to a private. "Ride back and tell the general what we've found. We may be about to be attacked at any minute."

The wind shifted just then and Peter could smell the sweet stench of death. He'd never gotten used to that smell. At least he had his medical kit for when they found wounded soldiers. Of course there would be wounded soldiers. Custer had hundreds of men with him; they couldn't all be dead. The private saluted and took off at a gallop while the patrol moved forward at a slow canter. On a little rise several hundred yards ahead, there were white patches among the brown and black and gray motionless horses.

The captain reached for his binoculars. "What in the hell is that?"

Peter watched the man look through the glasses, start, then look again before the binoculars fell from his nerveless fingers. His face turned a ghastly white. "Oh, my God." Peter tried not to breathe the stench, but he knew now what the white blobs were. "I—I think I'd better see if there's anyone left alive."

"We'll go with you," the captain said. "Everyone stay at the ready. This might be an ambush."

They rode in silence. The day was so quiet that except for the squawking, circling buzzards, even the horses' hooves seemed to echo as they rode past dead cavalry mounts and scattered bodies. Peter swallowed hard and reined in, looking down. The white blobs were naked, dead men, mutilated beyond recognition. The hot weather had added to the horror. Behind him, the captain, only a boy, took a ragged breath. "Everyone look around. There's bound to be someone alive here."

Behind him, Peter heard a soldier retching at the sights and smells. His own stomach churned, but he did not have the luxury of getting nauseated; there might be wounded men to attend to. Somehow, even as Peter dismounted, he knew there weren't, but out of force of habit, he reached for his medical bag anyway.

"My God, here's Colonel Custer," someone called.

Custer? No, the fair-haired favorite couldn't be dead. He was invincible, the boyish hero of the Civil War. Still, Peter wheeled and walked over to look. Yes, the bloated body was indeed the boyish hero. George Armstrong Custer half lay, half sat against a rock, most of his clothing gone. He almost looked asleep, except for the bullet hole in his head and chest. Peter squatted down and stared in disbelief. Custer was beyond help now. At least he hadn't been mutilated or scalped. Which was more than he could say for the others.

Peter swallowed hard and stood up, stepping over a dead horse and looking around. The bodies were mutilated and unrecognizable, and with no clothes to hide their nakedness, it was impossible to tell a colonel from a private.

A private waved at the others. "I've found Tom Custer."

Peter ran to look. The head had been smashed beyond recognition. "How in God's name can you tell?"

The other man pointed. "His initials are tattooed on his arm."

Peter looked. *T.W.C. Thomas Ward Custer.* He stood up, gazing at the ghastly scene. Most of the men had sold their lives dearly; empty cartridges and dead horses lay all over the terrain among the grotesque, naked bodies. "I hope to God my old friend is not among them," he said aloud.

The others had been walking about, staring at the bloated corpses.

The captain shook his head. "If he is, Dr. Lester, I don't know how you'd recognize him. These bodies are in such bad shape, their own mothers wouldn't know them."

Peter knew it was true, yet he had to look. He walked among the bloody, naked bodies, hoping against hope that he wouldn't find Austin Shaw and yet, Austin had ridden with Custer's troops. "My friend has brown hair and is about my size," Peter said.

A soldier laughed without humor. "That's only about half the men out here, Doctor."

"Maybe his body hasn't been looted," Peter said, remembering suddenly. "My family's jewelry store sold his family some fine things—an expensive sapphire ring and a gold watch. The watch has his father's initials on it."

Another soldier paused to roll a cigarette. "Anything like that, the Injuns have taken."

Peter's heart fell. "That may be so, but I'd like to be able to send his body home to his mother." He walked around, staring down at the mostly faceless corpses, both hoping and fearing to find Austin. Probably the other man was right; the Sioux had looted anything worth taking—there was no way to know which one might be Austin Shaw. In the distance, he could see General Terry's column coming at a gallop now that the scout had gotten to him with the message.

Peter paused next to one body, then another. Flies came up in a swarm and the smell made him gag as he stared at the scalped bodies. No one seemed to be wearing that sapphire ring. Maybe Austin had escaped. Maybe Austin was riding with another part of the column, maybe—

"Dr. Lester, come here," a private called.

Peter turned and went over to where the man knelt by a naked body that had been speared by a war lance. "Yes?"

"This man seems to have something in his hand—I saw it glint in the sun."

Curious, Peter watched the private struggle to open the man's clenched fist. When he got the hand open, a small object glittered in the hot sun.

Wordlessly, the soldier took it from the dead man's hand and gave it to Peter.

Peter took it, stared at it. A fine gold watch. His fingers trembled as he snapped it open and looked at the monogram. *R.L.S. Robert Lewis Shaw.* Yes, he'd know that watch anywhere. What would he tell Austin's mother?

He stared down at the naked, mutilated body. One thing he wouldn't tell Elizabeth Shaw was the truth. The corpse was swollen and unrecognizable except that it was about the right height. The man had been mostly scalped, but what hair was left was brown. There wasn't enough left of the face to tell if the victim had had hazel eyes.

Tears clouded Peter's vision as he snapped the watch closed and dropped it in his pocket. "I recognize this watch," he said softly. "My family's jewelry store sold it to his father. Oh, God, I hate to be the one to tell his mother. If she could see him—"

"But she won't," the captain reminded him. "When we can finally ship these boys home, the coffins will be closed and the families will never know what happened to them. We'll lie and tell them the bodies weren't mutilated."

"Of course," Peter and the others nodded in agreement. Peter turned away. He didn't like Elizabeth Shaw, but he could pity her now. Still, she would get medals and put on a great, showy funeral, probably with a silver coffin. All Boston would talk of her brave son and she would be the center of attention. Elizabeth Shaw would love that.

General Terry's column galloped up just then. The officer dismounted and looked around. "Good God! Any survivors here?"

Peter shook his head. "Yet there's not enough bodies for the whole regiment."

About that time, a white scout galloped up on a lathered horse. "Sir, there are soldiers barricaded on a bluff about four miles from here."

"What?" Terry whirled.

The other man nodded. "Looks like Custer split his forces, then ran into more Indians than he could handle."

"Doctor," the general snapped at Peter, "get yourself over there right away."

"Yes, sir."

Behind him as he mounted up, he heard Terry order, "Let's get these bodies decently buried fast—there's no telling how many thousand Sioux are still in the area."

"But sir," the captain objected, "the officers' families will want—"

"We can return later with coffins and ship them back East," Terry said. "Right now, we've got to find out how many Indians we're dealing with before we meet the same fate."

Peter didn't wait to hear any more. He took off at a gallop toward the bluff where the other soldiers waited. He reached to touch the watch in his pocket. Eventually, Elizabeth Shaw would get her son's body returned for a hero's funeral and she would never know that he'd been mutilated too badly to recognize. No one ever told women things like that; it turned war into gory, ugly business instead of snappy brass bands, medals, and fancy uniforms. War was hell, but when it happened far away, the survivors never knew how much agony or abuse a dead man had suffered.

White Wolf only vaguely remembered the rough ride being dragged in the travois as his people headed north. His woman rode the horse that pulled the travois and now and then she looked back over her shoulder and smiled encouragement at him. She was beautiful. His handsome son often rode alongside, nodding encouragement. *Cincala.* Colt, yes, it was an apt description for the boy. Other than that, he remembered nothing except that he had been wounded somehow and had a gash across his forehead. He glanced down at his beaded buckskin clothing, but that gave him no clue. Well, what did it matter? There had been an emptiness in his heart; he knew that somehow now his wife and son were filling that emptiness. He only knew that he was happy for the first time in a long while.

Once when they camped, he asked, "Where are we go-ing?"

"To the Grandmother's Land," Wiwila reached down and gently touched his face, "it lies to the north. Our great chief, Sitting Bull, will lead us there."

Grandmother's Land. Canada, he thought, and then won-dered how he knew that. White Wolf raised himself from the travois. "Why do we go?"

His son shrugged. "Soldiers will kill us if we don't."

Soldier. It sounded vaguely familiar, but no mental image came to him and he did not want to appear stupid by asking what a soldier was and why the people feared them.

By the time they had traveled almost to the Grand-mother's Land, White Wolf had recovered and sat a mag-nificent white stallion that Crazy Horse had given him as a gift. Once word came that soldiers had been spotted and he saw the fear and loathing on his woman's face. "I will not let the soldiers hurt you," he vowed. "I will fight them."

Yet there were many soldiers, and the Lakota and the others of the Seven Tribal Fires of the Sioux nation hid in the passing brush until the blue-coated column rode past. Again, a memory stirred, but White Wolf brushed it away. Of course he had memories; hadn't he been told that the evil soldiers had often chased and murdered his people? White Wolf couldn't recall that, but he had seen the fear in all the faces. When he saw the terror in his woman's lovely eyes, gray as a wolf's pelt, he knew that it must be true and that the soldiers were his enemy, too.

Finally they reached the northern country and there was much feasting and celebrating because everyone knew that the bad soldiers could not follow them here. That first night, White Wolf had shot a fat buck and added to the feast. He was invited to sit with the other warriors and he was glad when he saw the pride on the faces of his woman and son. Then the dancing began and there was much laughter and merriment because they were safe and could relax and live without always looking behind them to see if the dreaded soldiers were coming after them.

White Wolf drank some of the whiskey the warriors had gotten from a trader. It burned going down, but it made him feel all warm and relaxed inside. After a while, he joined in the dancing around the fire. Others yelled approval and encouragement as he paused before Wiwila and nodded for her to join him in the sensual, slow movements.

Later there was a women's dance where Wiwila chose him to dance next to her, the two of them wrapped in her shawl. He could feel the warmth of her skin against his and he had a sudden man's need. When they left the circle and faded into the darkness, he asked, "Where is our son?"

"He is sleeping tonight with his friends. They want to fish in the morning."

"Then tonight is ours." He caught her arm and turned her toward him. Strange, his past was a blank as if a curtain had been drawn down over it, and yet one thing he knew: he could remember making love to this woman, being in her arms, although he did not know when or where. "Help me, Wiwila, I worry that I remember nothing of my past."

She looked up at him. "Are you happy, White Wolf?"

He nodded, looking down into her beautiful face. "I think I have never been happier in my whole life."

"Then let the past go," she whispered and came into his arms. Their lips met and he held her very close against his wide chest as his mouth caressed hers. She let her lips part and with a shudder, his tongue slipped inside. Wiwila moaned softly and clung to him. For many winter counts she had dreamed of holding this man again, making love to him, and the only way that was possible was for him to forget his past and truly become White Wolf. She had prayed to the Great Spirit for her love's return; surely the Great Spirit himself must have interceded for her.

White Wolf swung her up in his arms. "I want you."

"And I want you." She reached up to kiss him as he carried her to their lodge.

Inside, a small fire blazed against the coolness of the night as she stripped off her doeskin shift. White Wolf stood looking at her, drinking her in.

She laughed self-consciously. "Do I please you?"

"Like nothing I have ever known." He caught her hand and pulled her to him, running his hands up and down her naked body. She closed her eyes, enjoying the caress. She had waited so many winter counts to again share his embrace. He stroked her hair, murmuring soft words to her in Lakota.

She looked up at him. He was still handsome although he now had a scar across his forehead. His hair was growing out long and the constant sun was darkening his skin. In a few months, he would no longer look like a white man except for the light hair and hazel eyes. Only then would she feel safe that no curious white might nudge his memory and he would once again be Captain Austin Shaw. Maybe it was wrong, but she loved him so much, she did not care. She and their son needed him and that was all that mattered to her. Besides, White Wolf was happy; anyone could see it in his eyes.

She kissed her way down his mighty chest and licked his nipple. He gasped with pleasure and held her face there a long moment before she pulled away and began to kiss her way down his body.

At this point, he tore away his breechcloth and stood there in the firelight, proud and erect as a stallion. She went to her knees and kissed the symbol of his manhood. "You are my man and will always be," she whispered.

He knelt, gathered her into his arms. "I am going to love you tonight as I must have loved you the night I put my son in your belly."

She remembered that night and sighed with happiness. "I am awaiting your pleasure, my warrior."

He took her to the soft robe and embraced her, kissing every inch of her while she writhed with impatience.

"I want you to complete me," she urged, "to be one."

Instead, he put his mouth on her breast, sending shivers of delight up her back as he licked and kissed there. Then he kissed between them and went lower. She lay back on the buffalo robe, watching him kiss his way down her belly.

Surely he wasn't going to kiss her there, but then he did, sending her into a frenzy of desire. "Please," she begged, pulling him down on top of her, "oh, please!"

Only then did he enter her, thrusting gently into her soft wetness while she dug her nails into his muscular back and pulled him deeper. She heard his gasp of breath as she locked her legs around his lean, hard body and bucked under him as he moved faster.

His rhythm was perfect, moving with her as she ascended the mountain of need and desire. She wanted more, and he seemed determined to give it to her. They were both panting and covered with a sheen of perspiration as they locked together. And then she reached a pinnacle of ecstasy too intense to withstand and she cried out, but no one heard because he slipped his tongue inside her mouth, tasting and teasing there until he, too, came in a hot rush as they lay locked and straining together for a long, long moment.

Afterward, he dropped off to sleep in her arms. But she did not sleep. She lay stroking his hair and wondering if he would ever remember his past. She must not let him do that; to do so would immediately cause him to leave her and return to that faraway place called Boston. For this reason, she had carefully hidden the fine ring with the blue stone. She knew she should throw it away—it was the last evidence linking Captain Austin Shaw with the man she loved as White Wolf. Yet she could not bring herself to do that.

Finally, she too slept. At dawn he made love to her again and it was as wonderful as it had been last night.

* * *

As the weeks turned into months and then years, the three of them were happy. White Wolf no longer asked about his past and he had become a great warrior, riding with the Lakota against their enemies, the Ute and the Pawnee. Once, as he bent over a stream, he was surprised at his image, so much like his pale-skinned son. Yet his hair grew long and his skin darkened gradually so that he was almost as dark as any of the warriors. Their son grew tall and strong and he rode proudly beside his father.

The weather turned cold and sometimes the tribe went hungry. The buffalo were fewer all the time. However, White Wolf was a good hunter and his lodge had meat when some of the others had none. Then, as in the manner of the Lakota, the best hunters shared their food with the less skilled hunters and their families. Finally, after five bitter winters had passed, Sitting Bull felt safe enough to lead his people out of the Grandmother's Land and back to the endless plains to the south. They were always on the lookout for the dreaded soldiers. White Wolf had never seen one up close; he only knew that they meant death and destruction and the Seven Council Fires of the Sioux avoided any contact.

It seemed he had always known the things that his people knew—how to track game, how to kill an enemy. When the weather turned hot, the people began to plan a sun dance. White Wolf was pleased and humbled to be offered an invitation. That meant that he was considered one of the Lakota and a skilled warrior. He, too, pledged much food and offerings and prepared to take part by going to a lonely place and doing without food and water until he had had a vision. In his vision, the great wolf came to him and warned him to avoid the white soldiers lest those enemies steal his happiness from him.

On the appointed day, he, too, gathered with the other

warriors who had pledged a sun dance. As his woman and child looked on proudly, he gritted his teeth and made no sound as the wooden pegs were inserted under the skin of his powerful chest. The drums began to beat and he was tied to the sun dance pole and began to dance, pulling against the skewers in his chest. It was painful, but others nodded and murmured approval as he danced long hours, pulling against the leather rope. He danced until he was weak, jerking against the skewers until they finally pulled from his chest, tearing the skin. Although he was ready to faint, he managed to stay on his feet and Sitting Bull nodded with approval.

"White Wolf, no matter your blood, you are truly one of the Lakota at heart. Your name will become a legend."

He nodded proudly as he stepped from the circle. The sun beat down hard and he was bloody and in pain, but nothing mattered except that he had survived the sun dance and was one of the most revered warriors of the tribe. His woman put herbs on his wounds and smiled at him. "I love you so much. There is nothing I wouldn't do for your happiness."

"You are my happiness," he whispered and smiled at her and his son who stood proudly in the doorway. Maybe it was the Great Spirit who had robbed him of his memory, but the past no longer mattered to him.

In the summer, the Lakota spotted a small herd of buffalo and readied themselves for the hunt. White Wolf was not sure he knew how to kill the great beasts with only a lance, but his fine white stallion seemed to know what to do as White Wolf thundered alongside and made his kill. Later he looked on proudly as Cincala made his first kill.

Wiwila nodded approval to both of them as the women watched from the sidelines. "Like father, like son," she said. "Our lodge will never lack for meat." She brought a travois and her skinning knife and began to cut up the meat. She would peg down the skin to make warm winter clothing and the meat would be dried for the winter. That night, there was a great feast such as the tribe had not seen in a long time and afterward, dancing.

When the dancing was finished, White Wolf gathered his woman into his arms and carried her out to a small dell near a stream and made slow, satisfying love to her until they were both exhausted. Later they slept in each other's arms and he thought as he dropped off to sleep that even the Great Spirit world where warriors went when they died could offer nothing better than this.

As the months faded into years, they saw few white people and their little band managed to avoid the soldiers. Although the word nudged at White Wolf's memory, he never saw one up close and was not even certain what a soldier was except that they were very bad and dangerous to his people.

Wiwila gradually stopped worrying that she would lose her man. White Wolf's memory had never returned and more and more with each passing month, he became Lakota in every way but birth. Wiwila should have known that such happiness could not last and might draw the jealousy of some of the wind or earth spirits, because finally there came a day when the secret was out.

Thirteen

Dakota Territory. Autumn, 1881

Captain Peter Lester led his patrol into the fort and swung wearily off his dusty horse in the late afternoon light. Sioux country. Right now, it maintained an uneasy peace. He nodded to his sergeant, who ordered the troops to dismount. Peter ran his hand through his thin, graying hair and sighed. It had been more than five years since the disaster at the Little Bighorn, but he would never forget that scene. Since he had identified Austin Shaw's body, Peter had been ordered to accompany that dead hero home for the finest funeral upper-class Boston had ever seen. He had returned Austin's gold watch to Mrs. Shaw, and at the funeral, a colonel and some politician had showed up to present her with a handful of medals. Elizabeth Shaw had looked almost pleased as she stood next to the fine silver casket. They hadn't opened it, of course—the body was too ravaged—but because of the monogrammed watch, there was no doubt the son of one of the wealthiest families in Boston was being laid to his eternal rest in Mount Auburn Cemetery.

Peter had an eerie feeling as he watched Austin's mother at the funeral. She seemed almost happy. There she'd stood, dressed in the finest custom-made mourning clothes, next to the expensive coffin with her son's medals draped proudly over her arm. She was the center of attention and the event had been on the front pages of all the newspapers. She was now the mother of a bonafide hero of the Little Bighorn.

The country, of course, was furious with the Cheyenne and the Sioux over the battle, even though the army, with the white citizens' approval, had been harrying and killing Indians for years. Libbie Custer, all draped in black, was certain that cowardly officers such as Crook, Benteen, and Reno had caused her brave Autie's death and she appeared at the investigation to say so. To support herself, Custer's widow went about the country lecturing and writing books about the West and her heroic husband. If any man disagreed, he could not say so publicly because the public had taken the brave beauty to their hearts.

The country had taken the disaster as a personal insult, coming as it did only days before the country's centennial. How dare those savages hand the army a stunning defeat just as the United States of America was preparing to celebrate its hundredth year?

An approaching dour major brought Peter out of his musings and he snapped a salute. "Captain Peter Lester reporting, sir."

The lean, weathered officer returned the salute. "You're a doctor, aren't you, Lester?"

"Yes, sir."

"Were you the officer in charge of this patrol?"

Peter sighed. "No, sir. His horse fell and Captain Jory broke his leg, so we dropped him off at the infirmary and I brought the patrol in."

The other nodded. "Too bad, but this is tough country. It's all I can do to keep most of my men from going off to look for gold in the Lakota lands."

"Makes it hard to keep the peace, doesn't it, sir?"

The major nodded. "I have to admit I feel sorry for the poor devils. They don't understand why we pressure them to sign and then we ignore the treaties ourselves and do whatever we want. When some of them come riding in to trade here, they look pretty hungry and ragged. We don't get much company here at the fort, Captain. Join me for supper?"

"Thank you, sir." Peter smiled. "I'll be along as soon as I get my men taken care of and get myself cleaned up."

The major told him where to quarter his patrol and left.

Peter was giving directions to his sergeant when he saw the small group riding into the fort.

"Good God," the sergeant shifted the chaw of tobacco in his beefy jaw, "Injuns."

Peter paused and stared at the spectacle. A small group of warriors was riding in. They were resplendent in feathers and paint, beaded moccasins, and fancy horses. The one who took his attention was a magnificent warrior astride a great white stallion, a bundle of furs tied to a pack horse behind him.

Peter was mesmerized by the warrior in his fine beaded buckskin pants, although his great chest was bare and sun dance scars were visible. This must be a respected brave of many coups, Peter thought with admiration as he watched them rein in close by.

There was something familiar about the warrior, Peter thought, then shrugged it off as ridiculous. He'd hardly seen a Lakota in months and he never remembered seeing one as tall and handsome as this one. The man wore feathers in his hair and silver bracelets on his arms. Then he looked directly at Peter. A chill went up Peter's back as he realized the man's eyes were hazel and his long hair lighter than the other men. Peter took a step forward, stunned and staring. It couldn't be and yet . . . "Austin?"

The other blinked, looking back at him. "I am White Wolf," he said slowly in English as if he were not used to using the foreign words.

Peter shrugged. "Of course, I must be loco. What am I

thinking? I identified the body myself and attended his funeral."

The other man said nothing, only stared at him with that stern, expressionless look of the Lakota. After a moment, the man turned his horse and led his small group away toward the trading post.

Peter laughed and turned to his sergeant. "I feel like a damned fool, thinking I knew that savage."

The other man shrugged. "He's got white blood, sir, that's for sure. We call 'em squaw men, those who desert their own kind and go live with the Indians. Although sometimes I almost envy them their freedom."

Peter nodded. He had already dismissed the strange warrior from his mind. "Well, I'm going to wash up and find my quarters. Pass the word that we'll be riding out again early tomorrow morning."

"Yes, sir," the sergeant said and saluted. "The men will be glad to have tonight at the fort, sir."

Peter turned to go. "See you in the morning then." He walked briskly toward the officers' quarters. He wasn't sorry he'd made this choice in life. Now that he thought of it, he'd rather be an army doctor than the wealthiest physician in Boston.

White Wolf finished his trading and gathered the matches, salt and other small items he had traded for his furs, insisting the group leave the fort before dark.

His friend, Pony Running, scowled. "Some of us hope to sneak off to the trader who carries firewater."

White Wolf shook his head. "That will only bring us trouble with the whites. We have our things—let us leave this place."

The others obeyed and within an hour, they were riding out of the fort. As they rode, White Wolf turned in his saddle and looked back over his shoulder, thinking about the white man. The blue of the uniform had stirred something in him. The man's face had seemed familiar, too, and he had found himself understanding the man's strange words in that tongue, although White Wolf had not known he knew that language. *Austin.* He said the word aloud to himself as he rode, and it, too, seemed vaguely familiar, although he was not sure what an "Austin" was. Perhaps he had seen the white soldier from a distance somewhere. His mind drew a blank, coming up against a stone wall of the past that he could not seem to penetrate. *Well, what did it matter?*

White Wolf dismissed the thought and concentrated on the trail ahead. The wealth and the good things of the whites had been evident at the fort. What the elders said was true— the *wasicus* were becoming as numerous as grains of sand and had much guns, blankets, and supplies. But that was not enough for them; they wanted all the land the Lakota rode, too. To be greedy was wrong among his people.

The village was planning a feast as White Wolf and his group rode into camp. His son came running to meet him, eager, yet aware that he was twelve winter counts old, on the way to becoming a man. "Did you see white men, Father? What were they like?"

"I saw them," he nodded as he dismounted and handed the reins of the great white stallion to his son. "Their coats are blue, but their skin is the color of a fish belly, not a fine brown like ours."

For the first time, he took a good look at his own hand as he gave over the reins and then he looked at his son. Both their skins were dark, but not as dark as the other Lakota. The boy had eyes as gray as a wolf, just like his mother's. *Why had he never thought about that before?*

Wiwila came running to meet him, although it was not seemly to be so affectionate in public to a warrior of many coups. "Oh, my husband, you are back."

She saw that his eyes were preoccupied as if he hardly heard her. "Did you bring me a packet of needles?"

He nodded.

Their son broke in. "Mother, he saw white soldiers."

She felt her heart skip a beat; she had always feared this. "Soldiers? What did they want?"

White Wolf shrugged and started toward their lodge. "Nothing. A new bunch of them is passing through."

Pony Running said, "Their leader spoke to White Wolf."

Her heart began to pound. "What—what did he want?" Her man stared at her curiously. "I don't know. He acted as if he knew me, but of course, he is wrong."

Her mouth went dry as dust. "When are they going away?"

White Wolf shrugged. "I don't know. It means nothing to us."

"Of course not." She forced a laugh as she took his arm and they walked toward their lodge. "The tribe itself moves tomorrow also."

Her man looked down at her fondly. "It can't be too soon for me," he said. "We all know that it is dangerous to camp too close to the soldiers."

Wiwila breathed a sigh of relief. She was not going to lose him after all.

That night there was a feast, with dancing around the fire. Cincala had gone off with his friends and she was glad when she saw the look in her man's eyes as he watched her. He wanted her as a man wants a woman. She danced in the circle with him, her arm brushing his until he signaled for her to leave the glow of the big campfire.

Her heart thudded hard as he lifted her, carried her to their lodge. Inside, he reached for her, his eyes telling her how much he needed her. She went into his arms, loving him as she could never love another man, and yet her heart, which should be full of happiness and relief, was full of terror and guilt.

He kissed her eyes, her face, her mouth in a slow, languid way that brought her blood to a boil and made her draw her breath sharply as his hands caressed and stroked her breasts. "No woman could ever give me the pleasure that you give me, Wiwila. I trust you with my love as I would trust you with my life."

She held him close, not answering for a long moment. He was here perhaps because he did not know he had another choice; she had not given him that choice, fearing if he knew the truth, he would not choose her. She must not think of that; she must think of how much she loved and needed him, how much their son needed him. She kissed him then, parting her lips and caressing his tongue with her own as she pressed against him so hard, he must feel her nipples against his bare, scarred chest. He drew in his breath sharply, then reached to pull off her doeskin shift even as he tossed away his buckskin pants and stood there outlined in the firelight in his powerful nakedness.

He bent his head to kiss between her breasts, then slowly worked his way down her bare belly until he was on his knees before her and kissed the mound of her womanhood. The sensation made her catch her breath and she couldn't stop herself from holding his head against her body, asking—no, demanding that—he kiss and caress her most intimate spot. The warmth of his probing tongue caused her to shiver and her knees to go weak. "My dear one," she whispered, "you turn a small fire into a raging inferno."

"And I plan it will consume us both," he whispered, his breath hot against her most intimate place as he caressed it with his tongue.

He went to the soft fur of their bed and pulled her down on top of him. "Make love to me, my beautiful Wiwila," he said.

She needed no urging. She kissed his face, his nipples, his belly. He pulled her up so that her breasts hung over his face and then he began to lave them with his tongue, sucking them until she thought she could stand the sensation no more.

His maleness was hard, throbbing, and insistent against her bare lower body. "Ride me, my Wiwila," he urged, "ride me and pleasure us both!"

Finally, sated and exhausted, they both pretended to sleep, but both lay staring into the darkness.

Her secret was as much agony as it had always been these five long years since he'd returned to her. She must be honest with him and tell him, but she knew that in doing so, she would lose him. "Are you awake?"

"Yes." In the moonlight shining through the lodge door, she could see his profile as he sat up. "I keep thinking about that soldier who looked so familiar to me."

He might unravel the mystery of his past, or he might not. Her heart told her to keep her secret and hope for the best. He was happy here, wasn't he? Yet all these years, their life had been built on a lie and one does not lie to those one loves. "If—if you did remember you knew him, what then?"

He looked down at her, puzzlement in his handsome face. "I don't know. Sometimes I wonder about the life I must have lived, since I have no memory of it before I awoke in your arms one summer afternoon."

She sat up, too, biting her lip. "White Wolf, you must know you are not the same as the other Lakota."

He sighed. "And that's what worries me. I can never rest in peace until I know what secrets lie in my past."

She took a deep breath. "Does the word 'Boston' mean anything to you?"

"Boston." He seemed to be rolling the word around in his brain. "It does sound familiar."

"You told me once it was a city back East."

He shrugged. "How could that connect with me?"

She swallowed hard to hold back the tears. "What—what if I told you you are a rich white man from that place?"

"How would you know that?" His face furrowed.

"Because you once told me."

He reached out and grabbed her shoulder, shook her. "All this time I have agonized over the blankness of my past and you knew this?"

The tears were rolling down her cheeks now—she could feel them. "I didn't want to lose you."

"Wasn't that my decision to make?" His voice had an edge to it and his grip tightened.

"You're hurting me."

Immediately, he let go, but his face stayed grim. "I'll wager you know more, don't you?"

She nodded, too emotional to speak. "There is one thing more." She reached into a small sack where she had kept the magnificent ring hidden. "There is this."

He made a gasp of surprise and jerked it from her hand, turning the fine gem over in his hand so that it caught the light. "It is beginning to return to me—all the pieces of this puzzle."

"Remember I did this for love," she gulped and then took a deep breath. "You—you were wounded at the battle of the Greasy Grass River five winter counts ago."

The light broke over his face and he made a small cry. "Of course! I remember now. I was going for help for Custer's men . . ." His voice trailed off and he looked at her.

"All dead," she whispered. "I found you injured on the battlefield."

His memory returned with a rush and for a moment, he was so furious with the girl, he thought he would strike her. To control himself, he stumbled to his feet, still clutching the ring. He remembered riding hard through a hot June afternoon, the many warriors gaining on him. Then he remembered the pain in his head and falling toward the ground. More than that, he remembered his whole history. "I am Austin Shaw of the Boston Shaws," he said aloud to himself. "I come from a rich and powerful family back East."

She nodded. "Yes."

He looked down at her, half in disbelief, half in fury. "You knew all this yet you did not tell me."

She was weeping now. "I feared to lose you!"

"And so you tried to bind me to you with lies, fearing that I didn't care enough to stay with you if I knew the truth. Damn you for distrusting me and lying to me! This is not the way true love is."

He turned and stalked out. She ran to the lodge door and watched him stride toward where his favorite horse was hobbled. "I'm sorry," she called after him. "Whether you are Austin Shaw or White Wolf, I'll always love you so!"

He did not look back as he saddled his horse, mounted up, and rode off into the darkness. She had never known such inner pain as she did now, watching him leave her forever. He could get to the fort on time, she knew. The captain who had recognized him would probably still be there. No doubt by noon tomorrow, Austin Shaw would be on his way back East, the only survivor of Yellow Hair's men. She had been wrong in trying to hold on to him this way. How was it an old Indian saying went? *You cannot hold a butterfly prisoner without crushing its wings. If you love it, let it go. If it loves you, it will return to you.*

There was no chance of that. White Wolf hated her for her deliberate deception, he'd made that clear. She didn't care what happened to her anymore, but what of their son? Perhaps White Wolf would come back for him and take Colt away to live among the rich whites and she would be all alone. Well, Colt should be allowed to make his own decision and he worshiped his father. She would get her just punishment. Wiwila went up on a small rise to commune with the Great Spirit and seek help in her anguish. She knelt there, hands clasped for hours, staring up at the stars and wishing that White Wolf loved her as much as she loved him.

Finally, there was a rosy pink glow in the eastern sky. It would be dawn soon and the Lakota would be moving their camp this day. While she was moving farther west, Captain Austin Shaw would be making arrangements to head east on the Iron Horse. *"Wakan Tanka nici un,"* she whispered. May the Great Spirit go with you.

She needed to see about her son, although she still wasn't sure what she would tell him about his father's disappearance. Wiwila started down the rise, through the small trees near a spring.

A sound. She started, wondering if it might be an enemy sneaking up on her or a wild animal. Then White Wolf rode into view on his great white horse and blocked her path.

She stared up at him. "If you have come to take our son with you, please kill me or berate me, but don't take him away from the only people he has ever known."

He looked at her a long moment, then dismounted. "That's not why I came back."

"You're still angry with me," she said. "All right, kill me or beat me for what I've done. I deserve your anger for keeping your past from you."

He strode toward her, then paused before her. "Beat you? Kill you? Would that change anything?"

"It might make you feel better."

He stood there, looking down at her as if making a decision. "I have been riding all night, thinking about the past five years and weighing that against the life I would have if I returned to Boston."

She waved him to stop talking. "I know the Lakota have little to offer by comparison to the rich, comfortable life that awaits you in civilization."

"What the Lakota has to offer is you—you and our son." His voice was low, gentle.

"What?"

He came to her then, gathering her into his arms. "I realized how much you love me, how very happy you've made me the past few years. Someone I loved very much a long time ago told me that if I ever found a once-in-a-lifetime love, I should run after it, not look back, and damn the consequences."

She laid her tear-streaked face against his bare chest, not daring to hope. "Austin—"

He put the tip of his finger against her lips. "Don't call me that. My name now and forever is White Wolf and I am a Lakota warrior." He kissed her then, deep and passionate, and she clung to him, fighting back the tears. It was all going to be all right now; he had made his choice. "And I am now and forever White Wolf's woman."

"Indeed you are." He swept her up in his strong arms and carried her to his horse. "Now let us race to meet the dawn together. I will give the ring to our son in case someday he wants to seek his other life." He kissed her deeply, passionately. "As for me, I will stay with my woman forever and there is no yesterday, only tomorrow."

"Only tomorrow," she echoed and clung to him as he carried her to his horse and they galloped out to meet the dawn of forever.

PART TWO
COLT'S STORY

Fourteen

Wounded Knee Creek, South Dakota
December, 1890

Cincala was not certain how the massacre started. First there had been the Ghost Dancing that had been on for months, trying to drive the white man from the Sioux lands. The whites seemed to sense the power of the dance and had brought in more troops to these desolate plains, but that had only intensified the peoples' dedication to the mystic ritual that had spread from one tribe to the next after the Paiute holy man, Wevoka, had begun it.

The Indian agent was nervous about the Ghost Dance that he suspected would end in a bloody uprising as tribe after tribe began the ritual that they believed would drive the white men from the face of the earth and bring back the buffalo and the Indians to power. Two weeks ago, the Indian police had been sent to arrest Sitting Bull and had killed him instead. Now there were no great leaders left among the Sioux. The mystic Crazy Horse had been dead fourteen winter counts now. These two renowned warriors had led the Sioux in the hour of their greatest triumph at the Greasy Grass battle against the hated Custer. The air was tense as the Indian agent called for more troops and the Seventh Cavalry arrived on the scene. All awaited the one small spark that might explode into another confrontation.

Cincala was now a man, more than twenty-one winter counts old, tall and strong and lighter-skinned than most of the other Lakota. He knew that somewhere in his past, his father, White Wolf, had been a soldier white man, but more than that he did not know because the subject was forbidden.

A month ago, his father, worried about the tension on the Sioux reservation, had taken the fine ring that had a stone the color of the sky, and hung it on a thong around Cincala's neck. "There may be trouble with the whites," White Wolf had said, "and this might save your life."

Outside their warm tipi, the cold wind howled. Cincala had looked at the ring, turning it over and over in his brown hand, then back to his father. White Wolf's skin was almost as brown and weathered as any Lakota warrior, but his long hair was brown, though turning to gray. His eyes were almost golden, not like Wiwila's, which were gray. Cincala, when he looked at his reflection in a stream, knew he favored them both. "My father, how might this save my life? I will use the bow, the rifle—"

"There may come a time that will not be enough." White Wolf shook his head and looked with loving eyes toward his woman. "The bluecoats are nervous about the Ghost Dancing."

"As well they should be," Cincala boasted. "It will soon wipe them from the face of the earth."

White Wolf's handsome, weathered face saddened. "Listen, my son, the whites will not be driven out. Every day they grow like grains of sand. Soon we will ride this prairie no more, but be penned up in places they choose like wild birds in a cage."

"How can that be?"

"Because I have lived long among them and I know their customs," White Wolf said. "Now I will reveal some secrets in case the time comes that you need to know. This ring is very valuable, worth much gold. There may come a time you need to bribe your way or sell it."

"Never!" Cincala declared and clasped it tightly.

"Listen to me, my son," White Wolf's voice was grave. "I have taught you the white man's language and also taught you to read that language by scratching lessons in the dirt with a stick."

"I know how to kill a running buffalo and how to kill an enemy," Cincala stuck out his strong chin stubbornly. "I have no need for white man's knowledge."

White Wolf shook his head. "It may happen that warrior knowledge is not enough. You have always known that I am really white and have a secret past?"

The boy nodded. "I knew I was not to ask about it."

White Wolf chewed his lip as if deciding how much to tell. "My son, if you are ever in desperate circumstances and your mother and I are not there to help you, know this: you have a grandmother in a faraway place called Boston. She is very rich."

"She owns many ponies?" Cincala was impressed.

His father laughed. "Better than that—she owns much gold to buy many ponies and lives in a fine, big house."

"I like living in a tipi," Cincala argued.

"Nonetheless, should there be trouble, her name is Elizabeth Shaw. Say that name over and over."

"Elizabeth Shaw," Cincala turned the name over on his tongue. "Is it big medicine?"

White Wolf nodded. "It is in Boston, where she owns many things. I don't know that she would help you, but if you get in trouble and I am not here, her name may be magic. Remember it well."

Cincala nodded and said the name again. He was only trying to please his father, of course; he had no interest in a rich old white woman, and this place called Boston did not interest him at all.

It was only a few days later that the army insisted that the Minneconjou leader, Big Foot, bring his followers into the reservation.

Wiwila shook her head when she heard the message carried from lodge to lodge. "It makes no sense, my husband, to try to move the people in such cold, snowy weather."

White Wolf shrugged and smoked his pipe. "The *wasicu* do not care that they make no sense. They obey orders like ants following in a line without question. I think the Indian agent does not understand the Ghost Dance and it scares him into calling for more soldiers. Old Big Foot is ill, maybe I can speak to the army chief and get the order delayed."

Wiwila looked toward Cincala. "Perhaps we should flee this camp."

"It won't do any good," White Wolf sighed. "There is no place to run any more. The whites have been grabbing our land all these years and finally, they will have it all. Life will not get better for the Lakota."

Wiwila reached out and touched his arm. "You could leave this place, go back to this city called Boston."

"And leave you behind? Never!" He put his arm around her shoulders protectively. "You are my life, Wiwila, and I have chosen you over what my civilization had to offer."

His father must know the white men's hearts well, Cincala thought bitterly, because only a few days later, in the midst of the cold, snowy weather, the tragedy happened. Old Big Foot had begun to move the tribe into the area that the whites decreed, with many nervous soldiers ringing the Indians, taking away their weapons. Some of the defiant young warriors like Cincala put on their ghost shirts that were promised to deflect the soldiers' bullets, then hid their knives and rifles rather than give then up.

His father's face changed when he saw the insignia on some of the bluecoats. "The Seventh Cavalry," he muttered, "not a good choice—they'll be looking for revenge. My son, you gather up our pony herd—I will go look for your mother, who is helping a woman giving birth in another camp. Do not give the soldiers any excuse to arrest you."

Cincala nodded dutifully, but in his brave heart was rebellion. He would not be treated like a sheep, to be herded and crowded into a pen at the bluecoats' say-so. Still, he separated from his father and began to round up the family pony herd and drive it toward the valley where the soldiers wanted the Sioux assembled near the little creek called Wounded Knee. The snow was deep and the weather very cold. Old Big Foot was near death, but trying valiantly to bargain for his people. The soldiers on the surrounding hills had the big guns they called Hotchkiss, the small cannons, and kept them pointed at the gathering people in the valley. Cincala sneered at them, thinking how nervous and afraid the soldiers looked. Real warriors should not be afraid of a bunch of hungry, ragged women and children. There weren't many warriors anymore and some of them were old and sickly, too. Up on one of the hills was a weather-beaten wooden building with a cross on top. Cincala remembered his father had pointed it out once as the place where the soldiers at the local fort worshiped their god.

The soldiers had demanded that the people turn in their weapons, but some of the young warriors, distrusting the white men's intent, hid their guns in their lodges. No one would ever be sure who fired the first shot, whether it was a soldier or a warrior, or maybe someone only accidentally discharged a rifle. It did not matter. In moments, the nervous bluecoats were turning their guns and the Hotchkiss cannons on the people in the valley. Women screamed, trying to gather up children and get them to safety; old men struggled with antique weapons to defend the women, but to no avail. Horses plunged and reared, toddlers screamed and were shot down as they struggled to run through the snow.

Cincala fired at the soldiers, determined to sell his life

dearly as around him people fell and bloodied the snow with their life's blood. Through the din of shots and screams, he remembered the acrid smell of burnt powder and the sweet scent of blood. He looked around vainly for his parents, but he was not certain if they had escaped. They might already be dead. Well, he would die like the Lakota warrior he was, even though the men were outnumbered. At that moment, even as he began a warrior's death song, he was hit. The shot spun him around, his arm feeling as if it were on fire. Cincala continued to pull the trigger even as he went down. He was only vaguely aware how cold the ground was and how bright his blood looked melting the snow with its warmth. He struggled to his feet again, fighting his way through the drifts. If he could reach a high point of ground, he would have a better chance of defending his people. As it was, the Sioux were helpless in the valley as the soldiers on the surrounding hills shot down into them like shooting fish in a barrel.

The wound in his shoulder made his arm too weak to pull the trigger, but he forced himself to keep fighting, even though the white cold around him was now a red haze of agony. Then he heard the crack of a rifle and pain tore through his thigh like a cut from jagged glass. He bit his lip hard to hold back the cry of pain. A warrior must not show weakness. If he could escape, he would live to fight the damned bluecoats again, but his leg would not work and his injured arm would no longer support the weight of the gun. He sank to his knees in the snow, lost in a haze of pain and cold. So this is how he would die. Cincala threw back his head and began a defiant warrior's death song as he reached up and clutched his fist around the ring. He would not have his father's magic stolen by the greedy soldiers. The noise of the cannons was a roar in his head that seemed to get louder and louder until there was nothing in his universe but cold and pain and noise. The last thing he remembered was how cold the snow was against his face as he fell.

Cincala did not know how long he remained in the Spirit World. When his mind returned to this earth, he lay on a dirty blanket on the floor of a white man's building, his fist tightly clutching the treasured ring. In a haze of pain, he tried to move, but was too weak to do so. Looking around, he saw faded red-and-green crepe paper hanging from the walls as well as a small, decorated cedar tree. At the front of the building on the wall was a large wooden cross and other things that celebrated the birth of the white man's savior as White Wolf had explained to him. He must be in that church overlooking the Wounded Knee valley. Around him, other wounded Indians moaned or suffered silently.

Two bluecoats approached his pallet. Cincala grabbed for a weapon, then realized he had none, nor even the strength to rise up off his blanket. All he could do was lie there and glare up at them. One of them was a balding officer with thinning gray hair while the other was a plump sergeant. They bent to stare at him.

"Poor devil," the officer muttered and his face was kind.

"What's he got in his hand, sir?" the sergeant said.

"Doesn't matter." The officer shrugged. He carried the magic doctor bag of the white man. "May God forgive us for what the army's done here."

The sergeant frowned. "Beggin' your pardon, Dr. Lester, sir, but you're too softhearted toward these damned savages."

The white doctor didn't answer as he pulled back the blanket and frowned at Cincala's wounds. Cincala could only glare back at him. Had these men come to finish him off?

Instead, the white captain reached to examine the torn

shoulder. His touch was gentle. "Savage? This one's at least half white."

"Aw, squaw men," the other grumbled, "sleeping with Injun women."

The doctor did not answer, his sympathetic gaze searching Cincala's face. "He looks familiar, somehow." He began to wash and bind Cincala's arm.

Cincala tried to pull away, but he was too weak. He must not accept charity from the white man; he was too proud. His father had said to use the fine ring for an emergency and perhaps this was it, to pay the white doctor man who was saving his life. Very slowly, Cincala jerked the string from his neck and held the ring out. *"Pilamaya.* Thank you," he said, struggling to translate his Lakota words into the less familiar English. "This for you."

"Good God." The doctor took the ring from Cincala's hand, his eyes widening. "Where did you get this?"

The sergeant scowled. "Reckon he stole it someplace."

"I did not steal it," Cincala gasped.

The doctor ignored the other white man, staring deep into Cincala's eyes. "You look like someone I know. Who is your father?"

Cincala shook his head. He would not bring trouble to White Wolf. He knew his father was an honorable man and had not stolen the ring.

The officer stared at him in disbelief and shook his head. "He looks like a soldier I knew a long time ago, but Austin Shaw was killed at the Little Bighorn. I identified the body myself."

"My father," Cincala blurted, then cursed himself for his impulsive words.

The other's kind face was a mask of shock and disbelief. "Is Austin alive?"

Cincala shook his head. His sorrow added to his pain. Surely White Wolf and Wiwila had not survived the massacre and even if they had, he knew his father would not want the white men to know who he was.

The kind officer sighed. "No, of course not. I identified him myself, but at least I've found his son."

Cincala watched Dr. Lester stand up, still staring at the ring in his hand. "This is the evidence that clinches it," the doctor said to the sergeant. "After we bind this man's wounds, I've got to send a telegram. Elizabeth Shaw is about to get the shock of her life!"

The ancient butler, Williams, handed Elizabeth Shaw the telegram which had just arrived. Still wearing the black of mourning although her son, Austin, had been dead more than fourteen years now, she put on her gold-rimmed spectacles and peered at it. Then she fainted dead away.

When she revived, she was propped up on the library sofa with anxious servants hovering about with tea and smelling salts. "Where is my telegram?" she shouted in her usual voice that sent weak-hearted maids scurrying for cover. The butler put it in her hand and she reread it. No, it couldn't be true, but yet it was signed by Dr. Peter Lester and he wouldn't jest about such things.

Elizabeth made a shooing gesture with her small, nervous hands. "Everyone get back to work—I am not paying you to lollygag around."

Most of the help fled the scene, but the old butler stayed, looking dubious. "Can it possibly be true, ma'am?"

"Maybe. Williams, call my lawyer on that new telephone thing and tell him I need to talk to him at once. And then you'd better call Bosworth down at the mill. He's not going to be happy to hear that I may have an unknown heir."

The old man limped out to do her bidding and Elizabeth got up off the settee, went to the window, and looked out. It was cold in Boston in January, but here in her fine mansion, it was toasty warm. She walked over to the cabinet where she kept Austin's watch. He had inherited the fine gold timepiece from his father and Peter Lester had used it to identify Austin's body at the Little Bighorn. Now both father and son lay beneath elaborate headstones at Mount Auburn Cemetery. The watch was on a little stand next to Austin's picture. She smoothed the wrinkles from her black silk dress. Technically, she could have given up wearing black long ago, but she rather gloried in being the mother of one of Custer's dead heroes. She knew people pointed her out on the street as Austin Shaw's mother and would retell the story of his heroic death against the savages.

Suppose there was some mistake. No, she thought and shook her gray head. Peter Lester had mentioned the family heirloom, the sapphire-and-diamond ring. Very well. A grandson. She was both excited and embarrassed to imagine one of the blue-blooded Shaws sleeping with some Injun girl. How old was the little savage? She reread the wire, but Peter Lester had not said. Austin had been killed in June of '76. Perhaps the boy was no more than thirteen or fourteen years old, still young enough to tame if she could find the right tutor.

A tutor. That settled, she rang for the butler with orders to send a telegram to Dr. Lester to ship the boy to her. Then she sat down at her desk to compose an advertisement. With any luck and some strict instruction from a stern taskmaster, her half-breed grandson might very well be civilized and turned into a proper Shaw.

A week later, Samantha MacGregor paused at the great iron gates of the Georgian mansion and checked first the ad and then the house number. Yes, this was it. The cold wind shook her and took her breath away as she grabbed onto the gate to keep from falling. It had been a long walk from town, but she had not had money for a carriage. Carriage? She had not even had a meal today and it was late afternoon. Last night, she had slept on a bench at the train station.

Sam was desperate, desperate enough to do what she had done—send a note to this house, asking for an interview. Sam knew the lady of the house would not be expecting a girl to show up, but if she talked fast, the family might reconsider. Yes, she was hungry and desperate. If she didn't get this position, she wasn't sure where she would sleep tonight.

The wind whipped around her again and Sam was colder than she had ever been in her life—colder and so weak, the landscape was beginning to fade before her. If she could just make it to the house . . . Picking up her worn valise, she took a tentative step. Inside, there would be warmth and maybe a cup of tea or even a bite to eat while she was interviewed. If she didn't get out of this weather, she might freeze to death before anyone noticed. Sam took another step, swaying on her feet. She had to make it to the door, she just had to. And then the wind cut through her again and she didn't have the strength to keep her balance and though she did her best, the snowy ground rushed up to meet her.

Fifteen

Elizabeth Shaw had paused by her upstairs sitting room window and peered out toward the gate. A girl stood there looking up at the house. The girl was quite young, perhaps not yet out of her teens, and very slender under the worn old coat. A strand of dark red hair had come loose from her scarf and whipped about her thin but pretty face. Another beggar, no doubt, who'd heard that the cook was most generous with supplies that belonged to Mrs. Robert Shaw. Annoyed, Elizabeth rang for the butler. "Williams, do you see that girl down there?"

He peered out. "Yes, ma'am. She looks a bit frail."

"Exactly. An Irish serving girl, no doubt, looking for a position. Boston is wrapped up in them these days. Go out and run her off."

"Run her off, ma'am? She seems near done in."

"You heard me," Elizabeth snapped. "But do let me know when a young man named Sam MacGregor arrives." She waved the note in her hand. "He's applying for the job as tutor and I don't know what he'll think of our family if he sees immigrant trash hanging around our gate."

"Perhaps I could feed her—"

"Feed her?" Elizabeth Shaw wheezed as she shrieked in a voice that belied her diminutive size. "You're as generous with my food as the cook. If this keeps up, word will get around town and we'll have all the riffraff coming to our gate. Go chase her off before the tutor gets here."

"Yes, Mrs. Shaw."

Even as the butler turned to go, Mrs. Shaw saw the girl stumbling toward the door. She was trying hard, but the chill wind was buffeting her and after another uncertain step or two, the girl collapsed in the snow on the lawn. "I knew it! Now what am I supposed to do?"

"If I may suggest, ma'am," the old butler came to the window, "perhaps we could perhaps revive her with a cup of tea and then send her on her way."

Elizabeth glared down at the form in the snow, the dark red hair blowing about. "Oh, all right. Otherwise, I'll have a body to deal with. Once you get her on her feet, send her back to town. We don't need any more servants."

Elizabeth turned from the window and paced up and down, wheezing a little. She really should follow her doctor's advice and loosen her stays, but she had always been so proud of her small waist. She glanced at the note in her hand again. Perhaps this Sam MacGregor would be the perfect tutor. She was getting desperate. All week, she had interviewed young men in vain. When each found out she was expecting them to tutor and civilize a young savage, fresh from the plains, none wanted the position, even though she had offered room, board, and a generous salary. Even now, her young grandson was on a train heading east and Elizabeth hadn't the least idea how to deal with him. Perhaps she had made a mistake and shouldn't have accepted the responsibility. Well, maybe Sam MacGregor would be the answer to her prayers.

When Sam came to, she was in a chair by a kitchen fire with a bunch of anxious faces peering at her.

"Lord love her, she's opening her eyes." A round-faced woman with white sausage curls wiped her hands on her apron.

"She's got pretty eyes," a young footman said. "Blue."

"Don't you be gettin' ideas," an elderly butler said as he offered a cup of tea. "Here, miss, there's sugar in it and plenty of cream. Cook here has some fresh bread just out of the oven with butter and strawberry jam."

Sam grabbed the warm cup with both cold hands and sipped it. She felt the warmth all the way to her toes. "I don't remember how I got here."

The butler studied her. "The lady of the house saw you fall in the snow out front and sent me to fetch you."

"She must be quite kind." Sam looked around and noted the help exchanged glances, but no one said anything. "I—I just tripped," Sam mumbled, and felt her face redden. The expressions on their faces told her no one believed her.

The cook handed her some fresh, warm bread. "What is a wisp of a thing like you doing out on this road in this weather? Are you lost?"

Sam licked her fingers before she thought, not wanting to miss a bit of butter. "No, I'm here to apply for a job if this is the right house. Is this the Shaws'?"

Everyone nodded and looked at each other.

"I must look a mess," Sam said and gulped the tea. "I've an appointment for an interview. May I tidy up?"

The others looked at each other blankly, then the plump cook took her arm. "Sure, miss, let us help you. Williams, go tell the old dragon she's here."

The butler looked dubious. He obviously wasn't sure what she was applying for.

"I'm Samantha MacGregor," Sam said. "I'm here about the tutoring position."

"Tutor?" the butler asked.

The servants looked at each other and chuckled.

"I don't see the joke," Sam said. She was feeling a little more spunky now that she had some food in her.

"My dear," the old cook said, "I'd advise you to leave now. You'll not get this job and you'd not like the lady of the house anyway."

"I won't leave!" Sam stood up and brushed crumbs off her worn gray skirt. "Please announce me to the lady. I'll at least plead my case."

She saw the doubt on all the faces.

The old butler said, "All right, miss, I'll announce you. I don't know what Mrs. Shaw will think—no one's stood up to her for years now."

Elizabeth Shaw looked up from her needlework as the butler entered. "Well, did you send that girl on her way and have you heard anything of Mr. Sam MacGregor? He's a little late for his interview. I like punctuality in my people."

The butler bowed. "The young lady has revived." He hesitated, as if choosing his words.

"Well, what is it?" Elizabeth snapped.

"Sam MacGregor awaits your pleasure."

"Oh? I didn't hear a carriage arrive. Very well, I'll interview him down in the library."

"Yes, ma'am." The butler bowed and left.

Elizabeth laid aside her needlework with a sigh. If this Sam MacGregor wasn't the right one, Elizabeth was not certain what to do next. Her grandson was due in on the train tomorrow. Elizabeth hobbled down the stairs and into the library, sat down before the roaring fire, then stood up as the big pocket doors slid open.

She paused, blinking. The slender girl in the faded gray dress came through the doors and hesitated. She was prettier and more delicate than Elizabeth remembered and her blue eyes were bright under the dark red hair pulled into a conservative French twist on the back of her neck. Elizabeth pursed her mouth in annoyance. "I thought I told the butler to give you some tea and send you on your way."

Sam took a deep breath, curtsied, and smiled, although the tiny woman opposite her did not smile back. The woman must be in her mid-seventies and she wheezed when she breathed. *Probably wearing a very tight corset,* Sam thought. "I wanted to thank you for having your servants rescue me. I—I tripped out there in the snow."

"Hmm." The stern face did not show any emotion. "All right, you've thanked me. Now I expect you'll be on your way before dark." Mrs. Shaw looked around the room as if expecting someone else.

"But I wanted to talk to you." Sam's heart plunged. The woman's cold eyes registered no sympathy or warmth.

"Look, miss, I don't mean to be rude, but I'm expecting someone, so if you'll be on your way—"

"I'm here for an interview." Sam took a deep breath.

"Interview?" The old lady shook her gray head as she advanced on the girl. "I'm not hiring maids or kitchen girls right now, so since I've made that clear, I—"

"Mrs. Shaw," Sam plunged in bravely, "you asked me to interview as a tutor. I am Samantha MacGregor."

"Samantha?" The old woman's face screwed into a frown. "I'm expecting a Sam MacGregor."

"That's me—my family always called me Sam."

"Why you, you charlatan!" The woman was seething. "How dare you try to pull such a trick."

"Perhaps I was not quite honest," Sam said, "but I was certain you would not grant me an interview if—"

Mrs. Shaw had already turned toward the door, ringing the bellpull frantically. "Williams, come here at once and throw this impertinent wench out!"

"Please, Mrs. Shaw, won't you at least talk to me?"

"No, I won't! I advertised for a male tutor. Williams! Williams, where are you?"

"I've been a governess," Sam said.

Mrs. Shaw paused, evidently uncertain. Just then the butler arrived. "Ma'am?"

"Please, Mrs. Shaw," Sam begged, "at least hear me out. I'm qualified for this position."

Mrs. Shaw glanced from one to the other, still angry.

The butler cleared his throat. "It's growing dark outside,

ma'am. If we send her away, she might freeze to death out by our gate."

"Let her take a carriage," the old woman snapped.

"I have no money for a carriage," Sam said. "I walked out here from town."

"Walked? Nobody walks." Mrs. Shaw made a nervous gesture of dismissal. "That's not my problem. Toss her out, Williams."

"Begging your pardon, ma'am," the butler said politely, "if she should freeze to death near our place and the papers got hold of it, it could bring some ugly publicity."

That seemed to give the old lady pause. "All right, I will talk to this devious wench." She motioned Sam to a chair near the blazing fire. Sam sank into it gratefully. The warmth felt good.

Mrs. Shaw whirled on her. "Later, Hemmings, my driver, will see that you get back to town in my carriage. Where are you staying?"

Sam paused, embarrassed to admit her desperation. "Last night, I stayed in the railroad station. I am completely without funds."

Mrs. Shaw looked exasperated.

"How can that be? Everyone has funds."

Sam shook her head.

The butler said, "Mrs. Shaw, perhaps you two could talk while I bring you some nice tea?"

"I will not hire her," Elizabeth Shaw said stubbornly, "but yes, I'd like some tea."

The butler bowed and left, closing the doors behind him, although Sam had a feeling that curious servants were lurking outside the doors to eavesdrop.

The dowager swept to a chair near the fire. "All right, why did you lie to me?"

Sam looked out the window at the falling snow. "I did not lie to you—I simply did not tell you everything."

"You must have known I was expecting a man. I cannot imagine a frail young girl taking on such a challenge."

Sam tried to smile, but the dowager did not smile back. "Mrs. Shaw, I am desperate for a job and since the advertisement has been running for a number of days, I thought you might be having a difficult time—"

"That's not true," Mrs. Shaw snapped. "Everyone would like to work at the Shaw home. I am prominent socially."

Sam looked at her frankly. "Then pray tell why has the position not been filled?"

"You are a bold, sassy piece!" Mrs. Shaw snapped. "You must be Irish."

Sam shook her head. "No, Scottish."

"Who are your people? Are you a local girl?"

Sam swallowed the lump in her throat, remembering. "No, I'm from Pennsylvania. My family was wiped out almost two years ago in the Johnstown flood." Everyone knew about the breaking dam. It had been in all the newspapers. More than two thousand people drowned, including her mother, father, and younger brother.

"Hmm." The stern, wrinkled face showed no sympathy. "Why is a pretty thing like you not married?"

She needed the job, yet she still had spunk. "That's an impertinent question," Sam snapped back. "Not that it has anything to do with my abilities as a tutor, but yes, I had offers. However, I would not marry a man I did not love just to have a roof over my head."

The old lady looked taken aback. "No wonder you are not married. Most men would not put up with such independence."

"That's their loss, then," Sam returned without thinking. She had already decided she would not get this job, so she would say what she thought.

The butler returned with the tea tray and poured. Sam took a cup and watched as he placed several tiny, delicate sandwiches and cookies on a plate and handed them to her.

She tried to eat slowly and daintily though she was still hungry enough to wolf them down. At least maybe she would get tossed out of here with a full stomach.

Mrs. Shaw watched her, her eyes cold until the butler left. She stared at Sam as if not quite sure what to make of her. Was that a shade of admiration in her eyes as she put on her wire-rimmed spectacles and surveyed Sam closely. "What is your training?"

Sam sipped her tea. "My mother was a lady of good family who ran away with a man her parents did not like."

Mrs. Shaw frowned. "And your father?"

Sam shrugged and smiled, remembering her parents fondly. "He was a poor carpenter. They married for love."

"Love!" The old lady snorted. "Marriage is a business arrangement. Your mother must have been addle-brained to trade position for love."

"She didn't think so and neither do I. Anyway, she taught me everything she had learned in a fancy boarding school. You'll find I'm well educated."

"Hmm." The old woman leaned back in her chair. Sam was not sure what Mrs. Shaw might be thinking, but at least she wasn't calling for the butler to toss her out into the snow. "Now," she said, "you say you have been a governess?"

Sam nodded and kept eating. Maybe she could grab some of the extra sandwiches to stuff in her pockets when this interview ended. "For two fine families."

"Good. Let me see your references." Elizabeth Shaw held out her hand.

So here it was. "Ahh, I have none," Sam said.

"You have none?" The old lady's voice was incredulous. "You dare to apply for a position with no references?"

"When one is desperate, one dares much," Sam said.

The old woman peered at her in disbelief. "And why do you have no references?"

Sam hesitated. "It was of a personal nature."

"A personal nature?" said the other. She seemed to be considering. "You are very pretty. I am guessing that the gentlemen of those families became too forward?"

Sam felt herself flush and looked into her teacup. "I was told by each they could make a lot of trouble for me if I did not submit to their advances, so I quit."

The old woman looked her over carefully. "Most young girls would not have been so brave. I'm surprised you did not bring me fake letters."

Sam looked her in the eye and shrugged. "Mrs. Shaw, gossip around town tells me you are a shrewd and successful woman, and therefore smart enough to check references."

Her words seemed to please the other. Elizabeth Shaw stood up and shook her head. "Still, you won't do. You won't want the position anyway when I tell you about it."

So she was undecided. Sam looked out at the snow blowing past the window. "Mrs. Shaw, I am desperate, try me."

"A number of young men have already turned this position down. It will be most difficult."

Sam's interest was piqued. "How old is this child?"

Elizabeth turned from the fire and looked at her. "The boy is a young savage, my dead son's chance encounter with an Indian girl."

"A savage?" Such a thing had not occurred to Samantha in civilized Boston. She had only expected some spoiled, petulant brat to deal with. Sam had a way with children, even difficult ones. Now she couldn't stop her mouth from dropping open.

Mrs. Shaw nodded. "Yes, a half-breed, wounded savage who'll be my only heir. He must be tamed and civilized."

"How—how old is he?" Sam tried to picture the boy. All she knew of Indians were those dreadful pictures of war-painted, half-naked warriors she'd seen in books.

"I don't know for sure. My son died at the Little Bighorn, but I have no way to know when he fathered this child."

Sam put down her teacup, fascinated. "Does this little boy want to come to Boston?"

"How should I know?" Mrs. Shaw snapped. "Wouldn't anyone want to come into a rich heritage and live in this fine home?"

"I would think so," Sam said.

"He has been badly wounded," the older woman said. "Other than that, I really know nothing about him and perhaps I am being foolhardy. Anyway, it's too late to change my mind—he's on his way here now. Dr. Lester had indicated the boy might die if he doesn't get better care."

"Poor child." Sam's heart went out to this waif, as orphaned and desperate as she herself. "Mrs. Shaw, I'd at least like to try. Some say I have a way with children. Surely there can't be much difference between a white child and a brown one."

Mrs. Shaw seemed to be thinking as she stared into the fire. "No one else has been willing to accept this challenge," she admitted finally.

"Small wonder," Sam said before she thought. In her own heart, she questioned whether she could handle this. Perhaps she should accept that ride back to Boston, sleep in the railroad station again, and look for another job. Now Mrs. Shaw looked a bit desperate. "He's arriving tomorrow. I'm not quite sure what to do."

Sam stood up, speaking with more confidence than she felt. "Mrs. Shaw, I am willing to try. You have nothing to lose by giving me a chance. If you aren't satisfied, then you can look for a male tutor."

"The pay won't be much."

Sam raised one eyebrow at her. "You have just told me that no one is willing to take on this job."

The old woman gave her a nod of grudging admiration. "You are a brassy, bold piece to bargain with me. I know you are desperate."

"And so are you," Sam shot back.

"All right. The position is yours until I can find a suitable male tutor." She named a salary that took Sam's breath away although she did not show it.

"Agreed." Sam smiled and stood up. It was only as she was being shown to her room upstairs that she wondered what on earth she had let herself in for. Then she listened to the cold wind howl outside and knew that she had had to accept this position. After all, she cheered herself as she unpacked her worn valise, how much trouble could an injured child be, even a savage boy?

Sixteen

Cincala knew it was something about the ring that caused it all to happen. That army doctor had gotten excited when he saw it and asked all sorts of questions before he handed it back. Wounded and weak, Cincala pretended he did not understand English, and indeed, he did not understand what the words "heir," "Boston," and "Mrs. Shaw" meant. However, a few days after the massacre, still clutching his father's precious ring, he found himself being loaded on a stretcher and taken from the church as the doctor gave the two burly soldiers who carried him strict instructions. He was too weak and in pain to resist as he was loaded first on an army wagon and then on an Iron Horse.

What to do? He supposed he was being taken away to the faraway prisons where the soldiers always sent warriors who were troublemakers. Cincala tried to plot an escape, but he was always under guard by the two soldiers and anyway, he was still weak and without enough warm clothing to survive if he should escape into the Dakota plains. He gritted his teeth against the pain and tried to get up, but his injured leg wouldn't support him and the soldiers forced Cincala to lie still.

After several days, the two soldiers unloaded him at a station so busy, it looked like a hive of ants; the buildings were taller than any tree he had ever seen. A soldier sneered as they put him in a horse-drawn ambulance. "You dirty savage, you don't know how lucky you are."

Where were they taking him? He tried to ask, but his captors only grinned. "You'll find out."

Samantha heard the bustle downstairs at the same time old Mrs. Shaw began to call for her. "Hurry up, Miss MacGregor, the ambulance is pulling up outside. My little grandson is about to arrive."

Sam took a deep breath and hurried down the stairs. Through the window, she could see the snow falling about the big, black carriage. She was more than a little apprehensive about whether she could deal with this savage child who was to be her responsibility. Mrs. Shaw had had a bedroom redecorated for the expected grandson in bright colors, clowns, and circus acts. At least she had not done it in toy soldiers, Sam thought with relief. After surviving the Wounded Knee massacre, the little Indian might not be pleased to see soldiers on his bedroom walls.

She pressed her face against the window, along with some of the maids and footmen, and watched one of the big soldiers come to the door. "Mrs. Shaw?"

"Yes?"

The soldier doffed his cap. "We've brought your savage according to orders." He sounded a bit peeved. "I just hope when he's well enough, he doesn't scalp you in your bed."

Mrs. Shaw looked baffled. "Surely you jest."

The soldier laughed. "Just you wait, ma'am. Turning a Lakota warrior loose in this house will be like turning a wolf loose in a chicken coop."

Tiny Mrs. Shaw drew herself up proudly. "He may be a savage now, but I intend to civilize my grandson so he can take over his heritage."

The soldier threw back his head and laughed as if that were a great joke. "Have you got several sturdy footmen?"

Mrs. Shaw nodded. "Yes, but I don't see why—"

"You will," the soldier promised again and turned to signal the other soldiers. "Bring him in."

Like the others, Sam went to line up beside the front door to greet the future master. She couldn't see much, just a form bundled up in blankets on a stretcher. "Ah, the poor thing," she breathed.

The soldier paused and grinned at her. "A pretty thing like you will be his first victim," he said.

Sam bristled. "I think I shall report your rudeness."

At that the soldier grew more humble, his jowls reddening. "Sorry, miss, but we're all tired from guarding this savage. I was afraid the whole time he'd get strength enough to cut all our throats and scalp us."

Just then, the soldiers unloading the stretcher brought it up the icy sidewalk and through the front door. All the servants leaned over to peer at its occupant. Sam took a deep breath and gasped as Mrs. Shaw said, "Oh, my God."

The soldier laughed again. "Remember, I warned you. Now he's *your* problem."

Sam stared at the man on the litter, almost unable to believe her eyes. He was a full-grown man, not a child, and what a man. He was half-naked with long, black braids. When this brown, virile savage turned his head and looked at her, she saw his eyes were gray as a wolf's pelt. He stared back at her, puzzled and defiant as a trapped wild animal, and she wondered what he thought about this commotion and whether he had any understanding at all of why he was here.

Mrs. Shaw stepped back in horror. "There must be some mistake. I'm expecting a young boy."

The soldier shrugged. "Our orders from a Dr. Peter Lester said this savage was your grandson, ma'am, and that you wanted him."

"But this can't be he," Mrs. Shaw insisted.

About that time, the handsome savage, who was clutching something that hung around his neck, came up on one elbow and unclenched his hand from that object. Sam gasped. On a string around his neck, the man wore the most magnificent blue sapphire ring surrounded by diamonds. It must be worth a fortune, Sam thought.

Mrs. Shaw made a small, strangled sound. "That's the Shaw family ring."

Sam thought the way they were all staring at the ring must have made the savage uneasy. He clasped it in his big fist again as if daring anyone to take it.

She felt both pity and fascination with the half-naked man. She touched her own chest. "Me Samantha." She then pointed at him and gave him a questioning look.

The soldier shook his head. "You're wasting your time, miss. I doubt he speaks much English."

Sam ignored the soldier and repeated her effort, smiling at the wounded man.

Finally, he blurted, "Cincala."

"Cincala," she repeated and turned to the soldiers. "Anyone know what that means?"

A second soldier scratched his head. "I think it means Colt in Lakota."

Colt, Sam thought. *He was more like a stallion.*

Mrs. Shaw looked totally done in. "I—I wasn't expecting a fully grown, dangerous savage. I'm sending him back to the reservation."

The lead soldier shook his head. "Our orders were to deliver him, ma'am, and we've done that. You don't want him, you'd better write the War Department or the Indian Agent or something. Good day, ma'am."

Mrs. Shaw took another look at the wounded savage and her voice became a hysterical shriek. "You can't leave him here, I tell you!"

"Them was our orders, ma'am," the first soldier said. "If I was you, I'd make sure some of the men servants know how to use a gun." As the household staff stood mesmerized, the soldiers all got in the ambulance and the horses started down the drive.

The big savage lay on his stretcher and looked around as if he would get up and run if he weren't so hurt and weak.

Mrs. Shaw turned to Sam, her face desperate. "What on earth do we do now?"

It was cold with the door open. Sam shut it and tried to think. She was as terrified as anyone of this wild beast, but she made a decision. "Well, first let's take him to his room and maybe you'd better call the footmen to guard him. We'll try to feed him and assess his wound. You'd better call the doctor."

"But this isn't the grandson I expected," Mrs. Shaw protested.

"Well, we've got him until you can figure out what to do with him." Sam heaved a sigh, still staring down at the prone savage clutching his ring. Even though he looked dangerous, his gray eyes held a trace of defiant fear, like a big wolf caught in a trap. Without meaning to, Sam's heart went out to him.

Behind them, one of the little maids began to whimper. "Ahh, we'll all be scalped in our sleep."

Sam whirled on her. "Oh, shut up, Molly. You can see the man's more dead than alive. He's not going to be able to stand up for a while, much less kill anyone." She signaled for the old butler. "Get the footmen to carry him up."

In a haze of pain, Cincala lay very still and watched the confusion as people ran about, making a lot of noise. He was still not sure why he was in this fine white man's house or what they intended to do with him. He would pretend to understand nothing until he figured it all out. In the meantime, it didn't appear he was in imminent danger of being killed or dragged off to prison, so maybe he would have a few days to regain his strength before he had to fight his way out of here and return to the Dakotas.

The white girl with the flame-colored hair who called herself Samantha was accompanying his stretcher as white men dressed in uniforms carried him up the stairs. They weren't soldier uniforms, but he realized they were under the command of the old white lady who was dressed in black. Cincala wasn't sure who the old woman was or what she wanted except that she had been interested in his ring. He vowed he would die before he would let anyone take it away from him.

The uniformed men carried him into a room, followed by the crowd of curious servants and the pretty white girl. Cincala looked around at the walls. The brightly colored decorations meant nothing to him. It must be a white man's joke. Strange men in funny, baggy clothes cavorted across the walls. The men wore bright warpaint and giant shoes. Little dogs balanced on balls and a line of strange gray animals with noses longer than their tails marched out of a large tipi with a colorful little flag on top. He didn't like the room at all. However, no one asked him what he thought. The uniformed men lifted him off the stretcher and onto a big, white bed. It was comfortable on his injured body and much softer than the buffalo robes he was used to.

The girl called Samantha looked down at him. "Mrs. Shaw, please get the doctor. You, Molly, bring me some hot soup."

Everyone hurried to do her bidding, but the old woman said, "I'll leave the footmen here."

Samantha shook her head. "Post them outside the door. I think he's afraid of them."

Afraid? Cincala was afraid of nothing, but he did not protest because he did not want her to know he understood the white man's tongue.

Everyone left the room and the flame-haired beauty closed the door and came back to look down at him. She seemed a little nervous and Cincala decided to make no sudden moves. He'd rather be in the care of this beauty than those footmen who looked like they'd beat him if no one was around. He studied her and realized she had eyes the color of the stone in his precious ring. She was fragile and slender in her plain gray dress, but she was beautiful. He decided that when he broke out of this place, he might take her along as a captive. If he carried her back to the Dakotas, it would be good to have a woman to warm his blankets.

The girl put her hands on her hips and looked at him. "My, you are dirty."

As he watched, she reached for some object from the bedside table that had two long, sharp blades and came toward him. He wasn't certain what she intended, but he would not lie here and let her cut him. It took all his strength, but he came up off the bed, quick as a rattler's strike, grabbed the object and the girl, then twisted her so that the sharp points were against her pretty throat. There was terror in those bright blue eyes, but she did not panic and scream as most silly white girls would have done.

Sam tried not to panic as she felt the tip of the sharp scissors against her throat. He was so close, she could feel his body trembling—whether from pain or being in a strange place, she could only guess. Anyone under such pressure might snap. He might try to use her as a hostage to escape from this house, even though he probably didn't have the strength to make it out the window and across the roof or down the stairs. Worse yet, if he tried to escape alone, he might kill her to keep her from yelling for help. She must keep a cool head. "It's all right," she gasped, "I was just going to cut your hair."

He held her against him even tighter, breathing hard, the sharp points trembling against her throat. She was not sure he knew enough English to know that she didn't intend to hurt him. Was he going to stab her? She wasn't going to give him the chance. Sam took a deep breath for courage and moved fast. Before he realized what she intended, she knocked the scissors hand away, whirled as she drew her fist back, and hit him hard—right in the middle of his shoulder wound. He cried out and crumpled in a dead faint, dropping the scissors as he did so. They rattled across the floor and Sam bent to retrieve them. He lay unconscious, his face distorted in pain. Her heart went out to him as she noted there was fresh blood on the bandage.

There was a knock on the door and the blowsy maid who had been afraid of being massacred in her bed, stuck her head in. "Here's the soup, miss." She peered in, her eyes big with wonder. "He's a handsome one. Isn't he dangerous?"

Samantha shrugged. "Not right now. Is the doctor on his way?"

"Yes, mum." The maid curtsied and left. There was something sarcastic in her tone as if she resented the new employee.

Sam hid the scissors in her skirt pocket. If he made another threatening move, she'd be ready for him. Still, her heart was hammering as she took a wet cloth and mopped his face. His skin was very pale and his pulse thready.

After a moment, he opened his eyes, his shoulder throbbing. Then he remembered what had happened. She was smart and brave for a white girl.

"Are you hungry?" she asked.

He ignored her, then turned his head and looked toward the window.

"You needn't bother," she said. "It's a long way to the ground and it's very cold outside."

He could wait, he decided, until he regained his strength. Of course he might be taking a chance that they were going to execute him before he could escape, but this certainly didn't seem like a white man's prison. Still, who knew how white men thought? They were very clever and devious. Hadn't they proved that many times with their treaties that they always broke? And this girl was not only clever, but brave. Cincala had counted many coups on tough warriors and had never expected to be bested by a spunky girl who now acted as if nothing had happened.

The girl settled herself next to the bed with the bowl and a spoon. "Here's some good soup." She held out the spoon to him.

It smelled so good that his mouth watered but he only shook his head. Maybe these clever whites were going to kill him by poison.

Sam looked down at the virile savage and saw the apprehension in his gray eyes. He looked gaunt and hungry, but he turned his head when she tried to feed him. "Look," she said, "it's good."

Again he shook his head.

It dawned on her that he might not know what it was. She took a spoonful herself. "Mmm. Good."

He looked at her a long moment as if waiting for her to drop dead, then nodded.

A thought occurred to Sam. "Would you like to do this?" She tried to give him the spoon, but he shook his head.

Of course, his right arm was injured and no doubt he was right-handed, she thought. She offered him a spoonful of soup. He took it. She offered him another. It occurred to her she was alone in a room with a half-naked savage who had held scissors at her throat only moments ago. He could do it again with her sitting this close. Her hand trembled a little, spilling soup on his bare chest. "I'm so sorry."

She reached for a napkin, wiping the soup off his big, brawny chest. This time, his big hand reached out and caught her hand, steadying it as she took the soup to his mouth. His touch unnerved her but she made no sign. This was a big, virile man and the way he was looking at her unnerved her even more. He grabbed the bowl from her hands and drank it down, soup dripping down both sides of his mouth, then wiped his mouth with the back of one brawny, brown arm. Sam was taken aback, thinking how primitive and uncouth he was. He handed her the bowl back and ran the tip of his tongue across his lips and she noted how full and sensuous his mouth was. "Well, I guess we'll have to start from scratch with your table manners."

Just then she heard someone puffing up the stairs and a pleasant, older man carrying a doctor's bag entered.

"Hello, I'm Dr. Diggs. So this is our wounded savage? You're taking quite a chance, young lady. If I were you, I'd have those footmen right here in the room with you."

She decided not to tell anyone about the scissors incident. "I'm doing all right. Besides, they seem to make him nervous and he's been through enough trauma all ready."

"Nonsense!" the old man snorted. "Savages don't have our sensibilities. My lord, he's dirty and half-naked. Oh, well, what can we expect?"

His arrogant tone annoyed Sam, but she stepped aside obediently so the doctor could lean over the patient. Immediately, the savage cowered against the bed and tried to move away.

Without thinking, she reached to put her hand on Cincala's shoulder. "He won't hurt you," she said softly. "He wants to look at your wound."

The doctor turned to peer at her. "He doesn't speak English, does he?"

Sam hesitated. "We don't think so, but I forgot that. Anyway, I think he's been through a terrible ordeal."

The doctor frowned. "I can't believe he's Mrs. Shaw's heir, although I'll have to admit he does have the family resemblance. Funny how soldiers take up with Injun girls."

She watched as he unwrapped the man's arm.

"He must be strong as an ox," the doctor muttered, examining the wound. "Another man would be dead by now."

Sam watched, knowing what the doctor was doing must be hurting Cincala, but the warrior gave no sign except that sweat broke out on his high cheekbones and he seemed to be clenching his teeth.

The wound looked ghastly. Sam had to take a deep breath to keep from fainting when she saw it.

The doctor glanced up at her. "You the governess?"

Sam nodded.

"Well, I doubt you'll be needed much longer. Mrs. Shaw says she'll send him back when she can make arrangements."

The savage smiled ever so slightly.

So he did understand English, Sam thought, and wondered who had taught him.

"Young lady," the doctor cleared his throat. "I'm going to work on that leg near his . . . well, you know. Maybe you'll want to leave the room. You look awfully pale. Are you going to be sick?"

Sam swallowed hard and turned away. "I—I'll stay. You might need something." If the savage attacked the doctor, at least she had her scissors, although she wasn't certain she could bring herself to stab anyone. She went to the window and stared out for a few moments at the drifted snow. Once she heard the patient moan ever so slightly. She whirled, concerned as the doctor pulled the sheet over him.

"He's a brave one," the doctor said as he began to gather up his things. "I've heard grown men scream when I've cleaned less serious wounds."

Sam looked at the half-breed's pale, drawn face. "Can't you do anything about his pain?"

The doctor led her aside and said in a low whisper, "Do you think he'd take anything I'd give him without a fight?"

Sam shook her head. "He'd probably think you were trying to poison him."

"If you can get him to drink some coffee, I can slip a little laudanum into it."

Sam bit her lip. "Will it make him sick?"

"No, just put him to sleep for awhile; give the footmen a chance to clean him up and cut his hair."

Sam took him outside the door and lowered her voice. "We can't cut his hair, that's very important to him."

The old doctor gave her an incredulous look. "How do you know that?"

"It doesn't matter. Anyway, if she's going to send him back, there's no point in going to the trouble, is there? There'd be hell to pay when he woke up."

She signaled Molly and told her to bring a pot of coffee, then watched the doctor add a little laudanum.

"It's up to you now, my dear."

Sam took a deep breath and went back into the room with the tray. The savage lay with his eyes half-open, looking weak and in pain. "You want some coffee?" He looked at her with suspicion and she poured a cup, moving it around under his nose so he could smell it.

He gestured that she should taste it.

"All right." She pretended to drink more than she did. "There, see? It's all right."

When he took it, his hand shook so badly, the liquid splashed on the sheets. She knew he must be in a lot of pain.

"Here," she said, "I'll help you." She leaned close, took the cup, and held it to his lips. He was very dirty, she thought, looking at his tangled and matted hair. She tried not to look at the bronzed, muscular chest, but his gray eyes watched her cautiously and she realized this man could break her in half if he decided he was going to escape. He must be thinking that, too, because he was staring out the window at the falling snow, then back at her as if judging her strength.

Sam stifled a yawn. "There are still guards outside the door," she reminded him, wondering how much he understood. All her instincts told her to go downstairs, confront Mrs. Shaw, and quit this job. She glanced out the window again. And just where would she go if she left in this cold weather with no prospects of any kind? Besides, if the old lady was going to send him back, she'd be out of a job soon enough. In spite of her fear and apprehension, her heart went out to this wild savage. Sam didn't think anyone in this household would be particularly kind to him if she left.

Gradually, the etched lines of pain faded in the strong dark face and the gray eyes flickered closed. Sam took the empty cup from his nerveless fingers and watched him. Asleep, he looked so vulnerable. "Poor fellow, I'm sorry we had to add to your pain."

Sam stifled another yawn as she went to the door. Mrs. Shaw was waiting outside. "Well?"

Sam closed the door behind her so as not to disturb her patient and led the tiny woman down the hall and out of earshot of the two burly footmen guarding the door. "The doctor talk to you?"

"Yes, and he advised me to send him back at once. I know some important people in Washington—"

"Mrs. Shaw, I don't know if he could survive another long train ride. He's very weak."

Mrs. Shaw wrung her tiny hands. "I must have been out of my mind to let him come here. I can never turn this savage into a Boston gentleman."

Sam sighed. "He seems intelligent. After all, he has your bloodlines. I'm sure he can be taught and he's very handsome."

"That's right, isn't it? If we could clean him up and cut his hair—"

"I wouldn't try cutting his hair," Sam blurted, recalling the scissors incident. "He's very peculiar about that. I think long hair must be the mark of a man in his culture."

"But I can't have him running around Boston looking like that. What will my friends say? What will they say anyway?" she moaned. "Why, Mrs. Vanderhof has already sent an invitation to her little daughter's birthday party."

"Hmm," mused Sam. "Well, he's too sick and weak for social events right now. Your friends will surely understand that. Maybe in a couple of months, after he's cleaned up and taught a few manners, he might be acceptable to the fine folk of Boston."

"If we all aren't murdered in our beds," Mrs. Shaw said.

"He's too weak even to get out of bed for a little while," Sam reminded her. "The doctor gave him some laudanum to make him sleep. Maybe the footmen can clean him up before he awakens."

She turned and looked toward the tough, scowling footmen. If the savage came awake while they were washing him, they might be brutal. "Never mind." Sam made a gesture of dismissal. "If I can have Molly, maybe we can manage."

Mrs. Shaw looked at her in dismay. "I couldn't expect a governess to stoop to do dirty work like a chambermaid."

"Look," Sam said, "someone has to do it and since he's asleep, I think I can manage. And by the way, the circus decorations seem to make him uneasy. Haven't you another room we can move him into?"

"Austin's old room. It's been closed up for years."

"Show it to me."

The old lady wheezed as she led Sam down the hall and opened a door. It was a man's room, Sam thought, done in leather and the colors of nature with paintings of horses on the walls. It smelled faintly of pipe tobacco. Without ever having known him, Sam liked the dead man. "I think his son will be happy in here. While he's still asleep, I'll have the footmen move him."

"All right then." Mrs. Shaw straightened her black silk skirt. "This has to be the most foolish thing I have ever done. Dr. Lester should have warned me he was sending a full-grown man. After the footmen move him, I'll send Molly up right away with warm water and towels."

Sam nodded. "If you'll wait in the library, Mrs. Shaw, we'll talk about this later."

The old lady left and Sam directed the footmen to carry the sleeping man into the larger bedroom. Soon Molly arrived upstairs armed with some washcloths and a pan of soapy water. Molly was not at all enthused. Her pretty face looked pouty. "Wash that savage? Coo, I didn't sign up for the likes of that."

Sam knew she couldn't do it alone. "Look, Molly, stop this nonsense. He's out cold, but he might not be if we stand here and argue about this for a while."

The girl frowned. "You think you're so important because you're a governess and I'm just a maid."

"We both work for Mrs. Shaw," Sam snapped. "Now be a little more helpful or I'll get you fired."

"You wouldn't!" the girl said.

"Just try me," Sam threatened and gave her a steely look, although she was bluffing. She was too kindhearted to see anyone tossed out without a job in January weather.

So the two of them went back in, closed the door, and very gingerly began to wash the man. When Sam wiped his face, she discovered that his skin was much lighter than she had first thought.

They washed him as best they could without turning him over. Sam wondered about the two scars on his chest and smaller scars here and there on his big frame. This was indeed a warrior.

Molly grinned. "What are we going to do about washing his . . . well, you know."

Sam felt herself flush as she stared at his ragged buckskin pants. "I had a younger brother I used to take care of. I guess he doesn't have anything I haven't seen before."

Molly's eyes widened as she looked from his crotch to Sam's face. "You suppose a savage's is any different?"

Sam had just been wondering the same thing. "I doubt it. Now we'll each grab a leg of his pants and pull to get them off him." As she turned back the covers, it occurred to her that if they kept him pantless, he'd certainly be less likely to try to go out the window and escape. Or would he? A savage might have no qualms about running through the streets of Boston bare-assed.

"As you say, mum." Molly's tone was overly polite.

They each grabbed a leg of his pants and pulled. The buckskin was dirty and ragged, Sam noted as they took his pants off. Underneath, where the sun didn't touch, his skin was much paler.

"Coo, would you look at the size of 'em," Molly gasped. "I seen a lot of men, but not built like this one."

Sam was already staring. This was a big man, all right, in more ways than one. She knew she should close her eyes and begin to wash his privates, but she couldn't stop staring at his manhood.

Molly smiled and winked. "Now, there's a man for you. I'll wager he's made some girls very happy. Savage or not, I'd welcome that stallion into my bed."

Sam was abruptly exasperated and not sure why. "That'll do, Molly. Go see if Mrs. Shaw can round up a nightshirt."

Molly nodded and left, closing the door behind her. Sam took a deep breath and grabbing up a soapy rag, hurriedly washed his lean loins and privates. Quickly she yanked the sheet up over his body.

About that time, Molly returned with the nightshirt, her eyes big and round as she stared with evident admiration at the savage. Somehow, that annoyed Sam no end. "That'll do, Molly. You can go now and I'll finish up. Tell Mrs. Shaw I'll report back to her when I finish."

The sassy girl made a face. "Who made you my boss?" she flung out as she exited the room.

Just what she needed—an enemy among the servants. Oh, well. Sam picked up the nightshirt. Just how was she going to do this? "Please," she whispered without thinking. The wolf-gray eyes flickered open. He reminded her even more of a wild creature. "I have a nightshirt. Let me help you put this on."

The savage shook his head.

"You can't sleep naked." She was scandalized.

"Sleep wrapped in buffalo robe," he mumbled in English.

Sam was stunned. So he did speak English. She had a sudden vision of this muscular, virile man lying naked, wrapped in fur. She wondered what that would feel like, especially wrapped in the fur with him. *What was she thinking?* She had never had such thoughts in her whole virginal life. "All right then," she sputtered, "you sleep any way you want. Rest now, and later one of the servants will bring you some more food."

"You bring," he ordered faintly.

In confusion, Sam fled the room. To the two big bruisers outside the door, she cautioned, "He's weak, but he's smart. Don't let your guard down."

One of the men laughed. "He's a stupid savage—he won't outsmart us."

"Don't say I didn't warn you," she said and left.

Downstairs, she found Mrs. Shaw sitting by the library fire, wringing her hands. "This isn't what I had in mind at all. I wasn't expecting to be sent a full-grown savage."

"He's only a half-breed, Mrs. Shaw," Sam said softly and was surprised to find she had a great deal of sympathy for the captured warrior. "And he's probably not more than twenty or twenty-one."

The old woman put her face in her hands. "Ah, the shame of it. My aristocratic son sleeping with some Injun girl."

Sam didn't say anything. In her mind, she pictured the savage upstairs naked and holding her in his embrace on a soft fur next to a fire. Was she losing her mind? "Mrs. Shaw, he is your grandson."

"I don't care." The stubborn old lady shook her head.

"I'll not have it, do you hear? I'll ship him back to that reservation."

Sam sat down across from her. "You can do as you wish, but you may have to wait a while. I think he was near death when he got here and another long train ride might kill him."

Mrs. Shaw got up and went to the side table, picked up a faded daguerreotype, and held it out. "Here's my Austin— do you think this savage looks like him?"

Sam studied the image. The handsome young officer in the daguerreotype didn't look too happy, but he was a perfect copy of the wounded boy upstairs, except the son's hair was black as a raven's wing. "They looks just alike, ma'am."

"It isn't fair, it isn't fair at all," Mrs. Shaw wailed and wrung her tiny, claw-like hands together. "My Robert is dead, my Austin is dead, and no one even knows where my other son, Todd, is. My only heir is a savage."

"Well, there are worse things," Sam said quietly, remembering with sadness. "My parents and my younger brother all died at the same time."

"That's different," Mrs. Shaw sniffed. "There was obviously no inheritance to consider or a fine family line to continue. Why, my relatives have been in this country since before the Revolutionary War."

So had Sam's, but that didn't matter now. "Mrs. Shaw, if he were cleaned up, educated, and civilized, he might make a fine heir indeed. After all, his bloodlines are good."

The lady brightened as she turned toward Sam. "That's right, isn't it? Blood will tell. If he's got Shaw blood, he's better than average. Why, I might be able to hold up my head in public once he's educated and we cut that long hair."

Sam shook her head. "I think we'd better leave his hair alone for a while until he gets used to the idea of being a white man."

Elizabeth Shaw seemed to be considering. "Do you think you could really do anything with this barbarian?"

Sam wasn't at all sure; in fact, she remembered now the strength of the man as she had struggled with him upstairs. He was both intriguing and dangerous. She hadn't had such mixed feelings since she had played with fire when she was a small child. "I don't know whether he can be educated or not, Mrs. Shaw, but I'd be willing to try."

In her heart, she thought, *we may educate him, but I'm not at all certain this savage can ever be tamed.*

Abruptly, she heard the doorbell ring and after a moment, a man's angry voice asking for his aunt.

"Oh, dear," said Mrs. Shaw, "I wondered how long it would take Bosworth to hear that my grandson had arrived."

"Who's Bosworth?" Sam began, but just then, the pocket doors flew open with an angry bang and a dapper, well-dressed man in his late forties strode into the room.

"Aunt Elizabeth, you're surely not going to go through with this?" His face was ruddy with anger and at first, he did not seem to notice Sam sitting by the fire.

Mrs. Shaw stood up. "I haven't decided yet, Bosworth. May I present Miss MacGregor?"

The handsome man seemed taken aback, but he quickly recovered and took Sam's hand to kiss it. "Well, Auntie, I had no idea you had such young, pretty friends." He looked at Sam and smiled, but his dark eyes didn't smile. They were as expressionless as a snake's.

"My nephew, Bosworth Shaw." Mrs. Shaw shrugged by way of explanation. "He manages the mills for me."

That seemed to bring the man back to his purpose. He turned back toward the old lady. "Dear Auntie, I thought when you mentioned this several weeks ago that it was a joke, bringing this savage child here to Boston—"

"He's not a child, Bosworth," Mrs. Shaw said, "and maybe that's the joke. He's a grown man."

"A man?" Bosworth recoiled in horror, throwing up his

beautifully manicured hands. "Are you telling me you've brought a full-grown savage into this house? Why, Auntie, he might murder you in your bed."

"I hardly think so," Sam blurted. "He's so badly wounded, it's a wonder he survived the trip."

The dapper nephew looked pleased. "Are you saying he may die?"

Mrs. Shaw snorted. "Don't be so callous."

"Aunt Elizabeth, it's only that I'm worried about you."

"You're worried about the inheritance," the old woman snapped. "Don't be so greedy, Bosworth. You have a good position with an exorbitant salary now that I have finally hired you as my manager."

His mouth came open in disbelief. "I can't believe you would think that was what I'm worried about. All of Boston thinks you have lost your wits."

"After all, this young man is Austin's son." Mrs. Shaw was defensive now.

"And how can you know that for sure?" her nephew challenged. "How do you know he's not some fake, eager to get his hands on your money?"

Sam liked the man even less and felt drawn to come to Colt's defense. "He doesn't seem to comprehend money," she said, "and I think he'd flee if he had the strength. Besides, he looks just like his father's picture."

"True," agreed the old lady, "and he has the ring."

"Poor Austin, I miss him so." Bosworth clucked sympathetically, but his eyes were as hard as obsidian. "Still, Auntie, you must understand that this savage could be dangerous. I insist you ship him back to the West."

"I'll make that decision myself, Bosworth, after we see how Miss MacGregor here does with my grandson."

The man looked at Sam with added interest. "Oh?"

"I'm the governess," Sam said, "hired to turn this rough savage into a Boston gentleman."

"You're on a fool's errand." The nephew laughed.

"We'll see," Sam snapped. "I'm at least going to try."

Bosworth turned toward his aunt again. "This isn't fair, you know. I've labored hard and long for you since I finally replaced Hiram Hall. Profits are way up."

"And I've given you several raises," the old woman answered. "More than enough to pay for all those fine suits you have custom-made and that expensive wine you favor. Enough! I'm getting a headache."

Immediately, he looked worried. "Oh, I'm so sorry, Auntie." His voice was low and smooth as silk. "You must believe I only rushed over here because I was concerned for your welfare—"

"You are concerned for the Shaw fortune, which you hope to inherit. Miss MacGregor, please show my nephew out."

Sam was only too glad to escort Bosworth to the front hall. He lingered there a moment. "Please convince my dear aunt that I'm sorry I upset her, but I feel it's my duty to protect vulnerable women from such a danger in the household. She's so naive and old-fashioned. Why, she just lately added a telephone, gaslights, and indoor plumbing to this old house."

"Thank you, Mr. Shaw, but we're not too concerned now."

He caught her hand and kissed it. Sam pulled away, but he seemed not to notice. "Really, my dear Miss MacGregor, this job is beneath you—nursemaid to a savage. I could use a girl in my office down at the mills. Do you by any chance know how to use a typewriter?"

Sam shook her head. "Sorry, no. Thank you for the offer, but I see this job as quite a challenge."

"I would think so." Bosworth chuckled. "Very well. I'm sure that stubborn old dear will soon realize she's made a big mistake and will send the savage packing."

"Maybe not," Sam said and liked him even less.

He grinned at her. "Be realistic, my dear. She's old and

has a bad heart. Right now, I'm her possible heir and I think after she tries to deal with this Indian, she'll realize no one can tame him. Someday soon, I'll be living in this fine house." He looked around as if envisioning it.

"Good day to you, sir," Sam said as she spun on her heel. "You know the way out." She was walking away when she heard the door slam behind her a little too loudly. Sam started up the stairway. As she went, she wondered if she had just made a very big mistake. If the savage was sent back West, handsome and elegant Bosworth Shaw would stand to gain everything and he was evidently attracted to her.

The next day, Bosworth sent his aunt a giant bouquet of flowers. Mrs. Shaw was noticeably pleased as she sniffed them and read the note aloud to Sam. *"I know lilies are your favorite, my dear aunt, as you are mine."* She smiled at Sam. "Isn't that sweet?"

"Hmm," Sam murmured.

"There's more." Mrs. Shaw looked again at the card.

I do hope you'll forgive me for my outburst as I was worried about your safety. Do remember me to Miss MacGregor and let me assure you both I'll do whatever it takes to welcome your grandson into the family.

Mrs. Shaw took a deep breath. "Perhaps I judged Bosworth too harshly."

Sam didn't say anything. The old woman must either be stupid or very susceptible to flattery if she couldn't see through her greedy nephew's motives. Not that any of the wealth mattered to the gravely injured man upstairs, but Sam saw quite clearly that the ambitious and cunning nephew intended to end up with everything the rich old widow owned.

Seventeen

Almost two weeks passed and Cincala improved as Samantha looked after him dutifully. She sat and mopped his brow with cold, wet cloths to bring his fever down and talked to him, even though she was not sure whether he actually understood or even heard her. She figured the sound of a soft, human voice might be comforting, so she explained where he was and why, who she was, who the old lady was who appeared to peer at him and shake her gray head doubtfully.

The doctor came and went, looking grave, but had to admit the savage was improving when he should have died if he'd been an average man. The maid, Molly, seemed to find all sorts of reasons to pop in, but was never around when Sam actually needed some work done such as cleaning the room or changing the sheets.

Sometimes, the young man opened his gray eyes and glared at Sam like a wolf with his paw caught in a trap from which there was no escape. Sooner or later, he would make an attempt to get away, Sam thought with a shiver, because she was certain Colt Shaw could be very, very dangerous if anyone got in his path. She was more than a little afraid and might have quit her job had she anywhere else to go. But whether she wanted to admit it or not, she felt a little sorry for him, lying weak and wounded in a white man's nightshirt with that valuable ring on a rawhide thong around his sinewy neck.

As he became increasingly aware of his surroundings, Molly popped into the room more often and Sam couldn't help but notice the way the crude immigrant girl's gaze lingered on him. Came the day he could sit up and look around; Sam drew a sigh of relief. He wasn't going to die after all.

Mrs. Shaw, fearing for the safety of everyone in the house, took to stationing a sturdy footman outside his door at night. She still spoke of sending the savage back to the Dakotas when he was strong enough to travel.

Finally, one day several weeks later, Colt Shaw was able to sit on the side of the bed and tried to stand.

"You shouldn't get up," Sam said, jumping up from her chair, "you're still too weak."

He glared at her and tried again.

"All right, if you're determined to be stubborn, lean on me." He draped one big arm around her small shoulders and gestured that he wanted to go to the window. So he understood more English than he was letting on, Sam realized. Well, she'd go along with the deception.

However, with his arm around her and him standing there in nothing but a night shirt, she realized how vulnerable she was and scolded herself for her impulsiveness. She should have called for a male servant. Still, she took a deep breath and helped him to look out the window at the wind blowing the snow across the estate grounds. "Too bad to be outside," she said and looked up at him.

Their faces were inches apart and his was inscrutable. Had he understood what she'd just said? She had no way to know. His closeness made her terribly uncomfortable and she led him to a chair and gestured for him to sit. He made hand signs that he'd like some pants. Sam shook her head.

Keeping him in a nightshirt made it more difficult for him
to escape.

"Are you feeling better?" she asked slowly and distinctly,
then felt silly for asking. He looked up at her, his gaze
moving up and down in a bold way that made her feel
naked. "Would you—would you like some tea?" She knew
her voice sounded too high and strained as she made a
gesture of sipping from an imaginary cup.

Cincala watched the pretty girl. What he would like was
to have her naked and sprawled in his bed. He must be
feeling much better to be thinking of women. Since they
did not know he spoke good English, they were careless
about talking around him and he was learning much about
this household that might help him escape. Slowly he nodded.

Sam's mood brightened as she went to the door, opened
it, and called to a servant to bring a tray of tea, sandwiches,
and little cakes. She was communicating with the savage
and maybe she could teach him a few more words of English. She sat down across from him and spoke slowly, using
many gestures. "I am Samantha MacGregor and I am going
to teach you everything you need to know to live in a civilized world. You are Colt Shaw and you are in your father's
old room here at your grandmother's house in Boston."

Cincala watched the girl and pretended to be struggling
to understand. Now that he was feeling better, it was hard
not to grin at her antics as she made a fool of herself, acting
as if he were either stupid or did not understand her language. She really was very pretty, though a trifle thin for
his taste. Maybe when he escaped from here, he would
kidnap the girl and take her with him. It had been a long
time since he had had a woman.

Sam stared into his gray eyes, wondering what his
thoughts were. "You will not be hurt here," she said. "This
is your grandmother's house and Elizabeth Shaw is a very
rich woman. You are going to have a luxurious life as a

white man once we cut your hair and buy you some fine clothes."

The savage scowled and shook his head; then he touched his long, black braids and shook his head again.

Sam remembered the incident with the scissors. "Okay, we'll let you make the decision about when to do that."

Never, thought Cincala stubbornly, but he said nothing. He did not want to live like a white man. He wanted to return to the Lakota, even if his parents were dead. But first, he would have to escape from this house and he thought he knew who would be willing to help him—that little maid.

Sam watched him and wondered what he was thinking as there was a knock on the door and Molly stuck her head in. "Ahh, is he awake now? I've brought a fine spread for 'em."

Her eager expression annoyed Sam. She stood up and went to the door to take the tray, but Molly was already pushing her way in, carrying the tray over to set it on the table next to Colt's chair. Sam frowned. "You can go, Molly. I'll deal with this."

Molly bustled about as if she had not heard her. "It's no trouble to pour it for him, fix him a plate."

Before either of them could stop him, the savage abruptly picked up the delicate china teapot, took off the lid, and proceeded to drink out of the top. Then he grabbed a handful of the tiny sandwiches and stuffed them into his mouth as the women watched.

Sam blinked. "Uh, I think the first thing I'll have to teach him are table manners."

"Coo!" gasped Molly. "Will you look at him eat!"

As they watched, the savage finished the food and wiped his mouth on his sleeve, then smiled at both women. Sam could only blink, but Molly smiled back and fluttered her eyelashes at him. "I'll wager I know what he'd like now."

Sam flushed. "Help me get him back to bed, Molly, and then get out of here."

Molly bridled. "You think I can't see you got your eye on him yourself, you prissy thing? I got as much right as you to end up married to the heir."

"Marry this savage?" Sam was aghast at the thought. She caught Molly's arm and led her to the door. "Watch your sassy mouth or I'll tell Mrs. Shaw."

She pushed Molly out the door and slammed it. Sam was horrified at the thought of ending up in bed with this virile savage. No doubt the old lady was already wondering if he could be civilized enough to even be invited to an afternoon social, much less married to some prim white girl.

When she went to help the wounded man back to bed, he indicated he needed to use the chamber pot. She went to the door and called for the butler or footman, but there were none about. She felt her face flush and tried to decide what to do. She was certain the savage was enjoying her dilemma. She might as well take the bull by the horns and introduce him to the modern bathroom. Sam got Colt into a robe, put his arm around her shoulders, and helped him hobble out into the hall. Thank goodness the bathroom was right next door. With some difficulty, they got into the bathroom, which because of Mrs. Shaw's wealth, sported the latest of porcelain technology. Sam gestured toward the big, claw-footed tub. "We turn the knobs and it fills with water."

She sat Colt down on the vanity stool and put the stopper in the tub, then turned on the faucets. His eyes grew wide as the tub began to fill. "Then," she demonstrated, kneeling by the tub, "you take the stopper up and the water runs out."

He bent his head as if to see the water running out on the floor.

"No," Sam said, "it goes down the drainpipes."

He turned to look with fascination at the toilet.

How to explain this to someone who had never seen one? She felt herself flush as she surveyed the fancy appliance with its wooden box near the ceiling and the long pull chain. Before she could say anything, Colt reached out and grabbed the chain. Immediately, it flushed and he jumped, then leaned forward to watch the water swirl in the bowl and disappear. "Big medicine," he said solemnly. "What good?"

"Let me—let me get the butler to explain," Sam sputtered and exited in a hurry to find the old man. Later, she helped Colt back to his bed.

Mrs. Shaw stuck her head in. "How is he doing?"

"We are learning about the finer points of civilization." Sam coughed.

"That's nice," the old lady said. "I'd hate it if he didn't know the difference between a shrimp fork and a salad fork and humiliated me at a party."

He'd probably drink out of the finger bowl, Sam thought, but she nodded encouragingly.

Abruptly, Colt smiled at the old dowager. "Grandmother," he said.

Sam was as surprised as the old lady, but Sam recovered first. "He understands a few words," she said.

Mrs. Shaw looked doubtful. "He's got a long way to go, I think."

"You don't know how long," Sam muttered.

"What?"

"I said I'd been reading about Long John Silver to him."

"Good. You'll teach him to read. He must be able to keep up with the stock market and business reports." The old lady went happily on her way.

Sam sighed at the thought of turning him into a polished gentleman worthy of upper-crust Boston society. Even now, he was wiping his face on his sleeve again. Oh, they had such a long way to go.

Cincala watched the fiery-haired girl. This could be very

amusing for the next several weeks. After that, when his leg wound healed enough so he could get around without leaning on someone, he intended to escape. He only had to appear cooperative and harmless while his leg improved and he made his plans.

One cold night, Sam was awakened by a small noise. For a long moment, she thought she had imagined it, then decided she had better investigate. In the darkness, she couldn't find her robe and she hesitated to light a lamp until she was certain there was no one in the room.

Again the noise and it was most certainly in the hallway. Wearing only a thin nightdress, she ventured out. Nothing. She paused and considered returning to bed. The hall was cool and she was shivering. Her intuition caused her to continue her journey.

At Colt's open door, she found the footman sitting against the wall, snoring loudly. Next to him lay a bottle. Sam picked it up, sniffed. Liquor, all right, but it also smelled of laudanum. She realized the savage had no access to either.

The door was ajar and even though she tiptoed in, she knew she would find the bed empty. A chill went up her back. The barbarian was loose in the house and someone had helped him by getting the guard drunk.

What to do? Were there weapons in the house? Were they all about to be slain in their beds? She must alert Mrs. Shaw and maybe send the butler for the police. Too bad Mrs. Shaw's telephone was still damaged and waiting for repair.

Perhaps the Indian had already fled. If so, he wouldn't make it far. The snow outside was deep with a gusty wind rattling the shingles and all he had on was a nightshirt.

Sam hurried down the long, shadowy hall toward Mrs. Shaw's room. Abruptly, against one wall, she saw a glint of light. What was that? Even as she realized it was the reflection of the moonlight on the sapphire-and-diamond ring, a hand reached out and grabbed her. Sam opened her mouth to scream, but that big hand clapped over her mouth and pulled her up against a hard, warm body.

"Be silent!" he commanded.

She was too terrified to scream even if he hadn't had his hand over her mouth. He pulled her up against him and she realized he was naked except for the bandage on his injured arm and thigh. She saw the outline of an open hall drawer and realized he'd been scavenging for clothes. "If you scream," he whispered, "you'll regret it. I've got to find some pants."

She nodded to show she understood. Very slowly, he took his hand away.

Sam was angry with herself for her own naivety. "Damn your hide, you could have told me you spoke good English."

"Why? I learned a lot while everyone thought I was a stupid Injun." His gray eyes bore down into hers and she was acutely aware of how big and brawny and naked he was and how near-naked she was. "I'm getting out of here tonight."

"Who—who helped you?"

"What's that to you?"

"It was Molly, wasn't it? What did you bribe her with?"

"This." He pulled Sam close and kissed her. No man had ever kissed her so passionately in all her sheltered nineteen years. For a long moment, she melted against him, only too aware that he was naked, the sheerness of her nightdress and how much man he was. His lips sought hers, tasting and teasing. She surrendered only a moment, molding herself against him, her heart hammering. His mouth was very warm and intense; his tongue caressed her lips in a way that made her want more. Abruptly, she came to her senses. *Was she insane?* She was in the embrace of a naked, desperate man and who knew what his intentions were?

Even if she screamed, the elderly butler wouldn't be much help and if the footman roused and cornered the savage, he might hurt someone.

She pulled out of his arms, breathless. "You can't get away—it's cold outside."

"I'll take my chances."

"You're a fool! I can't let you do this!" She opened her lips to scream, but he clapped his hand over her mouth, cursing softly. "I ought to break your pretty little neck!"

Oh God, he was going to kill her, and he was strong enough to do it, even though his wounds must still be tender. *Tender.* Suddenly she remembered that first day when they had struggled over the scissors. The way he was gripping her wrists now, she couldn't get her hands free. If she didn't hurt him bad enough to cause him to faint or cry out, alerting the household, he would probably retaliate by killing her. She had to take the chance, for his sake as well as hers. Wounded and still weak as he was and completely without knowledge, he wouldn't survive in the civilized jungle of the white man's big city. It was now or never. Sam brought her knee up suddenly and hard.

She never knew if she caught him in his thigh wound or his privates, but he cried out and turned her loose, doubling over in pain as she turned and ran down the hall. The noise must have awakened the whole household as lights came on and doors flew open. Feet pounded up the stairs. The groggy footman stumbled to his feet as Sam shrieked, "Quick! He's loose, but don't hurt him!"

The savage was still stumbling about, weak with pain, as three big male servants grabbed him and half-dragged, half-carried him back to his room.

The old lady stuck a sleepy head out her door. "What's happening?"

"Nothing," Sam smiled and tried to appear calm. "Just go on back to bed, Mrs. Shaw."

When the door closed, Sam turned her attention to the

servants struggling with the limping Colt. "Put him back in bed and someone get a leg chain."

The fugitive glared at her as if he'd like to cut her heart out.

"It was for your own good," she said. "It's cold out there and you're too hurt to travel."

"Thanks to you," he mouthed, but no one but Sam saw it as they dragged him back to his bed.

Sam lay awake long after the house had settled back down because she was still trembling. Whether it was from fright or the remembrance of the way he had held her, the taste of his mouth, she wasn't sure. She must quit this job tomorrow, she promised herself. Then she pictured Colt, alone in this strange place and still injured. She couldn't be at all certain what would happen to him if she left. Damn it, why should she care? He might have killed her last night. Yes, she made up her mind to give notice in the morning and recommend that Mrs. Shaw give up this insane idea of a civilized grandson and ship the savage back to the Dakotas as soon as possible.

When she opened Colt's door the next morning and peeked in, he appeared to be asleep. One ankle stuck out from under the covers, encircled by a chain attached to the sturdy brass bed. Her stomach churned at the thought that he was chained up like a wild animal. But that's what he was, Sam reminded herself as she closed the door and went downstairs. She hated to give up on a task once she had set herself to it, but even she now realized that she didn't have the key to taming this savage. She didn't think anyone did.

As she reached the bottom of the stairs, the butler came to meet her and said Mrs. Shaw awaited Sam in the library.

Sam nodded, steeled herself, and went in.

The old lady sat before a blazing fire, an ornate silver

tea service on the butler's tray before her. "Come in. Would you like some tea or coffee?"

Anything to delay this meeting. "Tea, thank you."

Mrs. Shaw motioned her to a comfortable horsehair chair near the fire. "Do you like butter or jelly on your scone?"

"Both, please." Sam settled herself on the chair and smoothed her worn gray skirt.

The lady handed her the treats on delicate, costly china and Sam tasted the flaky scone and hot tea and smiled with pleasure. After she enjoyed this food, perhaps she would have the fortitude to admit failure and resign the job.

"Now tell me what happened last night." The old eyes bore into her over gold-rimmed reading spectacles.

Sam hesitated. She was not good at lying. Abruptly, she forgot about her own situation and how she meant to resign. She only knew she didn't want to see the savage sent back to the reservation; he was too ill and weak. The trip would kill him. "I'm not sure."

"The butler found the liquor bottles," Mrs. Shaw snapped. "I've already sent the drunken rogue packing."

"I don't know anything about that," Sam said truthfully. "I think Colt might have awakened and needed help. He went stumbling down the hall where I found him in dire need and pain so I called out and everyone came running."

"Hmm." The grim lady did not look as if she believed the story. "Colt?"

"That's what his name means, remember? We keep calling him 'the savage,' but he does have a name."

Mrs. Shaw set down her teacup and sighed.

"Colt Shaw. I had no idea what I was getting into when I sent for him. We might have all been murdered."

"But we weren't," Sam reminded her. "He does seem very intelligent and his health is improving. I've got all sorts of plans and—"

"Oh?" The old woman blinked in surprise. "I had gotten the impression you might be about to give up on him."

Was she? She must be out of her mind, Sam thought as she found herself shaking her head. "I'm pretty stubborn once I start a task. I like to finish it."

The old woman peered at her over her spectacles. "I went by the office yesterday afternoon. My nephew is very worried about that savage being here in the house with an innocent girl such as yourself."

That leech with his oily smile.

"Mrs. Shaw, I'm willing to keep trying if you are and we just won't tell Bosworth about it until we see some results."

She seemed uncertain. "I'm sure my nephew has only my best interest at heart."

Sam didn't say anything. The old woman must be blinded by family ties. Sam didn't think Bosworth Shaw had anyone's best interests at heart except his own. "I will try hard, Mrs. Shaw, so you won't regret hiring me. Your grandson will take his place in Boston society and make you proud yet."

The thought was laughable if it hadn't been so sad, yet the old woman brightened. "I always dreamed of one of my sons taking over the family businesses, marrying into the best of Boston aristocracy. My husband always hoped someone in the family would run for office—governor or a senator."

Sam thought about the savage upstairs chained to his bed. She couldn't even imagine him in a suit, much less dancing a waltz with some elegant, snooty girl or sitting behind a desk. "I'd be pleased right now to teach him to use a fork properly without him trying to stab someone with it," she muttered.

"What did you say?"

"I said I'll try to teach him the difference between a shrimp fork and a salad fork."

"But everyone already knows that, don't they?"

Oh, this naive and sheltered old lady. "Not everyone."

Sam smiled a little too brightly. It was going to take a miracle to turn Colt Shaw into a civilized Boston gentleman.

"Imagine that. Nevertheless, after talking to my nephew yesterday, I've made a decision. I'll give you until late spring to see what you can do with him. After that, my Washington contacts have assured me they can have the army come get him and ship him back to the plains."

"Spring?" Sam was aghast. "That's not too far away."

"I'm planning a formal ball for late April or early May to introduce him to society. If you haven't made major progress by then, I'll cancel the ball, ship the savage back to the reservation, and you'll be looking for a new job."

Sam let the words sink in. They almost made her drop her teacup. "You mean, you expect me to get him ready for polite society in just a couple of months?"

"Is he not intelligent enough or are you not capable?"

Sam sighed and set her teacup down. "I'll give it my best, Mrs. Shaw."

As Sam went upstairs to check on her charge, she was almost certain her best wasn't going to be good enough. She wondered again who had helped Colt last night. She suspected it was Molly, but she didn't have enough evidence to give to the lady of the house and get the girl fired. Sam would just have to watch Molly closely.

Sam arrived in time to interrupt the pretty maid, who was fluffing up his pillows and smiling at him. He was returning the smile.

"That'll do, Molly, you can go now."

The girl glared at her and flounced out of the room, but not without a flirting backward glance.

Sam exhaled in exasperation. "Do you charm every woman you meet?"

He looked at her and blinked as if he did not understand.

"Don't give me that," Sam snapped. "I found out last night you speak excellent English."

He shrugged. "Have you told anyone?"

"No, but I should."

He frowned at her and looked at the chain on his ankle sticking out of the covers. "You did this."

She felt both sorry for him and apologetic to see him chained like a dog. "You'd have frozen to death outside."

"Better than this." He turned his head and stared fixedly at the wall, ignoring her.

"I am sorry, Colt. It's my job to civilize you. Mrs. Shaw would be very pleased to see you in a suit with your hair cut."

He glared back at her, his eyes cold as gray granite. "Warrior's hair. If anyone tries to cut my hair, I'll take scissors from his hand and cut his throat."

She had no doubt he meant it. He was clever. Maybe she could bargain with him. "Look, if you'll cooperate, I'll take the chain off and get you some pants and crutches so you can get around."

"Crutches?"

She gestured. "Wooden things. They fit under your arms, help you walk."

Colt seemed to think it over. "All right."

She was relieved at how easy that had been. "Fine. I'll get the key to the chain and I think the coachman is big enough that his clothes might fit you until Mrs. Shaw can get a tailor out here to make you some new things."

He actually smiled and it made her feel good. His hand went up to touch the ring hanging around his neck.

"Colt, tell me how you came by the ring."

He looked down at it hanging against his bare chest in the nightshirt. "My father gave it to my mother." She saw his face sadden as he took the ring in his hand and stared at it as if it brought back memories.

There was more to the story, she suspected, but because of his despairing expression, she did not ask. "I'm so sorry about his death."

He looked at her in surprise. "The whites are certain he is dead then?"

What kind of question was that? Sam nodded. "Mrs. Shaw says he was killed at the Little Bighorn."

Colt blinked, started to say something, then shrugged.

She stood up, retreating to the door. "You get well, Colt, and then we'll begin our lessons. Mrs. Shaw has given me a deadline on turning you into a gentleman."

"What is a gentleman?"

"You'll find out," she promised as she left the room. Somehow, she didn't think Colt Shaw was going to like his introduction to civilized life.

Cincala settled against his pillows and stared at the door after the fire-haired girl who had just left. He was experienced with women even though he was less than twenty-one winter counts old. He could sense she was both drawn to him and afraid of him. He remembered how she had felt in his arms last night out in the hall, fragile but oh, so much woman. When his lips had dominated hers, for a long moment, he had forgotten about escape or anything else except how she would feel under him when he took her body and made it his. She was a virgin, there was no doubt about that.

That pouty girl, Molly, would certainly help him as she had last night when he was ready to escape, but he had no real interest in her. The girl who made his loins ache was the spunky, slender one with the red hair. He remembered again how she felt through the thin nightdress and how her lips had tasted. If he got the chance, he might steal that fire-hair and take her with him. She'd make a good captive for his pleasure back in his lodge a thousand miles from here. In the meantime, he'd have to pretend to cooperate so the whites wouldn't suspect anything.

Sam was pleased at Colt's sudden change of attitude in the next several days as he was finally on his feet under the watchful eyes of two sturdy new footmen. They had unchained him, found him some clothes from one of the big men servants, and had the doctor bring over some crutches so Colt could get around. She conveyed all this to Mrs. Shaw down in the breakfast room. From upstairs, the sound of the toilet flushing and then flushing again and yet again.

"My word, what—?" The old lady gave Sam a questioning look as it flushed again and again.

Sam hid a smile. "Now that I've showed it to him, he keeps flushing it over and over just to watch the water swirl and disappear."

"Oh, dear. Well, he'll soon get over that, won't he?"

Sam shrugged. "Let's hope so. I thought I'd offer him some mental stimulation by bringing him downstairs. He's getting around nicely on his crutches."

The old lady looked doubtful. "Turn him loose?"

"I don't think he's planning on murdering anyone."

"There's knives and cleavers in the kitchen." Mrs. Shaw reminded her, nodding toward the back of the house.

"I'd forgotten about that. Well, I'll just keep a close eye on him."

"Is he speaking any English yet?"

The clever devil always did, Sam thought, but she only said, "His grasp of words is stunning. He must have your family's intelligence."

The old lady beamed. "Very well. Tutor him in any room you please. I just hope my nephew doesn't drop by while he's out. Oh, by the way, I've got the best tailor in Boston coming soon. It won't do to have a Shaw wearing servant's clothing."

Sam nodded. She excused herself and went upstairs to Colt's room. "Today, we begin our lessons seriously."

He frowned at her. "What do I need learn? I ride like wind, I can bring down buffalo or deer with one arrow. I can cut a man's throat in a heartbeat before he can cry out."

Sam shuddered. "I hate to disappoint you, but there won't be much throat-cutting required in Boston, except maybe in business."

He raised his eyebrows at her.

"Forget that," she said hastily, "it's a joke. Anyway, riding and being able to handle a gun might be important now and then. You'll probably even get invited to a fox hunt."

Colt grimaced. "White men eat foxes?"

Sam laughed. "No, of course not, they only hunt them."

"Why?" He looked puzzled.

Now it was Sam's turn to be puzzled. "Frankly, I'm not sure I know why—they just do."

"Very stupid," Colt said.

"Agreed," Sam said and smiled at him, relaxing a little. "This morning, we can take our lessons in the conservatory."

"What's that?"

"It's sort of like a garden with flowers and plants, but it's inside."

He looked puzzled. "All right."

She got his crutches and led him out the door. When they started down the stairs, she held her breath and caught hold of his arm. The muscles rippled in his arm and she realized how big and strong he was. If he did fall, she couldn't do much to help him.

Passing the library, Mrs. Shaw came to the door. "Ah, Samantha, I see our patient is on his feet. Are you making any progress?"

"Some," Sam said, turning to Colt. "Say hello."

Colt looked at the small woman in the doorway. "Say hello," he answered obediently.

Sam rolled her eyes and sighed. "I'm afraid it will take a while," she said to the older lady and motioned Colt to follow her on down the front hall.

It was a magnificent conservatory, Sam thought, but then, the Shaws could afford it. Colt's gray eyes were round as she led him inside and the pair settled themselves on the wicker furniture.

He looked about the jungle of greenery and flowers in open-mouthed wonder. "A forest in a glass house."

Sam shrugged. "Rich people can afford it."

"I've got a forest and green things back home and I'm not rich."

"You're mistaken about that," Sam said. "Your grandmother is very rich and so you'll be."

Colt snorted and looked around. "I don't like living like a white man. I'll return to the plains where I can ride like the wind and do as I please. Better than here."

She watched the yearning in his eyes and realized that he meant it. "You'll change your mind," she said, but wasn't sure he would. "Now I have a book and we'll start with reading."

"You read," he insisted.

"All right, then you try. 'The chicken walked along the road. It said cheep, cheep.' "

Colt regarded her gravely. "What is a chicken?"

Sam considered. There probably weren't any chickens out in a Sioux village. "It is a bird that white men raise to eat. Anyway, it doesn't matter. See this word? It stands for chicken."

He was enjoying himself hugely. He leaned closer to her and watched her try to scoot further away. "Why is chicken walking?"

She was too aware of just how close he was. "I don't know. The story doesn't tell us."

"Then why should I care?" He seemed to be leaning even closer to her as he studied the book.

She hopped up and moved to a chair across from him. "It's important you learn to read."

He regarded her stoically. "Why?"

"So you can read treaties and contracts. If all your people could read, the white men couldn't cheat them."

"Good reason." He watched her wipe a sheen of perspiration off her pretty face. He really ought to tell her he could already read—his father had taught him. However, it was much too amusing to watch her struggle to teach him. That meant she had to spend much time with him. Good. He intended to take her virginity before he escaped from this house. He gestured. "Can't see book from there. Sit over here."

She wished she could see inside his head. Perhaps she had only imagined he was crowding close. It might have been perfectly innocent on his part. "All right. There's many things you need to learn such as numbers, manners, dancing."

"We can both hold the book," Colt said and scooted nearer. He was sitting so close, she could feel the heat of his thigh through her dress. It made her feel very uncomfortable, remembering the night in the hallway when she had been pressed up against his warm, naked body. Now he put the book back in her hands and when their fingers brushed, it sent a tremor running through her.

"You cold?" he asked.

"No." Damn him, could this ignorant savage possibly realize what his touch, his body was doing to her emotions? No, of course not. She took the book and began to read aloud slowly, pointing out the words and how they related to the pictures. " 'And now the chicken meets duckie-luckie.' "

Colt watched the girl as she bent over the book. Since he was taller than she was by more than a head, he was looking down the front of her plain gray dress at the swell of her perfect breasts and at the back of her neck where tiny tendrils of red hair curled up on the nape of her creamy white neck. He fought a temptation to kiss that soft nape and deliberately crowded a little closer and felt her hesitate, her sharp intake of breath. Then she began to read again. He was too aware of the warmth of her against him and stifled an urge to put his arm around her small shoulders. He felt his manhood rise in the tight white man's pants and shifted uneasily, fighting a terrible urge to take the girl in his arms and kiss her, pressing her slowly down onto the settee where he could get his hand inside her bodice and work her skirt up. He had never needed a woman as badly as he needed this one.

Then he remembered his past encounters with Miss Samantha MacGregor. No doubt she'd either slam her fist into his shoulder wound or the one in his thigh.

"You try it," she said and looked up at him, her lips shiny and partly open.

"What?" Had she guessed his thoughts and was encouraging him?

"You try now," she said again and pressed the book into his hands.

His hopes fell and he stared glumly at the words. How could he worry about the duck and chicken meeting Ronnie Raccoon when his pants were so tight against his swollen manhood, he was almost in pain?

Sam turned her head and looked up at him. Desire was evident in his gray eyes. For a split second, she thought he was going to take her in his arms and kiss her. If he did, would she let him? Her own need shocked her and she stood up suddenly. "You haven't been following the story. Maybe we've done enough for the day—you're still weak."

He smiled up at her. "Soon you teach me to dance?"

She was pleased that some of what she'd said interested him. "As soon as your leg's better. Now you've had enough for one day. Dr. Diggs said you should get plenty of rest."

That night as she lay in bed sleepless, twisting and staring at the ceiling, she kept remembering those moments on the wicker settee, the warmth and the power of his big body. She had never had a man, but now she knew desire. This was insane, she thought, not logical at all. None of that mattered. All she could think of as she flounced about restlessly was whether he had been thinking about kissing her this morning. She ran the tip of her tongue across her lips and remembered the other night, her body aching with need. She closed her eyes and imagined what would happen if she sneaked into his room, offering to let him educate her in ways she suspected he knew well. No doubt he would pull her down on the bed, rip off her nightgown, and take her with a hunger and an intensity that she could only imagine. He was all man, virile and powerful.

Colt lay staring at the ceiling, too. He wanted the girl in his bed, under him, accepting his seed, returning his passion. He was skilled with women. He would delay his escape until his wounds were healed. Maybe he might even steal the red-haired girl and take her with him as his captive. In the olden days, warriors had done that often. He drifted off to sleep dreaming of Samantha lying under him, panting and gasping as he took her virginity.

The next day, he came to his senses and realized that even with the best of luck, he'd never make good his escape if he took the unwilling captive along. He'd charm that Molly girl into helping him.

However, it was late in *wicata wi,* the month the whites called February, when one night, Cincala finally got his chance to get away.

Eighteen

Cincala had not realized it would be so far to the train station and his ill-fitting clothes were thin against the February cold. He stood on the winding road outside the Shaw mansion and tried to find direction from the stars, but clouds hid them. He had had to bribe Molly with the sapphire ring for her help. He valued it more than life, but he was desperate and the greedy servant girl had coveted it.

He heard the creak of wheels on the icy road and saw a wagon moving slowly toward him. He stepped into the shadows until it had almost passed, then hobbled out and swing up on the back of it unnoticed. His injured leg throbbed from the exertion, but he gritted his teeth and ignored the pain, knowing he had only until dawn before his disappearance was discovered. The wagon wound its way into the biggest town Cincala had ever seen; white men and wagons were moving about, even though it was very late and the streets were lit bright as day by gaslight. Somewhere he heard the echo of train whistles. He climbed off the wagon and followed the sound.

His leg felt as if it might be bleeding again, but he kept walking until he came upon dozens of tracks and many trains puffing like evil spirits. Which one? He walked up to a train, hesitated. A white man with bushy whiskers and wearing a uniform held out his hand. "Ticket?"

Cincala shrank back. Uniforms meant trouble. "Where do I get a ticket?"

Bushy Whiskers scowled at him and gestured. "In the station, of course."

Cincala turned and went where the man pointed. The building was as crowded as an ant bed, the white people shoving and pushing past each other, babies crying, and in the background the trains pulled away from the station in clouds of dirty smoke, growling like big bears. A few people turned to stare at him, but Cincala ignored them and stood in confusion a long moment, then limped over to a line of people where he could see another man in uniform standing in a big cage handing out small papers. He wondered what the man had done wrong that had imprisoned him? Watching what others did, Cincala got in line. In a few minutes, he reached the man in the cage and waited expectantly. The man had a handlebar mustache. He scowled at Cincala. "Where to?"

Cincala hesitated. "The land of my people."

"Don't get smart with me," the white man snapped. "What city are you bound for?"

Cincala chewed his lip. He had no idea what city lay near the land of his people. "I don't know."

"Look, you," the man growled. "See the line forming behind you? I don't have time for jokes."

"I want a ticket to out West," Cincala said.

"Where in the West?"

Cincala shrugged in frustration. "I really don't know."

The man eyed Cincala's ill-fitting clothes and long braids. "Have you got any money to pay for a ticket?"

"Money?" Cincala wasn't quite sure what money was although it seemed to be a very popular word with white people. "I don't think so."

The other man cursed softly. "Then, you savage, how do you expect to pay for your ride?"

Cincala reached through the wire cage and grabbed the man by the collar. "Don't call me a savage."

Instead, the man began to shriek for help and the next thing he knew, Cincala was surrounded by policemen with billy clubs and whistles. He had done nothing wrong and he tried to tell them, but they were determined, and when he fought them, someone hit him across the head.

When he came to, he was being dragged into a cell and dumped on the dirty floor as the door clanged shut behind him. His wounds were aching along with his head as he stumbled to his feet. "Wait, there's a mistake, I was only trying to ride the Iron Horse!"

He grabbed the bars and shook them, but the men in blue uniforms had turned and were walking away. Cincala realized at that moment that he was not alone. Turning slowly, he saw there were half a dozen others in his cell, ragged, villainous white men who stared at him.

"Look at the Injun," one whispered.

"Hey, Injun," another said, "you got any money?"

Cincala shook his head. Money again. It must be important. Samantha would have taught him about such things if he had stayed. "How do you get money?"

The others laughed. "Are you jokin'? You steal it or work for it if you can't steal it."

"Hey, look at his braids," a fat one in front said. "Looks like some schoolgirl."

Cincala drew himself up proudly. "Warriors wear their hair this way."

A short man snorted. "Men don't wear their hair long— let's cut it for him. Anybody got a knife?"

A third took out a crude knife that looked like it had been fashioned from a scrap of steel. "I got one. Let's give him a haircut."

Cincala shook his head. "No. Leave me alone."

Instead, the whole bunch advanced on him. Cincala's hair was the only thing left of his Lakota heritage and he would not let these rascals turn him into a white man. "I will fight," he warned.

Evidently, they didn't believe him or thought there was safety in numbers because they kept coming. Cincala crouched and made ready to return their blows.

Out at the desk, the police captain looked up from his report. "What in the name of all the saints is going on back there in the tank?"

Officer O'Hara shrugged. "Might be that Injun we put in a few minutes ago. The boys is probably givin' him a welcome."

The policemen all laughed but the noise from the back of the station grew louder with a white man now calling desperately for help.

The captain sighed. "Can't stand any more racket—find out what's going on, O'Hara."

O'Hara obliged and was surprised at the sight that greeted him when he went to the back. The white men all cowered in a corner of the cell, some with black eyes and bloody faces. "What the hell is all this racket?"

The savage sat on his bunk and looked out at the chunky cop. His wounds were bleeding again inside his ragged clothes and he didn't know how long the whites would keep him here or if they would ever let him go. He nodded toward his cowering cellmates. "They want to cut my hair."

"Keep it quiet!" the uniformed man snarled. "The captain don't like noise." With that, he turned and left.

For the first time, Cincala was afraid. He was in a cage with a bunch of white men who plotted to hurt him and he didn't know how to get out or what to do if he did so. Leaving this Boston was much more difficult than he had imagined. Sam might help him, but she wasn't here. She'd been right; he didn't know how to survive in a white world.

* * *

Sam awakened before dawn with a sense that something was wrong. As she had so often, she got up, pulled on a robe, and went to check on her charge. His bed was empty. What to do? She went out into the hall, heard a noise downstairs. Now what? She considered screaming, decided against waking the whole house. She didn't think Colt would harm her, but she wasn't so sure what might happen if anyone got in his way.

Down in the back hall, she bumped into Molly, who was about to go out the back door with a small valise. "Stop!"

In the dim gaslight of the hall, the girl turned on her defiantly. "I've decided to quit this lousy job."

"In the middle of the night?"

Molly backed away. "I don't know where he is."

Sam advanced on her. "So you did have something to do with it. You running off with him?" The thought pained her.

"No."

"Then he gave you something for payment. What was it?" Sam caught her arm.

"I ain't givin' the ring back—he said I could have it," the girl whined.

They were standing outside the butler's door and the conversation must have awakened the old fellow, because he stumbled out in his robe and houseshoes. "What is all this?"

"Nothin'," Molly snarled.

Sam tightened her grip. "Give it back, or I'll have you arrested."

"He gave it to me, I tell you!" But Molly dug in her small purse and handed over the sapphire ring.

The butler looked at them both. "What's happened, Miss Samantha? Shall I call the police?"

"No." Sam shook her head and let go of Molly. "She's just leaving." She pushed the girl out the back door. "And don't ever show your face around here again."

Sam turned to the old man. "Williams, wake the coachman. Molly has helped the savage escape and I need to find him before Mrs. Shaw discovers he's gone."

The old butler looked doubtful, but he nodded and headed out the back door to the carriage house.

Sam ran upstairs to dress, still clutching the ring. Poor Colt, he must have been desperate indeed to trade his ring for Molly's help. Where would he have gone? It was a long way to town for a wounded man, but if he could make it, he'd certainly try to hop a train. Sam pulled on her clothes and ran out to meet the sleepy coachman and directed him to take her to the train station as fast as possible.

Cincala lay on his bunk, watching the others in his dank cell. He was in pain, but he knew if he dropped off to sleep, he'd be at their mercy. He was in a bad way, but he didn't know what to do next. This cell was too strong to break out of.

A policeman came down the hall, his big keys clanking. He stopped before the cell. "Hey, you—Injun. Someone's come to bail you out."

Cincala wasn't sure what the man's words meant, but he knew the man was opening the door. Cincala stepped out into the gloomy hall, wondering if he could make a run for it and get away.

The policeman grunted. "You know Mrs. Shaw?" He looked as if he couldn't believe it.

"My grandmother," Cincala said.

The other man looked skeptical but impressed. The Shaw name was a power in Boston, Cincala realized suddenly.

"Someone from Mrs. Shaw's mansion has come to get you," the officer said respectfully.

"I am free?"

The officer nodded and motioned Cincala to follow him to the front. The red-haired girl stood there looking harried.

"Hello, Sam," Cincala said and realized he was genuinely glad to see her. "How did you find me?"

She looked relieved to see him, too, but maybe she was only worried she would lose her job if he were gone. "They told me at the train station what happened," she scolded as she led him out of the building. "I had a devil of a time getting enough money together to come down here and get you without Mrs. Shaw finding out."

He felt so weak, he wasn't sure he could make it out to the fine carriage waiting in the snow at the curbside out front. "I was trying to get on the Iron Horse and go home. You were right, Sam, I don't know enough to survive in a white man's world. I don't even know what money is."

She sighed and looked up at him. "You poor devil. I got your ring back and sent Molly packing. Get in."

They both got in and he sagged against the fancy leather seat and sighed, relieved as Sam put the ring in his hand. "I am sorry I cause you much trouble."

As the carriage started, she shrugged. "It's my job."

"Oh." Somehow, he had hoped it might be more than that. He settled himself in the warmth of the fine carriage and admitted to himself there were good things about being from a rich and powerful family. It was a long way back to the house and his wounds were hurting. He laid his head back and closed his eyes. "They tried to cut my hair," he muttered.

"Look, Colt," she put her hand on his arm, "you haven't given the white life enough of a chance."

Her hand was small and fragile on his dark arm. He could feel it and it aroused something in him. "I don't like white life."

"But you've got wealth, social position, and a fine home, everything that all white people envy. Besides, you can't return to the West by yourself—you don't know how."

"You are right," he admitted.

"You see? You need to learn more about our civilization. That's what your grandmother hired me for."

"Does she know?"

Sam patted his arm. "No. With any luck, we can get back in without her ever finding out."

"You protect your job," he muttered and closed his eyes.

Sam watched his eyelids flutter. He must be asleep. "No, I protect you," she whispered, and then hoped he hadn't heard her. She must not get emotionally involved with her charge. In a few months, she would have taught him which fork to use and how to get about the city and she'd be moving on to another position—this time, hopefully, with references. The thought saddened her. While Mrs. Shaw was a cranky, selfish old thing, Sam loved the comfortable big house and the servants she had come to know. Maybe that could all be hers if she'd encourage Bosworth.

"Pilamaya," Colt whispered.

"What does that mean?"

"In my language? *Thank you.* I didn't know how to get out of that cage and you rescued me."

"It's my job," she said.

However, the way she was looking up at him made him think it might be more than that. They were both safe and warm and she was close; that was a comforting feeling. He closed his eyes and leaned back against the cushions.

Sam watched him. He appeared exhausted. She took off her cloak and put it over him, tucking it in carefully. The carriage turned a corner and he lurched to one side against her, his head on her shoulder. Big and strong as he was, she felt very protective of him. If she couldn't teach this poor, naive wild thing how to survive in civilization, he might not make it and what would become of him? She realized she cared very much about his happiness. If she had enough money, darned if she wouldn't order the coachman to drive Colt to the station, put him on the right train, and send him back to the Dakotas.

Immediately, she rejected the idea. She didn't have the money, and worse yet, with his unhealed wounds, Colt might not make the long, arduous trip successfully. His face, against her shoulder, was very close. Without meaning to, she reached out a hand and brushed the hair away from his forehead, gently kissing his cheek as she might a child's.

Cincala was not asleep, though his eyes were closed. He was vaguely aware of the girl's touch, of her kiss, soft as a butterfly's wings across his cheek. Her gestures moved something deep inside him that he had not known was there. The girl had gone to a lot of trouble for him and it might cost her her job, which he understood she needed badly. Also, if his conduct did not improve, the cranky old woman might also let Sam go. Cincala thought about everything. Yes, there were things he had to know to be able to buy a ticket and get on the right Iron Horse to the land of the Lakota. Sam could teach him these things. He decided that he would become a more willing pupil—at least until he knew enough to survive in a white man's world.

In less than thirty minutes, they were pulling into the drive of the big red-brick house, where they managed to slip inside without waking Mrs. Shaw. Sam sent him straight to bed and then retired herself. However, she couldn't sleep.

Sam turned and tossed restlessly, remembering the heat of him against her in the carriage, the feel of his dark cheek when she had kissed him. She hadn't expected to get emotionally involved with Colt Shaw. The thought shocked her. Well, she would keep it strictly business from here on out— student and teacher, and make sure it went no further than that, no matter what. It was a long time before she dropped off to sleep.

Cincala lay sleepless, staring at the ceiling. He was tired and weak. The girl had been right; he couldn't escape until he knew enough to deal with the white man's world. He resolved to learn as much as possible over the coming weeks so that next time, he could travel back to his people without trouble from the whites who worked at the Iron Horse stable.

It took him a couple of days to recover from his ordeal, but if Mrs. Shaw suspected anything, she never said a word. The servants, who liked Sam, kept their silence; the butler covered for her and told the lady of the house that he had fired Molly for her impertinence.

Mrs. Shaw sniffed and nodded. "I never liked that girl anyway. I always suspected she was Irish."

After a day or two, Cincala was sufficiently recovered so that he put on the ill-fitting white man's clothes, grabbed his crutch, and limped downstairs. There was no one about. He paused in the hallway, staring at the strange box that hung there. Just then, the wooden box with the round metal eyes began to make a terrible noise. Cincala froze, uncertain what to do about this danger. Using his crutch, he hit it and a piece fell, dangling from a black cord.

"Hello?" the box said, "Hello?"

It had eaten a woman! Next it might eat Sam. He must defend her. He limped into the big room that was full of books. He looked about for a gun, but all he saw was a small metal rod by the fireplace. Cincala grabbed it and hurried back to the attack. The unseen victim still called "Hello?"

He would make the magic box spit her out. Cincala struck the box over and over until it clattered to the floor with a great crash.

Sam and Mrs. Shaw ran into the hallway. Sam took in the scene at a glance. "Colt, what are—?"

"I killed the monster." His chest puffed with pride.

Sam looked from the savage holding the poker to the destroyed telephone, then to Mrs. Shaw, whose mouth hung open. "Uh, there's something else I forgot to teach him."

"Well, see that you do," Mrs. Shaw snapped. "Williams! Call the repairman."

In the midst of this confusion, a funny little humpbacked man arrived at the front door. He had a measuring tape around his neck and a mouthful of pins. Sam explained that the man was a "tailor," whose task it was to measure Cincala for some clothes. He took Cincala into a room, closed the door, and made many measurements, commenting on how broad the shoulders were and how narrow the waist.

Cincala stared at the little man as the tailor gathered up his things. "You make me clothes?"

The other nodded. "In about a week, they'll be ready."

"But I have no money," Cincala protested.

The little humpbacked man smiled. "Don't worry about it—your grandmother has plenty."

As the little man left, Williams entered and bowed. "Miss MacGregor awaits you in the conservatory."

He couldn't remember what a "conservatory" was. This house was so big. "Where is that?"

The butler gestured down the hall and Cincala limped in to join the red-haired girl, awestruck by the conservatory. It had much glass and was full of plants despite the cold, raw weather outside. "Here I am," Cincala said. "What would you teach me?"

She smiled up at him. "Sit down, Colt. Today, I am going to teach you some table manners."

He shrugged, thinking how desirable she was with the light catching her red hair. "All right."

The butler brought in big silver trays and covered dishes, then deftly began to serve. After he left, she started talking, showing Cincala how to deal with his food and shook her head when he picked up the sausages with his hands.

"No, no, no. You must use your knife and fork."

Cincala shrugged, speared a whole sausage on his knife, brought it to his mouth, and took a big bite.

Sam took a deep breath and sighed. "No, that's not the right way, Colt."

"Why is your way right and mine wrong?"

"Let's not get into a philosophy discussion. Now you watch me and do as I do."

Cincala didn't know what "philosophy" meant, but obediently, he imitated her. The fork was a clumsy thing. He wiped his mouth on his sleeve, but she held up her hand.

"Stop. Use your napkin."

He gave her a questioning look. "What's a napkin?"

She held up the small white square of cloth in her lap.

"But it's clean," he protested. "I'll get it dirty."

Sam gave him a despairing look. "So was your shirt before you wiped your mouth on it."

She went on talking, but he ceased to listen. What held his attention was the way the morning light reflected on her fiery hair. He decided she was the most beautiful, desirable white girl he had ever seen. She might be even more beautiful than the Lakota girls. Desire built in him as he watched her.

". . . you aren't listening," Sam's eyes sparked fire.

"Yes, I am," he insisted. "You are droning on and on about which fork to use when one is plenty for anyone."

"Your grandmother is going to want to give a formal dinner for you and you must not embarrass her. Right now, I wouldn't dare suggest we have an informal breakfast with her. Mrs. Shaw would probably faint when she saw you wipe your mouth on your shirtsleeve."

"It must not take much to make white ladies faint." He looked at her again and wanted her in a way a man wants a woman. "Will it please you if I learn which fork to use?"

Sam nodded. "She will think I've been doing my job."

"All right, I will try harder. But enough about forks," he said as he wolfed down the rest of the savory eggs and biscuits, "teach me about white man's money."

She scowled at him as he gobbled his food, but he was

hungry and he was tired of all this nonsense about silver-ware.

"Money?" she said. "You have plenty of it."

"I do?"

She nodded. "The Shaws have a bankful, I would think. You can buy anything you want."

"In my country," he said, "I was very rich, too. I could make a gift of many ponies for a woman I wanted."

"And did you have a woman?" Somehow, the thought bothered her.

He shook his head. "I was looking, but I had not yet chosen a wife."

The way he was staring so frankly at her brought a warm flush to Sam's cheeks. She cleared her throat awkwardly and picked up the little bell beside her plate and rang it. Immediately, the old butler appeared and began to clear the table. "More coffee, miss?"

"Yes, please. Bring us a pot, then leave us."

The old man glanced at Colt doubtfully, then obeyed.

Sam looked at Colt, ignoring the frank interest in his gray eyes. "Would you like another cup?"

He nodded.

"The proper response is 'yes, please.' "

"Yes, please." He felt like one of the silly dogs balancing on the balls in his first bedroom. When she poured it, he picked up the cup with both hands and gulped it.

"I see we have a long way to go." The girl's voice sounded as if her patience was being strained. "I'll pour you another cup, and—"

"But I don't want any more," Cincala said.

"Well, I'll pretend to pour another cup and show you the proper way to pick it up."

"It is all very confusing," he sighed.

She looked at him. His wide shoulders slumped and he sounded discouraged.

"You'll learn," she said with a smile. "Now you pick it up by the handle with one hand."

Cincala stared at the dainty cup doubtfully. If he dropped it, no doubt Sam would be displeased. He picked it up carefully, although the fine china felt awkward in his big hand. "Enough. Tell me about money."

She decided she could only try his patience so far. "All right. I'll go get my purse and we'll start." She left the room, satisfied that he'd had a change of attitude, for whatever reason, and things were bound to improve. When she passed the morning room, Mrs. Shaw looked up from her desk.

"Are things going well, my dear?"

Sam nodded with a more positive smile than she felt. "I'm sure your grandson will be ready for that grand ball you have planned."

The old lady frowned at Sam over her gold-rimmed spectacles. "I can't afford to keep buying telephones. If that story gets around, I'll be embarrassed before all the ladies of my club."

How like Mrs. Shaw not to be concerned with Colt's feelings at all. Sam was still thinking about this as she returned to the breakfast area in the conservatory. Did the old woman care a fig about Colt or did she only want a presentable heir?

"Now," Sam said as she sat down, "here's what a penny looks like."

As she laid the coin on the table, Colt scooted his chair close to hers, almost touching. She hesitated, decided not to make an issue of it.

"Does it buy much?"

She shook her head. "If you want to buy more, here's a silver dollar."

Colt picked up the big, shiny coin, examining it. "My people knock holes in these and use them for jewelry."

"In the white culture, it is worth one hundred of these pennies," Sam said.

"How many dollars does it take to ride the train?"

She was very aware of how close he was. She seemed to feel the heat from his big body. "That depends on where you want to go. I suppose the next thing I'll have to teach you is some geography."

He looked so interested, she got up and returned to the library for a book of maps. When she came back, she moved her chair away from his. Unfortunately, that made it difficult to share the book. Again, Colt scooted his chair close to hers. As they shared the book, his arm brushed hers time and again. Sam was too aware of the warmth of his arm, but she wasn't certain whether to make an issue of it or not. It might be very innocent on his part.

He peered at the maps. "Show me my country."

"Here." She put her fingertip on the Dakotas.

His hand touched hers. "Here? Is this far away?"

Sam withdrew her hand as she nodded. "We are right here." She put her finger on Boston. She could feel perspiration breaking out on her body though the room was cool. "Maybe we need to do something else for a while." She jumped up, slamming the book shut.

He seemed to be enjoying himself hugely. "Sam, teach me to dance."

"Your leg isn't well enough for that yet."

"Cincala would like to try anyway."

The way he was looking at her caused Sam to hug the book against her breasts as if hiding behind it. "All right, we could at least listen to music. I'm sure Mrs. Shaw has a phonograph in her music room. Come along."

As she walked down the hall, she could hear him hobbling after her. Damn him, he was playing with her—or was he? Maybe he was just behaving like an innocent savage. She wished she knew.

In a cozy corner of the big ballroom, Sam found a phonograph on a small table along with a box of wax cylinders. She took a chair and motioned Colt to one. "At this big party your grandmother intends to give soon, you'll have to impress the young ladies."

He looked at her very seriously. "How does a man impress a young lady among the whites?"

He seemed so interested, she wondered if he were smitten by one of the pretty maids in the household. As handsome as he was, he'd have no trouble luring one of them into his bed. The thought pained her, but she wasn't sure why.

"Sam?"

She came back to the task at hand with a rush. "Well, you have to have nice manners and be able to waltz."

"What is this waltz?"

"It's a dance. In a minute, I'll crank up the phonograph and we'll try it. Now first, let's do the introduction." She stood up and motioned him to his feet. "I'll be standing here fluttering my fan and talking to other young ladies and someone brings you up and introduces you to me. Now you take my hand, bow slightly, and kiss it."

"Would rather kiss her mouth," he said.

"No, no, no," she scolded in exasperation. "You can't just grab her and kiss her mouth—you'll shock her and ruin your chances. She'll probably slap you."

"Doesn't she want to be kissed?" He was looking down into her eyes in a way that made her uneasy, her heart beating a little faster as he took her hand and kissed the back of it.

Sam backed away, but he didn't let go. "Maybe, but she can't let you know that."

"Why?"

"Because you might think badly of her." She looked up at him, remembering the taste of his mouth.

"I wouldn't."

"Well, then, her friends and everyone else would." His hand was strong and warm, hers curled inside it as if it belonged there. "Now you let go of my hand and I curtsy and maybe giggle a little behind my fan and tell you how pleased I am to meet you."

The way he was looking at her set her heart to pounding. She had a sudden feeling he was going to pull her into an embrace. That wouldn't do, wouldn't do at all. With a determined yank, she pulled her hand free and backed away from him. "I—I don't think we ought to try the dancing today," she gulped. "Your leg isn't up to it."

"Try me." He did not blink.

She wasn't quite sure what to do. She both wanted and feared to go into his embrace. She wasn't sure whether she didn't trust him or herself for what might happen. "Maybe we'll just listen to the music."

Sam hurried to the phonograph and cranked it up, then put on a wax cylinder. "This is the 'Blue Danube Waltz.' "

He cocked his head in amazement. "Where is the music coming from? I see no players."

Sam shrugged. "I don't know how it works, it's on the wax cylinder somehow."

He watched it gravely. "The white man has very big medicine. You can have this music anytime?"

Sam nodded and stopped the machine, showing him how to put a cylinder on, crank the phonograph, and start it again.

"Now," he held out his hands, "you teach me to waltz."

Sam licked her lips. She was certain nervous perspiration was gathering on her upper lip. "Okay. I'll stand in front of you and show you the step, then you copy it."

He shook his head. "In white man's dance, doesn't he take her in his arms?"

"We'll do that another time," Sam said, avoiding his eyes. "Now watch me, you step this way—"

Instead, he took her in his arms.

She looked up at him, thinking how big and powerful he was. He was standing so close, she was certain she could feel his aroused manhood through her voluminous skirts.

The look in his gray eyes was intense—too intense. She managed to pull free. "That was not correct. If you hold a girl that way, she will surely be insulted and slap your face."

"Why?"

"Stop asking why," Sam snapped. "It's not proper, that's all. Now keep a respectable distance. I'll show you how to take the woman in your arms."

He scowled. "I know how to take a woman in my arms."

"Not so close," she warned. "There is a proper way to do it." Sam waited for the beat. "Now put your hand on my waist and take my hand in yours. Wait for the next beat and then I'll show you the step."

Instead, Colt pulled her closer still and kissed her. She knew she ought to protest, but his tongue was caressing the inside of her mouth and she could feel his hard chest against the tips of her nipples. It felt too good to move away, even if she could have. He kissed her thoroughly until she managed to pull back, gasping for breath, her composure shaken. "No, you do not kiss the lady when you dance with her. She will think you forward and might slap you."

"Why? Doesn't she like being kissed?"

She struggled and finally yanked herself out of his grasp, still breathing hard. "Even if she likes it, she must not let him know it."

"Why?"

She was exasperated both with him and herself. "I don't know why, I just know that's the way it is. Look, I think you're tired and we've done enough for today."

"Cincala is not tired." He shook his head.

"Well, I am," Sam snapped and strode over to turn off the phonograph. "In the future, you must not try to kiss the tutor—it is highly improper. Is that understood?"

"I thought you were teaching me the white man's ways?"

Was he toying with her or was he that naive? She tried to control her indignation. "If you do not behave, I shall quit this job. Is that understood?"

He nodded.

"All right, we shall return to the library and study read-ing. We are running out of time to get you ready for your grandmother's introduction to proper society."

"What is proper society?"

"Anyone your grandmother knows. Do you not realize, Colt Shaw, that when you are ready, you will have your choice of all the prettiest, richest young women in Boston?"

"Any?" The thought intrigued him. Were there any pret-tier than the fiery-haired girl?

"Yes," she nodded, "you'll be able to just pick any one and with your grandmother's money, you can have her."

"And she'll go back to my people with me?"

He watched Sam. She looked both sympathetic and pained. "I'm afraid not. There aren't many white girls who'd be willing to make that sacrifice."

"Want to waltz again," he insisted, eager to get Sam in his embrace. He wanted to hold her, stroke her, kiss her.

"I told you we are going to study reading now." Her voice was as steely as her face. She started out of the room toward the library.

Cincala limped after her. She had liked his kiss; he had known that by the way she leaned into him and her mouth had returned his caress. He decided then and there that he would have the fiery-haired girl in his bed before he escaped to the Dakotas again, and he wanted her soon.

Nineteen

Mrs. Shaw entered the small sunroom where Sam was taking tea early one morning on the last day of February. As always, the older lady wore an expensive black mourning dress. "It's going to be a nice day," she said, "and the tailor has sent a note that Colt's new clothes are ready."

New clothes. The words reminded Sam just how threadbare the blue wool dress she wore really was. "Good. Those old clothes the servants gave him are a bit worn and too small."

"Therefore, we shall all go into town for the fitting," the old lady said grandly. "We're due there at ten o'clock. Is he up to it?"

"I think so. At least he might enjoy getting out of the house. Would you like me to accompany you, Mrs. Shaw?"

"Certainly!" She peered at Sam over her spectacles. "You don't think I want to deal with the savage by myself, do you? After that, I want to take him out and show him where his father is buried so he can pay his respects." The old lady turned and left the room.

Colt soon joined Sam. There was something about him that gladdened her heart. It was because he was her pupil, she told herself. "Where have you been?"

He shrugged. "I've been up a long time. I watched the sun rise through the ballroom windows, then had breakfast with the servants in the kitchen."

Sam gulped. "I don't think I would tell Mrs. Shaw."

"Why not?" He looked puzzled.

"Well, she would think it improper."

"Improper to eat breakfast?"

"Improper to eat with the servants."

"Oh, why?"

Sam sighed. How did she explain about class distinction to this poor savage? "It's just one of those white people things—it doesn't have to make sense. Would you like tea?"

He shook his head, his rugged features mystified.

Then she explained about the day's events.

"My father's grave? How can we do this?"

"Well, we just drive to the cemetery after the fitting."

"Oh." Colt's brow wrinkled and he looked puzzled.

"Perhaps you're too young to remember him."

He didn't answer, and she wondered what he was thinking.

However, just before they were to leave the house, Mrs. Shaw took them both into the library. "Colt, I'm sure you hardly knew your father, but I've almost made a little shrine to him in here." She pointed out the daguerreotype of the handsome man in a cavalry uniform.

Colt picked up the photo and sighed. "White Wolf."

"No, no," Mrs. Shaw cried and took it from his hands. "He was Austin Shaw, my oldest son." She put the photo down and reached for the gold pocket watch. "This was Austin's, too." She dabbed at her eyes with a dainty hankie as she took the watch off its tiny stand next to all the medals. "This is how we identified your heroic father's body—my late husband's watch was still clutched in his hand."

"My father?" The savage looked baffled.

Sam watched him and wondered. Perhaps he had never seen a photo and wasn't sure what a pocket watch was.

"Yes," the old lady nodded, "and here's all the medals they gave me. He was indeed a hero."

Colt didn't say anything. He stared at the items as Mrs. Shaw smiled and put the gold watch back on its little stand.

There was a long moment of silence as Colt looked at the items. "White Wolf is dead?"

Had he not known that? But surely he had, Sam thought, mystified. Maybe he had thought the soldier had deserted the Lakota girl he had made love to.

"What a strange remark," Mrs. Shaw said.

At that moment, the elderly butler stuck his head in the door. "Beg your pardon, ma'am, but your carriage is here."

Discussion forgotten, the three of them went outside. It was a brisk but fairly nice day for late February, with the snow partly melted. Sam thought the Shaw carriage was one of the best; two beautiful black horses pulled it, the red wheels and the brass trim all shiny. Inside, the red velvet cushions offered deluxe comfort. In minutes, the carriage hit a brisk clip along the winding road until they were on the narrow, bricked streets of Boston. They passed a couple on bicycles.

Colt's eyes grew wide. "People on wheels?"

Sam nodded, amused. "Bicycles. You can learn to ride."

Mrs. Shaw stared out the window, too, her face aghast. "Just look at that girl in those shameless bloomers."

Sam felt inclined to defend the unknown woman. "In a full skirt, she might get caught in the chain."

Mrs. Shaw sniffed. "That's no excuse. Colt, you want one of those, I'll have one sent to the house. Perhaps one of the footmen can teach you to ride."

"One for Sam, too," he said.

Sam felt her face flush. "Oh, really now, Colt—"

"Very well," said Mrs. Shaw. "Someone has to accompany you if you join one of those cycling clubs."

Sam tried to picture herself on a bicycle and stifled a groan. It wasn't something she looked forward to.

Soon they arrived at a fine tailor shop and alighted on the brick sidewalk still wet from melting snow.

Mrs. Shaw glanced from Sam to her grandson. "Oh, dear, I'm not sure this was such a good idea. Some of my friends might see him and he's not ready to meet them."

"Nonsense," Sam said. "It will be good for Colt to get used to the town."

"But suppose some of my friends happen by and he embarrasses me?" She looked quite concerned.

Sam didn't like her very much for her snooty remark. "Your true friends know what the situation is. I'm sure all of Boston knows. Why would you care what your enemies think? After all, you can buy and sell most of them."

The old lady smiled triumphantly and her nose turned up. "That's right, isn't it? The Shaws are the top of society." Mrs. Shaw nodded and sailed into the tailor shop.

Sam motioned Colt to follow them. "I don't want you to get lost again," she whispered.

Cincala had pretended not to understand the exchange between the two women although it annoyed him that Sam was right. Ever since he'd tried to take a train and ended up in jail, he'd known escaping from this crowded city was going to be more difficult than he'd imagined. Besides, he would need money for a ticket. Sam had told him he was rich, but no one had given him any dollars. If he asked for some, they would all be suspicious.

Colt?" Sam called from the doorway.

"Coming." He looked up and down the sidewalk at the dozens of people hurrying past. It reminded him of a busy anthill. He didn't like crowds. With a sigh, he followed the women into the shop.

Sam settled herself in a chair beside Mrs. Shaw as the little humpbacked tailor greeted them and began to bring out the clothes. "Your grandson is such a joy to design for—he has the perfect form for a man."

Colt looked doubtful, but Sam nodded encouragement to him. "Now you'll finally have clothes that really fit you."

"And won't look like a poor, homeless tramp any longer."

Mrs. Shaw smiled with approval as the tailor held up each fine suit. "Do try them on. Did you get the boots?"

The tailor nodded. "Yes. The shoemaker just finished three pairs for him this morning. Come, young man," he said, "come into the back room and try these clothes on. We'll do a fashion show for the ladies."

Sam was not quite prepared for what she saw when Colt strode back into the room wearing the custom-made coat and trousers. "Sam, do I look silly?"

She could only shake her head in amazement. She hadn't realized how handsome he actually was until she saw him standing there in the finest fabric and good leather boots. The sapphire ring still hung from a thong on his neck.

Mrs. Shaw let out the breath she'd been holding. "Why, he looks every inch the gentleman. Austin would be proud."

Colt turned to look in the full-length mirror and seemed stunned by what he saw. "I look like a rich white man."

"Isn't it wonderful!" Mrs. Shaw gushed. "When we take him to the barber and get his hair cut—"

"No!" Colt whirled on her, his gray eyes blazing. "No cut hair."

Sam touched Mrs. Shaw's arm. "He hasn't quite reached the stage of feeling like a white aristocrat, even though he looks like one." To the angry Colt, she soothed, "Don't worry, your hair won't be cut until you're ready for it."

Colt shook his head. "Never."

Elizabeth Shaw opened her mouth and then closed it again. Evidently she was a woman who knew how to pick her battles. "When you're ready to accept your new role as an important white man and not before."

Colt nodded, seeming mollified as he turned to look in the mirror again. "These cost much money?"

The little tailor coughed and looked embarrassed.

"Colt," his grandmother said, "gentlemen do not talk about money. It isn't polite."

Colt appeared puzzled. "But how do I pay for these things if I have no money?"

The little tailor smiled and reassured him. "Don't let that worry you, young man. Mrs. Shaw has an account here."

Colt looked as if he were about to object, but Sam stood up and took his arm. "I'm sure you can pay for it from part of your trust fund."

"Quite right," the old lady agreed and stood up. "Eventually, I'll open up an account for you at the bank."

Colt looked pleased. "I'll have money in my pockets?"

Why was he so concerned about money? Sam wondered. She assured him he would eventually have money as Mrs. Shaw advised the tailor to deliver all the clothes and boots except what Colt was wearing. The tailor helped him into a fine overcoat.

"We'll be about the town some today," the dowager wheezed, "and I don't want to be seen with a ragamuffin."

The tailor escorted them to the door with a flourish. "It's good to see you out and about, Mrs. Shaw. I was always so fond of Austin—such a hero."

"Yes," she nodded gravely, "we're on our way out to the cemetery now to put flowers on the grave."

Cincala looked from one to the other, then to Sam, who also looked sad. *What on earth were these fools talking about?* However, Cincala did not bat an eye or give any notice that he understood their conversation. He stroked the fine wool of the new topcoat. It felt good to his hand and he liked the admiring glance Sam gave him. He could get used to wearing white men's clothes for the little time he had left to stay in this crowded city, he supposed, but they would never feel as comfortable as buckskin and moccasins. Some things from the white civilization he would miss, he admitted to himself: the big clawfoot bathtub with all the hot, soapy water; the fragrant, sweet gingerbread men that Cook kept in a jar in the kitchen. Most of all, he would miss Sam.

They got into their waiting carriage and drove away.

Cincala leaned back and stared down at his fine leather boots. He didn't really understand about the cemetery. Surely if White Wolf had been killed, they hadn't brought the body all the way from Wounded Knee for burial? But who knew what strange customs white people might have? Cincala missed his parents, but death was an everyday occurrence in the difficult life of the Sioux and Cincala was resigned to it. He looked at Sam and smiled and she smiled back, which made him glad deep in his heart. "When are we going to the mill?"

"Maybe tomorrow," the old woman said.

"They will show me how to make money at the factory?"

Both women nodded at him.

He was very pleased. He wanted to know how the whites made those pretty silver coins so he might learn to make them. Besides buying things like train tickets, they made very good hair decorations for all the Plains tribes. He wanted to take a sackful when he returned to his people.

"Also," said his grandmother and she frowned at him, "people will keep staring at you as long as you wear that ring around your neck."

Cincala decided he would pretend he didn't understand.

The old woman turned to Sam with an exasperated sigh. "You really do need to get through to him that men don't generally wear a piece of jewelry that's worth a king's ransom like that. It really belongs in a safe."

Cincala reached up and grabbed the ring, glaring back at her. "Mine."

Sam saw the hostility on his handsome, dark features and moved to dispel the tension. "Mrs. Shaw," she said softly, "it's all the security he has. I suppose your son must have given it to his mother."

"Some Injun squaw," the old lady grumbled. "My ancestors must be rolling over in their graves to think such a valuable piece of jewelry was given to some Injun girl. If that irresponsible little tart, Summer Van Schuyler, had accepted it instead of running away, Austin would have been married to her and she'd be wearing that ring."

Sam was not even sure who Summer Van Schuyler was. She glanced at Colt. He was understanding every word, Sam realized, looking at the angry frown on his high-cheekboned face. Any second now, there would be an outburst and she must not let that happen. "There's time later to speak of what to do about the ring," she soothed as they rolled along at a fast clip. "Someday he might want to give it to his bride. But anyway, he can wear it under his shirt and no one will realize it's there."

He would never let anyone take his precious ring away from him; it had too many memories attached to it. He watched the wheezy old lady lean back against the seat cushions and doze off, snoring loudly. Cincala moved so that his knee was brushing Sam's. She frowned at him, but he gave her an innocent smile and brushed his knee against hers again. She couldn't say anything without waking the old lady, and she knew it; he could see the frustration in the bright blue eyes.

Mrs. Shaw awakened as they stopped for the footman to run into a flower shop and bring back some white roses as she instructed. Cincala gave Sam a questioning look.

"People use them to decorate graves," she explained. He started to ask more, then decided against it. In a few minutes, their carriage pulled through ornate iron gates. Everywhere he looked, there were fancy pieces of stone stuck in the ground. The carriage stopped before some of the biggest and most ornate stones. Mrs. Shaw motioned for them to get out.

"Come along, you two. I want Colt to see where his father is buried."

Sam let the coachman help them out into the brisk day. The snow lay in melting patches on the dark earth around the stones. Colt looked puzzled, but he got out of the carriage and followed the ladies as they walked over to the fine granite monuments with angels adorning the tops.

"See?" the old lady said. "I spared no expense for such a hero. He's buried next to his father, of course."

Sam looked at the letters cut into the granite. "Austin Shaw, one of the gallant heroes of the Little Bighorn," she read aloud, "killed by savages on June 25, 1876."

Mrs. Shaw bent to lay her bunch of roses in the snow of the grave and smiled triumphantly. "I was never so proud of Austin as I was when I heard the news."

Sam blinked, realizing suddenly that perhaps the old lady had never really loved her son; his death and the glory and attention it had brought her were more important. Sam glanced over at Colt. He seemed puzzled by the grave.

Mrs. Shaw must have noticed his expression, too. "I suppose he really doesn't understand."

"In time," Sam hastened to say.

"Well, he isn't progressing as fast as I'd hoped. I won't live forever and he has to be ready to take over this empire when I go. Poor Bosworth had hoped to be my heir, but after I found my grandson, Bosworth is disinherited."

Bosworth, Sam thought with distaste, but she made no comment. She watched Colt's dark, handsome face. He looked absolutely panicked as if taking over the Shaw responsibilities was the last thing he wanted. "Colt will learn gradually," she hastened to say.

He gave her just the slightest shake of his head and Sam knew that nothing had changed. Colt Shaw intended to return to his old life the first chance he got. She realized abruptly how much she would miss him when he left.

Mrs. Shaw seemed oblivious to this as she peered up at the sky. "It's late—we really must be going." Wheezing heavily, she turned and headed back toward the carriage.

Sam started to follow her, but Colt caught her arm. "I don't understand," he said. "Who is in that grave?"

Sam was taken aback. What a strange question. "Don't you understand? Your father."

His dark face saddened. "And my mother, too?"

Her heart went out to him. "I don't think so." This elegant cemetery certainly wouldn't accept an Indian body.

"She wouldn't like that," Colt said. "After all, they were killed together."

"They were?"

"I don't know for sure, but I think so. I was too hurt to go look for them and then I was put on the train."

He must be confused. Sam wanted to ask more questions, but about that time, Mrs. Shaw called from her carriage, her voice annoyed and impatient. "Come along, you two, I'm not used to being kept waiting."

"We'll talk about it later," Sam promised. Colt took her arm and they walked back to the carriage in silence. She sat across from the old lady, and before she could protest, Colt had wedged himself into the seat next to her. The carriage pulled away and Mrs. Shaw made herself comfortable and began to doze, snoring loudly.

Her grandson promptly put his knee against Sam's again. She tried to pull away, but he crowded closer. She didn't dare protest for fear of waking the cranky old lady. Now his arm went along the back of the cushions behind her. What to do? "Stop it," she hissed at him.

"Shh!" he warned in a whisper, "you'll wake her."

Sam couldn't disengage herself or put up a protest without a lot of movement that would surely wake Mrs. Shaw. His thigh against hers was strong and warm. The arm circling her shoulders seemed protective, if not possessive. She had an urge to lay her face against his fine wool topcoat and enjoy the embrace. What was she thinking? He was her student and such behavior would be very unethical indeed.

His hand on the back of the seat reached out and played with a tendril of hair on her neck. His touch sent goosebumps up her back that spread through her whole body. She closed her eyes and pretended she was not at all affected.

He reached out, caught her chin in his big hand, and turned her face to him. She opened her mouth to protest, but he put his tongue against her half-open lips. She wished she could force herself to pull away, but his embrace had deepened and he was kissing her, his tongue caressing her lips.

Sam forgot about Mrs. Shaw; she forgot about the consequences; she forgot about everything except this kiss. She gave herself into it as her emotions took control over her common sense. She let him kiss her, his tongue invading her mouth, his arm holding her close as the other hand stroked her breast until she was gasping for air. When she managed to pull back, looking up at him, his gray eyes were intense as a winter storm. He looked as surprised as she, as if he'd had no idea kissing her could be as exciting as it had been.

"I want you," he mouthed the words.

A chill went through Sam's body. She didn't know if she was concerned or eager to experience the passion his stormy eyes promised. She shook her head.

"I will have you," he mouthed again.

Abruptly the old woman stirred and Colt moved away from Sam, back into his corner of the carriage. Sam took a deep breath, feeling her cheeks burn. How dare he be so familiar? But of course wealthy men took liberties with women employees all the time; hadn't she lost two jobs over it? She wouldn't lose this one. Sam vowed she would make it crystal clear to Colt Shaw when they could talk privately. On the other hand, she was a little afraid of being alone with him. Was she afraid of him or herself?

It was late afternoon when they got back to the mansion and Sam excused herself, pleading a headache. She had supper sent up to her room, and even the cook's best beef stew and chocolate cake couldn't cheer her up. She went to bed early and was careful to put a chair under the doorknob. She was awakened in the middle of the night by the knob turning. She lay very still, holding her breath and watching the knob turn in the moonlight. She didn't know what she would do if he came into her room. Would she scream or would she hold out her arms? No, she was not going to become a rich man's plaything like so many governesses were.

After a moment, the knob ceased turning and Sam drew a breath of relief . . . or was it disappointment? Her thoughts annoyed her. She determined then that she would go out of her way never to be alone with Colt and make it very clear that his advances were unwelcome. If she could just make it until the spring ball and Mrs. Shaw was happy with her grandson's behavior, she would leave these premises with glowing references, and maybe a nice bonus, and never look back.

The next day dawned brisk and blustery for the first of March. Sam was breakfasting in the conservatory alone when Colt came in.

"Good morning."

She gave him a curt nod without looking up.

"I just spoke to my grandmother and she says we're going to visit some of our businesses today."

"I have a headache—you two will have to go alone." She refused to look at him, glaring down at her plate, stabbing her eggs with her fork so hard that the china clattered. She imagined she was sticking the fork in him.

The butler entered. "And what would the master like?"

"Bring me the same thing the lady is having and a pot of coffee," Colt said.

Sam stole a look at him. He had begun to adjust to this

life as if he'd been born to it. Indeed, he looked like an aristocrat in his fine, custom-made clothes—or would have, were it not for the long hair.

"So, Miss Samantha, are you feeling so poorly this morning that you'd miss our outing?" She couldn't decide if he was genuinely concerned or being snide.

"We must get one thing straight," she slammed her cup down so hard, it rattled. "You are not to touch me again."

He gave her a disarming grin. "You didn't like it? I would have sworn from the way you reacted—"

"Never mind how I reacted," her voice rose. "It is not ethical for a tutor to get involved with a student and don't ask me to explain 'ethical.' "

"I thought it was fun," he shrugged. "I would like to do that some more."

"Then do it with the chambermaids," Sam snapped. "I'll not be used as a plaything. I've been through this before and I need the references your grandmother will give me."

He leaned toward her and whispered, "Let me kiss you again and I'll give you references."

She felt her face burn as the butler entered with silver trays. She could only hope he had not heard the exchange, but his face was immobile as he served Colt.

Williams left and Colt dug into his food.

"Cut your bacon up," Sam said without thinking, "and don't stuff your mouth."

He grinned and nodded. "You know, there are a few things I could teach *you*."

She had no doubt that was true. She was lost for a retort. She decided to change the subject. "You're in for an interesting time when you visit the mills today."

He didn't look too enthused as he ate. "What's a mill?"

"It makes fabric—blankets. I understand the Shaws made a fortune producing uniforms during the Civil War."

He cocked his head thoughtfully as he sipped his coffee

and smiled. "So I'll be able to afford several wives like a rich Lakota?"

Sam shook her head. "No, the whites will not allow you to have more than one wife."

Colt paused with his fork halfway to his lips. "What is the good of being rich if I can have only one woman?"

"Spoken like a typical man," Sam said. "Rich white men keep mistresses."

"Mistresses. What is a 'mistress?' "

Sam blushed in spite of herself, wondering how she had gotten into this conversation.

"Educate me," he commanded, pushing his plate back. He almost wiped his mouth on the sleeve of his fine waistcoat, then seemed to think better of it and used his napkin instead.

"Hmm, rich white men usually have wives but then they sometimes keep several beautiful women as well."

"Why?"

"Can't you guess why?" Sam flushed. She wasn't certain if he were truly that ignorant or just playing with her.

"It seems to me," Colt said gravely, looking at her, "that if he had the right wife, he wouldn't need a mistress."

"This is not a proper topic for discussion," Sam scolded him as she got up and left the table.

"Grandmother says to be ready by ten o'clock," he called after her.

Damn him anyway, Sam thought as she hurried up the stairs. Well, she'd see to it that he didn't sit next to her on this trip.

The carriage was brought around and soon they were traveling down the winding road and away from the estate. Mrs. Shaw rattled on and on about the ball and how everyone in town was hoping for an invitation. All Sam could think of was how threadbare her one blue silk dress was and how beautifully the other young ladies would be dressed. But of course she wasn't invited anyway.

She sneaked a look at him. Except for the long, black braids and the ring on a cord around his neck, he appeared every inch the handsome, highborn aristocrat in his custom-made suit with his broad shoulders and fine booted feet. When he caught her studying him, he smiled and winked.

Quickly, Sam glanced away.

Mrs. Shaw looked at her just then and frowned. "Whatever are you blushing at, my dear?"

"I—I wasn't blushing," Sam stammered, staring out at the passing scene. The trees were still bare and stark, but a hint of spring was in the air today. "I must be about to have the vapors—all this fresh air, you know."

There certainly wasn't much fresh air in the big brick mill, Sam thought with dismay as they entered there. It seemed dark and dirty. Huge machines roared, making fabric. The noise was deafening and the air so full of dust, they were soon coughing. Bosworth came out of his office, greeting his aunt warmly and kissing Sam's hand. "I'll be happy to show you around."

He led them to another building where the fabric was turned into garments. Sam had never been in a sewing factory before and she viewed it with dismay. The place was cramped and smelled bad. Hundreds of immigrant girls, some of them not much more than children, sat at sewing machines in long rows, stitching by dim light. "Oh, my!"

Bosworth obviously mistook her comment because he smiled and nodded. "Yes, it is impressive, isn't it? We're the biggest mill in the area for making blankets and the girls turn out hundreds of garments. We have a government contract to supply the Indian agencies."

Without thinking, Sam said, "Some of those girls look awfully young."

The old woman dusted off her fine black dress. "They're just nobodies and their families need the money."

Sam noted that Colt looked as disgusted as she felt. He said, "Girls sit all day, sew over and over?"

"Yes," said Bosworth proudly, "and, I might add, they are putting a pretty penny in dear Auntie's pocket. With these starving immigrants, we can get them for almost nothing."

They passed a row of sewing machines and thin, pale girls paused and looked up fearfully. "Get back to work!" Bosworth shouted. "We didn't hire you to loaf about."

Sam had to clamp her teeth shut to keep from saying something. Colt looked annoyed. Only Mrs. Shaw and her nephew looked pleased.

"Grandmother," Colt said, "the girls do not look happy."

"Happy?" Mrs. Shaw sniffed.

Her nephew sighed and looked at Colt as if he were not quite bright. "You do not understand—it is not our problem. It is my job to make all the money I can for my dear aunt."

The old lady beamed at him. "That's right, Bosworth."

Colt walked over to a large box overflowing with blankets and held one up. Sam could see that it was of very poor quality and so thin that she could see light through it.

Colt shook his head. "This is much like blankets the Lakota were always given—not very warm."

Bosworth shrugged and motioned them along the aisles. As they walked, he said, "That doesn't matter. You see, the less wool we put into them, the higher the profit margin. I realize you don't understand, but—"

"I understand," Colt scowled.

When they left the big room, Sam looked back. The thin, pale girls were staring after them with pure hatred and fear. It left her so uneasy that she barely heard the conversation. The old lady and Colt moved on down the aisle, but Bosworth caught Sam's hand. "I'd like to show you my office, Miss MacGregor."

"But the others—"

"They'll rejoin us." He took Sam's elbow and led her into his office. By contrast to the place the girls worked, this was elegant, with fine furniture and Oriental rugs. He reached out and closed the doors and immediately, it was quiet inside.

"We ought to join the others," Sam said.

"I thought you might like to see my typewriter." He nodded toward the machine on the desk.

"I've seen one once," she said. "Very handy."

He moved closer, took her hand. "You must know how attracted I am to you."

"Mr. Shaw, I am not one of your poor factory girls." Her voice was icy as she tried to step away from him, but his desk was right behind her.

"I know that." He caught both her hands in his and looked down into her eyes earnestly. "You're a lady, Miss MacGregor, and you'd make a fine wife for the heir to the Shaw fortune."

Colt? "I—I am astounded at your forwardness, sir."

"I'll make this quick, dear Samantha." He brought her hands to his lips and kissed them. "You surely know this savage will never inherit my aunt's money, but I've seen to it that I'm more than amply paid."

"As stingy as Mrs. Shaw is?"

"I won't tell her you said that." Bosworth winked at her. "There are ways in accounting for an ambitious man to feather his nest a little. Later, we could share her fortune and her fine house together." He started to take her in his arms and she resisted.

About that time, the office door flew open and Colt stood there, his eyes intense as a gathering storm.

Taken aback, Bosworth stepped away from Sam. "Oh, hello, cousin, we were just about to rejoin you."

Sam took this opportunity to escape. "Colt, I'll see you outside."

Cincala didn't like the man, but he only watched as Bosworth walked over and closed the door.

"Cousin, I've been hoping we'd have a chance to talk."

Colt watched him as he would watch a rattlesnake. "Talk? What do we have to talk about?"

The other man gave him a charming smile. "You misjudge me, Colt. I'm on your side. I know how unhappy you've been in Boston and I want to help you."

His sixth sense told him not to trust this man. "Help me? How?"

Bosworth grinned as he went to his desk. "Gossip tells me you tried to return to your people and didn't make it."

"I had no money for the ticket," Cincala said. "People keep telling me I'm rich, but I have no money."

Bosworth smiled disarmingly. "That's to keep you from leaving, don't you see?"

Abruptly it was crystal clear to Cincala and he nodded. "I am stupid not to see this."

"But I am your friend and I want you to be happy." Bosworth went to his desk, opened a drawer. "Here is five hundred dollars. Don't tell my aunt I gave it to you."

Cincala shook his head. "I cannot take your money."

"Oh, but don't you see?" Bosworth pressed the money into Cincala's hand. "This is really your money, earned by your grandmother's factories. Enjoy it."

About that time, there was a knock at the door.

"Bosworth," Mrs. Shaw called, "is Colt in there?"

Hastily, Cincala put the money in his pocket as Bosworth hurried to the door. "I was just showing him my office, Auntie. Come in."

The old woman entered, shaking her head. "Goodness, Bosworth, I don't know how you bear the noise of this place. Did we do well this past month?"

"Certainly, Auntie. I hired a very special accountant."

"Good. I'm hoping Colt will take an interest."

Bosworth gave him a knowing look. "Oh, he's interested, all right. We're becoming good friends."

"Wonderful. I was afraid you'd resent him, Bosworth."

"Me?" The older man looked hurt. "Why, I plan to help him in any way I can, right, Colt?"

Cincala nodded, feeling the dollars folded in his pocket. "Bosworth is good friend. We go now, Grandmother?"

She nodded and Bosworth accompanied them out to join Sam at the carriage.

As they pulled away, Cincala leaned back against the seat with a satisfied smile. Evidently he had misjudged Bosworth Shaw. Now that Cincala had money, he only had to await the right time to escape. However, as he watched the fiery-haired girl across from him, he knew he could not leave without her. No, she wouldn't want to live the harsh life of the Lakota. He'd have to leave her behind.

Twenty

Most of the week passed uneventfully as the pair continued their lessons. However, as they lunched alone in the dining room, Sam said, "It's warm for March. Maybe this afternoon I'll teach you to play croquet."

He looked at her blankly.

Sam wiped her mouth with her napkin. "It's a game girls can play in tight corsets and long skirts. It's a socially correct way to meet the best young ladies."

He scowled and laid down his fork. "No. Sounds like a dull and stupid game."

"I'm not too crazy about it myself, but there's only a certain number of young ladies in this city your grandmother will approve of and most of them will play croquet or maybe lawn tennis."

He looked at her and his voice was stubborn. "My grandmother will not choose my woman for me."

"Well, she'll help and it will be one who is suitable."

"What is this word 'suitable'?"

Sam stood up. "One who is as rich as you are and owns as many factories."

"Will she be pretty?"

"Maybe, maybe not." Sam shrugged. "That doesn't matter in a white society marriage."

"It matters to me."

"This is no longer open for discussion," Sam said. "We will learn to play croquet."

Sam sent a maid running for their coats and led him out the back door to the big walled garden where the stakes and wire brackets had been set up. She retrieved the mallets and balls from the carriage house. "Now, here is what you do. You must knock the wooden ball through the wire hoop and against that wooden stake—then someone else takes a turn."

"It looks dull," he complained.

Sam sighed. "You are trying my patience. It may be dull, but it's a game genteel young ladies can play."

"Do you like to play?" he asked and took a mallet.

"Well, I'm not crazy about it," Sam admitted, "but that's not the point. Now you take your mallet and hit the wooden ball, through the wire hoop."

Colt shrugged, positioned himself behind the ball and took a mighty swing.

"No! No!" Sam screamed, but it was already too late. The wooden ball went flying through the air and crashed through a carriage house window.

Colt grinned. "Do I win?"

She pursed her lips to control her temper. "I think maybe you don't get the idea. The ball needs to stay on the ground. You must hit it gently."

Colt shook his head in puzzlement and hit another ball. It went over the garden wall.

Sam sighed and leaned on her mallet. "No young lady will want to play with you if you don't go by the rules."

"Good."

So he was going to be stubborn. "Let's try something else." She gathered up the mallets and balls and laid them to one side. "Let us work on fine manners and what young ladies expect."

His face clouded. "No."

Sam could be as stubborn as he was. "This is something

you must learn. Now pretend you have just danced with a young lady."

His face lit up. "Waltz?"

She remembered how close he had held her—too close. "Not today. Now pretend you have just finished waltzing and the young lady says how hot it is and fans herself."

"Yes?"

"Well, that is your cue to ask her if she'd like some lemonade. Then she'll smile prettily, fan herself, and say yes, so you go get her some."

"Respectable young ladies expect men to wait on them?"

"Only 'til they're married," Sam said, "then the man gets all the privileges."

Colt scratched his head. "Very strange."

"I agree. Now you might ask her if she'd like to see the garden."

He looked around at the carefully manicured lawns and the flower beds that were not yet in bloom. "Has she not ever seen a garden before?"

"Silly, it's an excuse for the two of you to go out in the dark and walk around like this while making light conversation." Sam took his arm and nudged him into a walk. She tried not to think how strong and muscular that arm was. "Now you walk about the garden and talk of fashion and what social events are coming up."

"Sounds very dull," he grumbled.

"It's the way it's done," Sam insisted. "Then up ahead, you steer her toward a bench or a swing like that one there in the bushes and if she doesn't suggest it, you might ask if she'd like to sit a minute."

He made an exasperated sound as they walked. "If she's as stupid as she sounds, why would I want to talk with her further?"

"Slow down," Sam commanded, "you're dragging me. Remember, a lady takes small steps. Now we reach the swing." She turned and looked up at him, batting her eyes.

"Why, I swear, Mr. Shaw, it's such a long walk and I'm quite out of breath." She made a motion of fanning herself with an imaginary fan. "Now it's your turn."

He scowled and blinked.

Sam took off her coat with a sigh. "Colt, please try."

"Okay. Why, ma'am, would you like to sit in this swing a moment?"

Sam giggled. "Why, I just believe I might." She threw her coat over the back of the big wooden swing and sat down, patting the white seat. "Do join me, sir."

Colt plopped down in the swing so hard, it shook and the chains creaked.

"No, not that way—you'll bring the swing down. Now without me realizing it, you take my hand."

For the first time, the gray eyes looked interested. "How can you not know when I take your hand?"

"I'm only pretending I haven't noticed." Oh, she had noticed, all right. He was sitting awfully close and she was painfully aware of his nearness. "Now you carry on more polite conversation and flirt a little and maybe kiss her fingertips. Then you head back into the dance."

"That's all?" He was looking down at her—awfully close, too close.

"Well, if you're engaged, you're allowed to kiss her."

"What's engaged?"

"If you're going to marry her."

"I can't kiss her unless I marry her?"

Sam looked away. "Well, of course men do, but they're not gentlemen."

"Then it's good I'm not a gentleman," Colt said and before she was aware of his intentions, he took her in his arms and kissed her.

He had taken Sam by surprise and for a long moment, she could only sit there in the creaking swing, his big hands on her shoulders as he pulled her hard against him as his mouth devoured hers, forcing his tongue between her lips.

She knew she should slap him or murmur in protest or at least pull away, but for a long moment, all she could do was surrender and let him ravage her mouth with his own.

When she did manage to free her lips, she was breathless. "No, no, not like that. It must be a small kiss, a respectable kiss."

"To hell with that," he declared and he kissed her again, his big arms going around her to enfold her and hold her tightly. She had never been kissed like this before and she was giddy and breathless with the feeling even as his hand slipped inside her bodice to caress her breast. She moaned low in her throat, unwilling or unable to draw upon her willpower to stop this moment of passion.

Then his hand went to her skirt and up under it. She was keenly aware of the heat of his fingers on her knee but still she couldn't pull away even though that hand was caressing her thigh. "Please." She managed to free her mouth enough to protest and then his fingers reached her most private place and stroked there. A shudder of pleasure swept over her. "Please . . ." she murmured and she wasn't certain herself whether she was protesting or begging.

There was no telling what might have happened if the voice of the old butler hadn't cut through her consciousness. "Master Shaw? Miss MacGregor?" he called from the lawn. "Are you out here?"

Colt swore and Sam pulled away from him with a shuddering breath, quickly rearranging her clothing. She stood up and called across the bushes, "Yes, Williams, we were— we were just looking at the garden."

"Mrs. Shaw wants you both to join her for dinner," the butler called.

Colt didn't let go of her hand. "Food is not what I want," he grumbled.

Sam tried to disengage her hand. "This was highly improper for a governess. I'll not forget my place again."

He didn't let go of her hand but looked up at her with

gray eyes alight with passion. "I'm a rich man," he said, "and that means I can have any woman I want. I intend to have you, Missy."

"How dare you!" She slapped him hard, broke away from him, and, blinded with tears, ran toward the house.

Cincala stared after her a long moment before he shrugged and went inside to dress for dinner. Sam had built a fire in him that could only be put out one way. She had built the fire, but he knew how to put it out. He resolved to take her virginity before he left Boston.

At dinner, the old woman asked, "Where is Miss MacGregor?"

Cincala looked down the long table all lit with candles. "I believe she said she had a headache."

"Good. I really don't like her anyway; too uppity for hired help."

Cincala started to say something, then decided against it. He tried to remember everything Sam had taught him. The old woman must have been pleased because she actually smiled at him. "Colt, I believe you are doing well enough that I could go ahead and discharge that governess."

"Not yet." Cincala gave her his most endearing smile. "I still have need of her."

"Very well then." Mrs. Shaw put down her napkin. "I'll keep her until after the spring ball. Speaking of which, we're getting lots of replies. It seems our ball is the hit of the social season."

Cincala stifled a yawn. The ball interested him not at all. "That's nice."

"Do you know how to play cards? I thought we'd play this evening."

"Tonight?" His mind went to what he had planned for tonight: Sam under him, her fiery hair spread out on the white pillow as he taught her about passion. "I'm really rather tired."

"Nonsense. I insist."

There was no getting around it. Cincala went to pull back the old lady's chair and they adjourned to the game table in front of the library fire. He let her win and was amused by the triumphant look in her eyes. There was no softness in the old woman; besides that, she cheated.

Sam passed an uneasy night. First she lay staring at the ceiling, thinking that Colt was just down the hall. If either one of them was to go to the other's room . . . What was she thinking? She rolled over, reminding herself that she was only an employee in this household and it was her task to get Colt ready to take over the Shaw empire and marry a proper young lady of equal wealth and social standing. Sam didn't want to be one of those unfortunate governesses who became a minor dalliance for the young master as was all too common. If she had any other possible employment, she would leave this household at once, but without proper references from Mrs. Shaw, she would again be homeless and hungry.

All right, she promised herself, as soon as she had her charge properly launched so that the old lady would give Sam references, she would look for a new job, preferably one far, far from here—and Colt Shaw. Her dreams were as uneasy as her thoughts and over and over in her mind, he kissed her and took her in his arms.

Sam rose early and breakfasted alone so that she would not have to sit with Colt.

After yesterday in the garden swing, it would be very, very awkward for her. As she was sipping a third cup of tea, the old butler stuck his head in the door. "Mrs. Shaw requests you join her and her grandson for breakfast, miss."

"Mrs. Shaw isn't having breakfast in her room?"

The butler gave Sam a conspiratorial nod. "Surprised us all, too. Perhaps the young master is having a good effect."

He affects everyone, Sam thought, but didn't say so. She nodded and rose. She would have had to face Colt later today anyway, so she might as well get it over with. In the large dining room, she found Mrs. Shaw and Colt sitting at opposite ends of the long, ornate walnut table. "Ah, Samantha," Mrs. Shaw actually smiled and Colt stood up gracefully.

"Good morning, Miss MacGregor." He came around to pull out a chair on one side of the table for her.

"Good morning all." Sam didn't look at him as she took her chair. At least he was remembering some of the things she had taught him.

The butler poured Sam a cup of coffee as Mrs. Shaw peered at Sam over her gold-rimmed spectacles. "My grandson and I were just discussing guests for the ball. I've gone through my social register and come up with the names of at least twenty prominent young ladies we must add."

"Yes, of course." Sam sipped her coffee and stared at the flowers in the middle of the table. Now that the time was fast approaching, she didn't like the feeling in the pit of her stomach about Colt meeting a bunch of pretty young women to choose a prize brood mare for future Shaw off-spring.

Colt said, "Sam must come, too."

There was an awkward silence. Certainly the snooty old woman would no more invite a governess to her ball than she would a chambermaid.

Sam cleared her throat, tried to smile, and looked at Mrs. Shaw's stony face. "I'm afraid he does not yet understand about the layers of society."

"Apparently not," Mrs. Shaw said coldly.

Colt scowled. "If Sam doesn't come, I won't come."

Another uneasy silence and Sam turned and glared at him. Couldn't he see he was creating an awkward, embarrassing situation for her? "Colt, you see, it's not proper—"

"I don't give a damn," he said and put his coffee cup down so hard, it rattled in its saucer. "Sam comes to the party or I don't."

Sam looked at Mrs. Shaw helplessly, feeling her face flush.

"Very well," Mrs. Shaw snapped. "Perhaps he doesn't yet feel comfortable in polite society without you nearby to tell him which fork to use. You may attend, Miss MacGregor. I'm sure Nellie could use some help at the refreshment table."

"Oh, in that case, as an employee, of course I'll be glad to help out," Sam said.

Colt grinned.

That afternoon, they worked on arithmetic and geography. Sam felt very awkward. Every time she looked up, Colt was staring at her. "Could we practice waltzing again?"

"Not right now." She didn't want to end up in his arms and was uncertain whether she didn't trust him . . . or herself.

Colt frowned and shifted his big frame in the chair. "About the ball—I think I might not like the girl my grandmother might choose."

Sam shrugged. "She's bound to be very pretty and very rich—you can't do any better than that. Let's work on our arithmetic."

"So I can keep up with all my money my factories are making?" he frowned.

"Of course. That way, no one can cheat you."

He chewed his lip thoughtfully. "Yet Shaw Industries is cheating the Indians."

Sam didn't answer for a long moment. She suspected from the hints Bosworth had dropped that he might also be keeping false accounts, cheating the old lady who was probably naive when it came to business. Of course, without proof, Sam could not voice her suspicions. "Let us keep our minds on our schoolwork," she snapped, but it was difficult for her to do and every time she glanced up, Colt was staring at her with those storm-gray eyes.

That night, Sam bathed and brushed her hair a long time, her mind on her student. Yes, he was smart. It wouldn't be long before she smoothed off his rough edges. Once they got his hair cut, it would be impossible to tell Colt from any of the other young blades about town . . . except that he was dark, taller, and more handsome. After the ball, every eligible beauty in town would be after him. Sam couldn't bear to see that. No, immediately after the ball, she would look elsewhere for a position, although she would miss this big house and all the servants.

The house was very quiet as she went to bed, a full moon streaming through the window. The weather had been unusually mild and that boded well for the April ball. Sam had heard gossip in the kitchen that servants at other fine homes around town were telling about their young mistresses' delight or despair over invitations or lack of. The best dressmakers were backed up with orders for fine ball gowns for the biggest society event of this spring.

A noise awakened her and she blinked. Was that Colt standing silhouetted in her doorway? *Of course not, silly,* she scolded herself, *you're only wishing and dreaming.* And then the vision moved.

He closed the door, came over to her bed, and stood looking down at her. Only then did she realize he was wear-

ing only the bottoms of pajamas. She knew she should protest and scold him, or even scream. The sound stuck in her
throat.

He sat down on the edge of her bed. "Sam?"

She rose up on one elbow. "What are you doing in here?"
she demanded in a whisper. "If your grandmother finds
out—"

"You said as the master, I could have any of the girls I
wanted in my bed. I've decided I want you." He pulled her
to him and kissed her.

Of all the nerve. She pulled away from his hot, seeking
mouth, breathless and indignant. "I didn't mean—"

He kissed her again and lay down beside her, pulling the
cover back. Sam seemed unable to move as the kiss deepened, his lips gently pressuring hers to open to the caress
of his tongue, his free hand stroking up and down her slender body under her sheer nightdress.

Her heart pounded so hard, she was certain he could feel
it. She knew she should pull away from him and tell him
no. If she did so, would he stop what he was doing? Did
she want him to stop? Then he kissed her again and all she
could do was sigh in surrender and return his ardor with a
passion that matched his own. All these long weeks she had
wanted him and had fought that hunger, knowing he could
never be hers, knowing that she was grooming him for a
society in which she would never be welcome. His hand
covered her breast and caressed there and at that moment,
she lost all sense of reason as his fingers slid the sheer
nightdress down her shoulder and he bent his lips to her
breast. For just an instance in the moonlight, she saw his
dark profile above her breast, felt the heat of his breath on
her nipple and then his hot tongue licked around the areola
and his lips fastened on her nipple and she trembled.

"Tell me," he whispered, "tell me you have wanted this
as much as I have."

"You know I have. God help me for being such a fool,

but you know I have." And she forgot she had meant to resist him.

His lips brushed across her face in surprisingly gentle kisses then down her throat and between her breasts. Feverishly, she ran her hands up and down his hard-muscled arms, knowing she should stop him and send him back to his room, yet knowing, too, that she was powerless to deny him anything. She who had been the teacher was now the pupil as she clung to him.

He took her hand and placed it on his hard, throbbing manhood. "Tonight you will be mine."

He was built so big, she was shocked at the size of him. Mating with this primitive stallion would be an experience she would never forget. She hesitated and he must have felt it, because he whispered against her ear, "You can still send me away."

She knew that in the long run, she could not have him. Some society girl would share his bed soon and bear his children. All Samantha could hope for was this one stolen night and she knew as his hand stroked her thigh that this one night would be worth all the empty, lonely nights that lay in her future. "I love you," she whispered, "and tonight I regret nothing."

His hand stroked up her thigh as he kissed her deeply, lingeringly. She pulled him closer still. She could feel the power of his small hips, smell the scent of his raw maleness, and it excited all her senses. "Please," she begged, and was not even sure what she yearned for even as his fingers touched and stroked her most private place.

"My pretty teacher," he murmured as he pushed her night dress up and moved to lie between her thighs. "Tonight I will teach you."

It was still not too late to stop him, Sam thought. It was still not too late to save her virginity, rather than throw it away like some upstairs maid who'd become a plaything for the master of the house. Yet even knowing this, she only held him closer. "Teach me," she answered, "because I know so little."

In the moonlight, his gray eyes seemed as intense as any wild thing. She knew that this was hopeless; he could never be hers—Mrs. Shaw would see to that. And yet, she cared so much for him that she would take whatever time he might give her. He rose up on his knees between her thighs, one of his big hands on each side of her head. "You want this?"

"Yes, you know I do!" She reached to pull him down on her. He was so big, he hesitated against the portals of her velvet sheath, then slowly slid into her even as his mouth covered hers again. He was too big for her—she knew that as he began to enter her—yet she dug her nails into his lean hips and pulled him down. She must have him at least once and after that, she would live on the memories of this one glorious coupling. He came down on her hard, going deeply into her and her moan was muffled by his mouth covering hers.

He paused, breathing hard, and kissed her face. "I do not mean to hurt you," he gasped.

"Take me," she commanded, writhing under him, "take me! I've always wanted this as have you!"

He began to ride her hard then and she moved in perfect rhythm with him, overwhelmed by the feeling of his body locked in hers. The bed creaked with their thrashing and wild mating, but nothing mattered except that they finish this, satisfy this wild longing in both their souls. She did not think she could bear this increasing passion, but it went on and on. Then he paused and stiffened as she, too, reached the peak of sensation and she could feel him pouring his seed and his hot desire into her slender body. Was it only a moment or an eternity that they lay locked together, lost in ripples of sensation like ocean waves crashing against the shore?

Finally she sighed and he relaxed and collapsed on her

body and began to kiss her face. "I've been wanting to do this since the first moment I saw you, Sam."

She came to her senses with sudden horror. What had she done? She tried to wiggle out from under him. "Colt, I shouldn't have. This—this was as much my fault as yours."

He rose up on his elbows and brushed a red curl from her forehead. "Why not? Didn't you say the master of the house could have any servant he wanted?"

And that was all she was to him, she thought with sudden clarity, no more than a chambermaid he'd caught in an empty room to sate his lust.

"Get out of my room!" She began to beat on him with her small fists and he caught her hands in his big ones.

"You're angry?" He sounded puzzled. "But you've wanted this as much as I did. I've known that a long time—"

"Was I so stupidly transparent then?" She was crying now as he moved enough so she could push him away.

He stood up naked, looking puzzled and magnificent in the moonlight. "I don't understand—"

"Get out of my room," she ordered, "get out right now!"

He picked up his pajamas, turned and went to the door, then stood looking at her. "I want you again," he said simply.

"Well, you won't have me!" She almost screamed it at him. "It can't become more than a sleazy thing between classes and I won't settle for that."

He started to speak, but she threw a pillow at him, although she was furious at herself for surrendering to him. He shrugged and left and Sam hopped out of bed, running to put a chair under the knob, although she was certain from the look on his face that he would not be coming back. Whether it was that fact or the thought that she had just thrown away her virginity on a man she could never have, Sam didn't know or care as she threw herself across her bed and sobbed.

Everything in her told her to collect her things and leave before dawn, but she had no place to go and no references. Besides, Mrs. Shaw would want an explanation and Sam was not a good liar. She was expected to stay in this house until after the ball. All right, she would do that, but as soon as the ball was over, Sam would collect her pay and her reference and disappear out of Colt Shaw's life forever. She admitted to herself at this moment just how much she loved the half-breed savage, and it could only mean a broken heart for her. Sam buried her face in her pillow that seemed to still carry the masculine scent of him and cried most of the night.

Twenty-one

Sam could hardly bear to look at Colt the next morning, but she had no choice as she was summoned by Mrs. Shaw to join that pair for breakfast in the large dining room.

The old woman was wearing a mauve dress. That was so different from her usual black mourning that Sam could only pause and gape.

"Stop staring at me like a dolt," Mrs. Shaw commanded, "and sit down."

Colt came around the table to pull Sam's chair out and as she sat down, his fingers brushed her shoulders, but Sam ignored him. "I'm sorry, but the dress—"

"I have decided I have mourned too long," the dowager wheezed, "and mourning is not proper attire for a ball."

That was true. Sam looked at her plate so she would not have to look at Colt seated across from her.

Mrs. Shaw regarded her with disapproval. "My employees generally do not lie abed so late unless they are dying."

Which I'm sure you do not allow on your time, Sam thought, but she only said, "I—I did not sleep well."

"Dreams?" Colt said and when she glanced up, he was smiling. Was he mocking her?

Mrs. Shaw sipped her coffee. "Your eyes are all swollen. Are you coming down sick?"

"It might be a cold coming on," Sam said lamely and

picked at the plate of waffles and ham the butler placed deftly before her.

Elizabeth Shaw drew back in horror. "I hope it's not anything catching."

"I doubt it," Sam said and tried to eat.

Mrs. Shaw signaled for the old butler to serve her more strawberry muffins and butter. She regarded her grandson with affection. "Colt seems to be learning a lot, Miss MacGregor. You are to be congratulated."

Colt looked at Sam over the rim of his cup. "Perhaps I've taught Miss MacGregor a few things, too."

Damn him. Sam felt the blood creep up her face, but the old lady was intent on the pile of mail Williams had just brought to her on a silver tray. "We've been getting dozens of acceptances for the ball." She smiled as she began to open them with a silver letter opener. "I daresay it's going to be the party of the season."

Sam glared at Colt, who winked at her. "I'm sure, Mrs. Shaw, that all the young ladies can hardly wait to meet your grandson and vise versa."

"How true." The old woman nodded agreement. "He has the Shaw charm and is better-looking than his father. Couple that with the Shaw fortune, and he'll be the most eligible bachelor in Boston."

"I'm sure." Sam nibbled at her fruit cup and tried not to look at him, tried not to remember the torrid moments last night in his arms.

Colt looked from one to the other. "On the contrary, Grandmother, I'm still a bit unpolished in many ways. I was hoping Miss MacGregor could continue tutoring me."

If he thought she would stay around to pleasure him while he chose his elegant wife—

"Nonsense, Colt." Mrs. Shaw paused in looking at her mail. "You will soon marry and your new wife will have all the polish of the upper class. You will cut your hair and give her the priceless ring you insist on wearing around your neck and she will teach you the rest of the social graces."

Colt shook his head.

"All right." The old woman seemed to realize she'd moved onto shaky ground. "Maybe someday, when you accept your role as a Shaw and find the right girl, you'll change your mind."

Sam took in a deep breath of relief. Maybe she would be gone before another girl wore that treasured ring and Sam's heart was broken even more.

"Well," said Colt, rubbing his hands together with enthusiasm, "I can hardly wait for today's lessons."

Sam gritted her teeth, wondering if she could plead a sick headache.

The old lady nodded with approval. "Good. What will you work on today?"

Colt looked at Sam. "I thought we might practice dancing—I could be much better than I am for the ball."

Damned if she was going to end up in his arms so he could nuzzle her neck and send uncontrollable thrills up and down her back. "On the contrary, Mr. Shaw is already an excellent dancer." Ignoring Colt, she spoke to his grandmother, "I thought perhaps geometry or French."

Colt groaned aloud.

"Whatever you choose," Mrs. Shaw said, shrugging her tiny shoulders. "The maids are taking down all the draperies and cleaning the windows, and the decorators will be here this afternoon." She looked around critically. "It's about time I spruced the place up. I have to check on the orchestra and the extra champagne." She started to get up and Colt rose and went over to pull her chair out for her. The old lady smiled up at him. "You're going to be a Shaw after all—and quite a credit to me."

"But of course, Grandmother." He grinned.

Mrs. Shaw wheezed out of the room and Colt went to the sideboard to pour himself another cup of coffee.

Sam was alone with him and she didn't want to be, not after last night. "Well, that was quite a show."

"I'm sure I don't know what you mean." He sat back down across from Sam, grinning at her.

His grin set her teeth on edge. "This morning, we will study French."

He cocked his head at her. "You're angry with me."

"I think I have a right to be." She tried to keep her voice low so no one passing in the hall might hear, but she couldn't keep her tone neutral.

"I couldn't help myself. I don't think you could either. We both knew it had been building toward that since the first moment we met."

"I did not," she lied, staring at her plate. "I'm here in a professional capacity."

He shrugged. "If I had not pretended to be completely stupid and uncivilized, my grandmother would not have kept you more than a week or two."

"Pretended? Pretended?" Her voice rose.

"Oh, you are indeed a cad, sir!" Hurriedly, she tried to get up out of her chair and caught a skirt hem on its leg. As she fell, Colt was there, sweeping her up in his arms.

"If I may be of assistance."

She looked up at him helplessly as she struggled to right herself and stand alone. "Damn you, unhand me!"

"Tsk—tsk! Profanity from a gently bred governess." He yanked her to her feet and stepped back with reluctance.

"You would cause any woman to swear. I am going to my room. If Mrs. Shaw asks, tell her I've decided I do have a cold and may keep to my room all week." Sam stuck her nose in the air and sailed out of the dining room.

"Grandmother won't like that," he called after her. No answer. Glumly, he stared at the empty doorway. "And neither will I," he whispered. Without her, the dining room seemed lonely and empty. What difference did it make? He was leaving soon anyway. Sam had taught him enough that

he figured now he could get on a train and travel back to
the Dakotas without any trouble and Bosworth had provided
him with money which was now safely hidden in his room.
Cincala looked out at the windswept day that promised
spring was coming. He liked the prairie in the spring with
the new colts and the wild plum bushes in bloom. There
were two things that marred his outlook: his parents were
dead and somehow buried in this strange place, and he
would be leaving Sam behind. He couldn't tell her that, of
course; she might try to stop him. It was her job. It was
obviously out of the question to take her with him. He felt
more than sad as he went into the library to read.

Sam kept to her room all day and had her supper sent
up. She tried to read, but all she could think of was how
much she cared about Colt Shaw and how it had felt to be
in his arms. Nevertheless, that night, she carefully put a
chair under her doorknob, uncertain whether she would be
relieved or disappointed if he didn't try to come to her at
night.

It was very late but she was still awake when she heard
the knob turn and his whisper. "Sam?"

"Go away," she answered.

She was not sure what she expected or even what she
wanted to happen. She watched the door, half hoping, half
dreading that he would slam against it until he battered it
down, gather her up in his arms, and not take no for an
answer. Sam rose on one elbow, staring at the door. It was
all she could do to keep from getting out of bed and running
to open it and let him in. Was she willing to settle for the
crumbs of love from the rich man's table? It took all her
pride and control not to answer his whispered entreaties.

After a long moment, she heard footsteps walking away.

Sam managed to keep to her room for several days until
Mrs. Shaw was threatening to call the doctor to make sure

she had nothing contagious. At that point, Sam made a miraculous recovery and appeared at breakfast. Colt was quite cool to her and treated her in a businesslike manner while flirting shamelessly with the tall, pretty maid, Nellie. Nellie seemed quite pleased, though surprised, and it was evident the young master could sneak into her bed anytime he wanted to.

Well, that suited her just fine, Sam thought defiantly as she announced today's subject would be geography and headed for the library. Colt was all business, too, studying the books she handed him. Their fingers touched when she handed him a book and she hoped he did not notice how hers trembled.

A week passed and if Mrs. Shaw noticed the coolness between the two, she did not comment. Indeed, she was so busy with the details of the ball that she hardly had time for anything else. Bosworth Shaw called on Sam once, but she pleaded a headache and fled to her room.

She was a fool, Sam scolded herself. As clever and unscrupulous as Bosworth seemed to be, he might indeed end up with the Shaw fortune. As his wife, Sam could have a life of ease while poor Colt was shipped unceremoniously back to the West. Well, that was what the half-breed wanted, wasn't it? Anyway, Mrs. Shaw would never allow her heir to marry a lowly governess and Sam knew it.

Finally it was the night of the ball. Sam dreaded the event, but on Colt's insistence, Mrs. Shaw had ordered her to attend. She bathed and put on her worn pale blue silk, the only nice gown she owned, and the small cameo her mother had given her. She put her dark red hair up with satin ribbons and dabbed on a bit of delicate lavender fragrance. Then she pinched her cheeks to make them glow. Why was she going to all this trouble? Mrs. Shaw did not expect her to mingle with the guests; Sam was to help Nellie with the refreshments. If she could just do that and avoid Colt tonight, she would be fine, Sam decided.

Instead, she ran into him out in the hall as she started down the stairs. He looked so handsome, she gasped with surprise. He still wore his hair in braids, of course, but that was hardly noticeable with his fine, tailor-made, black broadcloth coat and scarlet silk cravat. The expensive leather boots shone on his feet. "Well, Miss MacGregor, you look absolutely stunning tonight."

She felt herself blush.

"Am I presentable?" he asked.

"Every inch a polished gentleman," she said.

He winked at her. "Well, maybe not such a gentleman in some company. Will you save me a dance?"

She started down the stairs. "It isn't really fitting. I expect I'll be helping out in any way I can along with the servants. Besides, your grandmother no doubt already has a hundred young ladies lined up for your inspection."

"No doubt," he laughed and caught up with her, taking her arm. "This is your first ball?"

"Yes," she admitted, lifting the hem of her skirt with her free hand. "This will also probably be my last, but I expect your social calendar is going to be very crowded."

"Will whites welcome a savage into their homes?"

"Mr. Shaw, you are no longer a savage—you are a very rich and handsome man, heir to one of the biggest fortunes in this state. Believe me, young women will be fighting each other to get your name on their dance cards."

He sighed as they descended the stairs. "Tell me again what that is."

"Each young lady will be wearing a dainty card and pencil on her wrist or in her purse. The most beautiful have so many young men standing in line to reserve dances, they can't possibly dance with them all."

"Sounds stupid," he grumbled.

"A lot of things in our civilization may be stupid and boring, but they are part of polite society," Sam said as they reached the bottom of the stairs.

Mrs. Shaw, resplendent in ivory satin, swept down upon them, all adither. "Oh, there you are! Colt, I want you to stand with me and greet our guests. So many eligible young ladies are dying to meet you." She scowled at Sam. "And you can go help Nellie arrange the silver."

Colt frowned. "I thought Sam would stand by us."

"Don't be silly," his grandmother snapped, "she's an employee, not much more than a maid. Why, we'd be the laughingstock of all Boston if we let her do that."

Sam saw that Colt was about to protest again. "Your grandmother is right," she put in quickly. "I'll do just fine helping Nellie." She turned and fled to the end of the big ballroom to one side of the entry. Here she could help arrange the silver punch bowl while watching Colt and his grandmother greet the arriving guests.

The orchestra at one end of the ballroom struck up a soft waltz and outside, the sound of arriving carriages came through the open windows.

"Law," exclaimed Nellie, bustling about, "it must be nice to be a fancy lady arriving for this ball and a chance to meet the young master."

"I'm sure it is," Sam said and tried not to watch Colt bowing low over a pretty blonde's hand as they were introduced. "But we'll never know what it's like to be a princess, even for one night."

Nellie turned and watched the next batch of tittering young ladies. "And just think," she said with a sigh, "someday soon, one of them will get to live in this fine house as mistress 'cause the old lady won't live forever and better than that, she'll get to sleep with the young master. I'll bet he's a good one in the covers."

Sam felt her face flame at the memory of his embrace. "You're quite out of line, Nellie," she scolded. "It's not for us to discuss the habits of our betters."

"I suppose not. I'll get the small cakes and the strawberries," Nellie said and headed for the kitchen.

Sam was left standing there, trying to look busy, while staying discreetly in the background. The position of governess in any wealthy household was a bit awkward. A governess wasn't on the low scale of a servant, and yet she wasn't on the social scale of the wealthy family's guests. From here, she could see Colt again bending low over the hand of a simpering young beauty wearing a fortune in pearls and imported pink silk. Sam gritted her teeth and fussed with the silver punch cups. There were going to be dozens of them tonight, hadn't she known that? Virginal, rich young beauties and Colt Shaw had the lineage to pick and choose among them. His wealth and background gave him that right. Hadn't she always known she could never have him?

"Hello, Miss MacGregor." Bosworth walked over, caught her hand, and kissed it. She tried to pull away, but he held on. "Ah, that song's one of my favorites. Would you do me the honor?"

"I'm really busy here—"

"Nonsense." He swept her into his arms, holding her a little too close, his face against her hair as they danced. "Mmm, you smell wonderful."

"Bosworth, don't. What will your aunt think?"

He laughed. "She'll think I'm smitten with you which I am. I'll still be around, you know, when the savage goes back where he came from."

The song ended and she managed to pull out of Bosworth's arms. "Colt can't go—she's seen to it that he has no cash."

Bosworth gave her a sly grin. "Oh, he has money, all right. Trust me on that."

How would Bosworth know that? Maybe he was just hoping aloud. "Thank you for asking me to dance, Mr. Shaw," she said in her coldest, most frosty tone. "Now I must get back to the refreshment table."

She returned to her post and stood there listening to the

music; the memory of that one night in his arms returned and she closed her eyes and remembered.

"Dozing off, Miss MacGregor?"

Sam started at the sound of Colt's voice. He stood at the refreshment table, towering over her.

"No, of course not."

"I do hope you'll save me a dance."

"Don't be silly. It would cause gossip to dance with a lowly governess, especially with all these silly young girls almost panting to dance with you." She pretended to be very busy, hoping yet dreading that he would walk away.

"You danced with Bosworth." His rugged face grew serious. "All those other girls really are pretty silly. I suppose I was beginning to think all of them were like you."

"Meaning what?" She looked up at him.

He shrugged. "Oh, I don't know. Intelligent, interesting conversation."

Sam looked away. "You'll find neither is essential in picking out a filly to produce your heir. Beauty, wealth, and fine bloodlines will be what your grandmother's looking for."

He grinned. "Don't I have anything to say about this?"

"Knowing your grandmother, I doubt it."

"Knowing me, could you really think I can't stand up to one old lady?"

Before Sam could answer, Elizabeth Shaw sailed across the floor, her face grim. "Colt, whatever are you doing? There are dozens of young ladies with your name written on their dance cards and you mustn't be rude." She grabbed his arm and led him away.

At that moment, two young beauties came over to the refreshment table and asked for champagne punch, both looking back over their shoulders at Colt's broad back.

"They say he's a real savage," whispered one.

The other giggled. "What do you suppose it would be like—well, you know?"

Both of them snickered and looked after him with sighs of longing.

Sam resisted the urge to splash champagne on both their elegant gowns as she dipped the punch. They ignored her as if she were part of the furniture.

Sam stood discreetly in the background as the music played and dozens of Boston's finest families gathered in little groups to gossip and dance. Colt stood head and shoulders over almost every man in the house and every woman seemed to watch him wistfully as he asked each lady to dance. The young girls were positively giddy over him, Sam thought, and she wondered if it was because he was a rich and handsome aristocrat or because of his legendary history of being a savage.

Mrs. Shaw came over to stand beside Sam. "Well, it's a more successful party than I imagined."

Sam agreed that it was a very nice party.

"My grandson is fulfilling all the hopes and dreams I had for my sons, but those ungrateful whelps would never do as I told them."

"I'm not sure Colt will be as easy to manage as you imagine," Sam said without thinking.

"Nonsense! He'll do exactly as he's told, marry the bride I choose for him, and take his rightful place heading up the Shaw empire."

Sam bit her lip to hold back her words. No one would be able to control Colt Shaw. He was dangerous and unpredictable, which made him fascinating.

Mrs. Shaw surveyed the crowd. "Hmm. There's the Calvin girl with the banking money, but that little blonde, that Foss girl, is heir to a bunch of shoe factories."

"Perhaps," Sam tried again, "you might consider letting Colt choose his own wife."

The old woman glared at her coldly. "When I get it down to two or three, he can pick among them. I will make the Shaw empire twice as big through my grandson."

It dawned on Sam then that Elizabeth Shaw had never really felt any affection for her grandson; she saw him only as a means to an end, a chance to keep the Shaw empire going. And she had been part of this ploy, Sam thought with horror, helping to civilize the carefree, savage heart so the old woman could mold him into what she wanted.

Elizabeth Shaw wandered off just then to greet several wealthy old ladies. About that time, the orchestra finished a number and Colt escorted a simpering young woman back to her seat. Then he turned and walked toward Sam. She looked about desperately, wanting to flee, but the area was crowded and there was no way she could make a fast exit.

Colt bowed low before her and took her hand. "Ah, Miss MacGregor, how is your pupil doing this evening?"

"Very well," she stammered. "If I didn't know differently, I would think you had always been part of this social scene."

The music started again.

"May I have this dance?" he asked.

"Colt, have you lost your mind?" Sam hissed. "There's a dozen young society girls standing out there waiting for their turn at you."

"Let them wait." He grabbed Sam's arm and propelled her out onto the dance floor.

"You're holding me too tightly—people will talk," she whispered frantically.

"Let them." He didn't release his grip as they circled the smooth wood floor. "I am, after all, the young host of this social event, am I not?"

"You are actually the guest of honor." She didn't dare tell him how Elizabeth Shaw was planning his life for him, yet hadn't she known it all along? In a way, she was ashamed for her part in it, and yet, knowing Colt as she did, she wasn't sure anyone could ever tame him. In his heart, there would always be a bit of the savage. She remembered his lovemaking and the thrill of his wildness.

"Do you want the banker's daughter or the shoe heiress? They're both at the top of your grandmother's list," she asked in jest.

Colt laughed. "Which two are they?"

She nodded toward two woebegone young beauties on the sidelines. "That striking brunette and the little blonde."

He snorted and whirled her about the dance floor. "They were both more stupid than a carriage horse. Frankly, dancing with you has been the high point of the evening."

"Thank you, I think," Sam said. "Your grandmother is glaring at us."

Colt shrugged. "It doesn't matter. If this evening is the best that white civilization can offer, I know I'm right about what I've decided to do."

"Do?"

"Yes, I know I can trust you with this information, Sam. I've decided to go back to the Dakotas."

"What?" She stopped dead on the dance floor.

"Keep dancing—people are staring," he said and swept her into his arms again. He smelled faintly of aftershave and expensive French soap.

"Colt, you can't. Your grandmother has great plans—"

"But she never asked me what I wanted to do. I miss the freedom, the vast wilderness my mother's people dominated. I suppose I could learn to live in the white man's world, but I like the Sioux world better."

Before she realized what he was doing, he danced her through the open French doors at the end of the ball room and out onto the veranda.

"Colt, we can't do this," Sam protested. "If anyone saw us go, there'll be talk—"

"I wanted to tell you good-bye," he whispered and then he kissed her.

Sam struggled only a moment, knowing she should pull away and insist on returning to the ballroom, but his mouth was so delicious and her senses were giddy with the nearness of him, the power of his big arms around her, crushing her to him. His hands stroked her bare shoulders as he kissed her eyes, her face, her hair. "Go with me, Sam," he said urgently, "go with me."

"Are you out of your mind? What would I do out there on the plains?"

"You'd make love to me, bear my children," and he kissed her again.

He couldn't be serious. She could taste the liquor on his mouth and wondered how much he had drunk. Tomorrow, he would realize what a great thing it was to be the Shaw heir and he would not remember tonight's conversation. But in the meantime, all Sam could do was cling to him and return his kisses, lost in the warmth and the strength of the man.

She heard a gasp and pulled away. Elizabeth Shaw stood in the doorway, glaring at them both. "This is highly improper—please come back in at once!"

"Of course, Grandmother," Colt said easily, but Sam began to stammer an explanation.

"We'll talk later," Mrs. Shaw said coldly and turned to march back into the crowd.

"Well, now you've done it," Sam said.

Colt shrugged. "You didn't really like working for my grandmother, did you?"

"You don't understand—I need the reference."

"Forget the reference and run away with me," he said as he led her back inside.

"I can't," she shook her head.

"All right. It's your choice." His voice was cool and remote as he bowed over her hand and went off to ask another girl to dance.

Late that night after the ball was over, there was a gentle tap at Sam's door as she put on her robe. Colt, she thought, and her heart began to beat hard. Was he asking her again to run away with him? If he asked, could she throw caution to the wind and go without a backward glance?

"Miss Samantha?" Nellie's timid voice.

What a disappointment. "Yes?" She opened the door.

"Mrs. Shaw would like to see you in the library." The thin, pretty girl hesitated, glancing around. "She's in a real stew, she is."

Sam sighed and pulled the belt of her robe tighter and squared her shoulders. "Thank you, Nellie."

Sam took a deep breath and walked slowly down the stairs, wondering if Colt was with his grandmother and what was about to happen.

She should have guessed. The old lady was in a towering rage, walking up and down the Oriental carpet, her wrinkled face ruddy with anger. "Well, you certainly took your time getting here!"

"I'm sorry, ma'am." Sam was certain her tardiness wasn't what this was about.

"How dare you! How dare you!" The old woman paused at her desk, opened the drawer, threw a small bundle of bills at Sam. "You are fired and you can forget about references."

"But Mrs. Shaw—"

"Don't but me, you—you strumpet, you! You've been carrying on with my grandson behind my back or were my eyes lying to me tonight?"

"I love him," Sam admitted and realized it was true. "But as far as any plotting and scheming—"

"You'd interfere with his making a good match, would you? And all the plans I've made for him—"

"Perhaps it is time Colt made his own plans," Sam snapped, "and for your information, I doubt they include me."

"I certainly hope not, you slut!" The old lady's rage was building until she seemed beside herself. "Take your money and get out of my house!"

Sam picked up the small bundle of bills. "Mrs. Shaw, I'm sorry if I've caused you any anguish, but I'm not sure your plans and Colt's are the same."

"You think I don't know that?" She almost screamed it at her as the old lady paced up and down. "I had him in here earlier and told him he was the beneficiary in my will, but he insists he's going back to the savages. I'm sure this is your doing."

"I assure you it is not," Sam said, knowing with a sinking heart that if he went back to the Sioux, she hadn't a prayer of ever holding him in her arms again.

"Are you calling me a liar, you strumpet? I want you out of my house before morning."

"Yes, Mrs. Shaw. I'm sorry things didn't work out for you and your grandson—"

"Get out! Get out!" the woman screamed. "Tomorrow, I'll try to reason with him again, but tonight, all that's important is getting you out of my house, you viper, you!"

Sam had never seen such a rage. If the old woman didn't calm down, she was liable to have a stroke. Anyway, there was no reasoning with her. Elizabeth Shaw was used to people doing exactly what she told them. With a sigh, Sam put the money in the pocket of her robe and left the room. Outside the library, she paused and listened. Behind her, the old woman did not even seem to notice she was gone. Sam heard books hitting the wall and fine porcelain shattering.

So she'd been fired for giving in to her heart and the man she loved and threatening Mrs. Shaw's plans. Perhaps the old woman would manage to talk Colt out of leaving. At any rate, Sam would never see him again. She went back to her room and began to pack. It didn't take very long; she owned so little. She would be out on the street again with a little money and no references. At least the weather was warmer than it had been when she'd first come to work here.

Cautiously Sam opened her door and picked up her little carpetbag. The house was silent and dark except for the tirade that was still going on in the library. She could hear old Mrs. Shaw shouting and throwing things. The servants were probably all cowering in their rooms. Sam felt suddenly free but sad. She had found the love of her life and was going to lose him. A poor governess might become the mistress of a wealthy man, but not his wife.

She waited a few minutes, wondering if she should write Colt a note. What was the purpose? She wasn't certain he would get it anyway. Yet she could not bear to leave without saying good-bye. Picking up her little bag, she tiptoed down the hall, hesitated before his door, and knocked. No answer. He might have drunk so much champagne that he was sleeping heavily. She knocked louder. Still no answer. From downstairs, the screaming and tantrum-throwing continued.

"Colt?" Sam whispered. "Colt, are you there?"

After a moment, she opened his door very slowly. Moonlight lit up the room and she could see his bed had not been slept in. Quickly, she went in and looked around. Many of his things were gone, as was he. Had he left without telling anyone good-bye?

She'd missed her chance. Now she knew she would be willing to follow him anywhere he wanted to go, she loved him so much. She slumped down on his bed and tried to think. He might be headed for the train station, or maybe not. Did he really want her? There was only one way to find out.

She picked up her little carpetbag, closed the door to his room, and went down the back stairs and out into the spring night. It was cool and Sam shivered. She'd always hated the cold because she was frail and thin. The Dakotas would be even colder than Massachusetts. She walked out to the winding road and started toward town.

Yet as she walked, she had to smile. There would be hell to pay in the morning when crabby old Mrs. Shaw realized

Colt had left and upset her selfish plans. Sam had been right about him; no one could tame his savage heart.

She was breathless when she finally reached town, although she'd had to stop several times to catch her breath. Even though it was late at night, the train station was bustling. Sam hurried up and down the platform, didn't see the familiar form. Then she went into the station and walked around, anxiously searching each face, asking questions. No luck. Maybe the ticket agent . . . By the time she reached the ticket window, she was so breathless, she couldn't speak for a long moment. The little man behind the window had gapped teeth and wore an eyeshade. "Where to, miss?"

"Did you—did you see a big, dark man?"

He yawned. "Lotsa men come through here. You need a ticket? If not, kindly move out of the way—there's a line forming behind you."

"He was Indian," she gasped, "handsome, wearing braids."

A light seemed to come on behind the rheumy eyes. "Oh, the savage? Yeah, I remember him."

A glimmer of hope came to her laboring heart. "Where is he? I've got to tell him—"

"He bought a ticket. You're too late—he's gone!"

Twenty-two

Cincala stepped off the train in the isolated little station in the Dakotas. A white conductor hurried up to him, looked him over, and asked with respect, "May I handle your baggage, sir?"

Now that he was dressed as a prosperous white man, Colt noted, he was treated with respect. "No, I can do it."

He picked up his one small bag and headed for the livery stable to rent a horse. His heart began to sing as he mounted up and rode out across the plains. Small, green plants were popping up and birds sang in the brush. Spring was coming to this wild, untamed country. He was back in the land he loved and as soon as he got out of these confining clothes and into a breech cloth and moccasins, he would once again feel like Cincala, the honored Lakota warrior. As far as he was concerned, Colt Shaw was part of his past. So was Sam. His heart saddened, but he pushed the memory of the fiery redhead out of his mind. His first task was to find his parents' bodies if they were dead and give them proper burial. He'd never believed they were buried in Boston.

As he rode into his old village, he was surprised at how ragged the people were, how hungry the children looked. The Sioux's circumstances hadn't gotten any better in the months he'd been gone. Had they always been so poor and beaten-down as they now appeared? He might never have known the difference if he hadn't been away in a prosperous white man's city. Cincala reined in before a ragged old woman. "Honored Old One, where might I find the chiefs of this village?"

She looked up at him, hostility in her dark eyes, and then seemed to see the Lakota in his face. "Cincala? Are you Cincala? We all thought you were dead!" She turned and ran through the gathering of tipis, shouting. "Everyone, come look! Rejoice! One of our own, Cincala, is returned from the dead!"

His heart pounding with excitement, Colt nudged his horse forward through the ragged line of lodges as people came out to greet him. At the edge of the row of tipis, a woman came out of a lodge and paused, staring at him.

Colt took a deep breath, not daring to hope. "Mother?"

She stared back at him as if wondering who this white man was who rode uninvited into the camp.

Tears came to his eyes as he reined his horse toward her. His vision blurred, but he would have known that beloved face anywhere. "Mother, it is me! I am home!"

For a long moment, there was no answer as he dismounted before the lodge. The woman watched him hesitantly, her black hair streaked with gray and her doeskin dress worn and stained. She blinked, looking up at him, at the ring hanging around his neck. "What white man asks . . . Cincala?" Her voice trembled. "Can—can it really be you?"

"It's me." He threw his arms around her. "I didn't think you were alive. I'm so glad to see you."

Just then, a man came out of the lodge, an aged warrior with long, gray-streaked hair. Only his hazel eyes and his lighter skin revealed that he was not Lakota. "My son? Are you back from the dead?"

Cincala faced his father, bowing respectfully in the Lakota manner. "My father, it is I, Cincala, returned from the big city of the whites."

White Wolf threw his arms around his neck. "We thought you killed at Wounded Knee."

"And I thought you dead, too." They hugged each other a long moment while Wiwila wept softly in the background.

"Come," White Wolf gestured, "we will sit before the fire and smoke while your mother prepares food. Soon we must give a feast of welcome. Tell me everything."

"First, let me take off these white man's clothes so I may feel like a true Lakota." His heart was pleased as he went into the lodge, changed into a breech cloth and moccasins, folded up the fine clothes and put them in his carpetbag, and returned to the fire. "What do you think?"

His father smiled and nodded. "You look like a true warrior, ready to ride against our enemies. Come sit; tell me how you ended up so far away."

Cincala sat down cross-legged while his father prepared a pipe and his smiling mother hurried about, brewing strong coffee and cooking meat. "When I was wounded, a doctor called Peter Lester found me. Then soldiers came and took me away, took me to a place called Boston."

"Ah, yes," White Wolf nodded and smiled. "I knew Peter a long time ago when I was a white man. You were sent to your grandmother?"

Cincala nodded. "She thinks you were killed at the Little Bighorn with Custer. She boasts about what a hero you were and how many Indians you killed."

White Wolf's face grew grave as he lit the pipe with a twig from the fire. "Why does she think that?"

"They found a body at the battle, a body holding your gold watch."

The older man frowned. "My watch was stolen. No doubt they have buried the thief in my place—some poor enlisted man, I suppose. How ironic that he's buried in that elegant cemetery where only bluebloods lie."

"Have you never thought of returning to Boston?" Cincala asked.

His father shook his head and looked with adoration at the woman busying herself beside the fire. "I have traded one life for another and I have never been sorry. Besides, I never felt my mother cared about me or about anything, really, besides the Shaw empire."

Cincala frowned and accepted the pipe. "She tried to civilize me."

"They must have done a good job of it," White Wolf smiled, "I hardly knew you when you rode up. Except for your braids, you look like a prosperous white man."

"A girl called a governess," Cincala sighed and thought wistfully about Sam, "she taught me."

"Ah," said his father as he took the pipe in turn, "you care about this girl?"

"Grandmother said Samantha was unsuitable. She said I should marry a society beauty with money."

"My mother has not changed, then," White Wolf said sadly as he smoked. "You can see why I could not go back—she would never have accepted Wiwila as my wife. Did you ask this Samantha to come with you?"

"Yes, but maybe she didn't love me enough." Cincala shook his head regretfully. "Besides, she is a very civilized, frail white girl. She could never survive our winters and our hard life."

"It is a hard life for whites," his father agreed.

Cincala stared off into the distance, remembering the warmth of Sam's fragile body in his arms, the taste of her lips. "It would have been expecting too much for her to give up everything in her civilized world to follow me." He touched the ring on the cord around his sinewy neck. He had wanted to give it to her. He looked around at the camp. "Have our people always been so poor and I just now see it?"

White Wolf looked around and nodded. "If anything, things are worse for all Indians, but especially the Sioux since Wounded Knee. If only we had someone who cared, someone with influence to talk to the whites, tell the Congress and the men in power how it is with our people."

Cincala nodded. "Myself, I am happy to be home."

Around them, people were still coming out of their tipis, talking excitedly and looking his way.

White Wolf grinned. "Word must be spreading that you are here, my son. All will want to hear about the white man's world. We must give a feast, except . . ." His voice trailed off and he looked away.

Cincala realized how poor the whole village was. "Father, I have money. I will buy supplies for the village and I will give a great feast to tell how glad I am that my parents are alive and well."

His mother looked up from the fire. "There will be many beautiful Lakota girls who will come," she said. "I see you still haven't given away the ring."

Cincala frowned as he reached up to touch it. In his mind, he saw Samantha MacGregor and he knew he could never love another as he had loved her. "If you don't mind, Mother, for a while, I'd rather not talk about a wife."

"But—" his mother began.

"Wiwila," his father admonished, "a white girl now rules his heart. Maybe someday he might change his mind, but right now, he does not think of another woman."

"Ahh!" His mother nodded sympathetically.

"In the meantime," Cincala wanted to change the subject, "Father, after we eat, I want to ride out across our land and feel the freedom of the air blowing in my face. Do you have a fine horse for me instead of this old rented nag?"

His father took the pipe and smoked a long moment, his face troubled. "I have a few fine horses left, but the plains are not so empty as they were before. White farmers are taking more and more of our land."

Cincala frowned at the news. "Does no one speak to the government about it?"

"I try, but they see me only as an old squaw man without any influence. My words fall on deaf ears."

Cincala considered this as he took the tin plate his mother heaped with meat and boiled corn. "We need someone back in civilization, someone of influence and money to plead all Indians' cause."

His father shrugged as he took a plate. "There is no such person. But let us talk of happier things. Tell me about Boston and what you thought of civilization."

As they laughed and talked, Cincala realized the white man's life wasn't as bad as he had thought. In fact, sitting here by the fire eating his meat out of a tin plate, he couldn't help but think of the elegant dining room with its comfortable chairs back at the Shaw mansion, the elderly butler serving him fine roast beef off a silver tray.

After they ate what little there was, he and his father went out to look at the horse herd and enjoy a long ride. The freedom of the wind blowing in his face, the lack of tight clothing, made him feel like an honored warrior again. If only he had Samantha by his side, he would be happy. "Perhaps we can go hunting," he said.

His father reined in. "Yes, we can do that, but there's not much game. The white settlers have killed it off."

"Then what do our people do all day?" Cincala asked.

White Wolf shrugged. "There is not much to do—loaf about and wait for the government to hand out rations, which are usually bad."

Cincala remembered the shoddy blankets Shaw Industries was manufacturing for the Indians. If he were in charge of those factories, the blankets would be of good quality. He would see to that.

They went hunting, but they bagged only a small rabbit.

His father said wistfully, "I miss the great herds of buffalo we used to hunt. Once they were like a brown sea rolling across these plains when I first came out here more than thirty years ago."

Cincala tried to picture that scene. Yes, he could remember buffalo as a small boy, but he knew that the last several years, the buffalo were almost gone.

After a long ride, they returned to the village. He thought again how ragged and unkempt everything was, how tired and thin the people looked. Had things changed so much in the time he'd been gone or was it he who had changed?

That afternoon, white men from the Indian agent's office distributed rations. Cincala was ashamed that his people had to stand in line like beggars for the wormy flour and the tough meat that was handed out. There were a few clothes and a stack of the thin blankets in a box marked Shaw Industries. Now he was ashamed of his white family. It did something to people to accept charity from others, he thought. Wasn't there something he could do? Not as Cincala, the Lakota brave, he thought ruefully as the people returned to their ragged village. The rich and powerful Colt Shaw could change things, but a Lakota brave, no matter his war honors, could not. He did not think kind thoughts about his grandmother. After talking with his father, he was certain the old lady had cared nothing for either of them and only wanted someone she could control to take charge of her empire. He was not even certain the old lady was capable of love. For that, he could only pity her.

That night, the village held a feast and there was dancing and drumming with plenty of food. It was much like the old days, Cincala thought happily as he celebrated and greeted old friends from the past. Too many of his friends were dead now, killed at Wounded Knee. Others had succumbed to white man's diseases over the past few months, or the white man's liquor. A number of shy, beautiful maidens looked at him discreetly and smiled. He knew they watched him, but his heart would always belong to only one woman, and the fiery-haired girl was not here. She alone made him feel regret about leaving the white man's world behind forever.

He slept once again in his father's lodge. The blankets on the ground that had once seemed so comfortable felt hard as rock and the memory crossed his mind of his white, soft bed at the Shaw mansion. Yet comfort was not worth the freedom he would have to give up to live under Elizabeth Shaw's control in Boston. Here Cincala was free as the wind, even if the Lakota and the other tribes were no longer as free and happy as they had once been. Yet that night, he did not dream of freedom; he dreamed of Sam and how her fiery locks spread over him like a red cloud as she lay on his mighty chest and kissed him.

Sam had stayed in the train station that night, trying to decide what to do next. So Colt had gone back to the Indians. Did he know how much she cared for him? Did he care? Perhaps she had only been a dalliance for the young savage. Not that any of that mattered. The question was, what was she going to do now?

As she sat on the bench, torn with indecision, she heard a sound of hurrying feet and looked up to see old Williams, the butler, rushing toward her. "Oh, Miss MacGregor, thank God I found you!"

"If Mrs. Shaw wants to bawl me out again," Sam drew her chin up stubbornly, "I won't take any more. After all, she's fired me once."

"Oh, no, miss, it's not that. We're trying to find the young master. Something terrible has happened at the house."

"What?" Now the butler had her full attention.

"It's Mrs. Shaw," the butler wrung his hands. "Not being disrespectful, but she has a terrible temper."

"How well I remember," Sam answered ruefully. The old woman had been raging and throwing things as Sam left.

"I think she's had a stroke. Can you come? No one knows quite what to do next, except call the doctor."

"Oh, my Lord! Of course I'll come." With the butler

carrying her bag, they hurried out to the carriage. Even though the driver whipped up the horses, the trip took more time than Sam would have liked.

They pulled up out front, the butler opened the carriage door for her, and she ran inside. She met Dr. Diggs coming down the stairs. The look on his face boded ill. "Doctor, what has happened?"

He shook his head. "I always told Elizabeth her temper tantrums would kill her if she didn't learn to control them. She's had a stroke. She's dead."

Dead. It took a long moment for the fact to sink in.

"Oh, I'm so sorry." Sam sagged limply onto a hall bench. "I'm afraid I was the cause of this latest one."

"Don't feel guilty, miss," the doctor shrugged. "She was famous for this. As I recall, she tried to control people by throwing these tantrums. Where is her grandson?"

Reality flooded over Sam. "I'm afraid he's gone back to the Indians."

"Refused this wealth?" He sounded incredulous.

"I think to him, it was a choice of money or freedom and he chose freedom."

The doctor smiled. "I'm afraid most of us civilized people wouldn't have the character to make that decision."

Sam grimaced. "And we called *him* a savage."

The butler, standing nearby, cleared his throat. "Miss MacGregor, I've taken the liberty of calling Mrs. Shaw's lawyer, but he can't get here until late tomorrow."

Sam sighed. Somehow she was being thrust into the role of the nearest relative. "Call Bosworth—he'll have to handle things until her lawyer returns. Has Mrs. Shaw no close friends we could call?"

She saw the butler and the doctor exchange glances. The doctor said, "Well, she had many social connections and, of course, all those people will attend the funeral, but no close friends that I know of."

"How pitiful," Sam whispered aloud. "All this money and no friends to make funeral arrangements."

"Miss," the butler said, "begging your pardon, but I think she left funeral plans in her desk, but the lawyer will have her will."

The will. Sam groaned aloud. "She intended to leave it all to her grandson, and I suppose she did. Not that it matters because he's rejected our civilization."

"Well, that's not tonight's problem," the doctor said and yawned. "It's very late and I'm tired. The maids are upstairs doing what's necessary. I've called the undertaker. Good night, all."

Sam realized suddenly just how weary she was. "Thank you for coming. I'll try to handle things until I reach her nephew or her lawyer gets back to town. Good night, sir."

Williams closed the door behind the doctor as he left and turned to Sam. "Will you attempt to notify young Colt?"

She didn't even want to think about Colt Shaw. "I suppose the lawyer will. The undertaker should be here soon. Then after that, there's nothing to be done until morning."

The butler nodded and disappeared and Sam trudged wearily up the stairs. She stopped at Mrs. Shaw's door, dreading it, yet thinking she needed to pay last respects. When she went in, maids had lit candles around the bed and covered the mirrors in that old custom. Elizabeth Shaw lay in state in her great bed and Sam realized now what a small woman she had been. It had only been her temper and ambition that had loomed large. "I'm so sorry," Sam said aloud, "so sorry you missed the love of your sons and your grandson. It could have been so wonderful for your old age. But you only saw Colt as a project, a savage to be tamed and turned into a fancy, civilized gentleman and he defied you."

The old woman looked as grim and angry in death as she had in life. Downstairs, the doorbell rang and Sam went down the stairs to talk with the undertaker. That finished, and knowing there was nothing more that could be done tonight, Sam went to bed and slept a deep, troubled sleep.

The next day, Mrs. Robert Shaw lay in state in a fine bronze casket in her own ballroom for mourners to come to call. Sam dreaded the day as she dressed in a plain black outfit and waited for the lawyer in the conservatory. Somehow, all the plants made it seem so much cheerier. The balding lawyer doffed his hat and bowed. "This is indeed an unfortunate occasion."

"Yes, it is," Sam said, ashamed that she couldn't really feel sorrow.

However, the lawyer didn't look too sad either as he shuffled through his briefcase. "Her heir is her grandson, Colt Shaw, since she disinherited her younger son, Todd."

"Yes, I understand the older son, Austin, was killed at the Little Bighorn."

The lawyer nodded. "Yes, quite a hero. Mrs. Shaw was quite proud of him, although I'm not sure she knew what to do with the young savage."

"She never really knew him at all," Sam said. "He had a great many good qualities that she didn't appreciate."

"Am I to understand he's disappeared?" The lawyer peered at her over his spectacles.

Sam nodded. "He and his grandmother couldn't see eye to eye on a lot of things and there was a fuss. He's gone back to his mother's people. Wealth does not impress him."

The lawyer looked impressed. "A rare human being," he said. "Still, I'll need to have him sign some papers, formally rejecting the family fortune."

"What happens to it then? Does it go to some charity?"

The lawyer tried to hide his smile as he shuffled through a pile of papers from his briefcase. "Oh my, no. You didn't know Elizabeth Shaw very well, did you?"

"Well enough," Sam said.

"Then you should know she didn't have a charitable bone in her body. When her grandson signs away the inheritance, it all goes to her nephew, Bosworth."

Sam blinked. "All of it? Nothing for the servants?"

He took off his spectacles. "A small bit, once young Shaw signs the papers, but it won't make up for losing their jobs now that she's gone. Maybe Bosworth will keep them on."

"I'm afraid he's no more charitable than his Aunt Elizabeth," Sam sighed.

The man laid some papers on the table. "I presume you know where we can find Colt Shaw to sign these documents?"

"I—I'm not sure. I'll have to give that some thought."

He stood up and bowed. "Then I'll leave you the responsibility of this task. The butler told me you were possibly the only one who might know. Someone needs to get word to him."

Who was there to do that? There might not even be a telegraph out there on the plains. Colt had broken Sam's heart and left in the middle of the night without so much as a farewell. No one could blame her if she did not accept responsibility for this errand. She stood up, too. "I suppose he should know she has died, but I'm certain he has no interest in the inheritance. However, he would want the servants to have whatever little she left them."

"He can sign these papers without returning to Boston," the lawyer said. "He can mail them back to me."

Maybe we could send a courier," Sam suggested, yet she knew that no hired messenger would ever have the nerve to venture deep into Indian country.

"I hope you will take this responsibility," the lawyer urged. "We'll talk later." He bade her good day and left.

Sam put her fingers to her throbbing temples as she stared after him. She wanted to run out the door and leave someone else to deal with this mess. This was not really her problem, but she felt duty-bound to do whatever she could. And though she didn't want to admit it, she knew it might be a final chance to see Colt one more time.

Two days later, at the large and ornate funeral, Sam faced Bosworth, who looked properly mournful in a new black suit as he stood by the coffin, greeting mourners as they filed past as if he were already master here.

Sam walked up and he caught her hand and kissed it. "Oh, my dear Miss MacGregor, my aunt's death is so sad."

She pulled her fingers out of his clammy grasp. "Yes, isn't it, though?"

Bosworth looked annoyed. However, he wiped his eyes with a flourish and lowered his voice. "Her lawyer is refusing to discuss details with me until later. I presume you know what is in the will?"

"I don't think this is the proper time to be talking about this," Sam whispered.

He grinned behind his handkerchief. "I can wait. Besides, I've got business of my own to take care of in New York for a few days. Perhaps I might be permitted to call on you when I return?"

"Let me think about it." Sam kept her voice cool. She did not want Bosworth to know about the documents she'd been given, but the way he was looking at her, there was no doubt he was still interested. The thought crossed her mind that if she married Bosworth Shaw, she could live a very comfortable and prosperous life after he received the inheritance. But the thought of marrying him made her gag. The money meant no more to her than it did to Colt.

That evening, Sam was on the train, headed to the Dakotas. Only when the crowded landscape faded into vast, sweeping plains did she realize the enormity of her task. The only clue she had was that she had once heard him mention a massacre at a place called Wounded Knee. As the train moved west, she stopped a passing conductor. "Please, do you know a place called Wounded Knee?"

The conductor stroked his handlebar mustache and shook his head with distaste. "Young lady, I don't know why you'd want to go there. It's a dirty place—nothing but hungry, ragged Indians in that area for miles."

"I need to go there," she replied stubbornly.

He looked at her with curiosity, but didn't ask. "No train there directly—you'll have to rent a buggy and drive the last few miles."

"I can do that. Just tell me what I need to know."

Two days later, she was sitting in that rented buggy, looking out across the vast, treeless prairie. Yes, this was Colt's kind of land, as wild and untamed as he was himself. She hadn't realized this savage land would be so huge, so trackless. She suddenly realized what a hopeless task she was facing. It was going to be impossible to find him.

Twenty-three

Cincala had adjusted to his old life in less than a week. Yesterday, his people had moved their camp again to a better site many miles from white encroachers. Although every time he touched the ring hanging around his neck he thought of Sam, he was happy now, happier than he had been as the young heir, Colt Shaw. He had packed away the white man's suit and tie and now lived almost naked, nothing in the warm weather but a loincloth, a pair of moccasins, and some feathers in his long, black hair.

In the warm spring weather, he often went riding with the other young braves or his father; no fancy English saddle, nothing but a spirited horse, a bit of blanket, and a twist of rawhide around the black stallion's jaw. He rode the vast prairie wild and free as he had always been and he ate what he hunted. At night, there were old, old legends to be told around the campfires and sometimes dancing as in the olden days.

Pretty young Lakota maidens flirted with him; his mother was urging him to choose one to warm his blankets for the long winter ahead, but his heart still belonged to the fiery-haired girl and he knew it would be a long, long time before he could think of taking another woman in his arms. No, it would not be a long time; it would be forever, his heart told him. His past as an elegant young blade seemed far behind him as if it had never happened. Within days,

Cincala reverted to the wild, free creature he had always been, and the only thing he really missed from white civilization was Samantha MacGregor.

One late afternoon, Cincala rode alone, ranging far from camp as he hunted. Habit drew him back along the trail toward the old village site. In the distance, he spotted a lone buggy. Who was it and what did the white want? At least it wasn't soldiers; they would be riding horses. He almost turned and galloped back to his village to warn people that a white stranger was coming, perhaps the Indian agent. Then he realized the buggy was stopped. Tense and on guard, Cincala rode toward it.

He realized as he drew close that the buggy had a broken wheel. There was no horse. Evidently the buggy's occupants had taken the horse and ridden for help. What was so confusing was that the horse tracks didn't head back toward town, they headed toward his old village.

Now why would a white man be so determined to reach a Sioux camp? Curious, he began to follow the hoofprints. The sun was hot, beating down on his bare back. Only his curiosity kept Cincala on the track. A white man coming to a Sioux camp was never good news. The weather was dry and dusty and Cincala stopped to drink from his canteen and wondered if the white man had a canteen. If not, he was in big trouble because there were no creeks in this area.

In another hour, he discovered the weary horse grazing alongside the trail. It wore a makeshift bridle and there were signs in the dust that the rider had fallen from his mount. Then he found small bootprints in the dust, unsteady and stumbling. Cincala grew even more puzzled. The bootprints were no larger than a child's. Surely a young boy wasn't out on this desolate prairie alone?

He caught the horse and took it with him as he followed the bootprints. Somewhere up ahead, he would find the young boy dead from heat and thirst—Cincala was sure of it. If he didn't find the boy's body and go to the Indian agent with an explanation, the whites would be muttering that the boy had been ambushed and killed by the Sioux and make ready to wreak vengeance on the Indians.

Cincala rode forward, mile after mile, growing more and more puzzled. This boy was certainly determined to make it to the Indian camp. All the signs showed that he had fallen, gotten up, and stumbled on. The white boy had more guts than brains, Cincala decided; still, he had to admire him for his brave stubbornness.

In the distance, he thought he saw a figure that disappeared from view and he decided the heat waves shimmering off the waving prairie grasses had confused him. Then the figure stumbled to its feet and began to walk again.

Cincala stared, frozen in disbelief. A woman. Could it be a woman out here all alone? That didn't make any sense. Then the late afternoon sun reflected off her hair which was the color of dark fire. He must be having a spirit vision of the girl who had meant so much to him. Not daring to hope, Cincala urged his horse into a gallop.

Sam knew she was almost done for as she stumbled and fell, then swayed to her feet to walk on across the prairie. It had been stupid to rent a buggy and start out alone. She had thought she could ride the horse on into the Indian village once her buggy broke down, but as she grew faint from lack of water, she'd lost her grip and fell. She had not had the strength to catch the horse and remount. Her lips were cracked and all she could think of was water, but she stumbled on toward where the whites had told her she might locate an Indian village. Her duty was to find Colt and give him the message. She might not make it, but she was going to die trying.

She tripped over a rock and fell again, struggling to get

up. Somewhere in her mind, it seemed she heard thunder. The sound grew louder and she felt a flicker of hope. Rain might save her if she could catch any of it. Then she realized it was the sound of a running horse. With great difficulty, she turned her head and saw a rider galloping toward her. For a moment, her heart leaped at the thought of rescue and then she realized the man wore only the briefest loincloth and moccasins as he sat the fine, black horse. A savage, she thought with alarm, a savage warrior and she was at his mercy. Sam tried to get to her feet, but she was too exhausted. There was no way she could defend herself, but she would not surrender without a fight.

Even as she reached for a rock as a weapon, the magnificent warrior rode closer. The late afternoon sun reflected on an object around his neck and her heart almost stopped. It couldn't be. Yet still the sun reflected off the blue sapphire ring. In her delirium, she must be imagining it. Yet she could not stop herself from screaming, "Colt? Colt, is it you?"

The bronzed man reined in, his fine stallion rearing as the savage pulled up short, staring back at her. Had he forgotten her so soon and reverted back to his old, untamed ways? Tears came to her eyes. She remembered again how handsome he was with his powerful physique, Sun Dance scars, and his long, black braids. "Colt?"

She waited for his reaction. Perhaps he would gallop away, thinking she might be bringing soldiers to capture him for his grandmother again. Her eyes teared up, loving him more than she had ever dreamed possible.

He rode closer, staring at her, then dismounted with a scowl. "You are a fool to come out here alone, and if you bring the soldiers to take me back to Boston, I will not go."

He watched her beautiful face as he dismounted and grabbed a canteen off his horse, then strode toward her. His heart was too full to speak further as he knelt by her side and put his arm around her frail shoulders, holding her as he gave her the canteen. What he yearned to do was embrace her, kiss those trembling lips, but he knew she must be bringing him trouble. Yet he loved her as he would never love again.

She paused, water dripping from her full, soft mouth, looking up into his gray eyes. "Thank God I found you," she whispered. "I didn't think I would."

She was safe now, she knew it, even though he still scowled down at her; she was safe in his strong arms. Her heart beat harder, and she wanted to reach out to him, but of course, she must remember he did not want her. He had fled without asking her to go with him. No doubt there was some Indian girl who held his heart.

He lifted her in his arms, looking down at her. "Why do you come here?"

Her pride held her back. He must never know how much she cared. "I—I have brought legal papers for you to sign."

Something in his rugged face changed and his expression grew remote. "All right. I will get you back to town and sign your papers so you can leave."

She blinked back tears. "Are you—are you happy?"

He nodded. "Very happy."

So she had her answer. All that remained was to tell him the news. Sam was suddenly very, very weak. She relaxed and allowed herself to lapse into unconsciousness.

Cincala stared down at the unconscious girl in his arms. Now what was he to do? His good sense told him to tie her on the extra horse and take her back to the white man's town so they could send someone after the disabled buggy. He had hoped against hope that she had come out here to tell him of her love; but of course, he was thinking like a fool. A frail white girl could never survive among the Lakota.

And yet he could not stop himself from bending his head

and brushing his lips across hers, remembering how it had been to make love to her. She was so small and vulnerable and he felt so protective.

What to do now? She needed food and medical attention, but it was a long way back to the white man's town and he did not want to turn this unconscious, defenseless beauty over to lustful strangers. He decided he would take her back to the Lakota camp. Tomorrow, when she was recovered, he would sign whatever papers had brought her here and put her back on the Iron Horse to return to Boston.

Gently, he carried her over to the horses. He mounted up, cradling her in his big arms. Then, leading the buggy horse, he turned his stallion and rode toward the Indian camp. She was soft and warm in his embrace as he rode, her dark, fiery hair spilling over his arm, her delicate face against his bare, bronzed chest. The thought occurred to him that he did not have to return her at all. Cincala could destroy the damaged buggy, trade off the buggy horse, and Samantha MacGregor would have disappeared without a trace. The whites would think she'd become lost forever out on the vast prairie. Cincala could keep her for his own to warm his blankets and bear his sons. The thought tempted him as much as her nubile body. Yes, that is what he would do. That settled, he kissed her soft lips again and holding her close, rode toward the Indian camp.

The curious but silent crowd came out as word spread through the village that Cincala had brought in a white girl with long hair the color of glowing embers. As Cincala dismounted, still holding her, his father met him.

"What—?"

"I'll answer questions later," Cincala said gruffly. "Right now, she needs help. Keep everyone away."

Brushing his mother's questions aside, Cincala carried Sam into his own lodge and laid her on a soft fur. He built a small fire in the firepit and put on some broth to cook. Then he went out for a gourd of cool water and a rag. The sun was slanting toward the horizon in the late afternoon as he returned and began to sponge her face. She moved ever so slightly and encouraged, he dribbled a tiny bit of water between her lips. She swallowed it, but her eyes did not open. The old blue dress she wore was dusty. He unbuttoned the bodice and found some folded papers there. Laying them to one side, he sponged the dust away until he reached the rise of her creamy, white breasts. Cincala hesitated only a moment before he unbuttoned her white lace bodice and washed those perfect breasts that his lips remembered so well.

In the dim firelight, her eyes flickered open and she looked up at him, her face furrowed with thought as if trying to discern where she was.

"Sam, you're all right," he assured her. "You're in my lodge. Tomorrow, I'll return you to the white man's town."

She looked up at him, feeling the gentle touch of his hand on her face. She had died and was in paradise, she thought. Heaven could not be better than this. She watched him fixing the broth at the fire and marveled at the ripple of muscle in his back as he moved. Yes, he belonged out here on this prairie; there was no doubt about it.

After a moment, he brought her a gourd full of strong, hot broth and when her hand could not hold it, he put his arm under her head and lifted her so she could drink it. Immediately, strength began to flow back into her body. Only then did she realize her bodice was undone and flushed as she hurriedly rebuttoned it. "I'm all right now," she said.

He handed her a tin cup of coffee and she warmed her hands around it as she sipped. "Where—where am I?"

"In my lodge at the Lakota village." He watched her and she wondered what he thought.

Now all the memories came flooding back. The papers, the important papers. "I was trying to find you."

His face brightened. "Oh?"

She nodded. "I've brought documents for you to sign. Did you find them?"

The hope in his gray eyes turned hostile. "Papers? Yes, I found them, but did not look at them."

There was no way to break the news gently. Sam took a deep breath for courage. "Colt, your grandmother has died."

He started, then frowned. "It is too bad. I am sad that I felt she never cared about me and wouldn't let me get close enough to let me care about her." He took a deep breath and frowned. "Is that what the papers are about?"

"Yes." She had hoped against hope that he would give some sign that he cared about her, ask her to stay with him. Sam would go anywhere, live under any hardship, just to be his woman. She could take the documents to town and mail them back. "You can sign away your inheritance if you wish and stay here with the Sioux."

He reached over and picked up the crumpled legal documents, staring at them. "I care nothing for being Colt Shaw, but I do not trust the white people who write this. I will sign nothing until my father reads it for me."

"Your father? But I thought—?"

"Never mind. There is much to explain, but you will have to promise not to tell the other whites."

Sam brushed her hair away from her face. If there were secrets, he might not trust her to keep them. If they were important enough, the Indians might not let her leave this camp alive. "You know you can trust me always."

His gray eyes softened and he took her small hand in his big one. "I know that, Sam. Who is to get the inheritance?"

Sam hesitated. "If you turn it down, your cousin Bosworth will get it."

He snorted with disgust. "Bosworth is no good, but I do not care if he gets the money. I have no use for it."

Sam ran her tongue along her lips, wondering how truthful she should be with him. "Bosworth wants to marry me," she admitted.

He turned her hand loose and laughed coldly. "So you will be a rich lady. That should make you very happy."

What would make her happy would be for Colt to tell her he loved her, ask her to stay with him forever. He meant more to her than the life of ease in Boston. She knew the plains could be merciless in its extremes of heat and cold, but if she could be his woman, she wouldn't care about the hardships. His lovemaking would keep her warm. *You're a fool,* she scolded herself; *he does not want you. In a few hours, you will have the papers signed and be on your way back to Boston to look for another job as a governess.* Her future without Colt stretched out, bleak and more grim than any prairie blizzard. There was always Bosworth, who'd now be very, very rich. She shuddered at the thought of his embrace; she'd rather be poor and hungry.

Colt stood up. "If you are feeling better, we will meet my father." He took her elbow and led her out of the tipi into the warm afternoon. As they walked along, curious people came out to watch her pass. Small, half-naked children, with big brown eyes stared at her, mongrel dogs barked, and in front of lodges, horses stamped restlessly and whinnied. Sam stared straight ahead, a little afraid of these silent, hostile Lakota. She remembered what Colt had told her about the massacre at Wounded Knee and wondered if these people hated her because of her white skin.

Yet Colt was totally at home here, his long-legged gait as easy and graceful as a cougar. He was a mighty warrior of the Lakota and savage as the environment he came from. How could she have thought she could ever tame him?

"Wait, I will get my father," he said and disappeared into a lodge.

Sam stood there awkwardly, keenly aware of the Indians gathering around to stare. Seconds seemed to drag into hours as she stood there. Colt must be telling his father about the grandmother's death and the legal papers.

After a moment, Colt came out of the lodge, followed by an older man. For a moment, Sam thought the other man was Indian, but when he straightened up, she realized that despite the buckskin clothing and the braided, gray-streaked hair, he was white. For a moment, she was confused. Then she stared into the older man's face and it was as if she were looking into Colt's. "You—you're Austin Shaw, aren't you?"

The man looked anxious, glanced at Colt. The young warrior put his hand on the other's shoulder. "He is now White Wolf."

The man smiled then, nodding to her. "Yes, I am Austin Shaw. You have come a long way, Miss MacGregor."

Sam shook her head to clear it. It was if she were seeing a ghost. Austin Shaw, the dead hero of the Little Bighorn, stood here alive and well, dressed as an aging Lakota warrior. "I'm afraid I don't understand. Why did you stay with the Indians?"

A woman joined them just then, a beautiful Lakota with only a little gray in her black hair. She was not all Indian, Sam thought, because her eyes were as gray as a wolf's pelt. Austin touched the woman's arm and smiled at her and in that look, Sam saw the answer. "You did it for love."

He nodded. "A long time ago, someone who was very dear to me told me that if I ever found a once-in-a-lifetime love, to run after it, damn the consequences, and not look back. I've done that with no regrets."

"Not many of us could do that," Sam whispered. She followed them inside the lodge and sat down on a log near the fire. "Did your son tell you why I've come?"

The older man nodded and sat down cross-legged on the

ground, motioning his son to sit also. The woman said, "I will prepare food," and disappeared outside.

Sam held out the legal papers. "I'm sorry about your mother's death."

White Wolf's face was immobile as he took the papers and stared at them without seeing. The firelight threw long shadows across his weathered features. "You know, she never really loved me—I think she was incapable of love."

Sam was not sure what the proper response was, so she did not answer for a long moment as he leafed through the papers. "You could return to Boston now and claim your inheritance," she suggested.

Austin Shaw shook his head. "My woman would not be happy there and after all these years, neither would I. Civilization is a thin veneer, Miss MacGregor, and I've lost most of it. Besides, everyone thinks of me as a dead hero, so I'd have a difficult time explaining how I survived the battle and deserted." Absently, he reached up to touch the livid scar across his forehead and Sam guessed the answer without being told.

"White Wolf," she said, "it is not my place to ask nosy questions. Since Austin Shaw is legally dead, the estate goes to his son. I come to bring the papers for Colt to sign, relinquishing everything."

White Wolf looked her over thoughtfully as if he had guessed this was only an excuse. "Someone else could have brought them."

She didn't know what to say to that. Was it that apparent how much she cared for his son?

"Hmm," he muttered, looking through the papers again. "This is a very important decision that will change his life, one he must not regret once he has made it. I think he will want to make medicine and commune with the Great Spirit before signing."

"Fine," Sam shrugged her shoulders, "except that I must be leaving."

Colt said, "It's a long trip to the white town and it will soon be dark. As I remember, the train doesn't leave until tomorrow afternoon anyway. You'd have to stay in a hotel and wait for it."

"Spend the night in this camp?" She didn't look at him. How could she tell him that she wanted to escape from him as quickly as possible so she wouldn't lose her dignity and beg him to make her his forever?

He must have misread her fears because Colt laughed sarcastically. "If you're afraid of the savages, Miss MacGregor, I assure you they'll not harm you. You'll be perfectly safe until tomorrow."

Safe? She didn't want to be safe. She wanted a wild, uncivilized coupling with this man like two wild things mating in the moonlight. After that, she would resign herself to losing him forever.

The silence deepened and she marveled as the lone survivor of Custer's last stand flipped through the pages she had brought. Finally he looked up. "I think it's all in order. I see my mother has been her usual selfish self in what happens to it all if Cincala doesn't accept it. Cousin Bosworth was always a greedy, dislikable man, but Mother couldn't see it. Woe to all the mill workers and the old servants at the house if he inherits everything, but I suppose it can't be helped."

She winced, remembering the manager of the Shaw factories. She could marry him and be very, very rich and comfortable for the rest of her days. She'd rather be poor and homeless. "You're right—if your son doesn't want it, Bosworth gets it all."

Colt scowled. "The money doesn't mean as much to me as my freedom."

The beautiful Indian woman returned and smiled at Sam. "You are the one my son speaks of?" she said softly.

Sam felt the blood rush to her face and saw the angry

look Colt turned on his mother, but she couldn't resist the impulse to ask. "He—he has spoken of me?"

Before his mother could answer, Colt blurted, "I give no thought to you," he snapped, "except when I think of those days laboring over a schoolbook, learning all the things civilized men must know. I hope you have found another job."

Sam cleared her throat, not wanting to admit she hadn't even looked. "Not yet," she said finally.

His mother smiled at Sam. "You should get a good man, have babies."

"I don't think so," Sam bit her lip and looked away.

Colt gave her a sarcastic frown. "Miss MacGregor is like most white women—she wants to be rich and successful."

She looked up at him then, and saw in his eyes that despite his harsh words, he was remembering the one night she had spent in his arms and she knew she would never find a passion like that again.

The silence hung heavy and awkward.

His mother said gently, "I have food ready."

She knew Colt watched her as she was handed a tin plate of stewed meat and corn and a cup of strong coffee. "This is very good," she said in surprise as she ate.

Colt smiled at his mother. "Wiwila is good wife."

Sam watched the older couple, saw them exchange loving glances. Austin Shaw was right; he could never return to Boston—everything he loved was here. She sneaked a glance at Colt. She would be willing to stay, too, if only he would ask her. No chance of that.

It was almost dusk when they finished. The older man said to Colt, "Why don't you take Miss MacGregor up on the ridge to watch the sun set? A prairie sunset is a beautiful thing to see. There's nothing like it in Boston."

Colt hesitated. Evidently, Sam thought, he did not want

to spend any more time with her than he had to. "I'm sure our way of life would bore her—our sunsets, too."

Sam bit her lip and looked away. "I wouldn't want to put you to any bother, Colt."

Colt stood up. "Come, Miss MacGregor, I'll show you a Sioux sunset and let you judge its beauty for yourself."

She didn't want him to touch her; she was not sure she could resist if he got too close to her, but before she could move, Colt took her hand and pulled her to her feet. "All right," she said coolly and began to walk with him up to the top of a nearby ridge. The red sunset slanting across the prairie grasses turned the landscape into a sweeping pink sea.

"It's beautiful," she said as they paused on the ridge, but she was focusing on the warmth of his big hand, the way it engulfed her small one. He said nothing and she was too aware of his nearness.

Finally he spoke. "You will not tell the secret about my father, White Wolf, when you return to Boston?"

She turned and looked up at him, shaking her head. "You know I wouldn't do that."

He nodded. "Strange—I never trusted white people, but somehow, I trust you."

She must not cry. She must not let him know how much she cared. It had been a terrible mistake to come up here alone with him. She tried to disengage her fingers, but he held onto them. She said, "I was surprised you left the house so suddenly that night, without telling anyone good-bye."

"I wanted to leave a note," he reached up and touched the ring on the cord around his neck, "but I couldn't put my feelings into words and I knew that Grandmother would never agree to my choice even if the girl would wed the savage she had tamed."

Sam's heart seemed to miss a beat. "Your grandmother fired me that night. She was in a towering rage over catching us out on the veranda together. I tried to explain that it was a mere dalliance on your part, but—"

"Is that what you think?" He was standing close enough to touch as the sun faded from view.

She could feel his nearness, see his strong silhouette as dusk gradually spread over the landscape. "Oh, Colt," she tried to control her tears, but they were coming anyway, "don't you know I've always loved you? I tried not to, because I knew she had plans to marry you to some rich society girl, but—"

"When I sign the papers," he reminded her tersely, "you can go back, marry Bosworth, and have it all. I saw the way he looked at you."

"I wouldn't marry that man even if he does end up with all the Shaw wealth. I'd rather be poor and stay here with you, if I thought you really cared—"

"Care? Of course I care!"

"But—" And then she could say no more because he swept Sam into his arms and kissed her like he would never let her go. She surrendered to his embrace, tears running down her face as she clung to him. "I love you. I love you so!"

He kissed the tears from her cheeks, her eyelids. "Enough to become the savage's woman?"

"I always was and always will be," she murmured and she kissed him again, her soft lips opening to his probing tongue as his hands caressed her. This man and this moment were all that mattered. Let Bosworth have all the wealth and be damned. Life with him would be luxurious, but life with Colt would be the zenith of passion and she loved him so.

"I want to make love to you as I did that one night," he murmured and he swung her up in his arms, kissing the hollow of her throat where the pulse pounded hard.

"Yes, oh, yes."

He laid her in the soft grass of the hollow in the lavender

dusk of evening and began to unbutton her bodice gently. "I have thought of nothing else since the only time I made love to you."

She was not ashamed of her nakedness as he slowly undressed her and she saw the approval and the desire in his gray eyes. He ripped away his loincloth and stood there, naked and proud.

She held up her arms to him. "My untamed one."

He came into her arms. "Oh, I'm tamed all right, although I never meant to be. You have done that, my darling." He kissed her, then deepened the kiss, his hands stroking her bare breasts. "I want you by my side forever and I want you to have my son."

She was ready to close the book on the past then and turn her back on civilization forever. Together they would take the legal papers to the town to be sent east. Hardship and hunger mattered little to her as long as she could sleep each night in Colt's arms. "We will stay here in the wilderness together," she murmured as he kissed her breasts, "your father is right; this is a once-in-a-lifetime love!"

He took her small face between his two big hands and kissed her lips and the tip of her nose. "My woman, whether I am Colt Shaw or Cincala, the Lakota warrior."

"Cincala's woman," she agreed and offered her breasts to him again for his tongue and his hands to enjoy. She reached out and grasped his manhood; he was rigid and throbbing with his need. "I want your son," she said, and spread her thighs for him.

He was hot and eager, reaching to rip away her lace drawers. Then he knelt and kissed her bare thighs. Her breath quickened, knowing where she wanted him to kiss and caress. His mouth went there, teasing and touching while she writhed under him. "Please," she begged, "please!"

"I love you." He mounted her, thrusting into her with a delicious slowness that made her twist restlessly. Unable to stand the exquisite sensation any longer, she reached to pull him down on her, wanting him to ride her deeper, harder.

She locked her legs around him, moving in perfect rhythm with his hard-driving thrusts as her own passion built and she begged for release. At the last possible moment, he locked his arms about her and they reached the highest pinnacle of passion at the same time, gasping and straining together for a long, long eternity of ecstasy.

At last they lay breathless in each other's arms. Dusk had turned to darkness as he was aroused again, this virile warrior, and he began to ride her again with renewed vigor until they climaxed while Sam dug her nails into his muscular back and begged him—no, demanded—more and more. Finally they were both sated.

"I love you," she whispered. "We'll be all right here. Nothing matters but that we be together."

"Together," he murmured, "yes, always together." He wrapped her in his strong, protective embrace and held her close. After a moment, he was aware that she slept.

Tenderly, he brushed the fiery hair from her eyes and kissed the tip of her nose. "My woman," he said, "my woman." All he had to do now was sign the papers and get them back to Boston. He should be happy now, but instead, he was increasingly uneasy. After a moment, he got up and stood looking down at the naked, sleeping girl with her fiery hair spread over the grass. He had forgotten how fragile she was. Samantha MacGregor would never survive the terrible winters of the Dakotas. She had no resistance to all the sickness that his tribe had endured for centuries or the hunger they often faced. The knowledge hit him then like a fist to the belly. He could not keep her here in his beloved prairie land. To do so would be her death sentence.

Cincala sighed and carefully covered her with her dress, then went to the top of the ridge to sit on a fallen tree and commune with the Great Spirit. What should he do? He wanted more than anything to keep her, but it would be selfish, knowing that after a year or two, she would surely die, even though she begged to stay by his side. No, he must send her back to Boston. A difficult life awaited her there, but not as difficult as it would be if she stayed in the Dakotas. He watched the stars and prayed to the Four Winds and the distant ancestors about what was right. She loved him enough to do whatever he asked, he knew that now. Perhaps marriage to Cousin Bosworth would not be so terrible and she would be rich and never have to worry about money again. She would not listen if he tried to tell her that, he knew, but he must decide what was best for the girl he loved.

Cincala thought about Boston. His heart was here in his untamed wild prairie, but anyplace with her would be enough. What to do? And he knew how very much he loved her when he realized that her happiness and her health meant everything to him. He made his decision then. All that was left to do was discuss it with his father. He started down the ridge. Halfway down, he saw his father coming toward him.

White Wolf said, "Where is the girl?"

Cincala nodded. "In the hollow asleep."

"Have you made your decision, my son?"

Cincala hesitated. "I love this land better than I love anything except our people and the fiery-haired girl."

"She would not survive long out here," White Wolf said.

"I know that. I am thinking of forcing her to return."

"Alone?"

He nodded. "She could marry Cousin Bosworth and be very comfortable the rest of her life with the Shaw fortune."

The older man ran his hand through his graying hair. "Is that what she wants?"

"She is too stubborn to listen to reason. I must make the decision for both of us."

"It is a very difficult decision to make. If she leaves here, she knows my secret."

"I know, but we can trust her."

"Can we? Are you so sure of her love?" White Wolf looked deep into his eyes.

"I am sure," he said. "I am very, very sure."

White Wolf gazed at the distant stars and Cincala watched his profile. "If Cousin Bosworth inherits the family wealth, he will use it to buy more power and grind people into the ground."

"Yes, I know." Cincala sighed with regret. "I saw the shoddy blankets our factories were making for the Indians. I would like to toss him out without a penny."

"Money is a very powerful thing," White Wolf said. "It could be used to pave the way to the governorship, maybe to the U.S. Senate."

Cincala blinked. "What are you saying, my father?"

"I am saying you have an obligation to your people, not just to your own happiness. If you had power and wealth, you could help all Indians, fight on their behalf."

Cincala shook his head stubbornly. "I don't like Boston and civilization very much."

"If you have the woman you love by your side, anyplace can be heaven on earth."

Cincala paused, letting the words sink in. He knew then what his decision must be. "Give me your knife, my father."

White Wolf hesitated, then reached for the sharp blade stuck in his waistband. "Here, my son. I know this is a hard choice for you, but it is yours to make."

Cincala took the knife, watching the blade shine in the moonlight as his father turned and walked slowly down the ridge. Cincala said a small prayer, knowing now what he must do. He turned and walked back toward the hollow.

Twenty-four

Cincala walked to the hollow and knelt, looking down at the sleeping girl, her hair like dark flame across the dry grass where she slept. The moonlight reflected off the knife in his hand.

Her eyes opened slowly and she looked at the blade in his grasp. Strangely, she had no fear, nor would she question his intent. "If you must kill me, go ahead," she whispered. "The love we have just shared was worth whatever it costs and I would rather die than return to civilization and live without you."

"I have made my choice and there is no turning back now." He took a deep breath, his hand shaking as if uncertain of his decision. As she watched in wonder, very slowly, he reached up and cut off one long braid, then the other. He tossed them to one side, then cut the thong that held the magnificent ring around his neck. "I have made my choice for your sake and the good of my people."

"What? I don't understand—"

"I am no longer Cincala. From this moment on, I am Colt Shaw, a white man from Boston. Will you wear my ring and marry me in the white man's way?"

She could only blink in confusion as she gathered her dress around her and looked up at him as he slipped the priceless blue ring on her finger.

"It is just the color of your eyes," he said with a nod. "A good omen."

"What are you doing? I thought you and I were staying—"

"No." He shook his head and reached to pull her to her feet. "We are going back to Boston."

"But you don't like Boston—"

"Hush." He took her in his arms. "I can learn to like it. Anyplace can be paradise with you by my side."

"Oh, Colt, I love you so!" She hugged him and tried to hold back the tears, knowing what this decision had cost him.

"There is still much to teach me," he said. "I intend to fire Cousin Bosworth, treat our employees better, and even run for political office. Can you get me ready for that?"

The joy in her face made him know he had made the right choice. "Yes, I can teach you," she said, laughing and crying at the same time, "and the inheritance can do so much good for the world."

He held her tight. "Then come, my love. We must say our goodbyes and ride to meet the train. There's a preacher in the white town who'll marry us."

"And I'll wire your lawyer from there and tell him to meet us with a carriage."

By early morning, they had said their goodbyes and promised to visit again, although they must always keep White Wolf's secret. As far as the world was concerned, all George Armstrong Custer's command had died at the Little Bighorn and it must remain that way.

White Wolf put his arm around Wiwila and waved goodbye. *"Wakan Tanka nici un,"* he said. "May the Great Spirit go with you."

Colt had put on his good clothes that he had worn from Boston. With his hair cut, he looked like a fine gentleman.

They rode away from the camp, waving back at the crowd of Lakota who had come to bid farewell.

The couple were married in town by a friendly preacher and then they caught the train.

When they stepped off the coach at Boston, the lawyer, Mr. Wimberly, was waiting for them. "I've got a carriage and I've contacted old Mr. Hiram Hall to stand by about taking the factories again."

"Good," Colt said. "What else should I know?"

"Well, your cousin has fired all the old servants."

"Find them all and rehire them," Colt ordered.

"This very afternoon," the lawyer promised.

"By the way, about Cousin Bosworth—have you told him I've changed my mind?"

Old Mr. Wimberly grinned. "I thought I'd give you that pleasure."

"Fine." He took Sam's hand and winked at her. "Where is my greedy cousin?"

"I believe he's at the house, planning how he will re-decorate it before he moves in."

Colt snorted. "I can hardly wait to see his face. But first, I must buy my bride a proper dress as befits the lady of the Shaw estate."

With Sam protesting, Colt and Mr. Wimberly took her to Boston's best shop and in minutes, she wore an exquisite black mourning dress as was proper. Colt ordered the dress-maker to begin a dozen new frocks for Samantha, including a blue one that matched the diamond-and-sapphire ring. Then they stopped by a barbershop to have Colt's hair trimmed and fine boots polished.

When he came out, he said to Sam, "How do I look?"

Sam laughed and hugged him. "Like a gentleman."

"And so I am!" He took her arm as they went out to the carriage and drove up the winding road to the Shaw estate.

As they stepped out in front of the red-brick mansion

with its great white pillars, Sam said, "Let me go in first." She hurried up the steps, leaving the two men behind her.

She opened the door herself and went in. Men were hurrying about, carrying scaffolds and paint. "Where is Mr. Shaw?"

"In the library, miss."

She was going to enjoy this. Sam strolled into the library, where Cousin Bosworth was turned away from the door as he scolded a workman. "You stupid oaf! I can afford the best and if you don't deliver it, I'll see you never work in this city again."

"Hello, Bosworth."

He turned, hesitated, and then his face lit up as he came toward her. "Samantha, my dear. So you've changed your mind and decided to become Mrs. Shaw?"

"I already am." She smiled sweetly up at him.

"What?" His cold eyes looked puzzled. "I'm afraid I don't understand—"

About that time, Colt strode in behind her. "Cousin Bosworth, you have a lot of gall to be redecorating my house without asking my opinion."

"*Your* house?" Bosworth's face turned ghastly pale. "Did you—did you say 'your house'? Why, you dirty savage—"

Colt crossed the room in three strides and hit the man in the mouth, slamming him backward against a desk. Bosworth brought his fists up to defend himself and Colt struck him again, sending the man stumbling backward over a pile of Oriental carpets.

About that time, old Mr. Wimberly entered. "He's right, Bosworth. You're in *his* house."

"Now get out, Bosworth!" Colt thundered. "You're not welcome here."

"But—"

"Get out before I throw you out."

Bosworth staggered to his feet, wiping his bloody mouth. "I don't get the inheritance?"

"Nor the girl either," Colt said. "She married me yesterday. And oh, by the way, you're fired as manager of Shaw Industries."

Bosworth looked toward the lawyer, horror in his eyes. "Can he—can he do that?"

"It's *his* company," Mr. Wimberly grinned. "Colt can do whatever he wants."

Bosworth groaned and stumbled out the door.

Colt Shaw looked every inch the fine gentleman as he straightened his cravat and turned to the astonished workman. "Tell everyone to quit work until my wife has time to make decisions. She'll redecorate this mansion to suit her."

The workman smiled. "Yes, sir, Mr. Shaw." He hurried out of the room.

Colt turned back to take both Samantha's hands in his own, then swung her up in his arms. "And now, Mrs. Shaw, I'm going to go back outside and carry you over the threshold in a proper manner as befits a newly married lady. Later we will throw the biggest wedding reception here that Boston ever saw."

The glint in his eyes told her what he had in mind in the master bedroom upstairs for the rest of this afternoon. "Whatever you say, my love," she whispered.

"Wimberly, don't you have business to attend to in town?" Colt asked.

The older man cleared his throat and nodded that he understood. "Of course, I must track down all the servants and give them the good news."

"And as you go," Colt said to him, but looking intently into his bride's eyes, "tell all those workmen to leave until further notice. And later, I want to talk to you about how one goes into politics."

"Politics?"

"Maybe a U.S. Senate seat or the governorship."

"A great idea!" And the door closed behind the old man.

"Would you like to move into the governor's mansion, my sweet?" Colt hugged her.

"Wherever you want to live, darling." Sam reached up to kiss Colt, knowing that she had tamed his savage heart and in doing so, had lost her own forever.

To My Readers

Was there really a lone survivor among Custer's men? That possibility has been an ongoing, intriguing legend. Dozens of men later claimed to be survivors, but only one man seems creditable: Frank Finkel. There was a book written about him called: *Sole Survivor, An Examination of the Frank Finkel Narrative,* by Douglas W. Ellison, Midstates Printing Co.,Inc., Aberdeen, South Dakota, 1983.

There is a classic novel on the subject by Will Henry titled *No Survivors.* Your public library may have a copy of this or my own favorite classic novel about Custer's Last Stand, *Bugles in the Afternoon,* by Ernest Haycock. Both these great old books are on the list of the 26 Best Western Novels chosen by the Western Writers of America.

I have walked the ground at all the historic sites of this story. The Washita site is now a national park here in southwest Oklahoma, the Little Bighorn battle site in Montana is a well known tourist attraction, and in South Dakota, grim Wounded Knee with its mass grave is still haunting me.

Why is the Little Bighorn still so intriguing to the public? I believe it has to do with the Seventh Cavalry's erratic and fascinating leader, George Armstrong Custer, who was and will always be highly controversial. He had been a great hero in the Civil War, becoming the Union's youngest general at the age of twenty-three, but he was dead at the age of thirty-seven. A great favorite with the ladies, he was handsome and brave to the point of recklessness. Custer was well known as an expert horseman; he also loved dogs and a good practical joke. If you are interested in his early life, I recommend a book by Lawrence Frost, *Custer Legends,* published in 1981 by Bowling Green University Popular Press.

There was a lot of controversy surrounding Custer's decision to leave the Washita battle without checking on the whereabouts of Major Joel Elliott. Maybe he abruptly realized there were a lot more Indians spread out along the river than he'd first guessed.

Also killed in this battle was Lieutenant Louis M. Hamilton, grandson of the famous Alexander Hamilton. Historians are still arguing over whether the captive Clara Blinn and her little boy, Willie, were killed in the crossfire of the battle or murdered by the Indians. Her heartrending note begging for rescue has been widely reprinted. Where is Clara buried? No one knows for certain, although I spent some time trying to find out.

An interesting note for Oklahomans: Captain David Payne, who was with the Kansas Volunteer column that was delayed in the blizzard, didn't arrive in time to assist the Seventh Cavalry in its battle. Later Payne would become better known as a leader of the "boomers," those who pressured Congress to open the Indian Territory to white settlement by illegally trespassing into the forbidden area. Ironically, he missed the land run, too, dying in Kansas before the run. Payne County, in the north-central section of Oklahoma, is named for him and he has been reburied in that county in Stillwater, home of Oklahoma State University.

Custer's Last Stand has had more written about it than any battle in American history with the exception of Gettysburg, the famous Civil War battle. We will really never know exactly what happened on that lonely Montana hillside although historians have argued over it for years. No one knows whether Custer was killed early or late in the fight, which lasted only a few minutes on that hot June Sunday afternoon. It is ironic that Custer chose to leave his

Gatling guns (early machine guns) behind because they were heavy and cumbersome. Whether they would have helped his troops is also debatable. Also, none of the soldiers were armed with sabers as they are in the most famous paintings of the fight. Most were carrying old Springfield rifles that often jammed, making them useless.

No one is certain of the exact number of Custer's men killed at the Little Bighorn. The bodies were so scattered, several were found as much as a year later some distance from the battle site. Three officers were never accounted for, although troopers later found bloody clothing with Lieutenant Sturgis's and Lieutenant Porter's names on them. However, no trace of Lieutenant Harrington was ever found, which probably gave rise to all the legends about a survivor. Also killed were the reporter, Mark Kellogg, and Bloody Knife, Custer's favorite Indian scout.

I've told you in an earlier book that Captain Keogh's bay gelding, Comanche, was found alive but wounded on the battlefield. Comanche became an honored veteran who was never ridden again by official decree. It is ironic that he was cared for the rest of his life by Gustave Korn, a veteran of the Little Bighorn fight, who was killed at Wounded Knee in 1890. Some say Comanche died of a broken heart in 1891 when given a new caretaker. On his death, Comanche was mounted by a taxidermist and today stands in a glass case at the University of Kansas in Lawrence.

Vic, Custer's mount at the battle, was either killed or captured, but his other horse, Dandy, who was with Benteen's pack train, survived and was given to Custer's father by Elizabeth Custer. If you have a particular interest in horses, I recommend an interesting book, *General Custer's Thoroughbreds,* by Lawrence A. Frost, 1986, J.M. Carroll & Co., Publishers.

Five Custer relatives were killed at the Battle of the Little Bighorn. George Custer himself is buried at West Point. His brother, Tom, winner of two Medals of Honor, and his brother-in-law, Lieutenant James Calhoun, are buried in the national cemetery at Fort Leavenworth, Kansas.

The very last survivor of Custer's entire Seventh Cavalry, Jacob Homer, died on September 21, 1951.

Elizabeth "Libbie" Custer lived until 1933, dying two days before her ninety-second birthday. She never remarried and spent the rest of her life guarding her dead husband's image while writing best-selling books such as *Boots and Saddles, Tenting On the Plains,* and *Following the Guidon.* Custer himself wrote numerous magazine articles and a book, *My Life on the Plains.*

So what happened to those who survived the battle? Ironically, the Indian triumph at the Little Bighorn brought more troops out, eager for blood. In 1877, Crazy Horse went to the Red Cloud agency with his young wife, who had tuberculosis, to seek help from the post doctor. While there, the soldiers attempted to capture him and throw him in a cell. Fighting to escape, the Oglala leader was bayonetted in the back and died a few hours later. There is a monument to Crazy Horse at Fort Robinson.

Sitting Bull and his group fled to the safety of Canada, where they stayed for five years, but finally returned. His followers joined in the religious craze for the Ghost Dance that nervous whites thought signaled the beginning of a new Indian war. In December, 1890, the army sent Indian police to Sitting Bull's home to arrest him. Suspecting treachery, the old man resisted and was gunned down by Indian police, along with two of his sons. I have walked this secluded site with my fellow members of the Order of the Indian Wars but it is not generally open to tourists.

What happened to Captain Reno? Blamed by many for not attempting to rescue Custer, Reno was court-martialed in 1877 after his problems with alcohol led him to be arrested as a "peeping Tom." He died of cancer in 1889 and was buried in Washington, D.C. He was later exonerated and moved to the Little Bighorn cemetery.

Trumpeter John Martin, the man sent with the message from Custer to Benteen asking for packs of ammunition, was the very last white survivor to see Custer alive. Neither Reno nor Benteen attempted to go to Custer's aid, since it might have been suicide to do so. Martin lived until 1922 and died in Brooklyn, New York.

Captain Benteen's family owned a music publishing company of which Stephen Foster was a client. A Southerner, he nevertheless joined the Union army. He died in 1898 in Atlanta and was buried there. In 1902, he was re-interred at Arlington National Cemetery in Washington, D.C.

Colonel Crook, known by the Indians as Gray Fox, was widely criticized for not attempting to get a warning to Custer after the devastating attack on Crook's forces at Rosebud Creek. Libbie never forgave Crook, Reno, or Benteen.

As far as Wounded Knee, no one is quite certain who fired the first shot that started the slaughter as the army attempted to round up the nervous Sioux. The Ghost Dance craze had spread throughout many tribes, created by a Paiute holy man named Wovoka. If the name sounds familiar, you met him as a small child in my earlier novel, *Nevada Nights.*

Wovoka (known to whites as Jack Wilson) was devastated that his peaceful religious ceremony had led to the deaths of so many Indians. He lived quietly the rest of his long life, died in 1932, and is buried in Schurz, Nevada. It is perhaps ironic that Wovoka's grandson, Captain Harlan Vidovich, became one of the famed Flying Tigers and was shot down and killed over China in World War II.

Another interesting note about Wounded Knee: Many of the Sioux women were shot as they fled and lay dead or dying through a blizzard before the army began to gather up the bodies, which were buried in a mass grave. Under one woman's body, they found her baby girl still alive. The Indians named her *Zintka Lanuni* (Lost Bird). A brigadier general, Leonard Colby, decided to adopt this child and sent her to his wife back East. The lady, a leader of the suffrage movement, reared the child. However, Zintka never quite fitted into white society and when she tried to return to her Sioux people, she no longer fitted in there, either. She had an unhappy life, playing an extra in Hollywood silent movies, working for a while in Buffalo Bill's Wild West Show. She died in her twenty-ninth year and was buried in California. In the year 1991, the Sioux decided that little Lost Bird needed to come home. She has been reburied at the Wounded Knee cemetery. The ceremony was attended by the great granddaughter of Iron Hail, the last Indian survivor of the Little Bighorn and Wounded Knee disasters. For further information, you might enjoy a biography titled *Lost Bird of Wounded Knee* by Renee Sansom Flood, Schrivner Pub., 1995.

Suggested other reading:

Brown, Dee, *Bury My Heart at Wounded Knee,* 1970, Holt, Rinehart, Winston, Pub.
Connell, Evan S., *Son of the Morning Star,* 1984, North Point Press, San Francisco
Hoig, Stan, *The Battle of the Washita,* 1976, U. of Nebraska Press, (previous printing Doubleday & Co.)
Sammarco, Anthony Mitchell, *The Great Boston Fire of 1872,* 1997, Arcadia Publishing, Dover, N.H.
Utley, Robert M., *Cavalier in Buckskin,* 1988, U. of Oklahoma Press, Norman, OK.

Many of you know that all my Zebra novels connect in some manner. You should remember Austin Shaw from my earlier romances, *Cheyenne Captive* and *Cheyenne Splendor.*

If you are on the Internet, I invite you to check out my

Web site that will always have information about me and my novels. http: //www. nettrends.com/georginagentry

If you prefer to write me, please send a stamped, self-addressed #10 envelope and I'll be happy to send you an autographed bookmark. Write: Georgina Gentry, P.O. Box 162, Edmond, OK 73083.

So what story will I tell next? In May 2003, look for my lighthearted, lusty Western romp *To Tame a Texan* about a feisty woman and an untamed Texas cowboy.

The cowboy is Ace Durango, handsome heir to the giant Triple D ranching empire in the Texas hill country. Ace can handle his cards, his liquor, and his women. Well, most women. This tough trail boss is about to tangle with one he can't handle and what's more, he doesn't even want to try. To put it bluntly, he can't stand the lady!

The feeling is more than mutual. Prim, uptight Lynnie McBride finds this untamed cowboy brute about as appealing as a buzzard. However, Lynnie is desperate to get to Dodge City for a suffragette meeting. How desperate? Enough to join Ace's cattle drive up the Chisholm Trail. No one asked Ace if he wanted her to come along and he's going to make it as miserable for her as possible. Trust me, she can make him pretty miserable, too.

Contact me or my Web page for the final title and release date later. Until then . . . *Pilamaya. Wakan Tanka nici un.*

Georgina Gentry